Also by Gerald Murnane

Stream System

Stream System

The
Collected
Short
Fiction
of
Gerald Murnane

FARRAR, STRAUS AND GIROUX NEW YORK

Farrar, Straus and Giroux
175 Varick Street, New York 10014

Library of Congress Cataloging-in-Publication Data
Names: Murnane, Gerald, 1939– author.
Title: Stream system : the collected short fiction of Gerald
    Murnane / Gerald Murnane.
Other titles: Short stories
Description: First edition. | New York : Farrar, Straus and Giroux, 2018.
Identifiers: LCCN 2017038359 | ISBN 9780374126001 (pbk.)
Classification: LCC PR9619.3.M76 A6 2018 | DDC 823/.914—dc23
LC record available at https://lccn.loc.gov/2017038359

Designed by Abby Kagan

Our books may be purchased in bulk for promotional, educational, or business use.
Please contact your local bookseller or the Macmillan Corporate and Premium Sales
Department at 1-800-221-7945, extension 5442, or by e-mail at
MacmillanSpecialMarkets@macmillan.com.

www.fsgbooks.com
www.twitter.com/fsgbooks • www.facebook.com/fsgbooks

1   3   5   7   9   10   8   6   4   2

Contents

Stream System

When the Mice Failed to Arrive

One afternoon in one of the years when I used to stay at home to mind my son and my daughter and to do the housework while my wife was away at her job, my son was caught in a thunderstorm. The storm broke over my suburb at half-past three, which is the time when schools are dismissed.

I had been alone in the house since half-past eight that morning, when my children had left for school. All afternoon I had watched from my windows while the clouds gathered. I had thought of the storms that broke every few days in summer over the city where I had lived from my fifth year to my tenth year. That city was a hundred miles inland from the suburb of Melbourne where I lived with my wife and my two children. In the thirty-three years since I had left the inland city, whenever I had seen the sky darkening by day I had remembered the storms that gathered outside my schoolroom window in the 1940s.

The storms of those years had always arrived at mid-afternoon. When a storm was overhead the teacher would have to switch on the lights in the darkened schoolroom. Before the first lightning flashed, I moved as far away as I could move from the schoolroom windows. At home I used to hide from lightning by lying on the floor under my bed. At school I could only press my face against the desk-top and ask God not to let the lightning strike me through the windows. I never thought of lightning as striking a group of children. I saw in my mind the zig-zag of gold stabbing down from the black clouds and piercing the heart or the brain of the one child who had been marked out for dying on that afternoon.

When I thought of myself being killed by lightning, I dreaded the confusion this would cause. After I had failed to arrive home at the usual time, my father would search for me along the streets that I had promised I would follow every afternoon. (Before my first day at school I had promised I would never turn aside from McCrae Street, Baxter Street, and McIvor Road. On the very few afternoons when I left those streets and walked for a little way along the creek, I supposed as I walked that my father was hurrying along McIvor Road while I was down among the bulrushes. My father had set out from home to meet me, I supposed. He had come to tell me that our house had been burned down or that my mother had been killed, but we had passed one another without knowing. On those afternoons I had almost turned back from the creek to make sure that my father was not somewhere behind me and walking away from me. And even while I wondered whether I ought to turn back, I thought of my father's arriving at the school and then turning back towards home but this time leaving the streets and walking along the creek for a little way because he thought I might have been loitering there whereas I was just then going back towards the school by way of the streets and passing my father again unseen.) When my father could not find me in my usual streets, he would think at first that I had turned aside to watch the water in the creek flowing swiftly after the storm. He would go down to the bank of the creek, and while he was looking for me among the bulrushes a priest from the presbytery next to my school would ride his bicycle along McCrae Street and

Baxter Street and McIvor Road on his way to my father's house to tell my father, who was not at home, that his only son had been killed by lightning.

I prayed that I would not be killed by the storm and that my father would not be lost and confused during the hour when the clouds had passed suddenly away to the east, and when the twilight that had seemed about to turn into darkness had turned instead into a bright afternoon with wet leaves flashing in the sun and steam rising from roofs. I prayed, and I was always spared, and I walked home while the gutters were flowing and the last of the black clouds were rumbling above the eastern horizon.

While the gutters flowed and the wet leaves flashed and the steam rose from iron roofs, I understood that I had been spared, but perhaps only for two or three days. The lightning that could have killed me was stabbing at the dark-green treetops far away past Axedale and Heathcote. By midnight the gold zig-zags would be shooting harmlessly into the Pacific Ocean. Days or even weeks later the clouds would settle quietly among the mountains of New Zealand or of South America. But somewhere behind me while I walked eastwards towards my home, another storm would soon arise.

I thought of each storm in summer as beginning far away to the east, in some bare paddock in the district around St Arnaud, where I had never been. (When I looked just now at a map of the state of Victoria, I saw that I have avoided all my life the countryside east of Bendigo. I was able just now to trace with my finger, beginning at Bendigo and moving north-west to Swan Hill then south-west to Horsham then roughly east to Castlemaine and then north to Bendigo, a quadrilateral enclosing more than five thousand square miles that I have never set foot in. Near enough to the centre of this quadrilateral lies the city of St Arnaud, whose name, whenever I heard it as a child, sounded like a preliminary snarl of thunder.)

When I thought of the beginnings of a storm, I saw a dark cloud rising from the earth in the way that the evil genie rose from the jar where he had been imprisoned for hundreds of years, in one of the illustrations that I often stared at in the pages of *The Arabian Nights Entertainment.*

In all his life my father never bought a book—for himself or as a present for another person. But a few books came into his possession from time to time. One of these was the book we called the Arabian Nights. Until I was thirteen years old, that book was the largest and the oldest book I had looked into. As a child I stared at the illustrations: plump, squat men with beards and turbans; giant Negroes with curved swords; donkeys cruelly burdened. I understood that the young women in the illustrations were meant to seem beautiful, but I was repelled by them. They had the huge dark eyes of Jersey cows, and their noses seemed to grow straight down from their foreheads. In the cities where all these people lived, the streets and lanes were narrow and gloomy; away from the cities the countryside was rocky and desolate; the sky, whether clouded or unclouded, was always grey.

I suppose the illustrations in the Arabian Nights were printed from some sort of engravings on stone or metal. But I know no more today about the carving of pictures out of metal or wood or stone than I knew when I sat in front of my father's book and thought of the Arabians, as I called them, as living all their lives threatened by storms. Today, if I happen to see in a book one of the sort of illustration that I call, rightly or wrongly, engravings, I remember myself having felt sorry sometimes for the whole of a nation called Arabia because its women were unattractive and its weather seemed always stormy afternoon. Or I remember myself having rested my eyes sometimes from focusing on donkeys or genies, and having tried instead to discover the cause of the greyness overhanging everything Arabian, at which times I began to see hundreds of fine lines forming an impenetrable mesh between me on the one side and on the other side the turbaned Arabians and their cow-faced young women.

From the time when I first learned to read printed words, I wanted to read the whole of the Arabian Nights. I wanted to see far into the strangeness and the greyness of Arabia. One afternoon in a year when I could still read no more than scattered words and phrases, my father came up behind me and warned me that I would learn nothing of benefit from the Arabians. He warned me that the Arabians did without shame what he and I and the people of our inland city avoided as the worst of sins.

One day in my tenth year I read for the first time the whole of a story from my father's Arabian Nights. At that time of my life I read books only in order to look for details that I could include in my dreams of myself living as a grown man in a mansion (with a lightning conductor on every chimney) behind a high fence of strong and interlocked wire in the bushland between Bendigo and Heathcote. One room of my mansion was going to be fitted out as a private cinema. On many a hot afternoon when the people of the districts surrounding my mansion were looking up into the glaring sky for the clouds that would be the first signs of a storm, I would be in my private cinema. The blinds on the windows of the cinema would be sealed against the light from outside. Modern electric fans would whirr in slowly swivelling cages. At rest in my cool twilight, I would watch what I called true films showing men and women doing without shame in far countries what the people in the districts around my mansion avoided as the worst of sins.

Of the story that I read in my tenth year I have forgotten every detail except one. I have not forgotten that a woman in the story, wanting to punish a certain man, ordered her slaves to strip the man and to flog him with the pizzle of a bull.

For long after I had first read that detail, I tried to believe that the stories of the Arabian Nights were not wholly fanciful. I tried to believe that somewhere in some country on the far side of the grey cross-hatching in books, a woman might once have looked at and named without shyness or shame the naked pink object that I pretended not to notice if it protruded from beneath the bull that moaned and shoved against the tall fence around the yard where my father's brother milked his Jersey cows while my father and I watched during our summer holidays. And after I had enjoyed the delicious shock of supposing that a woman might once have done those things, I dared to ask myself whether a woman in some story I had still not read might have put a delicate finger to the object while it rested in the hands of one of her slaves, or might even have curled all of her fingers around the object and lifted it away from the slave and then—and here I winced or hugged myself or gasped—stepped daintily towards the man who had been cowering naked all this time with his back to the woman and with his hands in front of his privates, and brought the long and quivering object down on his white buttocks.

If, on the far side of the grey world of illustrations in books, such things as these had been enacted even once, I thought, then I myself might one day watch such things being enacted—not merely in my mind while I read some antique book but on the screen of my private cinema, in my mansion protected by tall wire fences.

In many of the white spaces around the grey illustrations in my father's copy of the Arabian Nights, someone had stamped with a rubber stamp and an ink-pad, many years before I first saw the book, a black annulus enclosing the words: *Library of H. M. Prison, Geelong.*

My father had been a prison warder for twelve years before I was born and for two years afterwards. The last of the four prisons where he had worked during those fourteen years was the Geelong prison. In the month when I became two years old, my father ceased being a prison warder and moved with his wife and son from the city of Geelong to the city of Melbourne. During the last days of the fourteen years when my father was a prison warder, I was looking often at what is the only sight that I remember having seen during the two years when I lived in Geelong and what is also the earliest sight that I remember having seen during my lifetime.

I was looking down from the high landing of a set of wooden steps at the rear of my parents' rented house in the suburb of Belmont in the city of Geelong. I was looking first at the fence of grey palings at the bottom of my parents' yard, then at a row of sheds with grey walls and whitish roofs in the next yard. Each shed had at its front a wall of wire-netting. Beyond the wire-netting was a grey-white blur made by dozens of hens moving about in their crowded shed.

While I looked I also listened. At any moment of the day, many of the hens would have been silent. Those hens that were making a noise would have been making one or another of the several different noises that hens make in company. But from where I stood high above the sheds, I heard at every moment of the day a shrill and continuous sound as though every hen in every grey shed was forever complaining.

In each of the many places where he lived after leaving Geelong, my father kept a dozen or more poultry of the Light Sussex breed. Behind every house he lived in, my father fenced off three-quarters of the backyard so that his birds could have what he called a place to stretch their wings. My mother and I complained sometimes that the poultry trampled the grass and turned their yard into dust or mud, but my father would never lock his hens in a shed.

During the nineteen years of his life after he had left Geelong, my father seldom talked about the fourteen years when he had been a prison warder. Once, I asked my father where he had got the strange grey raincoat that he wore around the backyard on rainy days. He called the thing his oilskin and cape, and he told me that all warders wore such things in prisons on wet days. He said he had forgotten to return his oilskin and cape when he had ceased to be a warder.

One night when I was in my thirteenth year, I heard a radio program about a man who had killed three young girls in districts near Melbourne during the years just before I was born. I thought while I listened that the man and the girls were fictitious characters, but at the end of the program my father told me that what I had heard about had mostly happened. The name of the murderer was Arnold Sodeman, and he had been hanged in Pentridge prison, in the suburb of Melbourne where I was later born. My father had been one of the warders on duty on the morning when Sodeman had been hanged. When I asked how Sodeman had looked and behaved just before he was hanged, my father told me that Sodeman's face had turned a grey colour such as my father had never seen in the face of any other living person.

Until he died, my father kept among his shoes in the bottom of his wardrobe a piece of wood about the length of his forearm. The wood was slightly tapered and painted black. A circle of strong cord ran through the hole that had been drilled through the narrow end of the wood. The piece of wood was the truncheon that my father had carried while he was on duty at Geelong prison.

When my father had been dead for more than twenty years and I supposed that most of his friends had also died and that I would never learn any more about my father's life than the little I already knew, I read a short paragraph about my father in a printed leaflet.

The leaflet contained assorted details from the history of French Island in Westernport. About ten years after my father had died I began to notice newspaper articles describing French Island as a place for tourists to visit, but for fifty years before then, part of the island had been one of the four prisons in which my father had worked during his fourteen years as a warder.

I read from one paragraph in the leaflet that my father (whose surname had been misspelled) had been responsible, about ten years before I was born, for introducing to French Island the pheasants that still flourished there at the time when the leaflet had been compiled. My father had bred pheasants in cages at the prison and had released their young in the scrub around the island.

After reading the leaflet I wanted to know who had supplied to the compilers of the leaflet the item about my father and the pheasants. I learned from one of the compilers that the item had come from a woman (described as frail and elderly) in a suburb of Melbourne. I then wrote to the woman.

The woman wrote to me in faultless handwriting that she had known my father slightly. The item about the pheasants had come from her sister. When my father had been a warder in the prison on French Island, her sister had been living with her parents, who were farmers on the island. Her sister and my father had been good friends. Whenever the writer of the letter had returned to French Island to visit her parents in those days, she had supposed that my father was courting her sister. However, her sister had later left home to become a nun. The sister was still a nun. When the writer of the letter had told her sister that a leaflet was being compiled to inform tourists about the history of French Island, her sister had urged her to pass on to the compilers of the leaflet the information about the man who had introduced pheasants to the island.

The letter-writer had named in her letter the order of nuns that her sister had joined and the convent where her sister still lived. I knew about the order of nuns only what I had heard as a boy: that the order was an enclosed order whose members never left their convents. The nun who had been a good friend of my father had lived in a convent in a suburb of Melbourne since the year in the 1930s when she had left French Island, where my father was releasing young pheasant hens and cocks in the scrub. In all the years since then, the nun who had once seemed to her sister as though she was being courted by the man who later became my father would have received as visitors to the convent only the nearest members of her family. The visitors would have sat in the visitors' room, and the nun would have spoken to them from behind a steel grille set into the wall of the room.

I remember meeting my son at the front door on the afternoon of the storm and taking his schoolbag from him and giving him a towel from the linen cupboard to dry his face and his hair.

I remember making a cup of cocoa for my son while he took off his wet clothes and dried himself in the bathroom. I went into the bathroom afterwards and picked up the wet clothes and put the shirt and the singlet and the underpants in the laundry basket. My son stood in the loungeroom in front of the gas heater wearing his tracksuit and drinking his cocoa while I arranged his pullover and his trousers on the clotheshorse in front of him.

My son accuses me sometimes of having forgotten important details from the years when I used to cut his lunches and make his cocoa and tidy his cupboards and wash his clothes and read stories to him at night. I told him one day lately the very words that he had said to me on a certain afternoon seven years ago while he stood in front of the heater in the loungeroom and drank his cocoa, but he looked at me as though I had dreamed of the dark afternoon, of my twelve-years-old son being caught in a thunderstorm, and of the mice that had failed to arrive.

While I was writing the paragraph above that begins "I remember . . . ," I should have remembered that I would not have made the cocoa while my son was taking off his wet clothes. I would have waited until my son had done what he did every afternoon as soon as he arrived home. I would not have begun to make the cocoa until I had heard from my son's room the chugging and the hissing of the apparatus that he called his machine.

My son was an asthmatic who took medicines every few hours of every day. One of the medicines was a liquid that had to be inhaled in the form of a vapour. Three or four times a day my son sat for ten minutes with a mask of transparent plastic fitted over his nose and mouth. His medicine was in a plastic cylinder attached to the lower part of the mask. A rubber tube connected this cylinder to a pump powered by an electric motor. The pump forced air up the rubber tube and into the cylinder. How, I never understood, but the compressed air turned the liquid medicine in the cylinder into a vapour. Most of the vapour hung in the mask and was inhaled by my son, but some of the vapour escaped around the edges of the mask and out through the ventilation holes. When my son had first seen the strands of vapour drifting and curling around his face, he had called them his whiskers.

During his first five years my son was often in hospital. On every day when he was in hospital, I sat beside his bed through the morning and the afternoon while my wife was at work and my daughter was with neighbours.

The hospital was built on a steep hillside, and my son's room was on an upper floor. At one side of his room a glass door led to a veranda overlooking the valley of the Yarra. The season was always late autumn or winter when my son was in hospital, and the days were often foggy or rainy, and no one went out onto the veranda. On those days I would sit beside my son's bed, staring through the windows and across the veranda and trying to see the hills of Templestowe or the bushland around Warrandyte through the fog or the misty rain.

On foggy or rainy days I read to my son from his favourite books, from his sister's books, and from new books that I bought for him every day. I kept him supplied with paper and coloured pens and pencils, and if he was too tired to use them I drew pictures and made paper models in front of him. Each day on my way to the hospital I bought another Matchbox car to add to his collection. He and I put stuffed toys under the green coverlet on his bed and called the green mounds hills and undertook long, rambling journeys with toy cars through the pretend-landscape.

If the weather was fine and if my son was not struggling for breath, I took him out onto the veranda.

From the parapet of our veranda to the floor of the veranda above was a wall of strong wire mesh. My son and I pressed our faces against the wire. Sometimes the boy would be standing beside me and sometimes he would be riding piggyback with his chin resting on my shoulder. We stared at the motor traffic on the road far below, at the trains crossing the bridge over the road, at the girls in grey and blue uniforms in the grounds of Our Lady of Mount Carmel College, at the green hills of Templestowe, and sometimes—if the sky was quite clear—at the long dark-blue hump of Donna Buang, thirty miles away where the mountains began.

On the veranda my son was usually cheerful and looking forward to leaving hospital. He would talk to me about the things that he could see on the other side of the wire. I would wait for him to ask me the two questions that he always asked when he thought about the future. I would wait for him to ask why he suffered from asthma while so many other children breathed freely, and to ask when he would be free from asthma forever.

I had a stock answer for each of my son's two questions, but I did not merely answer in words. I had been trained as a primary teacher after I left secondary school. I had ceased being a teacher in the year before my son was born, but for ten years before then I had taught classes of boys and girls nine or ten years old. When I talked to my son or my daughter I liked to make use of my teacher's skills.

On the veranda of the hospital I said first to my son that every man was given an equal amount of suffering to endure during his lifetime. However, I said, one sort of man was given most of his suffering when he was only a boy. (At this point I would describe with my hands, in the air above my son's head, a shape that was meant to represent a dark-grey cloud. I would then fling my hands apart to represent the cloud breaking open, and immediately afterwards I would flutter my ten fingers in the air above my son's head to represent heavy rain falling on the boy.) The other sort of man, I said, had no suffering to endure as a boy. (I lowered myself a little way towards the floor of the veranda and tried to suggest a boy skipping lightly and carelessly.) Years passed, I said, and the two sorts of boys had grown into men. The first man, the man who had suffered as a child, was now strong and healthy. (I lifted my son onto my back and rushed towards the wire and made as though to tear it apart.) The second man, however, had not been prepared

14

for suffering. When suffering threatened this man, he fled from it and tried to hide from it and lived in terror of it. At this point, I set my son down on the floor of the veranda and moved back from him and became the man who had not learned to suffer early in life. I looked up into the air. I saw my own hand describing a broad circle just above my head, and I understood that the circle was a black thundercloud. Then I saw my own hand, with the index finger outstretched, darting downwards again and again through the air around my head. I understood that bolts of lightning were flashing all around me, and I fled.

The veranda of the children's ward had become, over the years, a dumping place for toys and furniture. Whenever I answered my son's question, I took care to be standing in a certain place. When I played the man who was frightened of suffering, I had only to scamper a few paces to the disused hospital bed that stood in the corner of the veranda. Then I crawled under the bed in order to escape from the lightning. But the bed had no mattress or bed-clothes on it—above me was only the network of fine steel that formed the wire base for a mattress. And my mime would always end with my grinning at my son from under the bed, as though the man who had fled now considered himself safe, while out of my sight just above me the index finger of one of my hands jabbed and probed at the gaps in the sagging mattress-base.

In answer to the other question that my son asked me, I would try to be cautious. No doctor had ever said more to my wife or myself than that a certain proportion of children experienced significantly fewer attacks of asthma after reaching puberty. But sometimes I would read in a newspaper about a runner or a jockey or a footballer who had been a severe asthmatic as a child. I would stick a photograph of the man to the door of our refrigerator where my son would see it every day.

In the winter of my son's seventh year his asthma was more severe than in any previous winter. Yet in the summer before that winter I had thought I saw signs that my son was on the way to overcoming his asthma. In hospital during his seventh winter, when he asked me the second of his two questions I became reckless. I told him that the worst was now over at last. Every year from that year, I told him, he would become stronger and his asthma weaker. Five years from that year, I told him, our dream would have come true: he would be free from asthma and breathing easily.

Fourteen years before my son's seventh year, I spent every afternoon alone in a room with the blinds drawn. The room was the lounge-room of a rented flat that had been described by an estate agent as a luxurious, fully furnished, self-contained flat suitable for a young business or professional couple. I lived alone at that time, and the rent for the flat was forty percent of my net earnings, but I had chosen to live in the flat because I was tired of sharing bath-rooms and toilets and kitchens with the queer, solitary men and women of the boarding houses and rooming houses that I had lived in since I had left my parents' house five years before.

The flat was at ground level, and the windows of the lounge-room overlooked a gravel driveway and part of the street and the footpath in front of the block of flats. I kept the blinds drawn in the windows of the loungeroom of my flat because I wanted neigh-bours and passers-by to think I was not at home.

Fourteen years before my son's seventh year, I was a teacher in a primary school in an outer south-eastern suburb of Melbourne. The outer suburb had once been a seaside resort separated from the suburbs that were then the outer suburbs of Melbourne by paddocks and swamps and market gardens. As late as the 1950s, the place where I taught as a young man in the 1960s was still chosen by some newly married couples as the place for their honeymoon. The block of flats where I lived with my blinds drawn was in the older part of the suburb, where the honeymoon couples had once strolled. The primary school where I was a teacher was on the edge of the suburb, on the side of a hill from the top of which it was possible to see not only Port Phillip Bay but also, far away in the south-east, part of Westernport and even, in clear weather, a grey-blue smudge that was a corner of French Island.

Most of the children of the school where I was a teacher lived more than two miles from where I lived. When I had first moved into the rented flat I wanted none of the children or their parents to know that I lived in their suburb. I did not want the children or their parents to know that I spent every afternoon and every evening and nearly every Saturday and Sunday alone in my flat. I did not want the parents especially to wonder why I seemed to have no friends either male or female or to wonder what I did during all the time while I was alone in the rented flat.

After I had lived in the rented flat for a few months, some of the children in my own class learned where I lived. The children were three girls nine years old who happened to be riding their bicycles along my street one Saturday morning when I was walking home with my weekend's shopping. The girls and I spoke politely to one another, after which I expected them to ride on their way. Instead, they followed me on their bicycles, at a distance of about twenty paces.

When I was inside my flat and the front door was closed behind me, I peeped around the closed blind and saw the three girls standing on the footpath and looking towards my flat. A few minutes later, while I was unpacking my shopping bag, a knock sounded at my front door.

I opened my front door and saw one of the three girls on my front porch. The other two girls were still standing on the footpath with the three bicycles. The girl on my porch asked me politely whether she and her friends could do some cleaning jobs for me in my flat.

I thanked the girl and told her that my flat was quite clean. (It was.) Then I said that in any case I was about to go out for the day. (I was not.)

I spoke softly to the girl and lowered my head close to hers. I did not want my words to reach the woman in the flat next to mine. I believed she was watching me and the girl from behind her drawn blinds. While I spoke to the girl I was pleased to see in her face that she was about to turn away and leave my door. But while I spoke I happened to look up and to see that a woman was passing in the street and looking hard at the solitary man who was whispering something to the small girl at the door of his flat.

After that day I would never answer any knock at my door. I did not want my neighbours or any adult passing in the street to think I was the sort of solitary man who was attracted to nine-year-old girls.

In fact, I was attracted to half a dozen of the nine-year-old girls in my class—and to two or three of the boys. Every day I looked from the sides of my eyes at the smooth skins of the girls, at the trusting eyes of the boys. I would never have dared to put so much as the tip of a finger on a child in a way that might have suggested something of what I felt for the child. All day while I taught my favourite children I wanted no more than that they should think well of me. But when I was safely out of their sight I often dreamed of the children.

I dreamed that my favourite children lived with me in a mansion surrounded by a tall wire fence in thick bushland in north-eastern Victoria. The children were no longer children; they were almost adults. They were free to live their own lives in the far-flung suites of my rambling mansion. I had never forced my company on them. I lived alone in my self-contained flat in a corner of the ground floor of the mansion. But the children who were no longer children knew that they were always welcome to knock at my door. I was always pleased to take them into the room where I sat behind drawn blinds on most afternoons and evenings watching black and white and grey films of men and women in far countries of the world doing without shame or shyness what I hoped my favourite children would never dream of doing.

In my classroom, fourteen years before my son's seventh year, I devised projects that encouraged the children to write about themselves. I wanted to know what memories of joy or sorrow were already stored in the children's hearts. I wondered what my favourite children dreamed about when I caught them gazing into the air.

One day I announced to my class that I had found a pen-friend for each of them in New Zealand. I announced that each child in my class would prepare during English periods for the next two weeks a long letter to be sent to his or her pen-friend. Each child would prepare as well, for sending with the letter to New Zealand, drawings and perhaps a photograph of the writer of the letter with family and friends and pets. When every child of the forty-eight children in the class had prepared his or her letter and accompanying material, I announced, I would make up a parcel and post it to a certain teacher in a large school in New Zealand. That teacher would distribute our letters among the children in his school. A few weeks later I would receive from New Zealand a parcel comprising a letter for each child in my class from a child in New Zealand, together with drawings and perhaps photographs.

The teacher in New Zealand was a man I had met two years before when he had been in Melbourne under the terms of a teacher-exchange scheme. Just before he had left Melbourne he had given me his address in New Zealand and had suggested that we should pair our pupils as pen-friends each year. In the first year after the man had gone back to New Zealand I had not taken his suggestion, but in the second year I suddenly thought of all the words that my pupils would write about themselves after I had told them that a class of children in New Zealand was waiting to read letters from them.

I ought to have checked first with the teacher in New Zealand before I began the project, but I was eager for my children to begin writing. After they had been writing for a week, I wrote a note to the New Zealand teacher to tell him that a parcel of children's letters would soon reach him. When I was ready to post the note to New Zealand I could not find the address of the teacher in New Zealand. I found in the notebook where I kept addresses the names and addresses of people I could not remember having met, but I could not find the address of the teacher in New Zealand, and he was the only person I knew who lived in New Zealand.

I ought to have told my class next day to put aside their letters and their sketches for the time being, even if I had not told them that I could not find the address of the New Zealand teacher. Then I ought to have found out the addresses of periodicals published for teachers in New Zealand and to have sent to the editor of each periodical for publication in the periodical a notice asking for pen-friends in New Zealand for a class of children in an outer suburb of Melbourne, Australia. But when I saw my children next day editing and rewriting their letters I could not bring myself to tell them that they might have been writing to nobody.

After that, I knew I could never tell my children what I had done. I could not even take steps to find another class in New Zealand for my children to write to. Each day for five days I read through the children's letters, correcting with light pencil marks their mistakes in spelling and punctuation. Each day I watched the children rewriting words and adding punctuation marks and then erasing my light pencil marks from their pages. Each day I watched children decorating with their coloured pencils the sketches they had made of their houses, their bicycles, the places where they went for their holidays. Each day I helped children to mount securely the photographs they had brought from home. Then, at the end of the week, I packed all the children's letters into my bag and took them to my flat and emptied them into a cardboard box on the floor of the built-in wardrobe in my bedroom.

When I had taken the children's letters from them I had warned the children not to expect replies for many weeks. I had told the children that they ought to forget that they had posted their letters, so that the replies would be all the more surprising when they arrived at last. And I had even said in class that I hoped my teacher-friend had not moved from his address and had not met with an accident since the year when he had given me his address in New Zealand.

The month when the children had given their letters to me was June. The school year did not end until December. From June until December of that year I offered my class every day some new diversion that would help them forget, I hoped, the letters that they had written to New Zealand. Some of the children seemed to have forgotten the letters after only a few weeks. Other children remembered the letters almost every day and reminded me that no answers had yet come back.

In September of that year I applied for a transfer to a school in a suburb on the other side of Melbourne. On the day after the last school day of that year I packed my clothes and my books ready for sending by taxi truck to my new address. I sealed and packed also the cardboard box that had been stored in the bottom of my wardrobe since June.

Before I sealed the cardboard box I spent an hour kneeling on the floor beside the box and tearing into small pieces every envelope in the box and every sheet of paper in every envelope. While I tore the paper I did not once look down at what my hands were doing. I did not want to read any name of any child or any word written by any of my children to one of the unknown children of New Zealand. When I had torn all the pieces of paper and when I was pressing the pieces into the box before sealing it, I remembered myself eight years before tearing paper into shreds and pushing the torn paper into the small cardboard boxes that served as breeding boxes for the mice that I kept in the shed behind my parents' house.

I had torn up the children's letters because I had thought of the box of letters falling from the taxi truck on the way from the children's suburb to my new address. I had thought of someone finding the box in the street and reading the names on the backs of the envelopes and then sending the envelopes back to the children who had been in my class, and I had thought of the children and their parents beginning to understand what had happened to the letters.

When I had begun to pack my belongings in my flat, I had

thought I would light a fire in the small yard behind my flat and would burn the envelopes and their contents. But then I had thought of pieces of burnt paper being lifted by the wind over the fence around the block of flats and being carried by the wind eastwards towards the houses of the children who had been my pupils. I saw in my mind piece after piece of grey paper with black penstrokes showing clearly against the grey, and all the grey pieces drifting towards the same children who had written messages on the pieces when they had been parts of white pages.

My son stood and drank his cocoa while I arranged his wet clothes on the horse. I told him his troubles were over for the time being. He was safe and dry in his own house after the storm; his machine had relieved his asthma; he could sit with me in the loungeroom and watch the last of the storm passing over the house.

My son told me that he had not had a hard day. He claimed to have had a rather pleasant day. His class at the high school had had almost a free afternoon. First, one of their teachers had been away sick, and then their science teacher had given them a free period in the last hour because the mice had not arrived.

For three or four weeks, my son said, the science class had been looking forward to the coming of the mice. The science teacher had told them she had ordered fifty mice from a laboratory. She had planned with the class beforehand a series of experiments. Small numbers of mice would be put into separate cages. Some mice would be allowed to breed. Each child in the class would be responsible for feeding and observing one of the cages of mice.

The mice had been due to arrive at the school, so my son told me, on that very morning, but they had failed to arrive. My son had cleaned the cage where his mice were going to be kept. He had set out a small heap of torn paper for the mice to use as lining for their cardboard nest-box. But the science teacher had announced to the class at the beginning of the last period of the day that the people supplying the mice had let her down. The mice had not come, and she was going to have to spend most of the science period telephoning to find out what had happened to the mice. While she was out of the room, the teacher had said, the class could use the time for private study. And then, so my son had told me, the teacher had left the room and he had spent the rest of the period talking with his friends or watching the approach of the storm.

While I listened to my son I felt a sorrow for some person or some thing that I could not have named. I might have been sorry for my son and his friends because they had waited so long for the mice that had not come. Or I might have been sorry for the teacher because she had had to disappoint her class, or because she had had to lie to the class (because she had neglected to order the mice, or because she had learned many days before that the mice would never arrive but had been afraid to tell her class). Or I might have been sorry for the mice because the taxi truck bringing them to the school had overturned during the storm, and the boxes containing the mice had tumbled out onto the road and had burst open, after which the mice had crawled around on the wet grey road, confused and bedraggled, or had been swept away in the fast-flowing water in the gutters.

Each time my son had said the word *mice* he had made faint signs with his eyes and his mouth and his shoulders. Probably no one but myself would have noticed the signs. He had turned his eyes just a little to one side and had stretched his mouth outwards just a little at each corner and had hunched his shoulders just a little. When I had seen that my son was making these faint signs, I had found occasion myself to speak the word *mice* and to make faint signs in return when I spoke the word.

The faint signs were the last traces of the signs that my son and I had made to one another during earlier years of his childhood whenever either of us had talked about mice or other small furred animals. During those years, whenever he or I had spoken the word *mouse* or the word *mice* in the other's hearing, each of us would have peered from the sides of his eyes and hunched his shoulders close to his head and stretched his mouth wide and held his hands in front of his chest in the shape of paws.

In earlier years I had always understood my son's signs as telling me that he was a mouse at heart. He was telling me that he was smaller than other children and made weak by his asthma. When I made my own signs in return in those years, I was telling my son that I recognised his mouseness and that I would never forget to put into his saucer each day a little heap of rolled oats and a cube of bread spread with vegemite and a scrap of lettuce, or to put a heap of torn paper into a corner of his cage when nights turned chilly.

When my son had made his faint signs to me on the afternoon of the storm, he seemed to be saying that he would always be partly mouse. He seemed to be saying that he had not forgotten my telling him five years before that he would be free from asthma after five years had passed; he had not forgotten, but he knew that what I had told him was not true. He seemed to be saying that he remembered every day what I had told him five years before; he had remembered it while he wheezed and gasped on his way home during the storm that had just passed over; but he knew that I had told him what I had told him only so that he could believe in earlier years that he would one day cease to be a mouse.

On the afternoon of the storm my son seemed to be telling me also that his life as a mouse was not unbearable; he had not been unhappy while he walked home through the rain; he was not unhappy now while he sat with me and watched the last of the clouds drifting towards the hills north-east of Melbourne. He seemed to be telling me finally that he was telling me these things because he understood that I too was partly mouse and would always be so.

During my fourteenth and fifteenth years I kept mice in cages in the cement-sheet shed behind my parents' house in a south-eastern suburb of Melbourne. Most of the mice were white or grey or fawn. A few mice were pied. I bred the mice selectively with the aim of producing only the pied sort. I kept the dozen or so female mice in one large cage, and the four or five males each in a small cage on the opposite side of the shed from the females. I had also two small breeding cages where a male and a female would be kept together until the female was swollen with young, at which time the male would be returned to his solitary cage. From each litter I kept only the one or two pied mice. The others I drowned. I put the unwanted mice in an old sock with a handful of pebbles and lowered them into a bucket of water. While I held the sock in the water I did not once look down at what my hands were doing.

I spent at least an hour every day in the shed alone with the mice. I fed the mice and cleaned their cages and set out torn paper for their nests. Then I studied the charts and tables showing the pedigrees of the mice, and I tried to decide which female and which male would be the next breeding pair.

During the hours while I was watching the mice I was also listening for certain sounds from the other side of one of the grey walls of the shed. I was listening in order to know when the woman from the house next door was in her backyard.

The woman was aged about thirty. She lived with her husband and her mother and her infant daughter. All of the family were Latvians and spoke to one another in a language that I supposed was Latvian. Whenever I heard the voice of the woman through the wall of the shed, I locked the door of the shed and crouched in the corner behind some of the cages of mice. I did in the corner what was all I could do as a solitary male who wanted to be one of a breeding pair. While I crouched in the corner I did not once look down at my hands. Instead, I pressed my ear to the cement-sheet in order to hear the voice of the woman talking in her own language. When I heard the voice I persuaded myself that the woman was talking only to me and talking without shyness or shame.

During November and December, most of the children seemed to have forgotten having written letters to New Zealand. Only one boy still asked me quietly every few days what I supposed might have happened to the parcel of letters. The boy was not one of my favourites, although he was one of the most intelligent in the class. He was not among my favourites because he was too often restless and talkative. One of his previous teachers told me that the boy was what he was because his father had been too anxious about the boy. The father was a teacher himself and had watched over the boy too closely.

Sometimes when this boy asked me about the letters during the last weeks of the school year, I thought he might have suspected me of having not sent the letters to New Zealand. I was thinking of this boy when I decided to tear the letters into small pieces before putting them into the taxi truck.

The place that I moved to was an upstairs flat with no yard where I could burn large quantities of paper. But soon after I had moved to the new place, I began to visit a man and his wife in the hill-country north-east of Melbourne. One Saturday when I visited these people, my bag was stuffed with the torn pieces of the letters to New Zealand.

I burned the pieces of the letters on a cloudy afternoon with a cool breeze blowing. The breeze, like nearly every breeze or wind in the districts around Melbourne, went from west to east. When all the scraps of the letters had been burned, I pounded the ashes with a stick. I wanted no fragment of charred paper to be left lying on the ground with a few blackened words still visible. Yet I had noticed, while the fire was burning, a few pieces of grey paper being lifted up and carried by the breeze over the nearest treetops.

The district where I stood, in the hills north-east of Melbourne, was at the edge of the mountains that were burned, in the summer when I was born, by the worst fires since details of the weather were first recorded in the state of Victoria. I had read that the smoke from those fires drifted all the way across the Tasman Sea and darkened the sky over New Zealand. I had read also that fragments of burnt leaves and twigs fell on some cities of New Zealand from the dark clouds that had drifted from the burning forests of Victoria, far away to the west. When I saw the fragments of grey paper being carried from my fire eastwards across the treetops, I thought of the fragments drifting down at last on New Zealand and one of the fragments happening to catch the eye of a boy or a girl of nine or ten years and of the boy or the girl making out a few words of a child's handwriting on the fragment.

Five years after the year when my son had been caught in a thunderstorm, and nearly twenty-five years after I had burned the pieces of the children's letters, I saw in a Melbourne newspaper a tiny photograph of the man who had been the boy who had been the last of the forty-eight children of my class to go on reminding me that the letters to New Zealand had not been answered. I had heard nothing of the boy since I had left the outer south-eastern suburb nearly twenty-five years before, but as a man he had become the South Pacific correspondent for the newspaper in which I had seen his photograph.

Underneath the tiny photograph of the man who had once been one of my pupils was a report that he had written in the language of writers for newspapers. I understood the man to be reporting that some people in New Zealand were afraid that a cloud of poisonous substances was approaching them from the east, and to be reporting also that some people in Australia were afraid that the same cloud would approach Australia after it had passed over New Zealand. The cloud had arisen far away to the east of New Zealand at a place in the Pacific Ocean where scientists from the country of France had exploded a bomb.

After reading the report in the newspaper I was not afraid of the poisonous cloud. I thought of the poisonous cloud as passing not from east to west but from west to east like the storms that had frightened me as a child and like the storm that had broken over my son and like the smoke from the bushfires in the year when I was born. I saw in my mind the poisonous cloud drifting down at last into the ocean near South America, where the last of the clouds had settled after each of the storms that had come up out of the paddocks near St Arnaud like the grey shape of a genie from the Arabian Nights.

Towards the end of my fifteenth year, my father told me we would soon be leaving the house that had behind it the shed with the walls of grey cement-sheet. The house where we were going to live had no shed behind it.

I understood that I would not be able to breed mice in the place where I was going to live. Nor would I be able to crouch against a wall while a woman spoke in a foreign language on the other side of the wall.

In the last weeks before I left the house with the shed behind it, I prepared to drown all of my mice and to tear up and burn the notebook in which I had recorded the pedigrees and the matings of the mice. While I was looking through the records I noticed that one of the male mice had not yet been used for breeding. Each of the other males had been moved at least once from his solitary cage to a breeding cage where he had been allowed to remain with a female until she was swollen with young. But one male mouse had been kept as a solitary male from the time when he had been taken as a half-grown male from his mother and his litter-mates.

I looked into the cage of the mouse that had been kept always solitary. The mouse was standing at the small panel of flyscreen wire at the front of the cage. I supposed that the mouse saw only a grey blur while he stood in the darkness of the cage with the fine mesh of wire in front of him and on the other side of the wire the half-light of the shed where I stood watching him.

The mouse pressed his nose against the wire and sniffed the air.

I knew that the solitary mouse had seen no other mouse, either male or female, in all the time since I had put him into his cage. But I wondered whether the mouse had sometimes smelled the smell of another mouse, either male or female, or had sometimes heard the squeaking of another mouse, especially the squeaking that came from a breeding cage whenever I first put a male and a female together there.

While I stood in front of the cage, I understood that I might leave the solitary mouse alone in its cage until the day when I drowned all the mice, and that I might keep the mouse alone even while I killed it. I understood also that I might take the mouse from its cage at that moment and put it into the cage where a dozen female mice were kept together and leave it in that cage, the one male among a dozen females, until the day when I drowned all the mice. And I understood that I might carry the cage of the solitary mouse to the other side of the shed. I might then place the cage so that the panel of flyscreen wire at the front of it rested against the panel of flyscreen wire at the front of the cage where the twelve female mice were kept together. I might then leave the cages in that position until the day when I took all the mice from their separate cages and drowned them.

Stream System*

This morning, in order to reach the place where I am now, I went a little out of my way. I took the shortest route from my house to the place that you people probably know as SOUTH ENTRY. That is to say, I walked from the front gate of my house due west and downhill to Salt Creek then uphill and still due west from Salt Creek to the watershed between Salt Creek and a nameless creek that runs into Darebin Creek. When I reached the high ground that drains into the nameless creek, I walked north-west until I was standing about thirty metres south-east of the place that is denoted on Page 66A of Edition 18 of the Melway Street Directory of Greater Melbourne by the words STREAM SYSTEM.

I could hardly doubt that I was looking at the place that was denoted in my map by the words STREAM SYSTEM. Yet I was looking at two bodies of yellow-brown water, each of which seemed

---

* "Stream System" was written to be read aloud at a gathering in the Department of English at La Trobe University in 1988.

roughly oval. When I had looked a few days before at the words
STREAM SYSTEM, each of those words had been printed on one of
two bodies of pale blue, each with a distinctive outline.

The body of pale blue on which the word STREAM had been
printed had the outline of a human heart that had been twisted
slightly from its usual shape. When I had first noticed this outline on
the map, I asked myself why I had thought of a human heart twisted
slightly when I ought to have been thinking of a body of yellow-
brown water of a roughly oval shape. I recalled that I had never seen
a human heart either twisted slightly or occupying its usual shape.
The thing that I had seen that was nearest in shape to the slightly
twisted heart was a certain tapering outline that was part of a line
drawing of an item of gold jewellery in a catalogue issued by the
Direct Supply Jewellery Company Pty Ltd in about the year 1946.

My father had five sisters. Of those five women, only one married.
The other four women lived for most of their lives in the house
where they had been children. In the years when I first knew my
father's unmarried sisters, who were, of course, my aunts, they
kept mostly to their house. However, my aunts subscribed to
many newspapers and periodicals and they wrote away, as they
called it, for many mail-order catalogues. During one of the summer holidays that I spent during the 1940s in the house where my
aunts lived, I used to sit for perhaps a half-hour every day in the
bed-sitting room of one of my aunts, looking through the hundred
and more pages of the catalogue of the Direct Supply Jewellery
Company.

The only gold object that I had seen when I first looked through
the catalogue had been the thin wedding ring that my mother wore,
but I did not consider my mother's ring the equal of any of the
items in the pages that I looked at. I questioned my aunt about
the many jewels that I had never seen: the gentlemen's cuff-links
and signet rings. I asked especially about the ladies' rings and
bracelets and pendants.

When I wanted to see in my mind the men and women who wore the jewels that I had never seen, I thought of the illustrations in the *Saturday Evening Post*, which my aunts subscribed to. The men and women in those illustrations were the men and women of America: the men and women that I saw going about their business whenever I looked away from the main characters in the foreground of an American film.

When I asked myself whether I would one day handle or even wear on my own body the jewels that I had never seen, I seemed to be asking myself whether I would one day live among the men and women of America in places far back from the main characters in American films. When I asked myself this question I seemed to be trying to see America from where I sat. When I tried to see America from where I sat, I seemed to be looking across seemingly endless grasslands.

When I sat in the cane chair in my aunt's room, I faced north. By turning my body a little in the chair I was able to face north-east, which seemed to me the direction of America. If the stone walls of the house around me had been lifted away, I could have looked north-east for half a mile across yellow-brown grass towards a slight ridge known as Lawlers' Hill. I could have seen beyond Lawlers' Hill only pale-blue sky, but if, while I sat in my chair, I could have thought of myself as standing on Lawlers' Hill and looking north-east, I would have seen in my mind yellow-brown grass reaching a mile and more north-east towards the next slight hill.

If I had wanted to think of myself as standing at the highest point that I could have reached if I had walked in any direction from my aunts' house, I would have thought of what lay behind me while I sat in my aunt's chair.

Behind the stone walls of the house was a paddock known as the Rye Paddock, which was about a quarter of a mile across. The fence at the far side of the Rye Paddock was a barbed-wire fence looking no different from the hundreds of barbed-wire fences in the district around. But that fence was a notable fence; that fence was part of the southern boundary of all the farms on the mainland of Australia.

On the far side of that fence the land rose. The land rose more steeply as it reached further south. The more steeply the land rose and the further south it reached, the less the land was covered by yellow-brown grass, but whenever I had walked on the rising land I had noticed yellow-brown grass still growing in tussocks, and I understood that I was still standing on a grassland.

About three hundred yards south of the southern boundary of the farm where I sat often with my face to the north or the northeast, the land rose to the highest point that I could have reached if I had walked in any direction from my aunts' house. At that point the land ended. Whenever I looked at that point I saw that the land had a mind to go on rising and to go on reaching south. I saw too that the grass had a mind to grow on the land for as far as the land might rise and for as far as the land might reach to the south. But at that point the land ended. Beyond that point was only pale-blue sky, and beneath the pale-blue sky was only water—the dark-blue water of the Southern Ocean.

If, while I was sitting in my aunt's room, I had thought of myself as standing at the high point where the land ended and as looking towards America, even then I would have thought of myself as seeing to the north-east only seemingly endless yellow-brown grass. If, while I was sitting in my aunt's room, I had wanted to think of myself as seeing more than seemingly endless grass, I would have had to think of myself as standing at some impossible vantage-point. If I could have thought of myself as standing at such a vantage-point, I would have thought of myself as seeing not only seemingly endless yellow-brown grass and seemingly pale-blue sky but dark-blue water on the other side of the yellow-brown grass and, on the far side of the dark-blue water, the yellow-brown and endless grasslands under the pale-blue and endless sky of America.

When I asked my aunt where I might see some of the pieces of jewellery illustrated in the catalogue, she told me that her married sister was the owner of a pendant. The pendant had been a wedding present to my one married aunt from her husband.

My married aunt and her husband lived at that time about four miles north-east across the yellow-brown grass. My aunt and her husband sometimes visited the four unmarried sisters. After I had heard about the pendant, I tried often to see in my mind what I expected to see one day below the throat of my father's sister in the same house where I had sat turning pages of illustrations of jewellery. I saw in my mind a gold chain and hanging from the gold chain a gold heart.

As a child I tried often to see myself as a man and to see the place where I would live after I had become a man. Often while I looked into the jewellery catalogue I would try to see myself as a man wearing cuff-links and signet rings. Often while I turned the pages of the *Saturday Evening Post* I would try to see myself as a man living in a place that was like a landscape in America.

I was never able to see myself as a man, but I was sometimes able to hear in my mind some of the words that I would speak as a man. I was sometimes able to hear in my mind the words that I would speak as a man to the young woman who was about to become my wife. And sometimes I was able even to hear what the young woman would speak to me from close beside me.

After I had been told about my aunt's pendant, I sometimes heard the following words as though they were spoken by myself as a man. *Here is your wedding present, darling.* And I sometimes heard the following words as though they were spoken by the young woman who was about to become my wife. *Oh! A pendant with a gold heart. Thank you, darling.*

When I had looked at the body of pale blue on which the word SYSTEM had been printed, I had seen in my mind the outline of a pair of female lips boldly marked with lipstick.

When I first saw such an outline of lips I was sitting in a dark cinema with my mother and my only brother, who was younger than myself. The cinema may have been the Circle in Preston or it may have been the Lyric or the Plaza or the Princess in Bendigo. The lips were on the face of a young woman who was about to kiss the man who was about to become her husband.

When I first saw such an outline of lips I had been watching the young woman so that I could afterwards see her in my mind. I wanted to think of her as the young woman who would become my wife when I had become a man. But when I had seen from the shape of her lips that the young woman was about to be kissed, then I had turned my head and had looked away from the main characters in the foreground. I had looked away because I remembered that I was sitting beside my mother and my brother.

In my aunt's room, trying to see in my mind myself as a man giving a pendant as a wedding present, I sometimes saw in my mind the outline of the lips of the young woman who was about to become my wife. But as soon as I saw from the shape of the lips that the young woman was about to be kissed, I looked away from the foreground of my mind. I looked away because I remembered that I was sitting near my aunt and that the other three of my aunts were in their rooms nearby.

When I had looked at the outline of the body of pale blue that consisted of the body labelled STREAM and the body labelled SYSTEM and the narrow body of pale blue connecting the two—that is to say, when I had looked at the two larger bodies and the one smaller body that together comprised the body of pale blue labelled

STREAM SYSTEM, I had noticed that the outline of the whole body brought to my mind a drooping moustache.

The first drooping moustache that I saw was the moustache of the man who was the father of my father and also of my father's five sisters, four of whom remained unmarried. My father's father was born in 1870 near the southern boundary of all the farms on the mainland of Australia. He was the son of an English mother and an Irish father. His Irish father had come to Australia from Ireland in about 1850. My father's father died in 1949, about three years after I had looked at the jewellery catalogue in his house. He would have been in the house while I turned the pages of the catalogue and while I thought of myself as a man giving a wedding present to a young woman, but he would not have seen me where I sat. He might have walked past the door of the room, but even then he would not have seen me turning the pages of the catalogue, because my chair would have been to one side of the doorway. I preferred to sit in places where my father's father was not likely to see me.

Whenever I have wondered why four of my father's five sisters remained unmarried, I have seen in my mind one or another of the four women sitting in her room and turning the pages of a jewellery catalogue or of a copy of the *Saturday Evening Post*. I have then seen in my mind my father's father walking to the door of the woman's room and the woman turning her head and looking away from what she had been about to look at.

But the drooping moustache of my father's father is not the only drooping moustache that I see in my mind when I look at the body of pale blue with STREAM printed on it and at the body of pale blue with SYSTEM printed on it and at the narrow body of pale blue connecting the two. I see in my mind also the drooping moustache of a man that I saw only once in my life, in about the year 1943. If the man had been still standing this morning where I saw him one afternoon in about the year 1943, I would have seen him this morning when I stood south-east of the yellow-brown water that was denoted by the body of pale blue and by the words STREAM SYSTEM in my map. I would have seen the man this morning because he would have been standing on the opposite side of the yellow-brown water from where I stood.

When I last saw the man with the drooping moustache, which was about forty-five years ago and near the place where I stood this morning, neither the man nor I nor any of the male persons around us saw a body of water either yellow-brown or pale blue in the place denoted by the words STREAM SYSTEM in the map of 1988. What we saw in that place was swampy ground overgrown by blackberries and with muddy drains leading into it. The drains ran downhill into the swampy ground from a shabby building of timber.

When I last saw the man with the drooping moustache in about the year 1943, he was standing near the shabby building of timber. The man was giving orders to a group of black and white fox terrier dogs and also to a group of men. Of the group of men receiving orders, three men were known to me by name. One was my father, one was a man known to me as Fat Collins, and the third was a young man known to me as Boy Webster.

I was allowed to watch the man giving orders to the dogs and the men, but I had been warned by my father to stand at a distance. Some of the men held in their hands hoses spouting water and some men held sticks for killing rats. The men with the hoses sent the water into holes under the shabby building. The men with sticks and the fox terrier dogs stood waiting for the rats to stagger out of their holes under the shabby building. Then the men with sticks would beat the rats and the fox terrier dogs would fasten their teeth in the necks of the rats. The man with the drooping moustache, who was the owner of the fox terrier dogs, shouted often at the men with the sticks to warn them against beating the dogs instead of the rats. The man had to shout often at the men with sticks because Fat Collins and Boy Webster and others of the men were by legal definition not in full possession of their minds.

The shabby building with rats living in holes beneath it was a

pigsty where about fifty pigs lived in small muddy pens. The liq-
uids that drained from the pigsty downhill into the swampy ground
that lay in 1943 in the place denoted by the words STREAM SYSTEM
were partly composed of leavings from the troughs where the pigs
ate. The food that was put into the troughs for the pigs to eat
was partly composed of leavings from the tables where the hundreds of men and women ate in the wards of Mont Park Hospital
on the high ground north-east of the swamp and the pigsty. Of
the men who stood around the pigsty on the day that I remember, all except my father and the man with the drooping moustache lived at Mont Park Hospital. My father spoke of the men
as *patients* and warned me to speak of them only by that name.
My mother sometimes called the men, out of my father's hearing,
loonies.

The man with the drooping moustache gave orders to the
patients only on that one day when he came to drive the rats from
the pigsty. My father gave orders to the patients every day from
mid-1941 to the end of 1943. During those years my father was
the assistant manager of the farm that was part of the Mont Park
Hospital for forty years until the cowyards and the haysheds and
the pigsty and all the other shabby buildings were knocked down
and a university was built in their place.

When no more rats seemed likely to come out from under the
pigsty, Fat Collins and Boy Webster and the other patients began
to aim the jets of water from their hoses at the dead rats lying on
the grass. The patients seemed to want to send the dead rats slid-
ing over the wet grass and downhill into the swampy ground. My
father ordered the patients to turn off their hoses. I thought that
he did this because he did not want the bodies of the rats to reach
the swampy ground, but in fact my father only wanted to keep the
men from wasting time. When the hoses had been turned off, my
father ordered the patients to collect the dead rats in kerosene tins.
The patients picked up the dead rats in their hands and carried the
rats in kerosene tins down the slope that leads today to the yellow-
brown water denoted by the pale blue in my map.

The outline of the bodies of pale blue resembles not only the moustache of my father's father and the moustache of the owner of the fox terrier dogs. Sometimes when I look at the outline of the body of pale blue that comprises the bodies labelled STREAM and SYSTEM and the narrow body connecting them and also the two small bodies at either side, I see in my mind the item of women's underclothing which is called by many people nowadays a bra but which I called during the 1940s and for some years afterwards a brassiere.

On my way this morning from my front gate to the place where I am now, I went, as I said before, a little out of my way. I followed a roundabout route.

After I had stood for a few moments south-east of the place that I am going to call from now on STREAM SYSTEM, I walked across the bridge between the two largest bodies of water. I walked, that is, between STREAM and SYSTEM. Or I walked, if you like, across the narrow connecting part between the two cup-shaped parts of a pale-blue (or yellow-brown) brassiere (or bra).

I kept on walking roughly north-west up the sloping land that had been forty-five years ago the wet grass where Fat Collins and Boy Webster and the other men had aimed their jets of water at the dead rats. I walked across yards where rows of motor cars stood and past the place that you people know as NORTH ENTRY.

Just short of Plenty Road I stopped. I turned and faced roughly south-west. I looked across what is now Kingsbury Drive at the house of red bricks on the south-eastern corner of the intersection of Kingsbury Drive and Plenty Road. I looked at the first window east of the north-eastern corner of the house, and I remembered a night in about 1943 when I had sat in the room behind that window. I remembered a night when I had sat with my arm around the shoulders of my brother while I tried to teach him what a brassiere was used for.

The building that I was looking at is no longer used as a house, but that building is the first house that I remember having lived in. I lived in that building of red bricks with my parents and my brother from mid-1941 until the end of 1943, when I was aged between two and four years.

On the night in about 1943 that I remembered this morning, I had found on a page of a newspaper a photograph of a young woman wearing what I thought was a brassiere. I had sat beside my young brother and put my arm around his shoulders. I had pointed to what I thought was the brassiere and then to the bare chest of the young woman.

I believe today, and I may even have believed in 1943, that my brother understood very little of what I told him. But I believed I had seen for the first time an illustration of a brassiere, and my brother was the only person I could talk to at that time.

I was talking to my brother about the brassiere when my father came into my room. My father had heard from outside the room what I had been saying to my brother and he had seen from the doorway of the room the illustration that I had been showing to my brother.

My father sat in the chair where I had been sitting with my brother. My father lifted me onto one of his knees and my brother onto his other knee. My father talked for what I remember as a long time. He spoke to me rather than my brother, and when my brother became restless my father let him down from his knee and went on speaking only to me. Of all that my father said I remember only his telling me that the young woman in the illustration was wearing not a brassiere but an evening dress, and that a young woman would sometimes wear an evening dress because she wanted people to admire some precious piece of jewellery hanging from her neck.

When my father told me this he picked up the page of the newspaper and tapped at a place on the bare chest of the young woman, a little distance above the top of her evening dress. He tapped with his knuckle in the way that he might have tapped at a door that stood closed in front of him.

This morning when I remembered my father's tapping with his knuckle at the bare chest of the young woman, I thought of the top part of the evening dress as being the body of pale blue labelled STREAM SYSTEM. I then saw in my mind my father tapping with his knuckle at the face of his father and also tapping at the yellow-brown grass where the dead rats had once lain before my father had ordered the patients to collect them in kerosene tins and to dump them in the swampy ground that was denoted, many years afterwards, by the words STREAM SYSTEM.

After I had looked at the building that was once the first house that I remember having lived in, I walked back to the slope of grass that had once been the place where the dead rats had lain but was now, according to my map, the bare chest of a young woman wearing an evening dress, the place where my father had tapped with his knuckle, the place where the young woman might have displayed a precious jewel, the face of my father's father.

While I stood in all those places, I understood that I was standing in still another place.

As a child I could never be contented in a place unless I knew the names of the places surrounding that place. As a child living in the house of red bricks, I knew that the place to one side of me was Preston, where I sometimes sat with my mother and my brother in the Circle cinema. I had been told by my father that another of the places surrounding me was Coburg, which was the place where I had been born and where I had first lived although I had never remembered it afterwards.

Whenever I stood at the front gate of the house of red bricks and looked around me, I seemed to be surrounded by grasslands.

I understood that I was surrounded finally by places, but grass-lands, so I saw, lay between me and the places. No matter what place I heard of as being in this or that direction away from me, that place was on the far side of a grassland.

If I looked in the direction of Coburg I looked across the grass-land that lay, during the 1940s, on the western side of Plenty Road. Where the suburb of Kingsbury is today, an empty grassland once reached for as far as I could see to the west from Plenty Road.

If I looked in the direction of Preston I saw the grassland slop-ing past the cemetery and towards the Darebin Creek.

If I looked in the opposite direction from the direction of Preston, I saw only the farm buildings where my father worked each day with the patients, but I had travelled once with my father past the farm buildings and the hospital buildings to a place where the land rose, and from there I had seen more grasslands and on the far side of the grasslands dark-blue mountains. I had asked my father what places were among those mountains and he had said the one word *Kinglake*.

After I had heard the word *Kinglake* I was able to stand at my front gate and to see in my mind the places on the far sides of three of the grasslands around me. I was able to see in my mind the main street of Preston and the darkness inside the Circle cinema. When I looked in the direction of Coburg I saw the dark-blue wall of the gaol and the yellow-brown water of Coburg Lake in the park beside the gaol. My father had once walked with me between the dark-blue wall and the yellow-brown lake and had told me that he had worked as a warder for ten years on the far side of the dark-blue wall.

When I looked in the direction of Kinglake I saw a lake among the mountains. The mountains around the lake were dark blue and the water in the lake was bright blue like the glass in a church win-dow. At the bottom of the lake, surrounded by the bright-blue water, a man sat on a gold throne. The man wore a gold crown and pieces of gold jewellery on his chest and his wrists and gold signet rings on his fingers.

I have mentioned just now three directions that I looked in

while I stood at the front gate of the first house that I remember having lived in. I have mentioned the direction in front of me, which was the direction of the place where I had been born, and I have mentioned the directions to either side of me. I have not mentioned the direction behind me.

Behind me while I stood at the front gate of the first house that I remember having lived in was the place where I described myself as standing on the first of these pages. Behind me was the place where I stood this morning looking at a body of yellow-brown water that had been denoted by a body of pale blue in my map, according to what I have written on these pages. Behind me was the place that was the slope of grass where the dead rats once lay; the place that was also the bare chest of a young woman who might have worn an evening dress so that she could display some precious jewel; the place that was also part of the face of a man with a drooping moustache; the place that was also a place just in front of the lips of a young woman who was about to be kissed. Behind me was still another place apart from those places. Behind me was the place that I came from this morning when I set out for the place where I am now. Behind me was the place where I have lived for the past twenty years—where I have lived since the year when I wrote my first book of fiction.

One day while I lived in the house of red bricks, I asked my father what place was in the direction that I have been calling just now the direction behind me. When I asked my father that question he and I were standing near the slope of grass that seemed to us then only a slope of grass that drained the water and other things from the pigsty into the swampy ground. Neither my father nor I would have seen in either of our minds bodies of yellow-brown or of pale blue.

My father told me that the place in the direction that I had asked about was a place called Macleod.

When my father had told me this, I looked in the direction that I had asked about, which was the direction ahead of me at that moment but which was the direction behind me when I looked in the direction of the place where I had been born, and which was also the direction behind me when I stood as I described myself standing on the first of these pages. When I looked in that direction I saw first grasslands and then pale-blue sky and white clouds. On the far side of the swampy ground the grasslands rose gently until they seemed to stop just short of the sky and the clouds.

When I heard my father say the word *Macleod*, I believed he was naming a place that had taken its name from what I saw in the direction of the place. I saw in my mind no place such as Preston or Coburg or Kinglake on the far side of the grasslands in the direction that was in front of me on that day. I saw in my mind only a man standing on a grassland that had risen towards the sky. The man stood on a yellow-brown grassland that had risen towards the pale-blue sky and had come to an end just short of the sky. The grassland had come to an end but the man wanted to go where the grassland would have gone if it had not come to an end. The man stood on the farthest point of the grassland just beneath the white clouds that were passing in the pale-blue sky. The man uttered a short sound and then a word.

The man uttered first a short sound like a grunt. He made this sound while he sprang upwards from the edge of the grassland. He sprang upwards and gripped the edge of a white cloud and then he dragged himself onto the cloud. His gripping and his dragging himself onto the cloud took only a moment. Then, when the man knew that he was safely on the white cloud that was travelling past the edge of the grassland and away out of sight of the man and the boy on the slope of grass below, the man uttered a word. This word together with the short sound made, so I thought, the name of the place that my father had named. The man uttered the word *cloud*.

During the years when I lived with my parents and my brother in the house of red bricks between Coburg and Macleod and between Preston and Kinglake, I often watched the men that my father called patients. The only patient that I spoke to was the young man known as Boy Webster. My mother told me not to speak to the other men that I saw around the place because they were loonies. But she told me I was free to talk to Boy Webster because he was not a loony; he was only backward.

I spoke sometimes to Boy Webster and he spoke often to me. Boy Webster spoke to my brother also, but my brother did not speak to Boy Webster. My brother spoke to nobody.

My brother spoke to nobody but he often looked into the face of a person and made strange sounds. My mother said that the strange sounds were my brother's way of learning to speak and that she understood the meaning of the sounds. But no one else understood that my brother's strange sounds had a meaning. Two years after my parents and my brother and I had left the house of red bricks my brother began to speak, but his speech sounded strange.

When my brother first went to school I used to hide from him in the schoolground. I did not want my brother to speak to me in his strange speech. I did not want my friends to hear my brother and then to ask me why he spoke strangely. During the rest of my childhood and until I left my parents' house, I tried never to be seen with my brother. If I could not avoid travelling on the same train with my brother I would order him to sit in a different compartment from mine. If I could not avoid walking in the street with my brother I would order him not to look in my direction and not to speak to me.

When my brother first went to school my mother said that he was no different from any other boy, but in later years my mother would admit that my brother was a little backward.

My brother died when he was forty-three years old and I was forty-six. My brother never married. Many people came to my brother's funeral, but none of those people had ever been a friend to my brother. I was certainly never a friend to my brother. On the day before my brother died I understood for the first time that no one had ever been a friend to my brother.

During the years when Boy Webster spoke often to me he spoke mostly about firecarts and firemen. Whenever he heard a motor vehicle approaching our house along Plenty Road from the direction of either Preston or Kinglake, Boy Webster would tell me that the motor vehicle would be a firecart. When the vehicle proved to be not a firecart, Boy Webster would tell me that the next vehicle would be a firecart. He would say that a firecart would soon arrive and that the firecart would stop and he would climb into it.

In the year when my brother died, which was forty-one years after my family had left the house of red bricks, a man was painting the inside of my house in Macleod. The man had been born in Diamond Creek and was living in Lower Plenty, which means that he had been moving roughly west from his birthplace towards my birthplace while I had been moving roughly east from my birthplace towards his. The man told me that he had painted during the previous year the insides of buildings in Mont Park Hospital.

I told the man that I had lived forty-one years before near Mont Park Hospital. I told him about the farm that was now a university and about the patients who had worked with my father. I told the man about Boy Webster and his talking mostly about firecarts and firemen.

While I was talking about Boy Webster the man put down his brush and looked at me. He asked me how old Boy Webster had been when I had known him.

I tried to see Boy Webster in my mind. I could not see him but I could hear in my mind his strange voice telling me that a firecart was coming and that he was going to get into the firecart.

I told the painter that Boy Webster might have been between twenty and thirty years old when I had known him.

Then the painter told me that when he had been painting one of the wards of Mont Park Hospital an old man had followed him around, talking to him. The painter had talked to the old man, who said his name was Webster. He told the painter no other name. He seemed to know himself only as Webster.

Webster had talked about firecarts and firemen. He told the painter that a firecart would soon arrive on the road outside the hospital building. He told the painter about the firecart every few minutes and he told the painter that he, Boy Webster, was going to climb into the firecart when it arrived.

The painter's father had been a tramways inspector until he had retired. The painter's father had since died, but the long green overcoat and the black hat with the glossy peak that the painter's father had worn as a tramways inspector still hung in a shed behind the house where the painter's mother lived.

The painter took the long green coat and the hat with the glossy peak to Mont Park Hospital and presented them to the old man known as Webster. He did not tell Webster that the coat and the hat were any sort of uniform. The painter simply presented the coat and the hat to Webster and Webster put them on at once over the clothes he was wearing. The old man known as Webster then told the painter that he was a fireman.

On the day before my brother died, I visited him in his hospital ward. I was his only visitor during that day.

A doctor in the hospital had told me that he was not prepared to say what particular illness had affected my brother, but the doctor believed that my brother was in danger of dying. After I had seen my brother I too believed this.

My brother was able to sit in the chair beside his bed and to walk a few steps and to sip from a glass, but he would not speak to anyone. His eyes were open, but he would not turn his eyes in the direction of anyone who looked at him or spoke to him.

I sat beside my brother for most of the day. I spoke to him and I looked at his face, but he would not speak to me and he would not look in my direction.

For much of the day I sat with my arm around my brother's shoulders. I believe today that before that day in the hospital I had not put my arm around my brother's shoulders since the evening in the house of red bricks when I had tried to teach my brother what a brassiere was used for.

From time to time while I sat with my brother, a woman in one or another uniform would come into the room. The uniform would be white or yellow-brown or one or another shade of blue. Whenever one of these women would come into the room I would wait for her to notice that I had my arm around the shoulders of the patient. I wanted to tell the woman in a loud voice that the patient was my brother. But none of the women seemed to notice where my arm was resting while I sat beside the patient.

Late on that day I left my brother and returned to my house in Macleod, which is nearly two hundred kilometres north-east from the hospital where my brother was a patient. My brother was alone when I left him.

On the following night I was told by telephone that my brother had died. My brother had been alone when he died.

At the funeral service for my brother, the priest said that my brother was now content because he had now become what he had been waiting for more than forty years to become.

On the Sunday after I had first thought of giving a pendant as a present to the young woman who was about to become my wife, the married sister of my father arrived at the house where I had sat looking at the jewellery catalogue.

One of my unmarried aunts asked my married aunt to show me her pendant. At that moment I looked at the part of my married aunt's body that lay between her throat and the place where the top of her evening dress would have been if she had been wearing an evening dress.

My married aunt was wearing not an evening dress but what I would have called an ordinary dress with buttons at the front. Only the top button of the dress was undone, so that I saw when I looked at my married aunt only a small triangle of yellow-brown skin. I saw no part of a pendant anywhere in the yellow-brown triangle.

When my unmarried aunt had told my married aunt that I had been admiring the pictures of pendants in the jewellery catalogue and that I had never seen a pendant, my married aunt moved one of her hands to the lowest part of the triangle of yellow-brown skin below her throat. She rested her hand in that place, and with the ends of her fingers she unfastened the second-top button at the front of her dress.

From the time when I had first heard that my married aunt was the owner of a pendant, I had supposed that the main part of the pendant was of the shape of a heart. When my aunt undid the second-top button of her dress I expected to see, somewhere on the skin between her throat and the place where the top of her evening dress would have been if she had been wearing an evening dress, a tapering golden heart.

When my married aunt had unfastened the second-top button at the front of her dress, she pushed apart with her fingers the two parts of the front of her dress and she found with her fingers two sections of fine golden chain that had been lying out of sight behind the front of her dress. With her fingers my aunt lifted the sections of chain upwards a little and then she scooped into the hollow of her hand the object that had been dangling at the end of the sections of chain. My aunt then lifted her hand out from between the two parts of the front of her dress and turned the hand towards me so that the object at the end of the sections of chain lay in the hollow of her hand where I could see it.

I understand today that the object in the hand of my married aunt was a piece of polished opal whose shape was roughly oval and that the object would have been of several shades of blue and other colours as well. But my aunt showed me for only a few moments what lay in her hand, and while she showed me the object she turned her hand a little so that I saw first what I thought was an object all of pale blue, then what I thought was an object all of dark blue, and then, after my aunt had slipped the object down again behind her dress, only the yellow-brown of part of the skin between my aunt's throat and the place where the top of her evening dress would have been if she had been wearing an evening dress.

Just before I began to walk this morning from Macleod towards the first house that I remember having lived in and the first view of grasslands that I remember having seen, I read something that brought to my mind the first body of blue water that I remember having seen in my mind.

I read in the pages of a newspaper that a famous stallion will soon arrive in this district. The stallion will arrive, according to what I read, from a famous breeding stud in the Vale of Tipperary, which is the part of Ireland where the father of my father's father arrived from when he arrived in this country.

The famous stallion will be used for serving more than fifty mares at the Mornmoot Stud, which is at Whittlesea, on the road between Preston and Kinglake. The name of the famous stallion is Kings Lake.

The only married woman from among my father's five sisters was the wife of a primary teacher. As a married woman she lived in many districts of Victoria. At the time when my aunt showed me her piece of polished opal of roughly oval shape, she and her husband were living about four miles inland from the place where I often sat with my back to the Southern Ocean and looked at the pages of a jewellery catalogue or of the *Saturday Evening Post*. The name of the place where my aunt and her husband lived is Mepunga East. In the same district is a place named Mepunga West. In maps of that district the word *Mepunga* appears only in the names of those two places.

Much of the text of *The Plains* was formerly part of the text of a much larger book. The larger book was the story of a man who had lived as a child in a place named Sedgewick North. If any map had been drawn of the district around that place, the map would have shown a place named Sedgewick East a few miles south-east of Sedgewick North. The word *Sedgewick* would have appeared only in the names of those two places.

The man who had lived as a child in the place named Sedgewick North had believed as a child that his district lacked what he called a true centre. Sometimes he used instead of the words *true centre* the word *heart*.

For some of the time while I was writing about the district around Sedgewick North, I saw in my mind some of the places around Mepunga East.

For most of his life my brother was said to be backward, but he was able to do some things that I have never been able to do.

Many times during his life my brother was able to travel in an aeroplane, which is something that I have never been able to do. My brother was able to travel in aeroplanes of different sizes. The smallest aeroplane that my brother travelled in contained only my brother and the pilot. My brother paid the pilot to take him through the air above part of the southern boundary of the mainland of Australia. While my brother was in the air he recorded by means of a camera and a roll of colour-film some of what he saw around him. I did not know that my brother had been in that air until after he had died. After my brother had died, the prints from that roll of colour-film were given to me.

Whenever I look nowadays at those prints I wonder whether my brother had become confused while he was in the air above the southern boundary of the grasslands of Australia, or whether the pilot of the aeroplane had tried to amuse or to frighten my brother by causing the aeroplane to travel sideways or even upside down through the air, or whether my brother had simply pointed his camera at what any man would see if he stood at the place in the air where the grasslands of Australia obviously have a mind to go.

When I look at those prints I seem sometimes to be looking at a place all of pale blue and sometimes to be looking at a place all of dark blue and sometimes to be looking at a place all of yellow-brown. But sometimes I seem to be looking from an impossible vantage-point at dark-blue water and, on the far side of the dark-blue water, the endless yellow-brown grasslands and the endless pale-blue sky of America.

Land Deal

After a full explanation of what my object was, I purchased two large tracts of land from them—about 600,000
acres, more or less—and delivered over to them blankets,
knives, looking-glasses, tomahawks, beads, scissors, flour,
etc., as payment for the land, and also agreed to give them
a tribute, or rent, yearly.

—JOHN BATMAN, 1835

We certainly had no cause for complaint at the
time. The men from overseas politely explained all
the details of the contract before we signed it. Of course
there were minor matters that we should have queried.
But even our most experienced negotiators were distracted by the
sight of the payment offered us.

The strangers no doubt supposed that their goods were quite
unfamiliar to us. They watched tolerantly while we dipped our
hands into the bags of flour, draped ourselves in blankets, and
tested the blades of knives against the nearest branches. And
when they left we were still toying with our new possessions. But
what we marvelled at most was not their novelty. We had recognised an almost miraculous correspondence between the strangers'
steel and glass and wool and flour and those metals and mirrors
and cloths and foodstuffs that we so often postulated, speculated
about, or dreamed of.

Is it surprising that a people who could use against stubborn
wood and pliant grass and bloody flesh nothing more serviceable

than stone—is it surprising that such a people should have become so familiar with the idea of metal? Each one of us, in his dreams, had felled tall trees with blades that lodged deep in the pale pulp beneath the bark. Any of us could have enacted the sweeping of honed metal through a stand of seeded grass or described the precise parting of fat or muscle beneath a tapered knife. We knew the strength and sheen of steel and the trueness of its edge from having so often called it into possible existence.

It was the same with glass and wool and flour. How could we not have inferred the perfection of mirrors—we who peered so often into rippled puddles after wavering images of ourselves? There was no quality of wool that we had not conjectured as we huddled under stiff pelts of possum on rainy winter evenings. And every day the laborious pounding of the women at their dusty mills recalled for us the richness of the wheaten flour that we had never tasted.

But we had always clearly distinguished between the possible and the actual. Almost anything was possible. Any god might reside behind the thundercloud or the waterfall, any faery race inhabit the land below the ocean's edge; any new day might bring us such a miracle as an axe of steel or a blanket of wool. The almost boundless scope of the possible was limited only by the occurrence of the actual. And it went without saying that what existed in the one sense could never exist in the other. Almost anything was possible except, of course, the actual.

It might be asked whether our individual or collective histories furnished any example of a possibility becoming actual. Had no man ever dreamed of possessing a certain weapon or woman and, a day or a year later, laid hold of his desire? This can be simply answered by the assurance that no one among us was ever heard to claim that anything in his possession resembled, even remotely, some possible thing he had once hoped to possess.

That same evening, with the blankets warm against our backs and the blades still gleaming beside us, we were forced to confront an unpalatable proposition. The goods that had appeared among us so suddenly belonged only in a possible world. We were therefore dreaming. The dream may have been the most vivid and enduring that any of us had known. But however long it lasted it was still a dream.

We admired the subtlety of the dream. The dreamer (or dreamers—we had already admitted the likelihood of our collective responsibility) had invented a race of men among whom possible objects passed as actual. And these men had been moved to offer us the ownership of their prizes in return for something that was itself not real.

We found further evidence to support this account of things. The pallor of the men we had met that day, the lack of purpose in much of their behaviour, the vagueness of their explanations—these may well have been the flaws of men dreamed of in haste. And, perhaps paradoxically, the nearly perfect properties of the stuffs offered to us seemed the work of a dreamer, someone who lavished on the central items of his dream all those desirable qualities that are never found in actual objects.

It was this point that led us to alter part of our explanation for the events of that day. We were still agreed that what had happened was part of some dream. And yet it was characteristic of most dreams that the substance of them seemed, at the time, actual to the dreamer. How, if we were dreaming of the strangers and their goods, were we able to argue against our taking them for actual men and objects?

We decided that none of us was the dreamer. Who, then, was? One of our gods, perhaps? But no god could have had such an acquaintance with the actual that he succeeded in creating an illusion of it that had almost deceived us.

There was only one reasonable explanation. The pale strangers, the men we had first seen that day, were dreaming of us and our confusion. Or, rather, the true strangers were dreaming of a meeting between ourselves and their dreamed-of selves.

At once, several puzzles seemed resolved. The strangers had not observed us as men observe one another. There were moments when they might have been looking through our hazy outlines towards sights they recognised more easily. They spoke to us with oddly raised voices and claimed our attention with exaggerated gestures as though we were separated from them by a considerable distance, or as though they feared we might fade altogether from their sight before we had served the purpose for which they had allowed us into their dream.

When had this dream begun? Only, we hoped, on that same day when we first met the strangers. But we could not deny that our entire lives and the sum of our history might have been dreamed by these people of whom we knew almost nothing. This did not dismay us utterly. As characters in a dream, we might have been much less at liberty than we had always supposed. But the authors of the dream encompassing us had apparently granted us at least the freedom to recognise, after all these years, the simple truth behind what we had taken for a complex world.

Why had things happened thus? We could only assume that these other men dreamed for the same purpose that we (dreamers within a dream) often gave ourselves up to dreaming. They wanted for a time to mistake the possible for the actual. At that moment, as we deliberated under familiar stars (already subtly different now that we knew their true origin), the dreaming men were in an actual land far away, arranging our very deliberations so that their dreamed-of selves could enjoy for a little while the illusion that they had acquired something actual.

And what was this unreal object of their dreams? The document we had signed explained everything. If we had not been distracted by their glass and steel that afternoon we would have recognised even then the absurdity of the day's events. The strangers wanted to possess the land.

Of course it was the wildest folly to suppose that the land, which was by definition indivisible, could be measured or parcelled out by a mere agreement among men. In any case, we had been fairly sure that the foreigners failed to see our land. From their awkwardness and unease as they stood on the soil, we judged that they did not recognise the support it provided or the respect it demanded. When they moved even a short distance across it, stepping aside from places that invited passage and treading on places that were plainly not to be intruded on, we knew that they would lose themselves before they found the real land.

Still, they had seen a land of some sort. That land was, in their own words, a place for farms and even, perhaps, a village. It would have been more in keeping with the scope of the dream surrounding them had they talked of founding an unheard-of city where they stood. But all their schemes were alike from our point of view. Villages or cities were all in the realm of possibility and could never have a real existence. The land would remain the land, designed for us yet, at the same time, providing the scenery for the dreams of a people who would never see either our land or any land they dreamed of.

What could we do, knowing what we then knew? We seemed as helpless as those characters we remembered from private dreams who tried to run with legs strangely nerveless. Yet if we had no choice but to complete the events of the dream, we could still admire the marvellous inventiveness of it. And we could wonder endlessly what sort of people they were in their far country, dreaming of a possible land they could never inhabit, dreaming further of a people such as ourselves with our one weakness, and then dreaming of acquiring from us the land which could never exist.

We decided, of course, to abide by the transaction that had been so neatly contrived. And although we knew we could never truly awake from a dream that did not belong to us, still we trusted that one day we might seem, to ourselves at least, to awake.

Some of us, remembering how after dreams of loss they had awakened with real tears in their eyes, hoped that we would somehow awake to be convinced of the genuineness of the steel in our hands and the wool round our shoulders. Others insisted that for as long as we handled such things we could be no more than characters in the vast dream that had settled over us—the dream that would never end until a race of men in a land unknown to us learned how much of their history was a dream that must one day end.

The Only Adam

It was the afternoon of the thunderstorm when A. finally decided to fall in love with Nola Pomeroy or try to shag her or do something special with her in some out-of-the-way place.

The clouds began piling up late in the morning. Storms in summer usually came from the south-west, where the ocean lay. But this one appeared from an unlikely quarter. A. watched it almost from its beginnings through the north windows of the school. Its black bulk was bearing down on Sedgewick North from the plains far inland.

After lunch the sky over the school showed nothing but bulging clouds that tore away continually and drifted like smoke on turbulent currents. A. had just seen the first of the lightning when Mr Farrant told the seventh grade that their film strip on Major Mitchell was ready in the cloakroom and asked them what they were waiting for. They filed out through the door. Mr Farrant called after them: "You, A., turn the projector and read the text and send the wrigglers and gigglers back to me."

The cloakroom was so dark that A. could not see who had gone into the lovers' corner. But the darkness made the pictures more sharp and clear than any he had seen before. He showed the map of south-eastern Australia with a wide blankness over nearly all of Victoria. He went on turning the knob. Mitchell's dotted line left the Murray River and thrust southwards. A.'s audience was unusually quiet and solemn. He supposed they were waiting for the first heavy drops of rain on the iron roof.

A. read aloud from the screen. Mitchell was so impressed by the rich and pleasant land that he named it *Australia Felix*, which meant Australia the Blessed. A. looked hard at a picture of level country with grass knee-high and huge gums grouped like trees in a botanical garden. It was hard to believe that such a landscape was part of his own State. Yet in the next frame Mitchell's dots had reached deep down into western Victoria. A. might even have said they were heading for his own district if he could have been sure where Sedgewick North should have been on the featureless map.

Still no one tried to joke or howl him down. There was not even a sound from the lovers' corner. A. wondered whether his own grade had at last found some history that took their fancy. Perhaps, like him, they were amazed to see an explorer approaching their own district—a famous man from their history course bearing down on their dairy farms and gravel roads.

The rain started. And a boy came up behind A. with some news that might have explained why everyone seemed quiet and thoughtful. It was not only the eighth-graders who were privileged to shag after school. One of the couples in the cloakroom at that moment had gone into the bush somewhere and tried it only the night before. A. hadn't caught their names for the noise of the rain on the roof. But he would find out soon enough because they were going to take up shagging every afternoon. And some of their friends might be joining them.

The storm was on top of them. The thunder and rain were so loud that A. gave up reading the captions. The scenes from Mitchell's journey passed over the screen without comment. The explorer had gone deep into *Australia Felix*, but there was still no mark on the map to show how near he might have been to any place that A. knew. The boy could only look at the land on the screen and wonder what he himself could discover to compare with it.

But he had to think, too, about the couple who had taken up shagging. The senior boys had always insisted that no one in A.'s grade was old enough to do it properly. A. had to admire the two, whoever they were, for sneaking off on their own to become pioneers. No doubt they had discovered a place where none of the older shaggers could disturb them or offer them advice. A. thought that all couples—lovers and shaggers—ought to do their own exploring and establish themselves in cosy nests all around the district. If he could have reserved Pomeroys' scrub for himself he would have enjoyed thinking of Sedgewick North as a network of concealed trails leading to hide-outs for enterprising couples.

The prolonged roaring of the rain died away. A. wound the film strip until it showed the familiar insignia of the Education Department of Victoria on a field of murky grey. No one booed as they usually did to complain that their film had ended. In fact, A. heard no sound from the darkness behind him. He thought what a fool he would seem if all the others had crept quietly away to plan their shagging in all the best landscapes of the district while he was still staring at what was left of the film strip.

But at least Nola Pomeroy was still in her usual place near the projector. A. glanced back and saw her looking as though she hadn't taken her eyes off the screen.

In the last half-hour before home-time the sky began to clear over the inland. There was even a shaft of sunlight pointing down at some lucky district near the horizon. Mr Farrant told A.'s grade to open their readers at the extract "On Pyramid Hill, Victoria, 1836," from *Three Expeditions into the Interior of Eastern Australia* by Thomas Livingstone Mitchell.

The pupils read by turns, and A. fidgeted while some farmer's son from Sedgewick North stumbled down the long rolling sentences that led to vistas of plains. Then it was Nola Pomeroy's turn. She was given the passage that A. had been hoping to read himself. But she was a good reader and, being a girl, she delivered her words with an earnestness that would have seemed ridiculous coming from a boy.

We had at length discovered a country for the immediate reception of civilized man, and fit to become the abode of one of the great nations of the earth. Unencumbered with too much wood, yet possessing enough for all purposes, with an exuberant soil under a temperate climate, bounded by the seacoast and mighty rivers, and watered abundantly by streams from mighty mountains, this highly interesting region lay before me with all its features new and untouched as they fell from the hands of the Creator. Of this Eden it seemed that I was the only Adam; and indeed, it was a sort of paradise to me.

A. kept himself from looking across at Nola. He watched instead the plains of *Australia Felix* projected onto the map of Victoria like an image from some memorable film strip. He watched himself reach a hand towards the waving grasses and scattered trees. But then a shadow fell on the map, and meaningless patches of light and darkness mottled his own skin. His outstretched arm had come between the source of light and the image he was after. And Nola herself might have been still behind him in the darkness.

In the last week of the school year even the rowdiest pupils were quieter and more decorous. Each morning before classes, the room was locked and the blinds were pulled down while Mr Farrant wrote up their final tests on the board. In the afternoon, while their teacher marked their test-books at his table, the upper grades filed into the infant school on the other side of the folding doors and practised for their Christmas Tree. Mrs Farrant played the piano, the upper grades sang the carols, and a select few of the younger children went through the actions of their nativity scene. Lolling against the infant-room walls under loops of coloured paper chains, A. and his friends sensed that the year was approaching some sort of climax.

They knew, of course, that the Christmas Tree was nothing much. It took place on the evening of the very last school day. The folding doors were pushed back and the desks stacked in corners. The parents and children faced each other across an empty space with the man-sized pine branch in its painted oil drum at the centre. The presents, one for each child, were heaped under the tree. The men of the School Committee, who had paid for the presents, sat on chairs beside Mr Farrant and referred to him as the Master of Ceremonies.

A. and his friends endured the carols, the nativity scene, the speeches, and finally the handing out of presents, all for the sake of the quarter-hour at the end. Then, while the parents had their tea and cakes around the tree, the older boys slipped outside into the dark and scattered. They ran and blundered and stumbled through the school garden, swinging their fists at anyone blocking their way, and made for mysterious hiding places. And even while the slower ones were still running, the howling began.

A. had first heard it years before, when he was much too small to join in. The big fellows had howled at every Christmas Tree since, and A. had tried it with them as soon as he entered the upper grades. He had known better than to ask what the rules were—he would have been told brusquely by the howlers that there were no rules. But he had learned, over the years, what a howler had to do.

You had to hide as far from the others as possible so that no one saw you when you let out your howls. You need not actually howl, but you must not make human sounds—and certainly not words. You tried to howl (or yelp or roar or crow) in turn with the others. This was hard to manage in the darkness, but if you were patient and listened carefully you heard a remarkable effect—

a long, almost rhythmic sequence of strange cries from near and far, with a place reserved for your own special call-sign.

A. was always glad just to find a corner for himself and to take part in the howling, but there were some who achieved much more. Some boys moved between one howl and another. They rather spoilt things if they stumbled noisily or showed themselves. But if they shifted their places unnoticed, you had a pleasant shock when their turn came. A howl that you had last heard from the end of the schoolground might ring out from behind a bush only a few paces away. Or a howl that you expected to come from nearby would reach you faintly from as far away as the pine plantation and leave you wondering how the bastard, whoever he was, had travelled such a distance between his howls.

Even the best howling sessions lasted only a few minutes. Then the school doors would open. The light from inside would spill out over the square of asphalt by the flagpole. Parents would come out to claim their younger children from the group of loiterers listening to the howling. The nearest of the howlers would creep in from the darkness and mingle with the family groups. Down past the pony paddock the farthest howlers soon noticed the gaps in the sequence and gave one last wild cry each and came quietly back. But A., whose parents were always the first to leave any gathering, had always climbed into the back of his father's utility still hearing one or two faint calls from the most daring of the howlers.

During each howling session A. tried to fix in his mind the strangest of the cries and the whereabouts, so far as he could judge, of the furthest howlers. He enjoyed the howling itself, but he looked forward to a far greater pleasure. He planned to question the others afterwards and to establish the exact routes followed by certain howlers across the dark schoolgrounds. If he could have learned enough, he would have drawn a detailed map showing the territory that each boy had seemed to claim when he stood in some unlikely spot and uttered his peculiar cry.

But A. had never been able to learn much more after howling than the little he knew from having been a howler himself. In bright daylight, with the same old paddocks around them, boys seemed reluctant to talk about the howling. They even seemed to dislike A.'s using glibly the word *howling* as though they and he had taken part in some annual ceremony. They seemed to want to pretend that a few tough bastards had run out into the dark to show off and a few others had followed them—and that was all.

A. invited Nola Pomeroy to the howling. He knew she could take no part in it. Not even the toughest eighth-grader would have led a girl away into the dark while her parents were just inside the school building. And no girl would have wanted to behave like a mad dog while she was dressed up for the Christmas Tree. What A. had in mind was for Nola to stand quietly outside on the asphalt and keep her eyes open.

Afterwards she might tell him the directions that the other boys had taken when they rushed off into the darkness. Days after the howling she might sit with him over his map of the schoolgrounds and the pine plantation and the nearest paddocks, marking with dotted lines the beginnings of the routes of all the howlers she had spied on. He would add some of his own observations from the hectic few minutes when he had blundered among the shapes and shadows she could not have seen. She might correct him occasionally, because she had been better placed to appreciate the whole event. But when they could not agree on a certain point they might well have to draw alternative diagrams.

On the night itself Nola walked a few paces away from the schoolroom porch and stood with her back to the windows. The first of the howlers were already leaping the lavender bushes and dodging between the dahlia beds on their way to claim their stations in the darkness. But A. moved slowly and deliberately away from the brightness of the schoolroom. He wanted to be sure that Nola observed him setting off into the obscure landscape of the howlers. If she had wondered sometimes why he had never got around to taking her into a pocket of roadside bush after school, she might now realise that he had much stranger places in mind.

He turned for a moment, and the sight of her alone against the brightness of the school windows made him pause. All year she had stood with him in the cloakroom and watched journeys of explorers in the patterns of shadows from film strips. Now there was darkness over Sedgewick North and as much as they could imagine of the rest of Australia, and Nola had placed herself in front of the brightest light for miles. The shadow she made reached far across the schoolgrounds. It merged into the unlit territory where the howlers were already following mysterious routes to their separate bases.

A. was less anxious to run out among the howlers. He moved further away from the school building, but not to search for any hiding-place among the unfamiliar shapes of shrubs and fences. He paused at what seemed the boundary of the aura from the lighted windowpanes. He wanted the girl behind him to make some movement or some sign that would suddenly alter the pattern of shadows around him. He wondered how much she might do to the scenery with just a gesture.

He looked back again. She was walking away; she was no longer between him and the light. And then the first howls were sounding, and he realised he had stood and wavered when he should have been running out into the dark to find his howling place.

It was too late for exploring. He dropped to the ground where he was. He wriggled and squirmed a little against the dry grass, thinking he might mark out with his body a place like a hare's that someone would stumble on and wonder about in the long, dreary days of the summer holidays.

The most notable of the howls that year could have come from anywhere. Once, it sounded so close that A. himself could have been held responsible. At other times it seemed to come from a place too far away for any boy to have reached. Someone was making the frantic bellow of a bull trying to get through a fence to a cow on heat. It was only the simple noise of an animal wanting no other landscape than the place where his female waited to be sniffed at and mounted. Yet out in the darkness it seemed to A., occasionally, something more.

Stone Quarry

I have just finished reading a piece of fiction about a man who insists on finding out how deep the bedrock is wherever he happens to be standing.

I would like to know the name of the woman who wrote the fiction. She has light-brown hair and interesting eyes, but her skin is rather weatherbeaten and her forehead is oddly wrinkled. I can never judge a person's age. This woman might be thirty-five or forty-five.

The woman's fiction is all in the first person, and the narrator identifies himself as a man. The author—the woman with the creased forehead—claims that the man in the story is based on her own brother, who suffers from what she calls an illness of the mind.

I will explain where I am and why I have to write this.

I am sitting at a battered garden-table on the back veranda of a ten-room stone house on a hilltop thirty-four kilometres northeast of the centre of Melbourne. A forest of rather skinny eucalypts grows all around the house and all down the steep gullies for as far as I can see. About once an hour I hear a motor car on the gravel road deep down among the trees. Mostly I hear the cheeps and tweets and ting-tangs of birds and the swishings of leaves and twigs in the wind. If I walk along the veranda I can just hear, through the thick stones of the wall, the tapping of a typewriter. At two other places along the stone wall I can hear the same faint sound. Far inside the house, and quite inaudible to me, two people are using electronic keyboards and screens. A writers' workshop is in progress.

The stone house belongs to a painter (a painter of quite ordinary views of desert and savannah, to judge from what can be seen on the insides of these walls). At this moment the painter is somewhere on the road to Hattah Lakes. But these details are not important . . . the artist's house is ours for the present.

We are six writers—three men and three women—who have undertaken to write and to show our writing to one another for seven days and six nights up here among the sounds of birds and the wind in the treetops. Five of us, so I believe, have had fiction published in magazines or anthologies. Myself, I am a poet (sparingly published) who is trying to break into prose. Our workshop is not meant to produce immediately a body of publishable writing. Our meeting here on this hill is meant to put us in touch with the deep sources of fiction.

Last night—Friday night—each of us had to write our first piece and then hand it to the person in charge of the session. This morning at breakfast each of us was given a copy of each of the five pieces written by our fellow writers.

In most writers' workshops the members sit around discussing their work; they talk about themes and symbols and meaning and such matters. The six of us do none of this. Ours is a Waldo workshop. The rules were devised by Frances Da Pavia and Patrick McLear, a husband-and-wife team of writers in the USA. In 1949 these two began a series of workshops at their summer house in Waldo County, Maine. Frances Da Pavia and Patrick McLear have both since died but they bequeathed their estates, including the house in Maine, to the Waldo Fiction Foundation, which continues to arrange annual workshops and to keep alive the Waldo theory of fiction in the USA and in other countries.

The rules for the Waldo workshops have hardly been changed since the first summer when the co-founders and four disciples shut themselves away for a week on a rocky peninsula looking across the water to Islesboro Island. As far as possible the writers have to be strangers to one another. (The co-founders were far from being husband and wife in the days of their first workshops, and after their marriage they were never again together as writers in the stone house.) Everyone is compelled to take a pen-name at the first session and to change that pen-name each day. But the most important rule is the absolute ban on speech.

In this matter a Waldo workshop is more strict than a Trappist monastery. Trappist monks are at least allowed to use sign language, but writers at a Waldo workshop are not allowed to communicate by any means other than the writing of prose fiction. Waldo writers may exchange any number of messages during their week together, but every message must be encoded in prose fiction. No other sort of message is permitted. Writers may not even allow such a message to reach them inadvertently: if one writer happens to intercept another's glance, the two must go at once to their separate writing-tables and write for each other a piece of fiction many times more elaborate and subtle than whatever lay behind either glance or was read from it.

Waldo writers are not even permitted to make the sorts of comment that writers in conventional workshops make about each other's work. Each morning in this house each one of us will pore over the latest batch of fiction, looking for scattered traces of our own stories in the manifold pattern of Waldo.

To preserve the ideal of unbroken silence, the Waldo manual recommends a certain gait for strolling around the house and grounds and a certain posture for sitting at the dining-table or on the veranda. The eyes are kept lowered; each stride is somewhat hesitant; arms and hands are guarded in their movements for fear a hand might brush a foreign sleeve or, worse still, a naked wrist or finger. House and grounds, naturally, are required to be remote and secluded. The co-founders' house, in the one photograph that I happen to have seen, seems to belong in an Andrew Wyeth painting.

The theory behind the vow of silence is that talk—even serious, thoughtful talk or talk about writing itself—drains away the writer's most precious resource, which is the belief that he or she is the solitary witness to an inexhaustible profusion of images from which might be read all the wisdom of the world. At the beginning of each workshop, every writer has to copy in handwriting and to display above his or her writing-table the famous passage from the diaries of Franz Kafka:

> I hate everything that does not relate to literature, conversations bore me (even when they relate to literature), to visit people bores me, the joys and sorrows of my relatives bore me to my soul. Conversation takes the importance, the seriousness, the truth, out of everything I think.

Every breach of the vow of silence must be reported to the writer-in-charge. Even so seemingly slight a thing as sighing within earshot of another person is a reportable offence, and the writer who catches a hint of meaning in the sound of someone's breath escaping is therefore expected not only to write before long about a fictional sigher and sigh but to draft a brief informer's report. Likewise, the sight of a mouth being drawn deliberately down at the corners or even a distant view of a head shaking slowly from side to side or of a pair of hands being pressed against a face—any of these can oblige a writer to amend the work-in-progress so that it includes a version of the latest offence against Waldo and of the report of the offence and any other documents to do with it.

A first offender against the Great Silence is punished by being sent to his or her room to transcribe passages from writers whose way of life was more or less solitary: Kafka, Emily Dickinson,

Giacomo Leopardi, Edwin Arlington Robinson, Michel de Ghel-
derode, A. E. Housman, Thomas Merton, Gerald Basil Edwards,
C. W. Killeaton . . . The Waldo Fiction Foundation keeps a register
of all those who for at least five years of their lives wrote or took
notes but talked to no friend or lover.

A second offence brings immediate expulsion from the workshop. The expulsion is never announced to the group, but suddenly
among the buzzings and clickings of insects and the chirrups of
birds on a drowsy afternoon a motor car engine starts up, and perhaps you notice an hour later that a certain pair of creaking shoes
are no longer heard in the corridors; or perhaps, standing at a certain point on the veranda, you see the same trail of ants flowing
up and down the yellowish stone and the same tiny spider unmoving in its cave of crumbled mortar but you no longer hear the faint
rattling of a typewriter through the wall; or later at the dinner table
a bread roll lies unbroken by a pair of hands that you formerly
watched from under your eyebrows.

Does anyone reading this want to ask why the workshop should
expel a person whose presence had made the fiction of at least
one writer daily more bulky and more complex? Anyone who
could ask this question has not even begun to understand what I
have written so far. But Waldo can answer for me. What might
have seemed to the objector a grave objection earns a sentence
in the manual. *Just the one room becoming empty will make the
echo of the fiction of the house more lingering still.*

No one questions the rules concerning silence, but newcomers
to Waldo sometimes wonder why no rule forbids a writer in a
workshop from sending urgent letters or manifestoes or apologias
after someone who has just been expelled. How can the purpose
of the workshop be served, the questioner asks, if the bereft writer,
instead of working at fiction, drafts long addresses to someone
who has seemed to undermine the basic principles of Waldo?

A little thought usually reassures the doubter. The writer in a
workshop has to deliver each day to the writer-in-charge not only
the finished drafts of fiction but any earlier drafts or page of notes

or scribble and certainly any letter or draft of a letter written that day. No one may send out from a Waldo workshop any letter or note or any other communication without first submitting it to the writer-in-charge. In short, the writer sending messages after an expelled fellow-writer may be writing to no one. Even if Waldo, in the person of the writer-in-charge, actually forwards the letters, there is no obligation to reveal to the person who wrote them the true name, let alone the address, of the person they were sent to. And the ritual bonfire at the end of every workshop is not just for all the writing done during the week but for all of Waldo's records—every scrap of evidence that might otherwise be adduced some day to prove that this or that writer once, under half a dozen pseudonyms, learned the secret of true fiction from an eccentric American sect.

So, the writer who spends the last days of a workshop trying to reach someone who once or twice glanced or stared in a certain way before being expelled—that writer will usually understand in time that no letters may have been forwarded or that the letters were forwarded but with the sender identified only by a false name and the address "Waldo." The writer who reaches this understanding will then be grateful to the body of theory and traditions personified as Waldo. For if the writer had had his or her way at first, much precious writing time would have been lost and perhaps the workshop itself abandoned while the two strangers made themselves known to each other in conventional ways. But, thanks to Waldo, the writer stayed on at the workshop and began the first notes or drafts of what would later become a substantial body of fiction.

Those novels or novellas or short stories or prose poems would be widely read, but only their author would know what they really were and who they were addressed to. As for that person, the one whose motor car had started up suddenly among the dry sounds of grasshoppers on a hot afternoon, that person would almost certainly never read any of the published fiction. That person would have been won over years earlier by the doctrines of Waldo, and in all the years since the founding of our group not a single apostasy has been recorded. The expelled writer is still one of us, and like every other follower of Waldo he or she would read no fiction by any living author. He or she might buy the latest books and display them all around the house, but no author would be read until that author was dead.

No living author would be read because the reader of a living author might be tempted one day to search out the author and to ask some question about the text or about the weather on the day when this or that page was first composed or about a certain year of the author's life before the first sentence of the text came into being. And to ask such questions would be not just to violate the most sacred tradition of Waldo; it would be as if to say that the old stone house by Penobscot Bay has never existed, that Frances Da Pavia and Patrick McLear are no more substantial than characters in a work of fiction, and that the Waldo theory of fiction—far from having produced some of the finest writers of our day—is itself the invention of a writer: a bit of whimsy dreamed up by a man at a writers' workshop and handed to the writer-in-charge so that a woman with light-brown hair and a frowning face would learn why the man had not yet told her how impressed he had been by her story of a man who worried about bedrock.

In an earlier draft of this paragraph—a draft that you will never read—I began with the words: "You may be wondering about that ritual bonfire mentioned a little distance back . . ." But if you had read those words you would have wondered not just how the words could have reached you if all the pages written during the workshop are ritually burned on the last evening; you would have wondered also who the word "you" referred to. If these pages are being written on the veranda of a stone house during a writers' workshop, you might say to yourself, why are they seemingly addressed to me: to someone who reads them in very different surroundings? For the pages are much too explanatory to have been written for the other workshop members—why would five followers of Waldo have to be told in the opening paragraphs of a piece of workshop fiction all the rules and traditions so well known to them?

But you have almost answered your own objection. You have spoken of this writing as fiction. This is the truth. These words are part of a work of fiction. Even these last few sentences, which can be read as an exchange between the writer and a reader, are fiction. Any thoughtful reader would recognise them for what they are. And the writers at a Waldo workshop are the most thoughtful of readers. When these pages are put in front of them, my fellow writers will not demand to know why they have to read an account of things already familiar to them. They will read with even more than their usual alertness. They will try to learn why I have written in the form of a piece of fiction addressed to strangers far away from this hilltop a piece of fiction that only they can read.

And yet, you still want certain puzzles explained. (Or, to put this more clearly, if you existed you would still want those puzzles explained.) If the ritual bonfire consumes all evidence of the workshop, why should I write as though these pages are going to be preserved?

My first impulse is to answer, "Why not?" One of the most cherished anecdotes among the followers of Waldo is of the writer who begged for a last few minutes while the other members of the workshop were already around the fire and making scrolls of their pages, tying bundle after bundle with the obligatory silk ribbons in the Waldo colours of pale-grey and sea-green, and tossing their bundles into the flames. During those last few minutes the writer crouched in the glow from the flames and scribbled over and over the same sentence for which the right order of words and the right balance among the subordinate clauses had still not been found.

With Waldo it is the spirit that matters rather than the form. No writer is stripped and searched before leaving a workshop. No luggage is forcibly opened on the front veranda on the morning

74

of departure. If you still believe that I am writing these words to be read by someone outside the workshop, then you only have to imagine my slipping this typescript under the heap of my soiled underclothes on the last night . . .

Now the danger may be that I am making Waldo seem a mere set of conventions to be varied if occasion demands. I assure you that Waldo weighs heavily indeed on me. Every page that I write here on this veranda will be tied, five nights from tonight, in the colours of ocean and fog and burned in the view of five writers whose good opinions I value, even if I may never learn their true names.

And I follow the way of Waldo even more strictly for having read sometimes, on the last day of a workshop, the implication that we are not meant to take Waldo seriously after all: that these monastic retreats with their fussy rituals, the manual with all its rules, the house in Maine, although they are, of course, part of a solid world, are only meant to work on the imagination of writers and to suggest how seriously one *might* take the writing of fiction in an ideal world.

At this point someone who had never heard of Waldo before reading these pages might need to be reminded that the isolation of Waldo writers is not relieved during hours of darkness.

The co-founders in their wisdom decreed that the writers in each workshop had to be strangers and that the numbers of men and women must be equal. Some people have concluded from this that we provide a literary introduction service. Perhaps one of my readers, even after the careful account I have so far given, supposes even now that only half the bedrooms will be occupied each night during this workshop.

Even if my suspicious reader, like all my readers, is only someone I called into being this morning on this veranda, still I consider myself bound to answer truthfully. In any case, what do I have to gain by writing anything but the truth in these circumstances?

I spent last night alone in my room. I cannot imagine why I

would not spend tonight and every other night of the workshop alone in my room—unless the whole of the history of the Waldo movement has been an elaborate practical joke of which I am the sole victim, and unless I am the only writer in this house who believes that if I were to try a certain door-knob tonight it should only be for the purpose of thrusting a little way into the darkness the thick bundle of all the pages I have written, with not even my true name on them, before I creep back to my room.

I cannot answer for any other writer, of course, but I hereby declare my faith in the doctrine that persuaded me to give up poetry and to come to this stony hill to learn how to write truly. I believe as a Waldo writer that my existence is only justified by the writing of prose fiction. And for inspiration I look to Campobello Man.

You Waldo writers reading this know very well who I mean. But my imaginary reader far from this hill could not have heard even the title of the book that explains everything.

Isles Fogbound: The Writer on the Wrong Side of America—have any of us read this book as it deserves to be read, and changed our lives accordingly? I am no better than any of you. I can expound the thesis of many a chapter, yet I have still not felt in my heart the joy that is promised in the last pages; I have still not seen the changed world that I ought to see all around me if only I could give myself wholly over to Waldo.

How can I think of everything I see as no more and no less than a detail in a work of fiction? I walked a little way down this hill before breakfast. From every outcrop of stones and gravel a small vine of *hardenbergia* grew: the same mauve that I look for in every garden I walk past in the suburbs of Melbourne. Yet I stared at the mauve against the golden-brown and could think of no place for it in any piece of prose fiction I might write. Perhaps the mauve and the brown belong in the fiction of another writer, and perhaps this is the sense of those ambiguous passages in the last pages of the inspired volume of Waldo.

When I knelt and touched the soil a surprising image came

to me. The flaky stones had the look and the feel of a thick layer of face-powder plastered oddly on her face by a woman not quite right in the head. A different sort of writer might follow this image wherever it leads.

Of all I have read in Frances Da Pavia and Patrick McLear I remember mostly the smaller details and the quirky propositions. From the accounts of the first workshops I remember the custom of making the newly arrived writers walk all around the rooms and corridors counting windows. They could consider themselves for the time being dwellers in the House of Fiction, but they ought to acknowledge that the house had considerably fewer windows than Henry James had asserted. As for the windows, even though I have never set foot on the North American continent I can see the dark-blue sky, the green of Penobscot Bay, and above all, the pearly-grey of the fogs—even the painted fogs on the double panes of the rooms for those who wanted to live Waldo doctrine to the fullest.

I am familiar too with all the contrivances that were fitted to the house for those who wanted to spy on their fellow writers by day or night. (In these temporary quarters we have no opportunity for the intensive spying that Waldo has always permitted without directly encouraging. A Waldo writer is urged not so much to spy as to feel always under close surveillance, and the spy-holes and carelessly hidden cameras all around the house in Maine are to promote this feeling. How many writers make use of these things Waldo officially does not trouble itself to learn. No one on this hilltop would have drilled through the artist's walls, but any-one would have been free to bring their own equipment with them, and one of you five readers of the first draft of this may be reading it not for the first time.)

I have only sometimes glimpsed the world through Waldo's eyes, but I have meditated often on the map of North America as Da Pavia and McLear taught me to see it. The people of the continent are mostly going in the wrong direction.

The people are all being carried blindly westward. They are all hoping to reach a place of bright sunlight where they will see enacted deeds befitting the end of a long journey. But the people are all going the wrong way.

The coast of Maine is almost the farthest place where a group of American writers can stand and declare that they have gone, literally as well as spiritually, against the prevailing currents of their nation. But even in the stone house in Waldo County, the writers wanted to say more than this; and so began the game of the islands.

The people of America are being carried blindly along in the path of the sun, but not the writers of Waldo. They huddle on their clifftop and set their faces towards Penobscot Bay. America, these writers say, is a book. They themselves may be situated within the pages of America, but they stand where they stand to signify that the subject of their own fiction lies behind the readers and even the writers of America.

The man who wrote under the name of Stendhal is supposed to have said in 1830 that he wrote his fiction for readers of 1880. Frances Da Pavia and Patrick McLear announced in 1950 that their fiction of that year was being written for the reader of 1900. (To make their arithmetic quite clear: they were writing in 1960 for the readers of 1890; and if the co-founders were alive today in 1985 they would have in mind the readers of 1865.) Towards the end of their lives Da Pavia and McLear thought of themselves as privileged to be drawing still nearer to the putative age when no word of fiction had yet been written. And just before their sudden deaths, our founders were preoccupied with the question what mode of fictional address the lucky writer would choose for that generation for whom a sentence such as *Call me Waldo* . . . and all that it could possibly mean were solid items of a factual world.

This is what first drew me to Waldo of all the schools of fiction I might have joined: this earnest undertaking by Waldo writers to shape their sentences not according to habits of thinking in their own day but as though each writer is writing from a separate island just short of the notional beginning of the mainland.

In the early years of the game the writers chose from actual islands. Before beginning a workshop each writer would consult large-scale maps of the coast. Then, on the first morning in the stone house and while the fog outside was still unmoving, table and chair would be carefully aligned so that the seated writer faced the blank double-page of America and a word would be whispered in the monkish room. For the remaining six days of the workshop, *Monhegan, Matinicus,* or *Great Wass* would mark the place where the true story of America was being written; where a writer that the writer in the room could only dream of found the words to write; where the invisible was on the point of becoming visible.

Although every page of fiction purporting to have been written at these places was burned in due course, still rumours and gossip hung around the stone house, and each new group of writers seemed to know which islands had been claimed in earlier years and which dwindling few had never been written from. In the last year before the game changed its direction, members of the workshop had to choose from mere rocks and nameless shoals. Then someone who claimed afterwards not to have noticed the dots and dashes of the international border swerving strangely southwest across the inked ocean wrote that he dreamed of someone writing dreamlike prose on Campobello.

What happened during the following week enriched the theory and traditions of Waldo, it was said, immeasurably beyond the hopes of the co-founders. (I prefer to believe that Da Pavia and McLear foresaw confidently the scope, if not the details, of the Campobello Migration and wrote about it in some of the best of their lost typescripts.) In a word, the writers for that week were divided quite by accident into two groups. The first had consulted in the Waldo Library (Can any of us in this house almost bare of books imagine what a treasury of recondite lore is the library in the original stone house?) an atlas in which coloured inks were used only for the nation or the state which happened to be the designated subject-matter for that page, surrounding areas being colourless, ghostly, almost bare of printed names. The second group consulted an atlas in which the colours reached to the very margins of every page, no matter what political or geographical borders crossed the page itself. So for one group Campobello—the island, the man supposed to be writing there, and the host of invisible possibilities behind the word itself—gave pleasure because it was perversely located in a place that a writer might actually visit if he or she was literal-minded enough to want to travel through the fog and even further along the schematic edge of America. (This group was further divided into those who recognised that Campobello Island is part of the Province of New Brunswick and those who believed it to be the utmost outpost of the State of Maine.) The second group, having seen a pale blob on their map and having deliberately refused to turn to the pages presenting a coloured Canada—not even to learn the name of the blob, supposed Campobello and everything arising from it to be the result of an ingenious invented cataclysm.

They supposed that at some time during the filling-in of the blank double-page of the continent and while the ink of America, so to speak, was still not dry, someone of far-reaching imaginative power had taken each page by its outermost edge, lifted the two pages upwards and inwards, and pressed them firmly together, even rubbing certain patches at random fiercely up against one another for simple delight.

How can the result of this be best described? America as a mirror of itself? America turned inside out and around about? America as a page in a dream-atlas? With this map in mind a writer could see in the forests of New England the colours of New Mexican deserts; could see, as I myself once saw (admittedly in an atlas published in England), the word *Maine* clearly printed near Flagstaff, Arizona, and the word *Maineville* near Loveland, Ohio. But of all the thousands of embellishments and verbal puzzles and aimless or fragmented roads and trails now added to America, what most appealed to the writers in the stone house was the simple notion of a Beautiful Plain as the primordial setting for fiction and the Handsome Plainsman as the original of all fictional characters, if not of all writers of fiction.

I could write an entire short novel on this subject, but I am only a minor poet taking his first stumbling steps as a writer of fiction; and in any case my first task is to finish this account of the most wonderful week in the history of Waldo.

After the bonfire of that week the writers meditated on the two versions of Campobello: the writer as finder of blank spaces on actual maps, and the writer as finder of quite new double-pages of maps. And what those writers never forgot was that the fiction from each of their two groups had been indistinguishable. The so-called Campobello Migration that followed meant simply that all Waldo writers were free from then onwards to locate the ideal source of their fiction in places even further east than New Brunswick or in places whose names or parts of whose names might have appeared on a map of Maine if certain pages of atlases were rubbed together, figuratively speaking, before their colours had finally dried.

The shadows of the nearest trees have now reached the yellow flagstones under my writing-table. The time is late in the afternoon. And just a moment ago I heard the sudden starting-up of a motor car.

The artist who owns this house left a badly written note explaining how to operate the pumps that bring water up the hill from the underground storage tanks, and for some reason he scrawled at the bottom: *Late in day find spot on back veranda with terrific view of Melb skyline so long no smog.*

As I write these words, a motor car is following the winding road downwards between these hard hills where off-blue *hardenbergia* sprouts wild between outcrops of dull-gold talc. In the motor car is a writer who believes wholeheartedly, as I believe, in the claims of Waldo fiction. The writer has submitted to being expelled from this house as the penalty for sending a message to a fellow writer by means other than the inserting of an allusion into a passage of fiction. If I am the person who was meant to receive the message, I can write truthfully that I have never received it.

I do not know the name of the person in the motor car. I will probably never know that name. If I could give all my time to reading all the fiction published in this country, I might read some day a passage recalling a piece of fiction I once read about a man who thought continually about the bedrock far under his feet, who studied the surfaces of all the stones he saw, who wanted to live only in stone houses, who would not have complained if he had been made to read fiction day after day, or even poetry . . .

The rules of Waldo allow me only until sunset to finish what I am writing. If this were only a piece of fiction devised to amuse a few writers with tastes and interests like my own—if not only Waldo and the man who wondered about bedrock but even the woman with the light-brown hair was invented for the benefit of a group of writers who have not yet been mentioned in these pages, surely now would be the time for me to explain myself.

Until I was nearly twenty years old I thought I was meant to be a poet. Then, in December 1958, I saw in the window of Alice Bird's secondhand bookshop in Bourke Street, Melbourne, a copy of *Ulysses*, by James Joyce. After reading that book I wanted to be a writer of prose fiction.

In those days I knew only two people who might have been interested in my change of heart. I told the two people what I had decided while the three of us happened to be standing under an enormous oak tree in the grounds of the mansion known as Stonnington, in the Melbourne suburb of Malvern. Stonnington at that time was used by the Education Department of Victoria as part of a teachers' college. I was a student of the teachers' college, working to qualify at the end of 1959 for the Trained Primary Teacher's Certificate, after which I would teach in schools of the Education

Department by day and write prose fiction during evenings and at
weekends.

After I had announced my decision to write prose fiction I
wanted to do more. I searched in libraries for information about
Joyce. Somewhere I found a sentence that I still remember today:
*He dressed quietly, even conservatively, beringed fingers being his
only exoticism.*

I went to one of the pawnbrokers in Russell Street, Melbourne,
and bought two cheap rings. Each was low-carat gold with a slab
of black onyx. I wore the rings on my fingers but I did not otherwise change my threadbare style of dressing.

The first picture I found of Joyce was a reproduction of a photograph that I have rarely seen since. I believed the man I considered the greatest of prose writers had had a forehead sharply scored
by lines of the same pattern—three parallel horizontals intersected
by a single diagonal—as the lines I had drawn in my fourth year
of secondary school in my general science notebook to represent
a layer of bedrock.

I hid my rings from my father. In my father's eyes, rings and
tiepins and cufflinks were of the style he called Cockney Jew. I hid
Ulysses also. My father could not bear to hear such words as *shit*
or *fuck* uttered in any context, and I assumed he would not want
to read them either.

My father has been dead now for twenty-five years. He left
behind him no prose fiction and no poetry, and not even a written
message for any of his family. But on the wall of a sandstone quarry
on the hill called Quarry Hill near the mouth of Buckley's Creek
in the district of Mepunga East on the south-west coast of Victoria, my father's surname and his two initials are still deeply inscribed above the date 1924. When my father carved his name he
was as old as I was when I made my announcement under the oak
tree in the grounds of the building called Stonnington.

In 1924 James Joyce was forty-two and *Ulysses* had been published for two years. The young man carving his name in the stone-
quarry had thirty-six years still to live; the man writing *Finnegans*

Wake in Paris had a little less than half that time ahead of him. The man in the quarry knew nothing then of Joyce or his writing and still nothing of them when he died.

I have enclosed with my last will and testament five sheets of paper inscribed with what I consider useful information for my sons. One sheet tells them how to find the inscription made by their grandfather who died ten years before the eldest of them was born. One or more of my sons may care to inspect my father's writing twenty-five years after my own death, and then to note how much or how little of my own writing can still be read.

Out of the quarry on Quarry Hill came the blocks of sandstone that went into the building of a house known as The Cove about one kilometre from the quarry and within earshot of the Southern Ocean. My father's father built the house and lived in it until he died in 1949. The house stands solidly today, but it is owned and lived in by people whose name I do not know. I have not seen the house for nearly ten years. I hardly ever think of it. I did not even think of it while I was writing about the stone house of Waldo by Penobscot Bay. This is not a story about a house but about the space where a house could have been. I only mention my grandfather's house in this story because the digging of the stone for that house gave my father a page for his writing that has lasted for sixty years.

All my life I have looked around me for outcrops of rocks or pebbles or for any jagged place where the true colour of the earth is exposed. Even the crumbs around an ants' nest will make me stop and look. I watch the cuttings beside railway-lines, the bare patches at the bases of roadside trees, and the dirt thrown up from trenches; I like to be able to think clearly about the colours underneath me as I walk.

The man I read about today is not interested in the colours of soil. He wants to be sure the bedrock is deep and true for as far downwards as he can imagine it. He believes in a world of countless layers, most of them invisible, and he believes that a fault in any one of the layers has an influence on every other layer. He believes that what some people call his mental illness is a fault in one of the subtle, invisible layers of the world at about the level of his own head. He believes that the ultimate cause of this fault is a terrible creasing of the bedrock far below.

The man I am writing about is a character in a piece of fiction, but the woman who wrote the piece of fiction is a living woman whose forehead creases when she writes or reads. Until a short while ago that woman was with me in this house, but now she has gone and I do not expect to see her again.

The woman with the furrows in her forehead has left the house because she has already read what I am writing. The woman came up to my table this morning while I was crouched on the hillside staring at the mauve *hardenbergia* and fingering the brownish, powdery rocks. The woman read my pages and understood more clearly than I understand why I am writing them. Then she left a message for me—a clear, unambiguous message not encoded in prose fiction and therefore in serious breach of the rules of Waldo. And then the woman handed all her paper and drafts to the writer-in-charge and left this house.

To finish this piece of fiction I would only have to write that after the woman had gone I went in search of her message and found it in the most obvious place—in the nearest thing to a library in this house. I would only have to write that one volume on the artist's miserable shelf of books was oddly stacked, as though drawing attention to itself . . .

The book is: *Berenice Abbott: Sixty Years of Photography*, by Hank O'Neal with an introduction by John Canaday, published by Thames and Hudson in 1982. On the front of the dust-jacket is a brilliantly clear picture of James Joyce at the age of forty-six. Two rings are clearly visible on his fingers. Inside the cover of the book the name Nora Lee has been written in ballpoint. My mother's mother had exactly that name but she owned no books. Towards the end of the book I found a photograph of a place called Stonington, which is on an island off the coast of Maine.

Or I might finish this piece of fiction by mentioning that I have always been drawn to writers who have felt their minds threatened. When I read Richard Ellmann's biography of Joyce in 1960 I studied carefully the account of his daughter's madness. I wondered whether Joyce could follow, as he claimed he could, the swift leaps in her thought.

One night in October 1960 I was drinking in the house of a man who boasted that he was welcome in the houses of famous artists in the hills north-east of Melbourne. Late in the evening, when the man and I were both very drunk, he drove me in his station wagon (it was the company car that he drove as a sales representative) first to Eltham and then along hilly back roads to the strangest building I had ever seen. I learned afterwards that the place was Montsalvat, but on that dark night in 1960 the man who took me there would only tell me it was an artists' colony. I learned afterwards too that the man I met in the stone castle was Justus Jorgensen, but I was introduced to him only as the Artist.

The Artist would have been justified in sending us away from his front door, but he let us in and dealt with us most politely. We must have talked for an hour, but all I remember is my learning that the Artist had been in Paris in the 1920s; my asking had he ever seen James Joyce; his telling me that he had; my asking had he ever seen Joyce's daughter, Lucia, and had she seemed in any way strange; his telling me that Lucia Joyce had been a beautiful young woman with no imperfection that he had noticed.

I might have ended this piece of fiction in either of the two ways outlined above, but of course I did not. I have thrown in my lot with Waldo. If I am any sort of writer I am a Waldo writer. If what

I write rests on any coherent theory it rests on those doctrines devised by starers into fogs and mutterers of names of islands on the wrong side of their country.

And so, trusting utterly in the wisdom of Waldo, and noting that the sun is at the point of sinking below the faint purple-brown blur which is the northern suburbs of Melbourne as seen from an artist's stone house far to the east of my own home, I end, or I prepare to end, this piece of fiction.

All the fiction I have written in the stone house has been an encoded message for a certain woman. In order to send this message I have had to imagine a world in which the woman does not exist and neither do I. I have had to imagine a world in which the pronoun *I* stands for the sort of man who could imagine a world in which he does not exist and only a man steeped in the theories of Waldo could imagine him.

Precious Bane

Ifirst thought of this story on a day of drizzling rain in a secondhand bookshop in Prahran. I was the only customer in the shop. The owner sat near the door and stared out at the rain and the endless traffic. This was all he seemed to do all day. I had passed the shop often and walked through the man's gaze; and during the moment when I intersected that gaze I felt what it might be like to be invisible.

On the day of drizzle I was inside the man's shop for the first time. (I buy many secondhand books, but I buy them from catalogues. Secondhand bookshops make me unhappy. Even reading the catalogues is bad enough. But the secondhand books that I buy do not sadden me. Taking them out of their parcels and putting them on my shelves, I tell them they have found a good home at last. And I warn my children often that they must not sell my books after I have died. My children need not read the books, but they must keep them on shelves in rooms where people might glance at them sometimes or even handle them a little and wonder about them.) The man had glanced at me when I came into his shop, but then he had looked away and gone on gazing. And all the while I poked among his books he never looked back at me.

The books were badly arranged, dusty, neglected. Some were heaped on tables, or even on the floor, when they could easily have been shelved if the man had cared to put his shop in order. I looked over the section marked LITERATURE. I had in my hand one of what I called my book-buying notebooks. It was the notebook labelled *1900–1940 . . . Unjustly Neglected*. The forty years covered by the notebook were not only the first forty of the century. Written "1940–1900," they were the first forty years from the year of my birth to a time that I thought of as the Age of Books. If my life had been pointed in that direction I would have been, just then, not sheltering from rain in a graveyard of books but inspecting wall after wall of leather-bound volumes in my mansion in a city of books. Or I would have been at my desk, a writer in the fullness of his powers, looking through tall windows at a park-like scene in the countryside of books while I waited for my next sentence to come to me.

I put together four or five titles and took them to the gazing man. While he checked the prices pencilled in the front leaves I looked at him from under my eyebrows. He was not so old as I had thought. But his skin had a greyness that made me think of alcohol. The bookseller's liver is almost rotted away, I told myself. The poor bastard is an alcoholic.

I believed, in those days, that I was on the way myself to becoming an alcoholic, and I was always noticing signs of what I might look like in twenty or ten years or even sooner. If the bookseller had pickled his liver, then I understood why he sat and gazed so often. He suffered all day from the mood that came over me every Sunday afternoon when I had been sipping for forty-eight hours and had finally stopped and tried to sober up and to begin the four pages of fiction I was supposed to finish each weekend.

In my Sunday afternoon mood I usually gave up trying to write and looked over my bookshelves. Before nightfall I had usually decided there was no point in writing my sort of fiction in 1980. Even if my work was published at last, and a few people read it for a few years, what would be the end of it all? Where would my book be in, say, forty years' time? Its author by then would be no longer around to investigate the matter. He would have poisoned the last of his brain-cells and died long before. Of the few copies that had actually been bought, fewer still would be stacked on shelves. Of these few even fewer would be opened, or even glanced at, as weeks and months passed. And of the few people still alive who had actually read the book, how many would remember any part of it?

At this point in my wondering I used to devise a scene from around the year 2020. It was Sunday afternoon (or, if the working week had shrunk as forecast, a Monday or even a Tuesday afternoon). Someone vaguely like myself, a man who had failed at what he most wanted to do, was standing in gloomy twilight before a wall of bookshelves. The man did not know it, but he happened to be the last person on the planet who still owned a copy of a certain book that had been composed on grey Sunday afternoons forty years before. The same man had once actually read the book, many years before the afternoon when he searched for it on his shelves. And more than this, he still remembered vaguely a certain something about the book.

There is no word for what this man remembers—it is so faint, so hardly perceptible among his other thoughts. But I stop (in my own thinking, on many a Sunday afternoon) to ask myself what it is exactly that the man still possesses of my book. I reassure myself that the something he half-remembers must be just a little different from all the other vague somethings in his memory. And then I think about the man's brain.

I know very little about the human brain. In all my three thousand books there is probably no description of a brain. If someone counted in my books the occurrence of nouns referring to parts of the body, "brain" would probably have a very low score. And yet I have bought all those books and read nearly half of them and defended my reading of them because I believe my books can teach me all I need to know about how people think and feel.

I think freely about the brain of the man standing in front of his bookshelves and trying to remember: trying (although he does not know it) to rescue the last trace of my own writing—to save my thought from extinction. I know that this thinking of mine is, in a way, false. But I trust my thinking just the same, because I am sure my own brain is helping me to think; and I cannot believe that one brain could be quite mistaken about another of its kind.

I think of the man's brain as made up of many cells. Each cell is like a monk's cell in a Carthusian monastery, with high walls around it and a little garden between the front wall and the front door. (The Carthusians are almost hermits; each monk belongs to the monastery, but he spends most of his day reading in his cell or tending the vegetables in his walled garden.) And each cell is a storehouse of information; each cell is crammed with books.

A few books are cloth-bound with paper jackets, but most are leather-bound. And far outnumbering the books are the manuscripts. (I have trouble envisaging the manuscripts. One of my own books—in my room, on the grey Sunday afternoon—has photographs of pages from an illuminated manuscript. But I wonder what a collection of such pages would look like and how it would be bound. And I have no idea how a collection of such bound manuscripts would be stored—lying flat, on top of one another? sideways? upright in ranks like cloth-bound books on my own shelves? I wonder too what sort of furniture would store or display the manuscripts. So, although I can see each monk in his cell reaching up to his shelf of books from more recent times, when I want to think of him searching among the bulk of his library I see only a greyness: the grey of the monk's robe, of the stone walls of his cell, of the afternoon sky at his little window, and the greyness of blurred and incomprehensible texts.)

There are very few Carthusian monks in the world—I mean, the world outside my window and under the grey sky on Sunday afternoon. But when I say that, I am only repeating what a priest told me at secondary school nearly thirty years ago, when I was dreaming of becoming a monk and living in a library with a little garden and a wall around me. Apart from the priest's vague an-swer, the only information I have about the Carthusian Order comes from an article in the English *Geographical Magazine*. But that ar-ticle was published in the 1930s at about the time when I was learn-ing to read in my other lifetime that leads back towards the Age of Books. I cannot check the article now because all my old mag-azines are wrapped in grey plastic garbage bags and stored above the ceiling of my house. I stored them there three years ago with four hundred books that I will never read again—I needed more space on my shelves for the latest books I was buying.

What I mainly remember about that article was that it was all text with no photographs. Nowadays the *Geographical Magazine* is half-filled with coloured photographs. I sometimes skip the brief, jargonised texts of the articles and find all I need to know in the captions under the photographs. But the 1930s magazines (in the grey plastic bag, in the twilight above the ceiling over my head) included many an article with not one illustration. I imagine the authors of those articles as bookish chaps in tweeds, returning from strolls among hedgerows to sit at desks in their libraries and write (with fountain pens and few crossings-out) splendid es-says and admirable articles and pleasant memoirs. I see those writ-ers clearly. I knew them well in the years of my teens, as the 1920s passed and the Great War loomed ahead. When those gentlemen-writers post their *belles-lettres* to editors, they include no illus-trations. The gentlemen actually boast of not knowing how to use cameras or gramophones or other modern gadgets, and their readers love the gentlemen for their charming dottiness. (I have never learned to use a camera or a tape-recorder, but when I tell this to people they think I am striking a pose to draw attention to myself.)

I do not think the Carthusians would have objected to a gentleman-writer's taking a few photographs of their monastery, so I assume that the author of the article trusted his words and sentences to describe clearly what he saw. The monastery was in Surrey, or it might have been Kent. This had disappointed me. When

I first read the article I no longer dreamed of becoming a monk, but I liked to dream of monks living like hermits in remote landscapes; and Surrey or Kent was too populous for dreams about peaceful libraries. The only place-name I remember from the article is Parkminster. I looked into my *Times Atlas of the World* just now and found no Parkminster in the index. (While I looked I vaguely remembered having looked for the same word more than once in the past with the same result.) Parkminster is therefore a hamlet too small to be marked on maps; or perhaps the monastery itself is called Parkminster, and the monks asked the writer not to mention any place-names in his article because they wanted no curious sightseers trying to peep into their cells.

But, in any case, the article was published in the 1930s, and for all I know, the Carthusians and their cells and the word "Parkminster" may have drifted off towards the Age of Monasteries and I may be the only one who remembers them, or at least what was once written about them.

Yet when I think of the man reaching up to his bookshelves, on a grey afternoon in the year 2020, I see broad gravel paths with trees above them: whole districts of paths with cells beside the paths and in every cell a monk surrounded by books and manuscripts.

The man at his bookshelves—the last rememberer of my book—not only fails to remember what he once read in my book but cannot remember where he last saw my book on his shelves. He stands there and tries to remember.

A lay-brother walks along an avenue of his monastery. Lay-brothers are bound by solemn vows to their monastery, like other monks, but their duties and privileges are somewhat different. A lay-brother is not so much confined to his cell. Each day while the priest-monks are in their cells reading, or reciting the divine office, or tending their gardens, the lay-brothers are working for the monastery as a whole: taking messages and instructions and even dealing, in a limited way, with the world outside the monastery. Each lay-brother knows his way around some suburb of the monastery; he knows which monk lives behind which wall in his particular district. The lay-brother even gets to know, in a general sense, what the hermit-monks keep in their libraries: what books and manuscripts they spend their days reading. A lay-brother, having only a few books himself, thinks of books and libraries in a convenient, summary way. He learns to quote in full the titles of books he has never opened or never seen, whereas a monk in his cell might spend a year reading a certain book or copying and embellishing a certain manuscript and thinking of it for the rest of his life as an enormous pattern of rainbow pages of capital letters spiralling inwards and long laneways of words like the streets of other monasteries inviting him to dream about their cells of books and manuscripts.

A lay-brother walks along an avenue of the monastery. He has an errand to undertake but he is in no hurry. This is not easy to explain to people ignorant of monasteries. Monks behind their walls observe time differently from the people in the world outside. While only a few moments seem to pass on an uneventful, grey afternoon outside the monastery, a monk on the other side of the wall might have turned, at long intervals, page after page of a manuscript. The mystery can never be explained because no one has been able to be at once both outside and inside a monastery.

So, the lay-brother is in no hurry. He stands admiring the vegetables and herbs in each of the gardens of the cells he has been instructed to visit. When each monk has come to the door, the lay-brother asks him a certain question or questions but with no show of urgency. The lay-brother will call again, he says, on the next day or, perhaps, on the day after. In the meanwhile, if the monk could consult his books or his manuscripts for the needed information . . .

There is more than one lay-brother, of course. There may be hundreds, thousands, all striding or ambling through the leafy streets of the monastery while the last of my readers runs a finger along the spines of his books and tries to remember something of my book. And although I think of the lay-brothers as walking mostly through a particular quarter or district of the monastery, I know there are districts and more districts beyond them. In one of those districts, I decide on the grey Sunday afternoon when I have to decide whether to begin my writing or to go on sipping— in one of those districts, in a cell with grey walls no different from all the grey walls in all the streets in all the districts around it, in a collection of manuscripts that has lain undisturbed during many quiet afternoons is a page where a monk once read or wrote what the man in the year 2020 would like to recall. The monk himself has forgotten most of what he once read or wrote. He could, perhaps, find the passage again—if he were asked to search for it among all the other pages he has read and written in all the years he has been reading and writing in his cell. But no lay-brother comes to ask the monk to look for any such page. Outside the monk's grey walls, no footstep sounds on many a grey afternoon.

The man cannot remember what he once read in my book. He cannot remember where among his shelves he once put away my thin volume. The man fills his glass again and goes on sipping some costly poison of the twenty-first century. He does not understand the importance of his forgetfulness, but I understand it. I know that no one now remembers anything of my writing.

So, on many a Sunday afternoon I leave my writing in its folder. I cannot bring myself to write what will become at last a greyness in a heap of manuscripts I can hardly imagine.

In the bookshop, I paid for my books and pocketed my change. The books were still on the table where the man had stacked them while he checked their prices. The man waited for me to take away the books so he could go on with his gazing, but I wanted to say something to the man. I wanted to reassure him that the books would be safe in their new home. I wanted to tell him that some of them were books I had wanted for a long time—unjustly neglected books that would now be read and remembered.

The topmost book was *Precious Bane* by Mary Webb. I touched the faded yellow cloth cover and I told the man that I had been searching for a long time for *Precious Bane*; that I intended to read it very soon.

The man looked not at the book or at me but out at the rain. With his face towards the greyness at his window, he said that he knew *Precious Bane* well. It had been a well-known book in its time. He had read it, but he hardly remembered it, he said, especially since his health was not what it had been. But it didn't matter, he said. It didn't matter if you couldn't remember anything about a book. The important thing was to read the book; to store it up inside you. It was all there inside somewhere, he said. It was all safely preserved. He lifted a hand, as though he might have pointed to some precise point on his skull, but then he let the hand fall again into the position where it normally rested while he gazed.

I took my books home. I entered the titles and the authors' names in my catalogue, and then I put each book in its correct place in my library, which is arranged in alphabetical order according to authors' surnames.

On the following Sunday, when it was time to stop sipping and to begin writing, I thought as usual of the man in the year 2020. He still tried and failed to remember a certain book, the book that I had written forty years before. But after he had walked away from his shelves and had sat down again to sip, I thought of him as knowing that my book was still safely preserved after all.

Then I thought of the monastery, and I saw that the sky above it had been changed. A golden glow was in the air; it was not so much the yellow of sunlight; more the dark-gold of the cover of Mary Webb's unjustly neglected book or the amber of beer or the autumn colour of whisky. The light in the sky made the avenues of the monastery seem even more tranquil. The lay-brothers on their way from cell to cell sauntered rather than walked. Each monk in his cell, when he reached for a certain book or manuscript, was utterly calm and deliberate. And when he held up a page to inspect it, the light from his window lay faintly gold on the intricate pen-strokes or the tinted initials, and he found with ease what he had been asked to find.

On that afternoon, and on many Sundays afterwards, I wrote while I sipped. When I next called at the bookshop I had been writing for six months of Sundays.

After I had paid the man for my books, I told him I was a writer. I told him I had been writing on every Sunday since I had last seen him. By the following winter I would have finished what I was writing. And by the winter after that, my writing would have been preserved in a book. I wanted the cover of my book to be a rich, gold colour, I told the man, although he seemed hardly interested. I did not care about the colour of my dust-jacket, but when forty years had passed and the jacket had been torn away or lost and my book had been stored in a far corner of a shop like his, I wanted the gold colour of its spine to stand out among the greys and greens and dark-blues of all the almost-forgotten books.

I told all this to the man while he went on gazing out into the sunlight as though it was still the same grey that he had gazed at when he told me about the books he could never forget. But this time the man would not reassure me. He was the last of a dying race, he told me. There would be no more shops like his in forty years. If people in those days wanted to preserve the stuff that had once been in books, they would preserve it in computers: in millions of tiny circuits in silicon chips in computers.

The man lifted his hand. His thumb and his index fingers made the shape of pincers, with a tiny gap between the pads of the two fingers. He held his fingers for a moment against the light from outside and stared at the crack between them. Then he let his hand fall, and he went back to gazing in his usual way.

On the following Sunday I did not go on with the writing that I had wanted to become a book with dark-gold covers. I sat and sipped and thought about circuits and silicon chips. I thought of silicon as grey, the grey of granite when it was wet from rain under a grey sky. And I thought of a circuit as a grid of gold tracks in the grey. I saw that the tracks of a circuit would have a pattern hardly different from the paths of a monastery. The circuits I thought of seemed rather more remote from me than any monas-

tery. But the pattern was the same. I could see only thin trails of
gold across the grey, but I supposed the gold came from close-set
treetops on either side of the long avenues of the circuit. The
weather over the circuits would have been an endless calm autumn
afternoon, the best weather for remembering.

I still could not imagine what sort of people would walk beneath the overspreading autumn-gold. But a few Sundays after I
had first thought about circuits, I began to write about a monastery where a page of writing might have been buried deep beneath
a stack of manuscripts in a grey room but that page would never
be lost or forgotten. As I wrote, I believed that my writing itself,
my account of the monastery, would rest safely forever in some
unimaginable room of books under gold foliage in a city of circuits.
That monastery, I wrote, was only a monastery in a story, but the
story was safe and so, therefore, was the monastery and everything
in it. I saw story, monastery, circuit, story, monastery, circuit . . .
receding endlessly in the same direction as the lifetime that would
have taken me towards the Golden Age of Books.

But as I wrote I came to see that the monastery was not, of
course, endless. Somewhere, on the far side of the monastery wall,
another greyness began: the greyness of the land of the barbarians, the streetless steppes where people lived without books.

Those people would not always stay on their steppes: the Age
of Books would not go on forever. One day the barbarians would
mount their horses and ride towards the monastery and turn backwards the history I had so often dreamed of.

I stopped writing. I poured another drink and looked far into
the deep colour in my glass. Then I read aloud what I had written
of my story, pausing now and then to sip, and after each sip to gaze
at the red-gold sunset in the sky over all that I could remember.

Cotters Come No More

My father had been dead for four years, but I would have resented anyone's thinking that the man walking ahead of me was the fatherly friend I needed. Yet the man was my father's younger brother and I admired him.

I admired him, for one thing, because he preferred to look at his land rather than farm it. He milked his cows at the proper hours; but on most afternoons, when he should have been out in his paddocks, he leaned on his garden gate and stared at the ibises on his dam or at the row of cliffs two miles away where the land ended. Or he sat at his kitchen table with an opened book propped against the teapot in front of him. He would read the book, but he would also watch the flies among the chop-bones and the streaks of tomato sauce on the plate at his elbow. Every so often he would bring an upturned drinking glass slowly down through the air towards a foraging fly. If he trapped the fly he would carry it in the glass, with the palm of his hand underneath, to one of the spiders' webs in the kitchen window. He would throw the fly into the web and then stand with his hands on his hips, observing.

While he walked ahead of me he whistled a piece of what he and I called classical music. I wished I could have named the music. My uncle would ask me eventually to identify it and would grin when I failed. I was the young man from Melbourne, where live concerts were presented in the Town Hall, and he was the yokel who listened to ABC programs on his battery-powered wireless set and who read books by the light of a kerosene lamp.

I could see no path across the paddock where we were walking, yet the man ahead of me made occasional detours as though he followed some old, leisurely trail. He had told me that morning I would learn something important before the day was out. He had his binoculars over his shoulder, and in his right hand he lugged his portable wireless. He might have been leading me a mile away from the road only to show me the nest of an uncommon bird. Or the chief event of the afternoon might have been his sitting down beside me on a hilltop, taking out of his trousers pocket the folded form-guide from the *Age*, pointing to a certain name among the fields of horses, and then fiddling with his wireless until I was just able to hear, above the crackle of static and the buzzing of insects in the grass, the call of a race more than a hundred miles away with the horse that my uncle had brought to my notice in the thick of the finish.

It was someone else's farm that we were walking across: a set of out-paddocks with no house in sight. The mob of yearling heifers that wheeled and galloped away from us might have seen no man near them for weeks. From the top of each low hill I saw a clump of scrub, or a swampy hollow with short green grass sheltered by man-high stands of rushes, and each clump or hollow seemed the very place where I would be sitting a few years later with a young woman beside me.

If I had been walking alone across those paddocks on that day, the young woman would have been someone I had met by chance in the clump of scrub or the swampy hollow. If I had been walking alone, a young woman would have been waiting in every clump and every swampy hollow for me to meet her by chance and then to spend ten minutes with her and afterwards to go on walking alone across the paddocks.

But I was not walking alone. I was walking a few paces behind my father's younger brother. And so the young woman on the patch of grass and out of reach of the sea-wind was my wife. A year before, I had proposed marriage to her in a sheltered place where the grass was short and green. A week before, I had married her. Now I was free to enjoy with her what I could otherwise have enjoyed with the other young woman, but I would have been much less ashamed if my uncle had turned suddenly and seen into my thoughts.

Walking behind my father's brother I looked out for the place that my wife and I might remember for the rest of our lives. The date was January 1954 and I was fifteen years old.

The man stopped walking. We sat down and rested. We heard only the slight sounds of the grass blown by the wind, and perhaps a faint rumbling from the ocean. I had my usual moment of dread that the man beside me might be going to say at last what the brothers of dead fathers said to nephews in novels and films: that my father should have been with us on that afternoon to walk on his native soil and to hear the ocean he had loved; that my father had been the finest of men, and I ought to follow in his ways even though I could never hope to equal him; and that he, my father's brother, was ready if I needed him to answer any question that a son might want to ask a father. The only families I had observed apart from my own were the families in American films. And I had feared since my childhood that my own people might one day throw off their usual reticence and begin to hug and kiss and confide in one another like any normal family.

My uncle lay on his side with his head resting on his fist and his elbow against the soil. His face was turned away from me. Near where I lay, but out of the view of my uncle, my wife of one week sat waiting for me among the tall grass. I surprised myself by not going at once to join her. I had thought I would enjoy being with my wife while my uncle was nearby and unsuspecting. But I was not so ready, when the time had come, to mock my uncle.

The man resting near me in the grass was a bachelor. As I understood the moral code of my family, my uncle's being un-married meant that he had had not much more contact with women than I had had. But the difference between us was that I would one day marry whereas he, so I had heard people say, would never marry. It seemed a little unfair that I could find in any of the paddocks around me the young woman I was sure to meet one day while he, almost forty years old, could see only an empty landscape.

He asked me after a while about my reading. I had told him already that I was top of my class in English literature and he ex-pected me, I knew, to recommend to him some modern author that he could then pronounce much inferior to the writers he called great. I played his game by talking about the poetry of D. H. Law-rence. I praised free verse, which I had only recently discovered and which I was sure would be too revolutionary for my uncle. He made his objections and I heard him out. But I had to say more. My uncle was the only man I knew who read poetry. Even if he laughed at me, I had to hear the theories I had kept to myself for so long propounded at last to an interested audience in a setting of grass and sky and distant cliffs.

I began to talk about the welter of impressions bombarding our senses and crying out to be preserved in the form of poetry. I made my uncle listen to the buzzings and trillings of the unseen insects around us, and to the snatches of bird-song brought to us by the wind. I pointed out to him that the sound of the wind in the grass was irregular and unpredictable. If he watched the grass he would see that the waves and furrows made by the wind were of no dis-cernible pattern. All this, I argued, should be the subject of poetry. He ought to read, and I intended one day to write, a poetry set free from the strict rules that ponderous and arrogant Europeans wanted to impose on the world. Where were we at that moment? I asked him rhetorically. We were at the very southern edge of an enormous land whose fund of poetic inspiration had barely been tapped. Neither he nor I knew of any poem celebrating the peculiar qualities of our little zone of bare hills lying between the emptiness of the Southern Ocean and the hazy plains inland. It was our responsibility to preserve in poetry what no one else had written about. And it was our right to be free to search for the most apt words unhindered by history or tradition. No one before us two had stood quite where we stood among those grassy hills or had seen and felt what we saw and felt. No one from before our time should cow us with their laws or customs. As poets and admirers of poetry we should be free. Only in free verse could a poet reveal his deepest feelings.

My uncle was staring into the middle distance, and I thought I must have said more than was decent between us. Perhaps the phrase "deepest feelings" had suggested to him that I saw a young woman at the heart of the landscape I was hoping to write about. And it was true that when I had mentioned free verse so often I was hoping my uncle would hear an echo of the phrase "free love," which neither of us could have spoken to the other.

But I could not have tolerated for long any tension between us. So, when he challenged me to recite some of the poetry I was praising, and I tried but could not get past the first five words of "Cypresses" by D. H. Lawrence, I was just as relieved to have given him an opportunity for jeering at me as he would have been relieved to jeer. I thought I was sounding the right note to end the matter when I claimed that even Lawrence himself would not have expected me to recite his poem from memory; that such poetry was meant to be elusive and ephemeral; that if I myself happened one day to compose a poem about the places we saw around us just then, I would not expect my reader to remember my poem any more exactly than I would remember afterwards the shapes made by the wind in the grass while I was speaking.

My uncle did not bother to untangle my propositions. He simply told me that his father, my late grandfather, had said about some men that instead of talking they opened their mouths and let the wind blow their tongues around.

Then my uncle began to recite a poem. He had a queer smile when he began, and a hint of self-mockery in his voice. But while the poem went forward I was too much interested in the words to notice any pose in the man reciting them. In any case, I had soon turned my face away towards the paddocks in order to make things easier for both of us.

It was a long poem that I had never heard before. Every line ended in a rhyme and every alternate rhyme was the same sonorous vowel, which the man reciting stressed and prolonged so that it seemed to persist through the poem like the drone of a set of pipes. One of the lines with this repeating rhyme was a refrain that came at the end of every stanza.

The man recited the poem without stumbling. I tried to hold on to some of the lines. I knew he would refuse to repeat even a word for me afterwards and would probably change the subject from poetry to racing, or would ask me what I thought was wrong with the youth of Australia.

At first, while he was reciting, I was able to grasp only the single repeating line. But I kept alert for the climax to the poem, and when my uncle slowed his pace and rounded his vowels I tried to memorise every word I was hearing. Later, while he unfolded the racing page and then while he sat reading, I stood out of his view and pressed my hands to my head and tried to keep the words in mind.

Stumbling among tussocks and hoping I looked as though I was merely checking how far we had come from the road or how far we were still from the sea, I learned by heart what I discovered more than twenty years later was not a stanza but an assortment of lines, some of them garbled. Even at the time, I must have known I was misremembering my uncle's poem; but I would have been satisfied just to keep for myself a form of words that would always

104

recall what I had felt when the man had sat erect with only the bare paddocks around him and had recited faultlessly.

I acquired, finally, what seemed to me a poem in itself: four perfectly measured lines with a mournful sound in their vowels and a vague, melancholic meaning about the whole.

> Remember now beside the wain . . .
> The days of old are o'er;
> This is our harvest of the plain,
> And we return no more.

And although the first three lines might not have been in their right places, I knew the refrain was safely in my mind.

The "wain" and the "o'er" and the quaint word-order did not irritate me. From the other stanzas I recalled other nouns with what seemed a medieval reference (arrows, horns, abbot, minster) and a syntax that persuaded me the poem was a very old ballad. I placed it somewhere towards the middle of the wide blank that lay between the French Revolution and the Fall of the Roman Empire. I considered the poem a genuine poem of its age: a lament by a poet with a good reason for lamenting.

Although I had dedicated myself to free verse I was pleased to admire my uncle's poem as a poem of its kind. Its faultless rhythms and unfailing rhymes would always seem to me (so it seemed to me in January 1954) the final perfection of a poetry that had had its day. I wanted to remember my uncle's having recited the poem defiantly with his back against the ocean on the south edge of the last continent to be invaded by free verse. I recognised something grandly inappropriate in the man's declaiming lines about jackdaws and minster towers after he had sat down to drag burrs from his socks and to squash flies in the corners of his eyes. While his neighbours were straining fenceposts or bailing hay, my uncle would have considered it his finest achievement of the day to have recalled every stanza of a poem that owed nothing to his surroundings.

Later that day I followed my uncle up to the cliffs above the ocean and searched with him for the bits of shells that he said were signs of Aborigines' cooking-places. We took turns looking through his binoculars at plovers and moorhens and dabchicks, and we found the nest of a white-fronted chat that my uncle had noticed fluttering among the rushes. We talked mostly about birds, and on another day I might have squirmed at his resembling some Most Unforgettable Character in a *Reader's Digest* article—the custodian of the lore of woods and fields inducting his nephew into the ways of the Great Outdoors. What kept me from thinking such thoughts was the line of poetry that stayed in my mind.

And we return no more.

The line from the poem told me that my father's brother was shut out—even if he would never have admitted as much in plain words—from what should have been his true country. No matter how many pleasant hollows and nesting-places he knew along the coast where he had lived all his life, he was barred from a much more desirable place. I thought I was rather acute at fifteen years in deciding that the country he had looked at but had later lost was the landscape where a man walked with his wife of only a few weeks.

My uncle had had girlfriends—three that I knew of. All three had been nursing sisters. My uncle had not had his girlfriends in close succession but at wide intervals during the ten years before I heard his poem. I remembered all three girlfriends. All had had pretty faces, but all three women had made me uncomfortable. They had talked a little too eagerly with me and had laughed a little too loudly when I said something clever. The first of the three had been probably in her late twenties and the latest in her middle thirties, but to me they had all seemed past their prime. Seeing one of these women in costly dress and hat, setting out with my uncle for a day at the races, or in slacks and sandals for a picnic at the beach, I had felt somewhat embarrassed. The woman and the man seemed to lack a certain dignity. If they looked into one another's eyes or if their hands touched even briefly, I seemed to have caught them at something childish. I preferred not to imagine what my uncle and his girlfriend talked about when they sat in his car for hours after their outings. And I would not even speculate as to whether they spent all their time together talking earnestly about their future or whether they played sometimes at being a young man and his girlfriend.

The end of each of my uncle's three romances had been roughly the same. He had come to Melbourne to visit my parents (or, in the case of the third girlfriend, to visit my widowed mother) and to sit at the kitchen table until midnight with his head in his hands explaining how easy it would be for him to marry and yet how selfish. It would be selfish because his duty was clearly to remain single for the sake of his widowed mother and his two unmarried sisters. A few weeks later the word around our house was that my uncle and his girlfriend had parted good friends. In each of the three cases, the former girlfriend had been engaged and then married to some other man within a year.

When I was fifteen it seemed clear to me that my uncle's girlfriends were his lost country. I myself had been relieved each time to learn that my uncle would continue to be a bachelor, but on the day when he recited his poem I allowed that he might have been thinking of one or another of those three nursing sisters. All three had married farmers, as it turned out, so that my uncle could have thought afterwards of the women as still strolling among paddocks and swamps and patches of scrub but not, alas, his own.

I thought of other lost countries. When my uncle had first begun to recite his poem I had looked sideways at his face. I would not have looked into his eyes. We were not a family for staring into eyes. But I had sneaked a look at his face from the side. I had caught myself looking hard at the tiny black sprouts of whiskers on his jaw. He would have shaved only a few hours before, but already the hundreds of black spikes were forcing a way out of him. I tried not to think of black hairs uncoiling from the skin on his belly. One night he had sent me from the lounge room into his empty bedroom to fetch something. I had seen the book on his bedside table—his nightly reading: the *Confessions* of Saint Augustine. In the paddock I swung my head away from him. Perhaps his bachelor's body was another sort of lost country.

Why was my uncle reciting the poem just then? Even at the time, I saw how hopeless it was for the grown man to appeal in any sense to the pimply boy who was—as the man surely knew—prevented by unspoken rules from answering. Any appeal must come to nothing. The boy could not have been expected to remember more than a few jumbled lines of the poem. The boy would probably never try to find the text of the poem among all the books of poetry on the shelves of the libraries of Melbourne. The poem itself was a lost country. The man had once learned it by heart, but the boy had heard it only once. The boy would remember afterwards only the pulse of the syllables and the drone of a certain vowel, as though he had tramped across a landscape and recalled afterwards only the sounds of his feet in the grass.

Perhaps I heard a warning sound in the poem. At the age of fifteen I would have disregarded any such warning, but my father's brother might have been reminding me that I was connected with that district of low grassy hills ending in sudden cliffs. With that district in mind, I would choose at last for my own poem some unfashionable ballad with a tone of regret. At that time I could only have thought of one kind of loss that deserved to be regretted in my own poetry. I could only have thought of the loss of the young woman I had seen already that day in every green, sheltered place. Even then, I could not have imagined myself losing her after first having found her—as my uncle seemed to have lost each of his three girlfriends. I could only have imagined myself losing my imagined young woman in the sense of failing to find her.

The young woman I had seen near me on that day, and on every day for five years past, was, I imagined, an actual young woman. She was someone who lived in Melbourne as I did but who had not yet met me. On every day of our lives the young woman and I each took a step, figuratively speaking, towards one another. Perhaps the young woman noticed in the corner of a page of a newspaper a certain advertisement. On the following day she would go a little out of her usual way in order to look through the window of a shop whose address she had read in the newspaper. Near the shop the young woman would meet another young woman: someone she had not seen for five years. A long chain of acquaintances connected this second young woman to a house that I would one day visit . . . In the meanwhile I was following my own roundabout but inevitable route. When the young woman and I had met at last, we would try to trace backwards all those steps we had taken. Seeing the patterns of our paths towards one another, we could never think of undoing what had been so neatly completed. If the poem I had heard had been warning me of a loss of my own, I could only have supposed that either the young woman or myself had taken a wrong turning. It was almost unthinkable, but our paths were not going to meet after all. Twenty years from then, or so my uncle's poem might have been warning me, I might have been a bachelor approaching middle age like the man who was trying to warn me. In that case, I could at least fall back on poetry such as his ballad of regretfulness.

At mid-afternoon my uncle and I turned away from the sea. We had left his car at the end of a grassy track two hours before; but in all our walking we had mostly wandered, and from the high cliff where we turned back I saw a glinting of the sun in glass about a mile away and supposed it was the windscreen of his Holden.

We walked back towards the car but through paddocks we had not crossed earlier. The nearest houses were still far away, in valleys sheltered from the sea-wind. The district was called Lake

Gillear, but no township or post office was denoted by that name. I had seen the lake. It was not much more than a large swamp. I had seen it years before on another outing with my uncle. The season had been winter then, and whenever I had said the words *Lake Gillear* afterwards the sound of the last vowel had made me remember the shuddering of the grey water while the cold wind had blown across it.

My uncle was leading me, I suddenly noticed, towards a piece of level ground on the sheltered side of a hill. If I had been more observant I might have noticed sooner the few signs of what the place had been: the traces of a track leading up to it; the older, wooden fenceposts marking where a gate had once swung; and the one fruit-tree—a quince, my uncle told me later—leaning to the ground among the boxthorn bushes and the rabbit-scrapes.

The decaying tree hid until the last moment the few broken bricks and the scattering of jonquils. As soon as I knew we were standing on the site of a house of which nothing survived but the ruins of a chimney, and that my father's brother had been intending all afternoon to lead me to that spot, I was apprehensive again. I thought I was in for a little ceremony—a rite of familial piety. I thought I might hear of some pilgrimage that the men of my father's family had kept up for years. But nothing of the kind happened.

I followed my father's brother into the level place where the grass was shorter and more yielding than the pastures around it. I felt the sudden dying-away of the sea-wind. The jonquils barely nodded. Of all the places I had observed that day, the green clearing with the hill behind and the shaggy tree in front was the most suitable for my meeting with a young woman.

My uncle had strode into the place with no change in his gait. He stopped only for long enough to glance around as though he had to deliver to someone afterwards a brief report on the crumbs of bricks and the neglected jonquils. Then he strode on again into the paddocks and towards the road.

I caught up with him and asked him off-handedly whose house we had just seen. He said I had just visited the home of the Cotters, who were among my forebears. The tone of his voice told me he had no banter just for the moment. But then, when I had already begun to see the Cotters as venerable husband and wife, my uncle went on to say that the Cotters had been his own great-uncles: two bachelor brothers of his grandmother who had spent the last twenty years of their lives in their cottage at Lake Gillear.

The influence of the Cotters reached me by way of the poem I had first heard a mile or so from their quince tree and jonquils. Following my uncle back to the road, I began to hear my remembered version of his poem being recited by what I supposed were nineteenth-century voices. When they reached the fourth of the lines they introduced a variant.

And Cotters come no more.

The reciters intoned their poem of regret, but I tried not to hear them. I thought of the green grass and the nodding jonquils and the shady tree. I thought of myself alone there with a young woman, perhaps my wife or perhaps not. The place was so sheltered and secluded that I could have recited poetry to the young woman or told her about the lonely Cotters before I took my pleasure.

We reached the road, which was a pair of faint wheel-marks in the grass. My uncle had left his car a hundred yards short of where the road ended and the coastal scrub began. While my uncle and I had been walking, someone had parked another car near the edge of the scrub. The other car was not a new Holden like my uncle's car but a shabby, canvas-topped car of some make I did not know—a young man's car.

Quite incautiously I craned my neck while my uncle was beside me. All in one moment I saw the rear door of the shabby car hanging open, I divined why it had been allowed to hang open and why I saw no heads and shoulders above the level of the seats, and I understood that my uncle had not only seen what I had seen but had seen that I had seen it.

And surely in the next moment I knew I was going to hear, during the many long pauses while my uncle and I travelled afterwards further away from the coast, the Cotters my forebears calmly reciting.

There Were Some Countries

Thereere were some countries so far from this city and so little spoken of among my acquaintances that no one objected when I summed up their terrain or their people in a few words. Nor did I object when I found equally brief descriptions of the same countries in reviews of books I would never read or in magazines I would never subscribe to.

This was not because I was impatient with the subtleties of actual geography. I believe I might have distinguished between the characteristics of each neighbourhood in Tashkent or Ulan Bator, if I had cared for such matters. But I preferred to discern, on the distant borders of the space I inhabited, countries that gave themselves away at a glance.

I assumed that I shared this preference with those who accepted my descriptions of remote places, and even with those who composed the sentences that served my needs. There was therefore no reason for me to question what I read not long ago in an American weekly: that the people of pre-war Romania were credited with a fondness for sexual perversions.

There may have been explorers who correctly predicted the whereabouts, and even some of the features, of the places they finally discovered. But I thought none of them could have placed his conjectured country so accurately as I had placed mine on my most private maps.

I had not known what name it would eventually bear, but I was familiar for many years with its folkways, and even some of its sorry history. During that time, of course, I was unable to verify my suspicions and intuitions. I hesitated a little before saying openly what was concealed among the close-set mountains deep within the borders of the land I knew.

I kept to myself some of my interpretations of its forbidding architecture, the awkward restraint of its dances, and the provoking fluidity of its language. And few people had the opportunity to dispute my explanations for the decline of some dynasty or the relentless persecution of some wayward sect.

But I never doubted the existence of the land, even when I least expected to learn where it lay. Whenever I was assured that it could not be located beyond this or that frontier, I only intensified my researches into its culture. I even surmised that some traveller had already uncovered in an actual territory the way of life that I knew as necessary to some nameless folk, but that his account of his travels had been suppressed or hopelessly mutilated.

When I read at last that brief reference to pre-war Romania, I believed I had learnt no more than the name of a country I had known since my school days. In those days I had begun to study what I called geography from my collection of second-hand *National Geographic*s. The illustrations of Europe were mostly black and white, and I used to hope that the men in shabby suits and the women in drab frocks were only wearing such clothes until they could replace the precious embroidered costumes they had lost in some bombing raid. The maps were too detailed to copy, but my teacher praised the page I reproduced from my school atlas showing three brightly coloured nations on the north-east shores of the Baltic and the free city of Danzig prominent nearby.

On the steep side of a mountain, in the country that I first found in those days, a ragged shepherd sprawled beside his flock. He was able to watch all day the comings and goings of villagers among the huddled houses across the narrow valley. But he himself lay almost unnoticed among the lowest reaches of a dense forest. In the languid hours of afternoon, the men and women moving in and out of his field of vision were mere blurs of limbs propelled by the same insistent energies that drove the wind through the branches above him or brought his snuffling sheep to the very grass where his legs rested.

The thoughts that occurred to this man might have seemed outrageous to anyone but myself. I had watched many a distant village in sombre illustrations and seen their inhabitants stripped of the invisible but bulky layers of moral fabric that I sensed about the people nearer me. The face of the man was haggard and creased. I knew he had done in his native valley what I would not have failed to do between far hillsides. And years before I knew that his homeland was called Romania, I called it, for convenience, Romania.

A group of farm-workers straightened their backs and rested for a moment from their threshing. Women and men stood elbow to elbow. The drudgery of their work in the shadeless sunlit field and the nearness of the keen-eyed older women should have protected the only girl I was interested in. And even though she looked willingly into the eyes of some passing traveller with a camera, the folds of the white shawl hiding half her face should have proved that she held herself aloof from the stocky scowling men around her. But I could devise only one explanation for the troubled expression that marred her delicate features. Young as she was, she had been besmirched already by the ruling vice of her race.

It was some time before I could calmly appreciate the extent of her predicament. But I came to see in her face the very blend of resignation and resentment and regret that would have been only a further incitement to her tormentors. I took those men, of course, for Romanians, and years afterwards found I had not been mistaken.

Like every other country I knew, Romania had its outcasts—its despised nation within a nation whose chief function was to bear the worst imputations that an already debauched citizenry could bring against its supposed inferiors. I was as repelled as any respectable Romanian would have been by the squalid ways of the homeless gipsies, even though I accused them of nothing I was not myself capable of doing in my whitewashed cottage, or gabled manor house.

I was ready to suppose that the gipsies in their wanderings saw aspects of a land that my countrymen and I had overlooked in our obsessive journeys across our territory. It was at least reassuring to learn in time that even the closest secrets of the gipsies were still preserved somewhere within the actual boundaries of Romania.

When I knew at last that all the lore and customs of Romania were in fact known to the Romanians, I might have felt an even closer kinship with my fellows, the saturnine men sipping their murky plum liqueurs while sunset reddened the Carpathian peaks above them. I knew now what was closest to their hearts. It was only what I had once thought so unlikely that I located it in the fancies of a people impossibly remote from me.

I might have enjoyed my own interpretations of the music of George Enesco or the writings of Eugene Ionesco. I might have begun my own investigations into the origins of Dada, knowing that Tristan Tzara was an expatriate Romanian. I should perhaps have been one of the few readers of Mircea Eliade who responded less to his scholarly essays than to his obscure remark that his life's work was inspired by his awed recollections of what he called Old Romania. And when I watched a certain popular film that was said to have made clearly visible something that had only been glimpsed in the landscapes of Australia, I might have been amused to hear, as an accompaniment to images of glaring skies and granite peaks and schoolgirls with Nordic complexions, the sound of Pan-pipes passed beneath the pursed lips of a native of Romania.

But none of these reactions occurred to me. For I had discovered the location of Romania by the wrong means altogether.

Alone at my desk in a side street of a suburb of Melbourne, I might suppose myself the only man of my nationality to own a copy of the selected poems of Tudor Arghezi, and certainly the only such man at a given hour to be savouring his bold imagery:

> *Statuia ei de chihlimbar*
> *Ai rastigni-o, ca un potcovar*
> *Minza, la pamint,*
> *Nechezind.*

But I could no longer enjoy my secret penetration of such matters, even knowing they were authentically Romanian. For I could not forget that the truth about Romania had been published in a magazine with a circulation of millions.

Bookstalls on every continent displayed its familiar cover. People who read no books still scanned its columns for something more coherent than the unremitting signals from radio and television. My prized information about Romania had been available to countless others. How many people, who never before could have visualised a solitary hillside in Banat, were now free to imagine whatever they chose in all the land from the Iron Gates to the banks of the Prutul?

It was no consolation for me to reflect that the Romania now exposed to general view was a land that had disappeared nearly forty years before. This was no assurance that my own discoveries in Romania had not been anticipated by others. For the best of my own insights had been obtained from places I never expected to visit. Now, as the passage of time made daily more remote the lands known as "pre-war," more and more of the curious might be encouraged to speculate about a Romania beyond reach of all of us.

I considered the possibility of excluding Romania from my thoughts. For of course I knew of other places where appearances scarcely concealed a way of life peculiarly suited to my own understanding. I could have gone back to the same magazines that first taught me about Romania and examined what it was that disturbed me in *Madagascar, Mystery Isle*, or what I found so oppressive in *Rambles in the Ryukyus*. But any satisfaction that I got from my study of those far places would have been threatened by the chance that some scholar or journalist had long since published what now passed for the truth about their corruption.

A simple course of action would have been for me to conceal all evidence that I once sympathised with the Romanians and arrived unaided at a knowledge of their strange habits. This would have safeguarded me from the accusation that I am poorly read and almost unaware of the wealth of information available for students of mountainous hinterlands.

For a time I chose to do just this. I consistently referred to Romania as though I had never dreamed of anything beyond the scant images that anyone might entertain of an outlandish, irrelevant landscape. Yet no one but myself seemed to observe any such restriction in their talk or their writings. I heard or read of scores of places with characteristics that could only have been discovered by a solitary observer with no more inspiration than an ambiguous text or an imperfect illustration. And few of those places seemed equal to Romania as I knew it.

I soon resumed my usual habits. I discussed, whenever I wished, those countries so far from this city and so little spoken of among my acquaintances that no one could object when I summed up their terrain or their people in a few words. I made no special mention of Romania. I was no longer anxious to interpret its strangeness for myself or for others. I believed that I, like everyone about me, was an exile from a stranger place still—the country that allowed us all to think ourselves exiles from a stranger place still.

Finger Web

This is a story about a man who visited Sydney only once in his life, in 1964. When I was asked to write this story I was in the middle of writing quite a different story about a man who visited Sydney only once in his life, in 1957.

I have visited Sydney only twice in my life.

When the man in this story first decided to visit Sydney, he did not think of himself as about to visit a large city four or five hundred miles north-east of his own city. Even when he said one Friday night in April 1964 to the men that he drank beer with every Friday night, "I'm thinking of going to Sydney for a couple of days," he was not thinking of himself as approaching a large city beside a semi-circular bridge with yachts sailing under it. If he had told the men in the hotel where he drank beer every Friday night what he was thinking of himself as doing, he would have said, "I'm thinking of walking up and down for a couple of days in a corner of a garden where a few dark-green ferns hang down in front of a wall of cream-coloured rocks."

After the man in this story had told the men in the hotel that he was thinking of going to Sydney, one of the men asked him where he would stay in Sydney.

The man in this story answered that he would stay with his married cousin in Granville. But this was not where the man saw himself as staying after he had arrived in Sydney. He had heard three years before that he had a married cousin living somewhere in Granville, but he had never thought of trying to find his married cousin. He told the men in the hotel that he would stay with his married cousin because he did not want the men to know that he was going to stay at the Majestic Hotel in Kings Cross.

The man in this story was going to stay at the Majestic Hotel in Kings Cross because one of the men that he played cards with and drank beer with every Saturday night had told him that the Majestic in Kings Cross was the place where he stayed whenever he went to Sydney for a couple of days.

The man in this story had said one Saturday night in March 1964 to the men that he was drinking beer with and playing cards with that he was thinking of going to Sydney for a couple of days. One of the men had then asked the man where he would stay in Sydney.

The man in this story had answered that he had never been to Sydney and he did not know where men such as himself stayed when they went to Sydney for a couple of days.

The man in this story had not felt comfortable when he said this, but if he had not said it he would not have learned where he might stay in Sydney, and in that case he would not have been able to go to Sydney.

The other men drinking beer and playing cards had each stayed for a couple of days in many places such as Sydney, but the man in this story had always lived in the room or the rooms that he called for the time being his own room or rooms in one or another of the suburbs in the only city that he knew. In March 1964 the man in this story had been frightened of what might happen to him if he went to Sydney for a couple of days. He had been frightened that the men and especially the women of Sydney might jeer or laugh at him because they saw about him some sign that he had never been to their city before. He had been frightened of the moment when he would have to walk up to a woman sitting behind a sort of walled desk such as he had seen in drawings of hotel foyers in cartoons and comic strips and would then have to ask the woman whether he could stay for a couple of nights in her hotel. (The man had not been so stupid that he supposed the woman behind the walled desk would be the owner of the hotel, but he understood that when he walked towards the woman both she and he would understand that she called all the rooms in the hotel for the time being her own rooms.) The man had expected that he might be too frightened to understand the words that the woman would speak to him from behind the walled desk, but he had expected that he would understand from the tone of the woman's voice that she had known from the moment when she first saw him creeping towards her walled desk that he had never been to her city before.

In March 1964 the man in this story had been frightened that he might have to spend his first day in Sydney walking towards one walled desk after another and asking one woman after another whether he could stay for a couple of nights in one of the rooms that she called for the time being her own rooms. But then the man had been pleased to learn that one of his card-playing and beer-drinking friends had stayed for a couple of nights at the Majestic Hotel in Kings Cross. The man in this story had then seen in his mind his friend the card-player and beer-drinker walking towards the walled desk in the foyer of the Majestic Hotel. Then the man had heard in his mind his friend's asking the woman behind the walled desk whether he could stay for a couple of nights in one of her rooms.

The man in this story believed that he himself could walk towards a walled desk and could speak to the woman behind the walled desk in somewhat the way that his card-playing friend would have walked and spoken in the Majestic Hotel. The man in this story had learned five years before how to drink beer and to play cards and to tell jokes in somewhat the way that his friends did these things on Saturday nights. In March 1964 the man believed he could now learn how to approach a woman behind a walled desk in the foyer of a hotel in a city that he had never visited before.

The men who drank beer and played cards every Saturday night with the man in this story were all unmarried. Each of the men spoke sometimes as though he had had many girlfriends in the past and as though he would have many girlfriends in the future, but none of the men spoke on any Saturday night as though he had a girlfriend for the time being. The man in this story sometimes spoke as though he would have many girlfriends in the future but he never spoke as though he had had even one girlfriend in the past. The man in this story thought of the other men as his friends because none of them had ever asked him why he spoke somewhat differently from them.

The men who drank beer on Friday nights with the man in this story were all married men. When the man in this story told the married men one Friday evening in April 1964 that he would stay with his married cousin in Granville if he went to Sydney for a couple of days, the man had already heard in his mind what the married men would have said if he had told them that he was going to stay at the Majestic Hotel in Kings Cross. The man had already heard in his mind the married men asking him questions about striptease artists and prostitutes. He had already seen in his mind the married men grinning at him while they asked their questions.

The man in this story told the married men in the hotel that he was going to Sydney for a couple of days to look at the sights. He did not tell the married men that he hoped to spend each of his couple of days in Sydney walking up and down past a low wall of cream-coloured stones in a Catholic monastery. The man did not tell the married men that he was going to Sydney in order to talk to a cousin of his who was unmarried and was studying to be a priest in a Catholic monastery where a few ferns hung down over a low wall. The man did not want the married men to know that he himself had been brought up as a Catholic, although he had not called himself a Catholic for the past five years and had not gone into a Catholic church during those five years. The man especially did not want the married men to know that he was going to Sydney because he foresaw himself beginning to call himself a Catholic again and to go into Catholic churches again as from January 1965, and because his cousin in the monastery was the only man or woman who might have been interested in hearing from him that he foresaw these things.

The man's cousin was two years younger than the man and had been studying to be a priest since he had left school. The man and his cousin had gone to the same secondary school in a suburb of the city where the man still lived. The two boys had seldom spoken to one another at school, but as from May 1961, which was three years and three months after the man's cousin had gone to the monastery in a suburb of Sydney, the man had written a letter every month to his cousin. Sometimes the man had sent with the letter a few handwritten pages of poetry.

In 1961 the man in this story had drunk beer with a few married men in a hotel every Friday night and had drunk beer and played cards with a few unmarried men in a bungalow behind the house of the parents of one of the unmarried men every Saturday night. On every other night the man had sat in the room that he called for the time being his own room and had drunk beer and read books and had sometimes written a page of poetry. One night in May 1961 the man had wanted to send a few of his pages of poetry to some man or woman who would read the pages and comment on them. The man knew no man or woman in the city where he had always lived who might want to read his pages of poetry, but he had thought that his cousin in Sydney might want to read a few of his pages. Before that night in May 1961 the man had never written to his cousin, but afterwards he had written to his cousin every month and had sometimes sent with his letter a few of his pages of poetry. The man's cousin had answered all the letters sent by the man and had sometimes commented on some of the pages of poetry.

One night in March 1964 the man in this story had written in one of his letters to his cousin that he was thinking of going to Sydney for a couple of days in order to tell his cousin something important.

The cousin had written back to the man that he would be welcome to visit him in the monastery. The cousin had sent with his letter four small colour prints of photographs of parts of the monastery. The man had looked only once at three of the colour prints, which showed parts of the outsides of buildings, but he had looked often at a colour print showing part of a low wall of cream-coloured stones with a few dark-green ferns hanging down in front of the stones.

Sometimes during the five years when he had not called himself a Catholic and had not gone into a Catholic church, the man in this story had wondered whether he himself ought to have been studying to be a priest in a monastery. Even though he claimed not to believe in the teachings of the Catholic Church, he had sometimes wondered whether he was the sort of man who could only have been contented as a priest in a monastery. The man had wondered about this whenever he had tried to persuade a young woman to become his girlfriend but had failed.

Whenever the man in this story had wondered why he had never been able to persuade a young woman to become his girlfriend, he had foreseen himself learning at last, in about December 1970, that he was the sort of man who would never persuade any young woman to become his girlfriend. He had then foreseen himself doing things other than trying to persuade one young woman after another to become his girlfriend and thinking of things other than having one or another young woman as his girlfriend. He had foreseen himself walking up and down in a corner of a garden and thinking only about the stones and the green leaves in the garden. He had then wondered whether the garden where he foresaw himself walking up and down was the garden of a monastery.

When the man in this story had first seen the colour print showing part of a low wall and a few ferns, he remembered his having foreseen himself sometimes walking up and down in front of such walls and such ferns. He then foresaw himself and his cousin walking up and down in front of the low wall and the few ferns on each of the couple of days when the man was visiting Sydney.

When the man in this story foresaw this he did not hear in his mind himself telling his cousin that he, the man in this story, had foreseen himself walking up and down at last in a corner of the garden of a monastery. The man heard in his mind himself telling his cousin that he, the man, was going to live, as from January 1965, in one or another country district far away from the suburbs of the city where he had always lived and that he, the man, was going to call himself a Catholic in that country district and was going to attend the Catholic church in that district on every Sunday as from January 1965.

In 1964 the young man in this story had been for five years a teacher in primary schools in the suburbs of the city where he had always lived. During those five years he had chosen in his mind one after another young female teacher that he would have liked to have as his girlfriend. He had talked with each of these young women and had become friendly with one after another of six of them. At one time or another he had asked each of these six young women to go with him to a cinema or to a house where a party was taking place or to a race meeting. Three of the six had agreed to go with him where he had asked them to go. One of these three had agreed twice afterwards to go with him where he had asked her to go. But not even this young woman had agreed to become his girlfriend.

Whenever the man in this story had chosen in his mind one of the young women mentioned in the previous paragraph, he had believed that she had not been brought up as a Catholic and had never been into a Catholic church. He had wanted his girlfriend not to be bound by the Ten Commandments as they were interpreted by the Catholic Church. But in February 1964 the man had begun to believe that he would never find a girlfriend from among the young women who were not bound by the Ten Commandments as they were interpreted by the Catholic Church.

One Sunday morning in February 1964 the man in this story had tried to learn why he had had to drink beer and to play cards with married men and unmarried men on almost every Friday night and Saturday night for five years, when what he had wanted to do on each of those nights was to be alone with a young woman who had agreed to be his girlfriend.

On that Sunday morning the man had assembled in his mind the six young women that he had become friendly with during the previous five years. The man saw the young women as standing in a line while he walked slowly past and looked at their faces and tried to understand why none of them had wanted to become his girlfriend. After he had looked at the face of each of the six young women, the man in this story had decided that each of the young women had been too knowing. The man had been older in years than each of the young women, but each young woman had been too knowing to want to be the girlfriend of the man in this story.

The man had next decided, in February 1964, that each of the six young women had been too knowing because she had not been bound by the Ten Commandments as they were interpreted by the Catholic Church. A month later, in March 1964, the man in this story had decided that the only young women who would not have been too knowing to want to become his girlfriend would have been young women who had been brought up as Catholics and who still called themselves Catholics and went into Catholic churches every Sunday. When the man had decided this, he decided to leave the suburbs where he had lived all his life and to live in a country district where he would call himself a Catholic and would go into a Catholic church every Sunday.

The man could not leave the suburbs at once. He had to stay until December 1964 at the primary school where he was a teacher. But he was free to apply in writing at any time during 1964 to be transferred to a primary school in a country district as from January 1965.

In March 1964 the man in this story had begun to spend part of each evening reading the pages headed ADVERTISED VACANCIES— PRIMARY SCHOOLS DIVISION in the *Education Gazette and Teachers' Aid* published by the Education Department in the city whose suburbs he had always lived in. While he read those pages he looked often at a map of all the country districts as far away as two hundred miles from that city. While he looked at the map he moved his index finger along the black lines denoting main roads. While he moved his finger he saw in his mind himself travelling in January 1965 from the suburbs where he had always lived to the country district where he would sit in a Catholic church each Sunday morning and would choose in his mind the young woman who would not be too knowing to want to become his girlfriend.

After he had moved his index finger in this way, the man in this story would move his index finger along the grey lines denoting lesser roads. While he moved his finger he saw in his mind himself travelling in January 1967 or January 1968 with his wife from the country district where they had been married towards the remote country district where they would live in a small weatherboard house beside the primary school where the man would be the sole teacher. In time, the finger of the man would come to rest at a point where two of the grey lines intersected. While his finger rested at this point the man would see in his mind himself and his wife living for year after year in the weatherboard house beside the weatherboard school at the remote crossroads. The school and the house that he saw in his mind were painted cream with dark-green trimmings like every school and every teacher's house in country districts for two or three hundred miles around the city where the man in this story had been born.

During the five years before 1964, while the man in this story had been living in the suburbs where he had always lived and had been choosing in his mind young female teachers in each school where he himself was a teacher, the man had believed that he would not always be a teacher in a primary school. He believed that he might become in the future a copy-writer in an advertising agency or an editor in a publishing firm or a manager of a book-shop. He understood that he was not qualified to become any of these, but whenever he was walking towards his room or rooms late on Friday night or Saturday night he would see in his mind first one or another young woman becoming his girlfriend then himself finding that his having a girlfriend caused him to feel more knowing then himself writing a paragraph of advertising copy or a poem or a short story that would be awarded first prize in a competition and at last the head of an advertising agency or of a publishing firm or of a firm of booksellers reading the prize-winning words and deciding to employ the man who had written the words.

But when the man in this story had decided that he would marry a young woman who would not be too knowing to want to become his girlfriend and who would be bound by the Ten Commandments as they were interpreted by the Catholic Church and that he would live with her in a house painted cream and dark green in a coun-try district, then the man had understood that he was also decid-ing that he would remain a teacher in a primary school for as many years as he could foresee. The man had understood this because he understood that his having a wife who had not been too know-ing to want to become his girlfriend and then his wife would not cause him to feel more knowing and so to write paragraphs of ad-vertising copy or poems or short stories.

When the man in this story wondered during March 1964 what he would see in his mind during all the years when he would live in a house painted cream and dark green, he foresaw himself walk-ing up and down for a few minutes every evening in the garden of his house and seeing in his mind networks of black lines and grey lines with dots of cream and dark green at their intersections and following with his finger in his mind first the black lines and the grey lines that he had already followed to the dot of cream and dark green where he was walking up and down at that moment and then the black lines and the grey lines that he might follow in later years towards other dots of cream and dark green in the network of black and grey that would surround him for as many years as he could foresee.

In May 1964 the man in this story travelled to Sydney in a carriage of a railway train. Outside the railway station in Sydney, the man asked the driver of a taxi to take him to the Majestic Hotel in Kings Cross. Inside the Majestic Hotel the man walked towards a walled desk that was not so high as the walled desks that he had previously seen in his mind. The woman behind the walled desk was so much older and looked so much more knowing than the women in his mind that he was hardly afraid of her jeering or laughing at him.

The man took the key that the woman gave him but he did not listen to what she told him about breakfast and dinner in the hotel. The man had decided before he had set out for Sydney that he was not going to sit in a dining room of a hotel where the young women of Sydney might see how much less knowing he was than themselves.

The man in this story went to his room in the Majestic Hotel in Kings Cross and put his bag on the bed. He took out of the bag and put on the small table near the bed the book that he was reading at that time: *Marius the Epicurean*, by Walter Pater, in the Everyman's Library edition. Then he took out of the bag and put on the table his map of the country districts for as far as two hundred miles around his city and one of the bags of sultanas and dried apricots and cheese that he had brought for eating in Sydney. The man ate the sultanas and dried apricots and cheese while he looked at the map. Sometimes he rested his index finger at a point on the map where two black lines or two grey lines or a black line and a grey line intersected and he saw the two lines intersecting in his mind and at the place where they intersected a dot of cream and dark green.

At noon on his first day in Sydney the man in this story walked out of the Majestic Hotel in Kings Cross and looked for a bus that would take him to one of the railway stations of Sydney. He stood on the footpath and watched two buses pass him. He saw on the other side of the windows of each bus young women who seemed no older than himself but much more knowing. He saw in his mind himself climbing the steps of each of the buses and asking the driver or the conductor a question that would cause the young women in the bus to smile or to laugh.

The man in this story travelled by taxi from Kings Cross to Central Station. From there he travelled by railway train to Turramurra on the Hornsby line. From the railway station at Turramurra the man walked through streets of houses with large front gardens. At each intersection of two or more streets the man looked at the directions that his cousin had written in his latest letter to the man. After walking for twenty minutes, the man came to the monastery and rang the front doorbell and was shown into the parlour to wait for his cousin.

The cousin of the man in this story came into the front parlour of the monastery and shook the hand of the man. The cousin asked the man whether he wanted to talk in the front parlour or in the garden of the monastery. The man said he would like to walk up and down on a quiet path in the garden.

The cousin led the man to a path between a lawn and a wire fence with a tennis court on the other side. The two men walked up and down and talked. The cousin talked about his life in the monastery. The man talked about his life as a teacher in a primary school.

While the man walked up and down and talked, he looked around him for a cream-coloured wall with a few dark-green ferns hanging over it. He saw part of a cream-coloured wall in a corner of the garden on the far side of the lawn, but he saw no ferns hanging down.

After the two men had walked and had talked for two hours, the cousin took the man into the front parlour of the monastery and then brought the man a cup of tea and some biscuits on a tray. The man then knew that the time allowed for his visit had almost passed.

While the man drank his cup of tea, his cousin told him that he felt very happy in the monastery because he was close to God. The man in this story then understood that his cousin was waiting for him to say that he felt unhappy in the suburbs of his city because he was not close to God.

The man in this story told his cousin that he was unhappy in the suburbs of his city and that he was thinking of going to live in a country district as from January 1965. The man thought that he would tell his cousin on the following day that he was thinking of going into a Catholic church as from January 1965 and of choosing a young woman who would agree to become his girlfriend.

The man left the monastery in the late afternoon and travelled by railway train from Turramurra to the centre of Sydney and then by taxi to the Majestic Hotel in Kings Cross. In his room he ate sultanas and dried apricots and cheese while he looked at his map of country districts and sometimes rested his index finger at a point where lines intersected.

On the second day of his couple of days in Sydney, the man in this story did the same things that he had done on the first day until the moment in the parlour of the monastery when his cousin asked him whether he wanted to talk in the parlour or in the garden. The man then said to his cousin that he would like to walk up and down on the opposite side of the garden from where they had walked on the previous day. The man did not tell his cousin about the cream-coloured wall or the ferns hanging down.

The man and his cousin walked up and down on the opposite side of the garden from where they had walked on the previous day. The cousin told the man that he would be ordained in February 1965, after which he would feel even closer to God. The man asked his cousin where he would live after he had been ordained. The cousin said that his superiors might send him either to a monastery in another suburb of Sydney or to a monastery in a country district but that he would feel equally close to God wherever he lived.

The man in this story then told his cousin that he was thinking of going to live in a country district as from January 1965 and of going into the Catholic church in his district every Sunday.

The cousin told the man that this was wonderful news. The cousin seemed to the man to believe that the man was thinking of doing these things because he wanted to feel closer to God.

While the man and his cousin had been talking, the man had been looking at the low stone wall beside the path where he and his cousin were walking up and down. He believed that the wall was the same cream-coloured wall that had stayed in his mind since he had first thought of going to Sydney, but he had not seen any dark-green ferns hanging down in front of the wall. He had seen ferns and other small dark-green plants growing in the beds of soil that reached back from the top of the wall, but none of those plants hung down over the wall. The man had seen also in the beds of soil signs that someone had pulled small plants out of the soil only a few days before.

The man in this story asked his cousin who it was that looked after the garden around the monastery.

The man's cousin answered that he and the other students for the priesthood looked after the garden during some of their recreation periods. The cousin then pointed to the beds of soil above the low stone wall and said that he and the other students had cleaned up that part of the garden only a few days before.

The man in this story walked up to the low wall of cream-coloured stones. The wall reached as high as the thighs of the man. The man looked at the bed of soil close to the top of the wall and at the cracks between the topmost cream-coloured stones. He was looking for the soil that had held the roots of the few dark-green ferns that he had often seen in his mind.

The man reached out a hand towards the wall. His cousin told him not to touch the wall and not to put his hands near the soil behind the wall. His cousin told him not to forget that the garden of the monastery was in one of the northern suburbs of Sydney, which was one of the districts where the funnel-web spider lived. The cousin said that he and his fellow-students always wore boots and thick gloves while they worked in the garden because the bite of the funnel-web spider was deadly. The cousin pointed to a crack between two cream-coloured stones in the low wall and he said that such a crack was often the hiding-place of a funnel-web spider.

The man in this story remembered a joke that he had heard from one of the card-players and beer-drinkers on a Saturday night in April 1964. One of the card-players and beer-drinkers had asked the others had they heard about the young woman who had been bitten on the funnel by a finger-web spider.

The man in this story heard jokes every Saturday night while he played cards and drank beer. Whenever he heard a joke that made him laugh, the man would put his cards face-down on the table and would take out and unfold a piece of paper that he carried in his pocket every Saturday night. Then the man would write a few words on his piece of paper. On the night when he had heard the joke about the young woman and the spider, the man had written the words *finger* and *web*.

On most Friday afternoons in the hotel, the man would amuse the married men who were his fellow-teachers by taking pieces of paper from his pocket and unfolding the paper and looking at the words written on the paper and trying to remember the jokes that he had heard on the previous Saturday night. On the Friday after the man had written the words *finger* and *web* on a piece of paper, he saw the two words on the piece of paper that he had unfolded in the hotel. The man remembered at once the joke that the words had been meant to recall to him, but he looked at the words as though he could not remember, and he told the men other jokes but not the joke about the young woman and the spider.

The man in this story had not told in the hotel the joke about the finger-web spider because he had thought of the married men surrounding him as much more knowing than himself. The man had been afraid that one of the married men would not smile after he had heard the joke but would say that he knew of no part of a woman's body that was shaped like a funnel and would then ask him, the teller of the joke, to explain what part of the woman's body he had had in mind when he had told the joke.

In the garden of the monastery, beside the cream-coloured wall where the deadly spiders were said to live, the man in this story did not tell his cousin the joke about the finger-web spider. The man did not want his cousin to think that he, the teller of the joke, was boasting of how much more knowing he was or of how much more knowing he would be as from the day in 1966 or 1967 after he had married the young woman that he would have chosen for his girlfriend in the Catholic church in his country district.

Late in the afternoon of his second day in Sydney the man in this story said goodbye to his cousin and travelled by railway train from Turramurra to Sydney and then by taxi to the Majestic Hotel in Kings Cross. In his room he ate sultanas and dried apricots and cheese while he moved his finger along the lines of his map.

On the following morning the man left the Majestic Hotel for the last time and travelled by taxi to the railway station in Sydney where he had arrived three days before. The man found the window seat reserved for him in the Melbourne train and sat down. He opened the free map that was provided for each passenger and began to study and to follow with his finger the route that the train would follow from Sydney back to Melbourne. When the train began to move, the man looked around him and saw that the only passenger sitting near him was a man in the window seat on

134

the opposite side of the carriage. This man seemed a few years older than the man in this story and was wearing the uniform of a soldier.

Early in the afternoon the man in this story became tired of studying his free map. He thought of talking to the man in the window seat opposite, but when he looked across the carriage he saw that the man in the uniform had gone.

The man in this story suspected that the man in the uniform had gone to some part of the train where beer was being sold. The man in this story wanted to drink beer and to talk to other men. He had not drunk beer while he had been in Sydney. He had not wanted to walk alone into a hotel and to order a single glass of beer from a woman older and more knowing than himself and then to stand drinking the beer alone among groups of married men or of single men older and more knowing than himself.

The man in this story got up from his seat and walked through the carriages of the train until he came to a carriage where women were serving food from behind a tall steel counter. Men were sitting on tall stools in front of the steel counter, and every man had not only food in front of him but a can of beer.

The man in this story glanced around him but went on walking through the carriage. He did not want to stand and to stare at the men and the cans of beer and so cause the women behind the steel counter to believe that he wanted to drink beer among the men but was afraid to approach the women.

The man was afraid to approach the women because he did not understand the rules for drinking beer at the steel counter. On his way through the carriage he saw a notice behind the women warning him that liquor would be served only with meals. He did not want to eat a meal that had been prepared by the strange women. If he had wanted to eat a meal he would have eaten the last of the cheese and the dried fruits in his bag. Yet most of the men on the tall stools were eating only cheese. Most of the men had in front of them a few pieces of cheese and a few dried biscuits.

The man in this story would have asked one of the women for a few pieces of cheese and a few dry biscuits if he had been sure that that was all he had to do in order to buy a can of beer. But the man was afraid that the women behind the steel counter would require him to pass some other test before they would sell him the can of beer. And even if he had to pass no other test, he was afraid that he might use other words than the customary words when he asked one of the women for the cheese and the biscuits and the beer, and that the woman would then understand that he had never before asked for cheese and biscuits and beer on the train from Sydney to Melbourne.

The man in this story was walking past the last section of the steel counter on his way out of the carriage when a man in a soldier's uniform asked him if he wanted a beer. The man in this story recognised the man in the soldier's uniform as the man who had sat near him earlier.

The man in this story sat on the tall stool next to the man in the uniform and leaned an arm on the tall steel counter. The man in the uniform smiled and made a sign with his finger to one of the women behind the counter. The woman smiled at the man in the uniform and hurried towards him. The man in the uniform told the woman to bring a can and a plate for the man in this story. The woman smiled again and went to fetch the can and the plate, but the man in this story understood that the woman had smiled only at the man in the uniform and that she was hurrying to fetch the can and the plate only because the man in the uniform had asked her. When the woman put the can and the plate on the counter near the man in this story she did not look at him, and the man understood that she would have jeered at him if he had not been sitting beside the man in the soldier's uniform.

The man in this story learned from the man in the soldier's uniform that he was a soldier. The two men talked and drank beer from early in the afternoon until early in the evening, when the train had crossed the Great Dividing Range and was approaching the northern suburbs of Melbourne. Sometimes the man in this story ate a biscuit or a piece of cheese from his plate so that the women behind the steel counter would not think he despised the food that they served. The soldier ate none of the biscuits and none of the pieces of cheese on his plate. In the early evening, when the two men had drunk the last of their cans, the plate beside the man in this story was empty and the plate beside the soldier was still covered with dry biscuits and pieces of cheese, yet the woman who took away the two plates smiled at the soldier and did not look at the man in this story.

During the afternoon the man in this story learned that the soldier resembled him in some ways. The soldier had been brought up as a Catholic but no longer called himself a Catholic or went into Catholic churches. The soldier had a cousin who was studying to be a priest in Brisbane. The soldier did not have a girlfriend. The soldier thought sometimes that he would like to live in a country district. However, the man in this story understood that the soldier was about seven years older than him, that he had had several girlfriends in the past, and that he was much more knowing.

During the afternoon the soldier told stories to the man in this story. Many of the stories were about men doing things that the man himself had done; they were stories about men drinking beer or playing cards or travelling to cities where they had never been before. Some of the stories were about things that the man in this story had once hoped to do but had since given up hope of doing; they were stories of men having one girlfriend after another. Some of the stories were about men doing things that the man in this story had never hoped to do; they were stories about men travelling to foreign countries and fighting as soldiers.

Twenty years after the man in this story had listened to the soldier on the train between Sydney and Melbourne, the man was drinking beer and playing cards with three married men and four married women of the same age as himself. The man asked the

seven married persons how many of them remembered the war
between Australian soldiers and Communist terrorists, as they
were called, in the jungles of Malaya fifteen years before the war in
Vietnam.

None of the seven married persons could remember the war
in Malaya. One of the married women said that the man in this
story had not remembered but had dreamed of the war.

The man in this story said that he not only remembered the
war in Malaya but also remembered himself dreaming of the war.
When he had been a student at secondary school, the man said,
he had read about the war in newspapers and had been afraid that
the Communist terrorists would win the war and would conquer
Malaya and neighbouring countries and would then invade Australia. He had been especially afraid, the man had said, that he
would have to become a soldier and would die fighting the Communist terrorists in the jungles or on the plains of Australia before he had persuaded a young woman to become his girlfriend.

While the two unmarried men drank beer and talked at the steel
counter, the soldier sometimes told the other man that he had seen
some terrible sights in the jungles of Malaya. After the soldier had
said for the first time that he had seen some terrible sights, the
other man supposed that the soldier was trying to decide whether
or not to tell him a certain story about a certain terrible sight.
After the soldier had said for the third or the fourth time that he
had seen some terrible sights, the other man supposed that the
soldier had decided not to tell him a certain story. But in the early
evening, when the train was approaching the northern suburbs of
Melbourne and when each man was drinking his last can of beer,
the soldier said he would tell the man a little story.

The soldier told the man in this story first that the jungles of
Malaya were far-reaching and thick and dark green and without
roads. While he was telling this to the man, the soldier moved the
tip of his finger inwards a few inches from one point after another

on the circumference of an invisible circle on the top of the steel counter. The soldier moved his finger inwards each time but then lifted the finger away before it reached the centre of the invisible circle. While the soldier moved his finger, the man in this story saw one road after another coming to an end in the remote country districts of Malaya.

The soldier told the man that the Communist terrorists had lived for many years in the jungle. Some of the Communists had built villages that seemed invisible among the dark-green leaves. The soldier and his mates had been trained to search for the invisible-seeming villages and then to kill all the Communists and to destroy all the invisible-seeming houses in the villages.

One day the soldier and his mates had found the largest number of Communists and the largest village that they had so far found. The village had seemed invisible because it consisted not of buildings but of caves. The Communists had built an invisible village of caves in a tall, cream-coloured cliff deep inside the dark-green jungle.

Before the soldiers could enter the village of caves, they had to fight the Communists who lived there. The Communists had fought to defend their invisible-seeming village but in time the soldier and his mates had killed every Communist.

After the soldiers had killed the last of the Communists, so the soldier had told the man in this story, the soldier and his mates had entered the invisible-seeming caves in the wall of cream-coloured rock.

When he had come to this point in his story, the soldier in this story began to move his index finger from place to place on the top of the steel counter. The man in this story understood that the soldier was not now trying to make him see a map in his mind but was afraid. The man understood that the soldier was afraid of telling the end of his story because it was the story of something that had changed him from one sort of soldier and man into another sort.

When the man in this story had understood this, he became

afraid. He was afraid that what he was about to hear would be something that would change him from one sort of man into another sort. He was afraid that after he had heard what he was about to hear he would go back to the room that he called for the time being his own room and would put away his map of country districts and would tear up the list of schools where he might have taught as from January 1965 and would be afraid afterwards to live anywhere but in the suburbs of the city where he had been born and afraid even to visit his cousin in the monastery or his married cousin or anyone else in Sydney or in any city other than his native city.

The soldier stopped moving his finger from place to place on the top of the steel counter. He looked through the window of the railway carriage at the lights of the northern suburbs of Melbourne. Then he told the man in this story that he and his soldier-mates had found in one of the caves in the cream-coloured cliff about twenty young women. The young women had been kept as prisoners by the Communists who had been killed by the soldier and his mates. The young women had been taken prisoner in a village in a remote country district. The soldier and his mates had passed through the village on their way to search for the invisible-seeming village of the Communists. The soldier and his mates had found all the houses of the village burned and all the people except the young women killed.

The soldiers had soon decided that they could not leave the young women living in the invisible-seeming cave. But then they had decided that they could not take the young women back to the village where the houses had all been burned and the people had all been killed. The soldiers had then assembled the young women and had looked at the face of one young woman after another. The soldiers had then decided to kill the young women. The soldiers had then fired bullets into the heads of the young women and had left the dead bodies of the young women in the invisible-seeming cave in the cream-coloured cliff in the jungle.

When the soldier in this story had told the man in this story that the soldiers in the soldier's story had looked at the face of one young woman after another, the soldier had not told the man how the faces of the young women had looked. Instead the soldier had told the man that he could imagine how the faces of the young women had looked. The man in this story had then seen in his mind that the faces of the young women had looked as though the young women were much too knowing.

First Love

Somewhere today in a suburb of Melbourne is a man who calls himself a writer of fiction but who writes, in fact, a sort of diary of the man he wishes he could be. The man I am writing about likes to pose as an eccentric. Before an interview he will always ask to be asked about his odd habits and preferences. And he especially likes to be asked if he has done much travelling lately.

When that question is put to him, the man says he hardly ever travels, and certainly never to the places that other people choose as their destinations. He says he has never been in an aeroplane and he has only once crossed the River Murray in a northerly direction. And while his interviewer pauses to wonder about all this, the man adds that he does all the travelling he needs to do in his mind—in his dreams. (It is quite in character for the man to use words such as *mind* and *dreams* loosely like this. He has very vague notions of what he consists of. His inner life, if it could be so called, is a continual wandering through a maze in which the walls are images of the places he has never travelled to.)

If the people who are always declaring that God is dead are really yearning deep down for God to appear and to put his arm around their shoulders, then the man who keeps on telling the world that he never travels must be secretly waiting for a well-wisher to present him with a passport and a sheaf of travellers' cheques and to tell him to sit back and relax because he's going to be whisked away to all the places his nomadic heart has always yearned after.

Where would the stay-at-home choose to go if this journey of a lifetime was put in his way? What means of travel would he use? And would he travel alone, or would he have a companion when he crossed the Great Dividing Range?

I see that I have answered one of my questions already. The man of this story has always thought of travel as taking him first north-wards across the Keilor Plains towards Mount Macedon.

Since he does not own a motor car, our man will have to take a Bendigo train on the first leg of his long-awaited journey. And he thanks you politely, but he wouldn't dream of putting anyone to the trouble of wandering off with him, or even saying good-bye. Just write down your address and slip it to the traveller before he sets out, and you might find yourself from time to time reading a rambling report of his travels.

Like most children of my time and place, I travelled on passenger trains drawn by steam locomotives across the countryside of Victoria in the years just after the Second World War. I would like to be able to describe the look and the feel of the carriages that I sat in from early morning until far into the hot afternoon. But lately I read again part of the story "First Love" by Vladimir Nabokov, which always reminds me that I have no memory for furniture or fabrics or interiors.

The narrator of "First Love" travelled on the Nord Express from St Petersburg to Paris in the years just before the First World War. The author of that story, looking across the same number of years that I now look across to my own railway journeys, wrote in the 1940s of the embossed leather lining of the compartment walls, the tulip-shaped reading lamps, the tassel of the blue, bivalved night light . . . As against all that, I can only recall the mild stickiness of the dark-green leather seats and of the bulbous armrests that had to be pulled out and down from recesses between the shoulders of the passengers.

I seem to have no memory for interiors. I am so little aware today of the insides of all the houses I have lived in that the rooms of those houses might have been only shelter from the wind, or shade from the sun, or places to hide in while I wrote and read. And instead of trying to remember railway compartments, I might as well complain about all the blank spaces that stayed in front of my eyes when I should have seen landscapes all around me on my travels across the countryside of Victoria.

But there is one other detail from the Melbourne-to-Bendigo or the Melbourne–to–Port Fairy: just one grey and brown memory to sit drably beside the tasselled night light or the mitre-folded napkins in the dining car of the Nord Express. In each compartment, above the green leather backrest and just below the metal latticework of the luggage rack, the wall was inlaid with three photographs behind glass of scenes from Victoria.

The weather outside the compartment was nearly always the heat of January, but the skies in the photographs seemed anything but blue, and I was glad not to be tending towards them. Even beach scenes (Cowes, Lorne, Frankston) with crowds in the water and well-defined shadows under the Norfolk Island pines could not convince me. There was only the sunlight around me and the sunlight I was headed for; there was no other sort.

It would be too easy to say that the photographs made me gloomy because they were old. Of course the canvas-topped motor cars and the moustached men in waistcoats were from my father's childhood, and one of the clouds high above was likely to be a tobacco-juice colour where dampness or something worse had got through a crack in the glass and had spread. Yet the word *old* meant hardly anything to me. What saddened me was to think how *far* from me those forests closed over the roads; those matchstick piers tapered away into milk-white seas without waves. I must have been seeing already in its simplest form the map of the world that has since grown in front of my eyes from just a few translucent panels like coloured glass prettifying my path to something so elaborate that I hardly remember any other sights behind it—any other world that these winding corridors and confusing windows might have been copied from.

The map grew out of one simple proposition. I speak of it tactfully as a proposition, but it has always seemed self-evident to me. In all the world there has never been, there is not, and there will never be any such thing as *time*. There is only *place*. What people call time is only place after place. Eternity is here already, and it has no mystery about it; eternity is just another name for this endless scenery where we wander from one place to another.

Before I begin to explain what follows from this, someone reading these traveller's notes is sure to remember a neat little sentence from an advertisement for a motion picture of a few years back. (If I were writing exclusively for those who understand the secret dominance of place, I would have put the word *away* instead of *back* in the previous sentence. My world has no *forward* and no *back*, only a place here and a million million other places near or further away.) Someone will remember the neat little sentence and will think I am only repeating what that sentence says.

The sentence actually comes from the book of fiction that the film-makers got their story from. The past, says the neat little sentence, is a foreign country: they do things differently there.

How poetic, and how promising this must have seemed to people preparing to watch a motion picture. Just when the movie-watcher might have thought all the countries in the world had been thoroughly photographed, here was a new sort of foreign country waiting to welcome camera-people and sightseers and tourists.

How wrong we were to think of history as lost to sight, the movie-watchers would have said; history is really a folk-festival in an exotic country, and history books are just a more wordy sort of travel brochure.

I went to my bookshelves just now and found a Penguin edition of *The Go-Between* by L. P. Hartley. On the front cover is a picture of a hard-faced woman wearing a long white frock and holding a parasol and standing on mown grass among green branches. On the back cover is this sentence (among others). *The cover shows a scene from the MGM-EMI Film Distributors Limited Release* The Go-Between *starring Julie Christie and Alan Bates, also starring Margaret Leighton.*

After I had read the sentence on the back cover I looked again at the picture on the front. I am looking at the picture now. I ask myself: this woman named Julie Christie or Margaret Leighton—is she in a foreign country? And if she is, I ask myself, do they do things differently there? And if the answer to each of these questions is "yes," should I call the foreign country the *past*?

These are questions I cannot answer. As soon as I look at the woman named Christie or Leighton, I see her strolling among the trees and flicking her parasol impatiently about her. Now she speaks; and although she looks anywhere but in my direction, I know her words are aimed at me.

Granted, she says, she is in my power to some extent. But I have power only over what I see. And all I can see is the long frock, and the parasol being flicked in anger, and the haughty and unsmiling face; whereas she can see the house behind all these lawns and trees, and she sees the people of the house, who are her equals as I can never be.

I look around me at this shabby room, and then through the window at the unkempt cotoneasters and the long sodden grass that was once a lawn, and I have no doubt that the woman who speaks to me—for all her haughtiness and her parasol and her long, elaborate frock—is in my own country.

But of course she is in my country, someone will object. She is in my country because she is not a woman named Christie or Leighton but an image of a woman—in fact an image of an image of a woman, or something even more complicated.

Instead of answering my objector just now, I turn from the picture on the cover to the text inside the book. According to the log that I keep of my reading, I read the text of *The Go-Between* in January 1977. But of all the text, I can only remember today about ten words spoken by a man to a boy. I remember none of the characters and nothing of the action. I could open the book at any page today and read it as though for the first time. But to prove to my own reader that this investigation is without bias, I hereby announce that the passage I will now read is the passage beginning on the seventh line of the seventy-seventh page.

And the heat was a medium which made this change of outlook possible. As a liberating power with its own laws it was outside my experience. In the heat, the commonest objects changed their nature.

These are the very words I read when I opened the book at the place chosen entirely by chance. The book is supposed to be about a foreign country called the past, yet every word in the passage I found belongs to the story I am writing at present. The reader will find every one of those words in context towards the end of this story. The words happen to describe something from the most memorable afternoon of my life.

I have nothing further to do with any objections. Not only is there no such thing as the past; there is almost certainly no such thing as a foreign country. Now, instead of wasting precious space with speculations about theoretical countries, I will go on writing about the here-and-now.

And I am going to write in the language of this world instead of the jargon of an imagined world ruled over by those invisible and sinister science-fiction tyrants Time and Change. It is the present now all over the world. It has always been the present and it always is the present. I use the word *present* only for old time's sake. What I should write is not It *always is the present* but It *always is.*

What is? All this scenery, of course: all this scenery multiplied endlessly around me wherever I look.

I am writing to you from the compartment of a railway carriage. In front of me, and somewhat above the level of my eyes, part of a pale road crosses a sandy hilltop. A motor car is stopped on the road—a motor car with a canvas roof and with side-windows of something tough and yellowish that is not glass. A man stands beside the motor car; the man has a thick moustache and wears a waistcoat and a watch-chain beneath the jacket of his suit. The man stands between me and a blur of sand-dunes and distant sea and hazy clouds. Across the width of the road at the man's feet are the words: *Warrnambool with Lady Bay.*

I am writing to you from the compartment of a railway carriage. In front of me, and exactly level with my eyes, a yellow-brown grassland rises and falls, bulges and sags, and moves continually from left to right. At its right-hand side the grassland is disappearing, bulge and hollow by bulge and hollow, behind the grey felt hat with the peacock feather in its band and the clean-shaven face and the three-piece suit of a man seven years younger than myself. At its left-hand side the yellow-brown grassland is being continually renewed, but the man with the peacock feather in his hatband is saying to me that from where he sits he can see the end of the Keilor Plains and the beginning of Mount Macedon.

I am writing, as usual, from the compartment of a railway carriage. In front of me, and somewhat above the level of my eyes, the sky is pale blue at its lower level and even paler at the upper edge of my view. The sky is moving from left to right. At its right-hand side, the pale blue is disappearing behind the grey sea and the grey-white sky of Warrnambool with Lady Bay. At its left-hand side, the pale blue is being continually renewed.

I am still writing from my railway carriage. The man in front of me, with the peacock-blue in his hatband, is my father, who was born at Allansford, Victoria, in 1904 and died at Geelong, Victoria, in 1960. His grave is in the Warrnambool cemetery, which overlooks the estuary of the Hopkins River at the eastern end of Lady Bay. From my father's birthplace to the site of his grave is a walk of perhaps two hours along the Hopkins, the most placid of rivers, from the shallow place of green rushes and smooth stones that was once a ford for the pioneers Allan to the wide, calm lake between grassy hills, cemetery, and sea.

From my father's birthplace to the place where we buried him is an afternoon's stroll, but the man with the rich blue in his hatband has travelled for most of his life in every State of Australia, and backwards and forwards across the Great Divide. He is sitting now, this endlessly travelling man, with the advantage that most travellers like to secure for themselves: he is facing his destination. I do not have this advantage. I am facing my father, and the man with the moustache and watchband, and Warrnambool with Lady Bay.

The man of the blue-green feather is telling me his travels are nearly over. He is taking me to a place we will neither of us want to leave. Today we have left Melbourne for good; from now on our home is Bendigo. And already from where he sits, my father says, he can see the end of the Keilor Plains and the beginnings of Mount Macedon. Soon we will cross the Great Divide and go on to live for the rest of our lives in Bendigo. I, of course, have not yet seen the Great Divide. I have still not even seen the end of the plains.

149

I am on my travels in this world of place after place, and my father is travelling with me, not to mention the old-timer on the road at Warrnambool with Lady Bay. The last of the plains have disappeared behind my father and his grey hat with the peacock-coloured feather. The last of the sky over the plains has disappeared behind the man at Warrnambool with Lady Bay.

Where else would I be but in this railway compartment? In front of me, and level with my face, is a slope of Mount Macedon. The slope is covered with forest, which is being renewed continually on its left-hand side. I can see no sky. The lower slope of Mount Macedon is disappearing where the plains have disappeared—behind my father. And the upper slope of the mountain is going where the sky over the plains has gone—behind Warrnambool with Lady Bay.

I am in the railway compartment where I am always. The forest is not being renewed, any more than the plains were renewed in place after place. My father tells me we have crossed the Great Divide. He says our home now is a country of gentle hills scattered with ponderous trees. He says a new sort of weather is settling over us once and for all.

The sky in front of my eyes is blue only. The sky is so blue and so far-reaching that I have never seen it disappear behind my father or behind any scenery.

Please assume that I am still in the railway compartment for as long as I go on writing about my travels. And please do not ask how I can be in two places at once. If the wooden-faced woman in the white frock is allowed to be waving her parasol not a thousand miles from where the little Russian boy stares at the blue night

light somewhere on the plains of Europe, then I too am somewhere on my travels.

I am lying on my back and looking at sky. I am lying among dark-
green glossy stems of rye-grass on the unmown land beside a small
weatherboard hall in Neale Street, Bendigo. Under my head and
body the soil is trustworthy. Even through the thick grass the feeling reaches me that this soil deserves to be trusted. I have learned
to trust absolutely the strong, gravelly soil of Bendigo.

At the moment I am not thinking of soil. I am looking at the
sky and wondering what to make of its blueness.

From where I lie, I can see more deeply into this sky than I have
seen into any other. I seem to be looking at a part of the sky so
deep it is not meant to be looked at. I am looking at a blue so blue
it is turning continually, far inside itself, into another colour.

My father is standing near me, but I cannot see him because I
will not take my eyes away from the sky. My father is grazing his
chestnut gelding, which is still a maiden after a long career in racing. I cannot see the horse, but I can hear its teeth tearing at the
rye-grass.

My father tells me the sky is the blue that it is because we are
on the other side of the Great Divide. He says the sky over the
places where he and I were born is not the true colour. Over Melbourne and Warrnambool the sky has been watered down; the sea
has drained the true colour out of the sky. But here at Bendigo the
sky is its true colour because it has nothing but land beneath it—
and not just any land but soil and grass that are mostly golden
orange, which of all colours brings out the richest from blue.

I discuss with my father the true name for the colour of this
sky of the inland. My father finds rather conveniently near his
feet a few small flowers of a kind I have always taken for weeds.
He tells me that these are cornflowers and the sky is cornflower
blue.

I cannot quite see in the sky overhead the blue of the flowers my father calls cornflowers. Yet I am pleased that my father has claimed to see that sort of blue. I understand that I am free myself to see in the sky a colour from earth.

I have to admit that the sky here, north of the Great Divide, is an incomparable blue, but its colour makes me sometimes uneasy. The deep, pure blue is a little too deep and too pure. I would lie more comfortably on the soil of Bendigo if I knew that the powerful blue is not all there is to the sky.

And so, privately, I decide that the sky over the inland leads back to a layer of lilac. Although no such thing has yet appeared to my eyes, I declare my belief in a delicate lilac underlying the deep blue. With my head resting against the soil, I trust that the sky will ultimately give way to the colour I see in the clusters of small flowers (each cluster shaped like a half-opened parasol) on the roof-high shrub behind my house each year when the first north winds blow.

I am standing on the solid soil of Bendigo and staring at the sudden shining or dulling of tiny creases and rumplings in a silk jacket as they catch or lose the light from high in the darkness above the Showgrounds trotting track. The silk jacket is worn by a man with a faintly Chinese face. His name is Clarrie Long, and I wish I had used that name instead of Harold Moy for the jockey in the first work of fiction I ever wrote, and the name Bendigo instead of Bassett for the city in north-central Victoria where that work of fiction is set.

Clarrie Long's jacket and the jackets of the five other drivers are the first racing colours I have seen, but I know already that I am going to study racing colours for the rest of my life. I will still stare at skies and lilac bushes, but only to help me understand racing colours.

I am sitting at my table in a room of a house in a suburb of Melbourne. On the south wall of the room, just to the right of the window, a page of a calendar shows rows of black numerals in white squares below a picture with the caption: *Snow gums on the Gorge Nature Trail, Mount Buffalo National Park.*

A week ago I asked a man who has lived for much of his life at Kangaroo Flat, on the south-west outskirts of Bendigo, what he remembered of the photographs in the old country trains. He said without hesitating that he remembered mostly pictures of snow and ice and granite boulders and the Chalet at Mount Buffalo. That man has never seen this room. He had no way of knowing that I would sit down one day to write about the interiors of compartments on the Bendigo train in a room with a scene from his own railway journeys above me on the wall.

The father of the man from Kangaroo Flat, by the way, died as my own father died—suddenly in his fifties. Each of the two men was, in his own way, a good Catholic; so each body lies now—the body of my father beside the calm, brown Hopkins and under a pale-blue sky, and the body of the man from Kangaroo Flat in the trusty soil of Bendigo and under that unforgettable blue—waiting, in the words of the Apostles' Creed, for the resurrection of the body and life everlasting.

I am sitting at my table, with my back to Bendigo, and facing the window in the south wall. The sky outside the window is the colour of the water in Bass Strait, with grey-white clouds appearing continually from behind the calendar-picture of Mount Buffalo. I am wondering how I have come at last to be staring at a sky no different from the sea after all the richness I have seen in skies.

I am sitting at my table and reading a letter from a man who has gone to live in Tasmania. For the sake of those people who have to read a story about the past as though they are watching a motion picture, I will mention here, and in each of the remaining scenes of this story, a calendar with the ordinal number of a year showing on it or else a scrap of newspaper with the date showing in the corner. In this scene, the page of a calendar marked 1986 is visible. (I am not scornful of the people who want to know this sort of detail. Even though time has been abolished from my world, some of the old words have been left in place, like signposts pointing to towns long since submerged under man-made lakes.)

In his letter from Tasmania, the man writes about the peculiar colour of the sky over the place where he now lives. He writes that some of the pale blue has drained away into the green of the plain around his house. I wonder how anyone could write in this way about Tasmania. But then I look through my collections of maps, and one map is drawn to such a scale that I see the man now as having found the one district in all Tasmania that can rightly be called plains.

The man who wrote the letter was born in the hills near Hurstbridge, Victoria. This is the district that I called Harp Gully in a work of fiction. The narrator in that work of fiction looked forward to spending the last part of his life at Harp Gully.

The man who now lives in Tasmania has written a work of fiction of his own set in a place called Harp Gully. Before he wrote his fiction he asked me if I would allow him to use the name Harp Gully, but I told him no one should claim to own the name of any place in a true work of fiction.

I am standing at my table in the room with a window on its south side. The sky is a watery colour, but I am not wondering whether the blue has been lost to Bass Strait or to the green plains of Tasmania. I am looking at two rhombuses, each measuring diagonally about 1.5 centimetres, cut from silk of the same colour as the sky outside the window at my back. I am holding one of the pieces of pale-blue silk between a pair of tweezers and trying to fit the piece into a collage of pieces of silk. When this and the other rhombus of silk are in place, the pattern of the collage will be complete and I will then cover all the pieces of silk carefully with a sheet of transparent and adhesive plastic. All the pieces of silk have been cut with a blunt razor blade from ribbons of silk bought at Myer Northland.

The shopping centre known as Northland is built on what was once the first patch of open grassland I saw and afterwards remembered having seen. The grassland was visible from the windows of the yellow bus that travelled between Bundoora and the East Preston tram terminus when I lived at Bundoora in my third and fourth years and just before I was taken to live at Bendigo.

The finished pattern of coloured silk, held firmly under the clear plastic, is the best likeness I have prepared of the colours that represent me.

I do not own a racehorse or a share in a racehorse. Even if I had the money to buy the least share in a horse, I would use the money instead to buy ten or twenty sets of racing silks, each of which would be a slight variation of the colours I have almost decided on in this room with the south-facing window and the calendar showing the numerals 1-9-8-2. Having bought the racing colours, I would spend the rest of my life studying each of the different patterns in different lights. I would study the patterns in this room in June or July, with a watered-down sky behind me. I would study the patterns in a room facing east in March, when the light of summer has begun to soften and I can make out separate dark-blue treetops on the first of the folds of hills between here and Hurstbridge. And I would study my patterns by a window facing north in September, when the first hot wind blows over Melbourne. ("Please do not close the window," said the Reverend Doctor Backhaus to his housekeeper in Brighton, Victoria, on a hot afternoon in the last year of his life. "That wind is the north wind," said the exile. "It comes from Bendigo.")

Only one room in this house has a window that looks north, and before this calendar in the corner is taken down from the wall, men shouting day after day in a foreign language will have torn down the old garden outside that window and built things called units in the bare dirt. But the sunlight in September will still reach the window, and the north wind will still flap the orange-gold holland blind.

One day, all the other people in this house will have gone away and left me to do what I have always wanted to do. For most of my life I used to think I would spend my days, after I had been left alone, draping over beds and chairs and floors all the variously coloured jackets and sleeves and caps from the collection of racing-silks bought with the money that a different sort of man would have called his life's savings. I used to see myself walking backwards and forwards in every room, always with my eyes on the silks, and stopping suddenly at any one of twenty different places to study some combination of colours in yet another light. The man I used to see in all the rooms of this house, in the light of windows looking towards all the places where the sky or the soil or the flowers or leaves of plants have mattered to me—that man is (I write *is* rather than *was*, because he is present to my eyes again) about to choose after fifty or sixty years of study the pattern of colours that has always been his own, although he has taken a lifetime to recognise it.

This is the man I used to see, especially in the room facing north, where masking-tape holds the edges of the blind against the window frame, and the light through the blind is the same light which is all that Doctor Backhaus sees now of the place he wants to go back to before he dies, because his housekeeper has drawn the blind against the sun and closed the window against the wind from the other side of the Great Divide.

This is the man I used to see. But now, at this moment against a backdrop of 1-9-8-2, with a tiny patch of sky-blue silk between my tweezers, I wonder why I have to put this sky-blue in the place reserved for it high up on the sleeve, so that the brown sleeve will have a sky-blue armband.

Clarrie Long leans comfortably back in the seat of the sulky behind the horse Great Dalla near the fence around the outside of the gravel track for bike races or trotting races at the Bendigo Show-grounds. Clarrie Long is talking to my father, who is a spectator on the other side of the fence from Clarrie. No calendar is conveniently near, but my father probably has in his hand a program for the Easter sports meeting. Or someone seeing all this as a scene in a foreign country might notice a scrap of the *Advertiser* blown along the gravelly ground with the numerals 1-9-4-6 on a corner.

Clarrie Long and my father are talking, but I am not listening. I am beginning to feel a grave lack of something.

In many other places with many other calendars on view, I will feel this same lack. I will then believe I have to look into the face of woman after woman (preferably when her eyes are not on me), as though I might see there what I lack. Here, however, under the lights around the Bendigo Showgrounds, I believe I lack a silk jacket and cap of my own colours.

Clarrie Long's jacket is brown with pale-blue stars. Under the lights of the Showgrounds, the pale blue is unevenly silvered like many a sky in all the years I am going to spend away from Bendigo.

I am aware of more than colours. A row of buttons runs down the front of Clarrie Long's jacket, with each button wholly wrapped in silk and most buttons brown but some, because the stars of the pattern are scattered at odd intervals, silver-blue, and one unforgettable button parti-coloured: a border town with differing flags on either side of the main street; or a poor mulatto brindled and haunted by his separate links with earth and sky.

The spread of the pattern over buttons and seams tells me that devisers of racing silks take no account of garments—or even, perhaps, of the men who fasten the colours onto themselves. The man and the garment are meant to be hidden behind the colours and the pattern. And the man and the garment I may never see again, but the pattern I will go on seeing.

In all the places where I feel my lack, with calendar after calendar by window and sky, I try to see my own pattern. Mostly I see Clarrie Long, with faintly Chinese features, and the wife of

Clarrie Long, the first woman I have seen who looks like a film star and the woman who appears as Mrs Harold Moy in the book in which Bendigo is called Bassett. I see the pattern of colours of the man whose wife is the first woman I have seen wearing sun-glasses. I see the wife watching a trotting race by daylight at another Bendigo Easter Fair, with images in her dark glasses of the man in the brown with pale-blue stars: the man who has fitted the colour of sky into the colour of soil.

I ask my father what he sees in the sky, and he turns to the small symmetrical shapes of the cornflowers.

In place after place, in front of every sort of calendar throughout my life, I scrape coloured pencils against white paper. I make one or another of nearly a thousand small sketches of a pattern suitable for my racing colours, and then I take each sketch to the open window, or I draw the blind, or I stare with my eyes wide open, or I cock my head and squint at the colours and the pattern.

Now, at last, I am here in this room with a window looking towards the sky over Tasmania, and the sky itself being continually renewed from the direction of Warrnambool. I have a scrap of blue ready to insert into the last of the thousand patterns I have made in place after place. I have decided on my colours at last. I am no longer sketching with pencils. I am about to make a pattern of silk pieces under clear plastic and to keep my colours where I can see them every day.

My colours are lilac and brown with two small patches of what I call sky-blue.

But before I insert the sky-blue to complete the pattern, I stop to wonder why my father looked down at the cornflowers instead of looking more deeply into the sky.

I am standing, or I am lying on my back, or I am sitting in a railway compartment. Wherever I am, I am staring into the sky and waiting for the blue to turn into some other colour. And now I hear the voice of a woman.

A scream, the echo of a scream, hangs over that Nova Scotian village. No one hears it; it hangs there forever, a slight stain in those pure blue skies . . . too dark, too blue, so that they seem to keep on darkening a little more around the horizon—or is it around the rims of the eyes?

I hear these words in many places, wherever I stop to look at the sky and to wonder what I can learn from blue. The words were written by Elizabeth Bishop, but I have lost the piece of paper telling me where she first wrote them. I found the words in the book pages of the *New York Times*, which are sent to me by ship across the blue half of the world.

No matter what colour the sky, I can nearly always hear the scream behind it. I hear the scream, and I think how easy it would have been for my father to tell me the sky is the colour of the mantle of Our Lady.

I see myself looking high above me in Saint Kilian's Church, Bendigo, or in the Sacred Heart Cathedral, Bendigo. I am looking among the colours of windows for the blue which is Our Lady's colour. I am whispering to Our Lady that she is my mother and that I love her, but secretly I am looking in the glass around me for colours other than the mournful blue of Our Blessed Mother. At heart I dislike the hunched woman, and I dread to hear her sniffling and moaning, and to see her white tunic or shift, or whatever she calls the thing under her blue mantle, all stained and damp from her sorrowing.

But my father does not name Our Lady. And just now I notice for the first time in my life that my father in all his life never mentions Our Lady or any such woman.

I hear the scream where I lie on the utterly reliable soil. I hear the scream, but I have to see many more places beneath many more calendars before I understand that what I hear is the scream.

I get up from the grass, and I climb the fence from the yard behind the hall into my own backyard. I kneel down on the bare soil under the lilac bush and I go on with my task of building a dream-racecourse and naming dream-horses to race on it and devising for the owners of dream-horses jackets and sleeves and caps of dream-silk patterned with dream-colours.

I go on with the task that occupies me for the rest of my life.

The patch of sky-blue drifts down from my hand, down past the page of a calendar showing a month in 1982, and down to the carpet, which happens to be an earth-brown colour. I leave the patch of sky-blue lying on the brown where it fell, and I pick up the other patch that was going to be the other sky-blue armband. I drop this patch too from the height of my upraised hand, and this sky-blue, like the other, drifts down past a month of 1982 and settles on the earth-brown.

The patches of blue are far apart on the brown carpet, and each patch is a rhombus, which is not a conventional star-shape. But I leave the patches where they have fallen, and I even press them—firmly, but not fiercely—with my shoe deep into the earth-brown.

I stand at the table with swatches of silk and a razor blade, and I cut out and fit together and seal under the transparent plastic the lilac and brown colours that have satisfied me since. I have no more to do with the colour of screams or of sorrowing women. All that matters of sky has drifted down and has settled on the brown of Clarrie Long's jacket. I no longer feel my old lack. Now I can stand in my dream-colours beside Clarrie Long. And if the wife of Clarrie Long should happen to look at me once again from behind her dark glasses after all these years, she would see the two men as equals—he in his soil-and-sky, and I in my soil-and-lilac.

In the railway compartment the lights have come on—yellow-white and dull. We are in the tunnel under Big Hill, which my father assures me is the last outcrop of the Great Divide. In the windows is an image of our compartment with darkness around.

First Love

In the story "First Love," which I still read every year or so for its railway journeys, the narrator is travelling towards Biarritz. From my reading I understand Biarritz to be such a place that if brown-white photographs were fitted to the walls of compartments of the Nord Express, more than one of those scenes would show the *plage*, the straw-hatted children, the ladies with parasols (all these are in Nabokov's story), and a grey-white mist or sea-spray or cloud drifting over the land like a curtain blown inwards by a warm wind (this is not mentioned by Nabokov).

I am sitting in semi-darkness in an inner suburb of Melbourne, watching one of the last motion pictures I will see. A man has persuaded me to watch this motion picture because one of its scenes is of cliffs and valleys richly coloured and said to be unlike any landscape on earth.

I watch the oily colours being continually replenished, and I remember the glass marbles I used to hold up against the sunlight in Bendigo. But the colours in front of my eyes are daubed on some kind of pane, while the colours in Bendigo were in the deepest part of the glass.

When the artist wanted a glass marble to photograph for the jacket of my first book of fiction, I allowed him to handle a few of the marbles that I first collected in Bendigo beneath a calendar showing the ordinal number preceding by two the number on the calendar described in the first sentence of the book of fiction with the glass marble (and the shadow of a second glass marble) on its jacket. I have kept my collection of marbles with me since I was taken away from Bendigo in the fourth year after I arrived there.

The artist chose for the photograph for the jacket of my book a marble of the sort called rainbow.

Much more than the coloured oils and dyes on glass, a scene near the end of the motion picture stays in my mind: a scene in which a very old man sits alone in a room coloured white and pale shades of brown.

I am sitting on a wooden seat on a patch of lawn outside Bendigo railway station. My father and I have reached the end of our journey. Nobody has come to the station to meet us, but my father was expecting nobody, and now he has left me here on this patch of dead grass while he goes to look for a telephone.

I look at the strange blue of the sky and I feel the hotness of the wind. I am only a small child, but I understand what it is to have arrived in a foreign country.

And the heat was a medium which made this change of outlook possible. As a liberating power with its own laws it was outside my experience. In the heat, the commonest objects changed their nature.

I tell myself I am living from now on in Bendigo. I will never again live in Melbourne, where I was born. I tell myself this while I wait for my father to come back to this patch of dead grass and dry soil and then to take me into the heart of the city which some sign or some printed caption has already told me is known as the Golden.

My hair is thin and my skin is wrinkled; I have come to the end of my travels. I am sitting on a wooden seat on a patch of dead grass and dry soil outside Bendigo railway station. I have just arrived by train. No page of any calendar is conveniently nearby. It would be unthinkable for any such page to be in sight.

Alfred Jarry once wrote that in order to dwell in eternity, one has only to experience two separate moments at the same moment. I believe this is true whether a moment is a unit of something called time or a unit of place.

I am among the very last, gentle hills to the north of the Great

Divide. The place where I am I have called for most of my life the other side of the Divide, but it is here.

Before I opened the book at random, I remembered only one detail from my reading in 1977 of *The Go-Between*. A boy on holidays from school is attending a gathering, where songs are being sung. One of the leading men at the gathering, trying to encourage people to sing, calls on the boy to sing the latest from school.

I remember no details of the love affair and not even the names of the lovers. But I have not forgotten the oddity of a grown man, with a full and busy life spread out around him, asking a schoolboy what can be seen from the edge of the world.

Long after I had finished, so I thought, the writing of this piece of fiction, "First Love," and only one week before I saw the final proofs of "First Love," a man who has lived for much of his life at Kangaroo Flat, as one of the characters in "First Love" is said to have lived, gave me a copy of a booklet, "Goldfields Shepherd: The Story of Dr Backhaus" by Frank Cusack, published by the Diocese of Sandhurst. (Sandhurst was once the official title of the place that has always been called by its inhabitants Bendigo.) I found in the booklet four sentences that clearly belong in "First Love." Those sentences now form the following paragraph. When I had first read about Doctor Backhaus's wanting in Melbourne to feel the north wind from Bendigo, I had supposed that he died in Melbourne.

". . . already Dr Backhaus was very weak. However, weak as he was, he insisted on returning to Sandhurst. It was there he wished to die and be buried. He rallied; somehow the long, slow trip by train was accomplished, and he was taken to the house of his old friend John Crowley in Wattle Street. There he lingered a day or two . . ."

The title of the story by Vladimir Nabokov refers to a small girl the narrator meets on the beach at Biarritz. I first thought of mentioning Nabokov's story in this story when I remembered the blue, bivalved night light, which is the sort of thing I myself can never remember. I thought that was the only connection between the two stories, and I was bothered by a certain untidiness.

As I explained much earlier in this story, I used to read only the early part of "First Love"; the railway journeys interested me much more than the coastal city. All the while I was writing my own story, I thought of Nabokov's story as leading only towards a small girl under the white sky overhanging Biarritz in the years on the other side of the First World War.

Today I read carefully to the end of "First Love." I read, in the second-last sentence, of the narrator's remembering something about the clothing of the girl that reminded him of the rainbow spiral in a glass marble. I read, in the last sentence, of the narrator's holding the wisp of iridescence, as he calls it, and not knowing where to fit it into his story. And I read, in the space beneath the last words of the story, the word *Boston* and the inscription from a calendar *1948* which tells me the author was wondering where that rainbow belonged in the same year in which I packed my glass marbles in a cloth bag in a tea-chest to be loaded onto a furniture van, because my father was taking me back towards Warrnambool and taking me, as he told me then and as I believed for long afterwards, away from Bendigo forever.

Velvet Waters

During the last two hours of the last Saturday before Christmas Day in 1959 and then during the first four hours of the Sunday following that Saturday, a man aged twenty-one years and seven months walked up and down the footpath of the Lower Esplanade in St Kilda, opposite St Moritz ice-skating rink.

During the last two hours of the Saturday and the first two hours of the Sunday other persons walked on the footpath of the Lower Esplanade, but the other persons walked away and out of sight while the man who was walking up and down went on walking up and down until he was the only person walking on the footpath of the Lower Esplanade.

The Saturday had been a hot day and the Saturday night was a warm night. During the last two hours of the Saturday and the first two hours of the Sunday the man walking up and down heard voices of male persons and female persons from the beach below the wall at the edge of the Lower Esplanade, but after the second hour of the Sunday the man no longer heard voices. During the third hour and the fourth hour of the Sunday the man heard only slapping sounds made by small waves on the beach.

The man was walking up and down the footpath because he was waiting for his best friend, who was a man five months younger than himself. His best friend had promised to meet the man opposite St Moritz at midnight on the Saturday.

Once every minute during the first four hours of the Sunday the man looked north along the Lower Esplanade, hoping to see his friend driving south in his brown Volkswagen sedan. On the Saturday evening the man and his friend had each put a suitcase of clothes on the back seat of the Volkswagen sedan. The friend had then driven the man to St Moritz and had promised to meet him again at midnight. The two men had agreed that they would set out in the Volkswagen sedan from the Lower Esplanade at midnight and would arrive before first light on the Sunday at the holiday flat that they had rented at Lorne on the Southern Ocean. The man walking up and down had hoped to sit on the balcony of the flat and to watch the sun rising out of the ocean on the first morning of his holidays, but the sky was already growing pale on the Sunday morning while he was walking on the footpath and waiting for his friend.

The man was almost sure that his friend was at a party that his friend had told him about. His friend had promised to leave the party before midnight but the man on the Lower Esplanade was almost sure that his friend was still at the party.

The man on the Lower Esplanade knew where the party was taking place. It was taking place at the corner of St Kilda Road and Albert Road, in a two-storey house in a terrace of houses. The house where the party was taking place and all the other houses of the terrace were knocked down three years later, in 1962, and a building known as the BP Building was built where the houses had stood.

The man walking up and down could have walked from the Lower Esplanade to the house where the party was taking place. He could have walked there in about forty-five minutes and with no risk that he would reach the house and would be told that his friend had set out no more than forty-five minutes ago for the Lower Esplanade. The man knew the exact route that his friend would follow from the corner of Albert Road and St Kilda Road to the Lower Esplanade. On every Saturday night during the previous six weeks, the man had sat beside his friend in the front seat of the Volkswagen sedan while his friend had driven by the same route from St Moritz to the house where the party would later take place. On those nights the man beside the driver had stared at the streets that he was passing through and had kept silent while the driver had talked to the two female passengers in the rear seat.

The two passengers were a woman aged about forty and her daughter, who was a girl aged either six weeks or five weeks or four weeks or three weeks or two weeks or one week less than sixteen years. The man beside the driver always knew how many weeks less than sixteen years the girl was aged. After the girl and her mother had left the car and had gone into their house on every Saturday night, the driver had told the man beside him the number of weeks remaining before the girl would become sixteen years of age. Every week the driver had said that the girl was his girl-friend but that the mother of the girl would not allow him to take the girl out until after her sixteenth birthday, which would be celebrated at a party on the last Saturday night before Christmas Day in 1959 at the house that was knocked down twenty-five years ago.

The man walking up and down did not walk towards the house where the party was taking place because he had been told that he would not have been welcome at the party. His best friend had told him that the party was only for close friends of the girl and her mother. Four weeks before the party the man's best friend had warned him not to mention the party in the hearing of the girl or her mother, in case they should think that he was hoping to be invited.

The owner of the Volkswagen sedan had first seen the girl on a Saturday evening in March 1959, when he had been aged twenty years and five months and she had been aged fifteen years and three months, although he had not known her age at that time. The owner of the Volkswagen sedan and his friend had been skating on the ice at St Moritz and looking at young women in the crowd of skaters around them. The owner of the Volkswagen sedan had pointed to a person that neither of the young men had seen before. The friend considered the person a girl rather than a young woman and guessed that she was not even fifteen years of age. She had clear, pale skin and blonde hair that looked almost white. Her arms and legs were thin and her thick woollen sweater seemed flat at the front. Her face had an expression of aloofness. When she saw the two young men looking at her she looked at them for a few moments but her expression did not change. The friend of the young man who had first noticed the girl thought that her face looked interesting but he did not go on looking at her after she had looked at him. The young man who had first noticed the girl went on looking at her after she had looked away from him.

During the last hour of daylight on the last Saturday before the winter solstice in 1987, the man who had walked up and down at St Kilda in December 1959 walked along a concrete path beside Spring Creek at Hepburn Springs in the Central Highlands of Victoria.

The man was not walking alone. He was walking beside the man who had been his best friend from 1951 until 1965. The men were still good friends but the first man no longer thought of anyone as being his best friend. The two men had been friends since they had first met in a junior form of a Catholic secondary school in East St Kilda thirty-six years and five months before the day when they walked beside Spring Creek at Hepburn Springs.

Five paces behind the two men on the concrete path the wives of the two men were walking together. Behind the two wives two other wives were walking together, and behind the two other wives the husbands of those wives were walking together. The four husbands and the four wives had arrived at Hepburn Springs on the previous day in order to celebrate the twenty-fifth anniversary of the wedding of the man who had been the owner of a brown Volkswagen sedan in 1959 and the woman who had been the girl that he had noticed among a crowd of skaters on the ice at St Moritz in St Kilda in March 1959.

The husband and the wife who had first seen one another twenty-eight years and three months before had been married for twenty-five years and five months, but the other three married couples had not been able to celebrate the anniversary until the husband and the wife had returned to Melbourne on a visit from Vancouver, where they had lived for fifteen years in the suburb of Kitsilano on a hill overlooking part of English Bay, and where they intended to live for at least eleven more years until the man had retired from his position as lecturer in the history of the Pacific Basin at a university. The other three married couples all lived in suburbs of Melbourne but they had travelled to Hepburn Springs in order to celebrate the wedding anniversary on the Friday evening and the Saturday evening.

The four married couples had chosen Hepburn Springs because they believed it to be a restful place among trees and near water at a distance from Melbourne such that any of the couples could have driven back to their houses within two or three hours if their children or a neighbour or the police had telephoned them and asked them to return home at once. The couples had chosen Hepburn Springs also because the wife who lived in Vancouver had told one of the other wives three months before in a letter from Vancouver that her husband had spent part of his summer holidays at Hepburn Springs in every year until the year when he was aged seventeen years but had not been to Hepburn Springs since that year.

Of the eight persons walking beside Spring Creek, only two persons had not previously been to Hepburn Springs. These two were the man who is the chief character of this story and his wife, who had first seen one another twenty-four years and four months before and who had been married for twenty-two years and five months.

During the last four hours of the Friday and the first two hours of the Saturday, the four men and the four women had sat in the bed-sitting room of the cabin allotted to the couple from Vancouver in the grounds of the hotel where all four couples had been allotted adjoining cabins. The men had drunk beer or whisky and the women had drunk wine or soft drinks. The four men had sat on chairs on one side of the double bed and the four women had sat on chairs on the opposite side. Sometimes one of the men or the women had talked to all seven other persons but for most of the time the men had talked to one another on their side of the bed and the women had talked to one another on the opposite side.

The man who had once walked up and down for six hours beside the sea at St Kilda believed while he walked beside Spring Creek that he had talked more than any other of the seven persons who had sat around the bed of the couple who had been married for more than twenty-five years. For twenty-seven years and six months the man had not been able to stop himself from drinking beer continually or from talking continually whenever he had been in a place where beer was being drunk. For twenty-seven years and six months, whenever the man had wakened after a night when he had drunk beer and had talked continually he had not been able to remember what he or any other person had said or had done after the third hour of his drinking. On many mornings when the man had tried to remember, the latest thing that he had remembered was his having decided during the third hour of his drinking and talking that he would later take aside a particular person from among the persons around him and would confide to that person something that he had not previously confided to any other person.

While the man walked beside Spring Creek during the last hour of daylight on the Saturday, he remembered his having decided during the second-last hour of the Friday that he would later take aside the wife of his oldest friend and would confide to her something that he had not previously confided to any other person. The man remembered on the Saturday that he had understood on the Friday that he would not take the woman aside in the bed-sitting room where the eight persons sat around the double bed but would take her aside on the Saturday afternoon beside Spring Creek. The man remembered on the Saturday that he had understood on the Friday evening that the eight persons were going to spend the Saturday afternoon beside Spring Creek and that he had believed on the Friday evening that he and any other man who wanted to drink beer on the Saturday afternoon would take a parcel of cans or stubbies of beer to a grassy place beside Spring Creek and would sit there and drink beer. The man remembered on the Saturday that he had decided on the Friday evening that he would get up from his grassy place at some time late on the Saturday afternoon and would stroll with the wife of his oldest friend among the trees beside the creek and would confide in her there.

The man was not able to remember on the Saturday evening any further things that he had understood or had believed or had said or had done during the last hour of the Friday or the first two hours of the Saturday, but he was able to remember everything that he had said and had done on the Saturday afternoon because his oldest friend had asked the seven other persons at noon on the Saturday not to take beer or wine or whisky with them to Spring Creek. The man who had spent his holidays at Hepburn Springs in the summer of every year for seventeen years until 1955 told the other persons that he was taking them to Spring Creek so that they could drink the water from the mineral springs, which would be far better for them than any alcoholic drink.

The man who had hoped to drink beer beside Spring Creek in the afternoon of the last Saturday before the winter solstice in 1987, when he was aged forty-nine years and one month, had first drunk beer in the afternoon of the last Sunday before Christmas Day in 1959, when he had been aged twenty-one years and seven months. He had not drunk beer before then because he had been afraid of what his mother might have said if she had learned that he had begun to drink beer even though his father, who had died in 1949, had never drunk any alcoholic drink. The man had first drunk beer on the balcony of a holiday flat at Lorne while he sat alone and stared between the tops of trees towards a patch of dark-blue ocean. The man had never previously been to Lorne and had never previously spent his summer holidays anywhere but in the district of Allansford, where the Hopkins River flows between grassy paddocks in the south-west of Victoria.

The man and his best friend had arrived outside the holiday flat at eight o'clock on the Sunday morning and had carried their suitcases from the Volkswagen sedan up a steep driveway between tall gum trees and into the holiday flat. The owner of the Volkswagen sedan had brought into the flat not only his suitcase but six bottles of beer. The other man had wondered why his friend had brought the beer. So far as the other man knew, his friend had never drunk any alcoholic drink because he was afraid of what his parents might have said if they had learned that he had begun to drink such drinks even though his parents had never drunk them.

The man who had brought the beer explained that the beer was a present from the mother of his girlfriend. When he had been about to leave his girlfriend's birthday party at ten minutes to four on that morning, the mother of his girlfriend had given him the six bottles from the supply that she had bought for the party. The man who was leaving the party had reminded the woman that he did not drink beer. The woman had then told the man to give the beer to his best friend for drinking at the first of the parties that the two men would surely arrange in their holiday flat at Lorne.

The friend of the man who had brought the beer had felt reckless when he had learned that the beer was a present from the woman aged about forty. The man who had been presented with the beer had learned from his friend, three hours before, that the woman had been, fourteen years before, one of the women known as American war brides. Fourteen years before, the woman and her infant daughter had left Melbourne and had travelled in the first ship that had carried passengers from Australia to the United States of America after the end of the Second World War in order to rejoin the American man that the woman had married when he had been a soldier stationed in Melbourne during the Second World War.

The man who had been presented with the beer had seen his mother staring at a picture in the Melbourne *Argus* on a morning when he had been a boy aged seven years. The picture was a reproduction of a photograph of a ship moving away from Station Pier and out into Port Phillip Bay. A crowd of young women leaned over the rails of the ship, holding streamers or waving their arms. The mother of the boy had said that the young women were the first shipload of war brides leaving for America. She had then said that the young women would be smiling on the other sides of their faces after they had arrived in America and had found that their Yank husbands and boyfriends were no longer interested in them.

On the morning when he had seen the picture of the war brides, the boy who was going to receive a present of six bottles of beer fourteen years later from a woman who had been one of the women in the photograph reproduced in the *Argus* hoped that his mother was wrong.

In 1945, when he was a boy aged seven years, the chief character of this story had believed that most young men fell in love continually with young women but that most young women consented to be loved by men rather than fell in love with them. When a young man had fallen in love with a young woman, so the boy had believed, the young man tried to persuade the young woman to become his girlfriend or his wife by dressing in a suit and offering her a bouquet of flowers or a box of chocolates or even by kneeling in front of her and pleading while she sat with her face turned aside. Sometimes the young woman would consent to

173

become the girlfriend or the wife of the young man; sometimes she would go on sitting with her face turned aside; sometimes she would slap the face of the young man. The boy himself fell in love continually with girls of his own age and foresaw himself falling in love continually with young women when he had become a young man.

When the boy aged seven had seen the picture of the war brides, he had believed that he was looking for the first time at young women who had fallen in love in the same way that he fell in love continually. While he had looked at the picture he had seen in his mind a group of the war brides stepping ashore in one after another of the seaports of America and he had hoped that each of the young women would step into the arms of an American man who loved her. He had then seen in his mind further groups of war brides travelling by steamboat along the river systems of America or by railway train through the mountains or across the plains of America. The steamboats had stopped at jetties far upstream and the trains had pulled into depots far inland, and one after another of the war brides had stepped out into the sunlight and had looked around for her boyfriend or her husband. The young woman who had travelled further from her home than any other war bride had stepped down from the railway carriage at a place where plains of grass reached in every direction from the railway tracks to the horizon. The young woman had looked around her in every direction, hoping to see her boyfriend or her husband.

The boy in Melbourne, Australia, had turned away from the picture in the *Argus* because he had not wanted his mother to guess what was in his mind. Then the boy had knelt on the grass in his mind in front of the young woman in his mind.

The chief character of this story and his best friend had sat together on the grass beside the lake at Caulfield Racecourse on many fine Sunday afternoons during the years from 1951 to 1955, when they had been students at secondary school. The boy who became later the young man who noticed the girl on the ice at St Moritz and later still the man who had been married for more than twenty-five years to the woman who had been that girl had ridden on his bicycle to the racecourse from the suburb adjoining the southern boundary of the racecourse. The boy who considered the other boy his best friend had ridden on his bicycle to the racecourse from the suburb adjoining the southern boundary of the other boy's suburb.

At the racecourse, which was always deserted on Sundays, the two boys had at first talked and smoked cigarettes with other boys from their school. On some Sundays one of the other boys had shown to the group of boys a few pages torn from a magazine. The boys had seen on each page a reproduction of a black and white photograph of a naked young woman sitting or standing or lying in such a way that her face and breasts were visible while her groin was hidden from their view. After the group of boys had separated on those Sundays the chief character of this story and his best friend had sat on the grass and had stared at the water of the lake.

On most of the Sunday afternoons when the two boys had stared at the lake a breeze or a wind had blown from the south-west, which was the direction of Port Phillip Bay, and had made small waves in the water of the lake. While the two boys had sat on the grass above the shore of the lake the boy from the further suburb had sometimes heard the faint slapping sound of a wave as it broke.

Whether or not the two boys had looked earlier in the afternoon at reproductions of photographs of naked young women, the two boys had always talked about naked young women while they had sat beside the lake. While the two boys had stared at the water each boy had told the other what he would do in the future with one after another naked young woman beside a lake or a stream or a bay or the ocean. Each boy had then promised that he would confide to the other in the future whatever he had done with each naked young woman.

While the boy from the further suburb had ridden on his bicycle away from Caulfield Racecourse on each fine Sunday afternoon he had not been able to foresee himself doing in the future the things that he had talked about beside the lake. The boy from the further suburb had foreseen himself in the future falling in love with one after another young woman and foreseeing himself in the further future confiding to the young woman something that he had not previously confided to any other person.

After the four husbands and the four wives had put their bags and their suitcases in their cabins behind the hotel at Hepburn Springs on the Friday evening, they had gathered around the fire in the lounge of the hotel. While the husbands and the wives were seating themselves the man who is the chief character in this story had asked each of the other seven persons what he or she would like to drink. The man had then gone to the bar of the hotel and had bought two pots of beer, two glasses of beer, a shandy, a glass of white wine, a Coke, and a glass of Hepburn Springs mineral water. The man had then carried the eight drinks on a tray back to the lounge.

While the man who had bought the drinks was handing them around to the seven other persons, the man who had been married for twenty-five years and five months had said that the last of the guests had now arrived at the fashionable winter resort somewhere in the Rocky Mountains. The man had said that the four chief couples would now go on drinking and talking continually until after midnight and that the scene in the early hours of the Saturday morning would be of men grabbing the fronts of one another's shirts or shouting at their wives or whispering into the ears of other men's wives or putting their hands on the knees of those wives or sitting alone and mumbling that they had been unhappy as children, and of women shrieking at one another or slapping the faces of their husbands or of other women's husbands.

The seven other persons had laughed at this, but the chief character of this story had only smiled. The chief character of this story had supposed that the seven other persons were thinking of themselves as characters in an American film. He had supposed that six of the seven persons watched American films often and that his wife, who had watched hardly any films since she had married him, still remembered the American films that she had watched more than twenty-two years before.

The chief character of this story had watched hardly any films during the twenty-two years since he had been married, but he remembered some of the films that he had watched more than twenty-two years before. When the seven other persons in the lounge of the hotel had laughed and had seemed to think of themselves as characters in an American film, the chief character in this story had smiled and had thought of himself as a character in a Swedish film.

During 1945 and 1946, when the chief character of this story had been aged seven and eight years, he had been taken by his mother to a picture theatre once in every two or three weeks and had watched American films; during the years from 1947 to 1958, when he had been aged from nine to twenty years, he had been taken by his mother or had gone alone to a picture theatre only two or three times in every year and had watched mostly American films and occasionally an English film; during the years from 1959 to 1962, when he had been aged from twenty-one to twenty-four years, he had gone alone to a picture theatre once in every two or three weeks and had watched films from European countries; during the years 1963 and 1964, when he had been aged twenty-five and twenty-six years, he had gone to a picture theatre once in every two or three weeks with the young woman who later became his wife and had watched American and English films; during the years from 1965, when he had become a married man, to 1987, when he had visited Hepburn Springs for the first time, he had gone to a picture theatre with his wife and his children once in every two or three years and had watched films but had not cared to learn which country the films had come from.

During the years from 1965 to 1987 the man who went to picture theatres only once in every two or three years had sometimes noticed in his mind an image from one or another film that he had watched many years earlier. If the image had been from an American film, the man had not looked at the image. The man had wanted only images from Swedish films to appear in his mind. The man had believed that images from American films would cause him to try to behave as though he had been alone with many girls and young women and women during his lifetime. The man wanted to behave as though he had sometimes walked between trees and had sometimes sat beside a stream or a lake with the young woman that he had fallen in love with.

The man who had begun to drink beer for the first time on a Sunday afternoon when he was aged twenty-one years and seven months had learned that the previous owner of the beer had previously been an American war bride during the second hour of daylight on that same Sunday, while he had been travelling in the brown Volkswagen sedan owned by his best friend across the plains south-west of Melbourne and while he had been playing in his mind a game that he had first devised as a child.

Since 1945, when he had been aged seven years, the chief character in this story had played a game that he called as a child Water of the Plains whenever he had travelled south-west of Melbourne. On the last Sunday before Christmas Day in 1959, when the chief character in this story had travelled south-west from Melbourne about fifty miles to the city of Geelong on Corio Bay and then about fifty miles further south-west to the small town of Lorne on the Southern Ocean, he had previously travelled south-west from Melbourne on about thirty occasions. On all of those occasions he had travelled south-west from Melbourne to Geelong and then about a hundred miles west-south-west to the district of Allansford, where the brother and sisters of his father lived.

During all the years when the chief character in this story had travelled south-west from Melbourne he had played the game Water of the Plains at different places between Melbourne and Allansford. The first of these places was a place about five miles past the town of Werribee and about twenty miles short of the city of Geelong. Whenever he had passed the town of Werribee on his journeys south-west from Melbourne, the chief character in this story had looked ahead as though he was seeing the landscape for the first time and as though he expected to see nothing but plains of grass until he first saw Corio Bay. About five miles past Werribee he would go on looking ahead as though he still believed he was surrounded only by plains of grass, but he would watch from the sides of his eyes for the few trees on the banks of Little River.

During the years from 1945 to 1958, whenever the chief character in this story had played the game Water of the Plains about five miles past Werribee he had known he would be able to play the game at three or four further places before he arrived at the district of Allansford. When he had played the game about five miles past Werribee on the morning of the last Sunday before Christmas Day in 1959, the chief character in this story had known that he would not be able to play the game later during that day because he was going to travel from Geelong not across the plains and the low hills towards the district of Allansford but through coastal scrub and the edges of rain forest towards Lorne. The chief character in this story had also believed that he would never again play the game on the plains or among the low hills between the city of Geelong and the district of Allansford because he would never again visit the brothers and sisters of his father in the district of Allansford.

While the Volkswagen sedan had travelled through the suburbs south-west of Melbourne the driver and the passenger had been silent. After they had passed through the last of the suburbs and had begun to cross the plains towards Werribee, the passenger had asked the driver what he had done with his girlfriend when they had been alone together on the Saturday evening and early on the Sunday morning. The driver had answered that he and his girl-friend had talked together.

After the two men had travelled through Werribee the passenger had asked the driver what he and his girlfriend had talked about when they had been alone together. The driver had then told the passenger what has already been mentioned about the mother of the girlfriend of the driver in the third section of this story.

The passenger had then asked the driver where the mother of his girlfriend had rejoined her husband when she had travelled to America as a war bride and where she had lived with him in America. The passenger had hoped to hear that the woman had travelled far inland after she had reached America by ship and that she had rejoined her husband and had lived with him in one of the Great Plains states. At the same time, the passenger had begun to play in his mind the game that he had always begun to play in his mind whenever he had travelled past Werribee.

When the driver had said that the war bride had left Australia by ship, the passenger had begun to pretend that he was surrounded only by plains of grass and yet to watch from the sides of his eyes for the few trees beside Little River. While the passenger had gone on pretending and watching from the sides of his eyes, he had heard the driver say that the mother of his girl-friend had left her ship at a seaport on the west coast of America and had travelled with her infant daughter by railway train to Chicago.

Whenever the chief character of this story had played the game Water of the Plains in his mind in previous years he had been travelling in either a motor car driven by the youngest brother of his father or a carriage of a railway train. Whenever the man had seen Little River in previous years he had seen it for a few moments from either a road bridge or a railway bridge before he had seemed again to be surrounded only by plains of grass. Then he had played the last part of the game, which had been to try to see the image of a clump of rushes or of a pool of water overhung by leaves or of a bed of stones with shallow water trickling between them in his mind as though the thing that he saw had been not an image in his mind but a detail that he saw on the plains of grass surrounding him.

While the chief character of this story had played the first part of his game in the Volkswagen sedan in December 1959 he had wished that he and his best friend had not been travelling towards Lorne and the Southern Ocean. The two men had agreed eleven months before that they would spend the last two weeks of 1959 and the first week of 1960 at Lorne. The two men had agreed that they would look at young women on the beach and on the streets of Lorne and would approach some of the young women and would invite them to drink coffee in a coffee lounge in the main street of Lorne or on the balcony of the holiday flat. But while the two men had been travelling between Werribee and Little River, the passenger had wished that someone had built a few years previously a caravan park on the level land near the west bank of Little River. If someone had previously built such a park, so the passenger had supposed, then the passenger could have persuaded the driver to turn aside from the road at Little River and the two men could have spent their holidays in a caravan among trees near the west bank of Little River.

On most days of their holidays at Little River the owner of the Volkswagen sedan could have driven his car to Melbourne and could have been alone with his girlfriend in the house at the corner of St Kilda Road and Albert Road while her mother was at work in the city of Melbourne. On some days the man could have driven his Volkswagen sedan to Melbourne and could then have brought his girlfriend back to Little River and could have been alone with her in his caravan in the caravan park.

While the owner of the Volkswagen sedan was travelling to or from Melbourne or was alone with his girlfriend in Melbourne or at Little River, the other man could have walked each day along the west bank of Little River and away from the caravan park. When this man had walked far away from the road and the railway line he could have stepped between a few trees and then down the bank of the river and towards the water. Any person looking out at that moment from a motor car or from a carriage of a railway train and believing that he or she was surrounded only by plains of grass and a few scattered trees might have supposed that the man far out on the plains had knelt or had lain down in the grass between a few trees, but the man would have been approaching a clump of rushes or a pool of water overhung by leaves or a bed of stones with shallow water trickling between them.

The passenger in the Volkswagen sedan had often looked at pages of his atlas of the world showing maps of regions of the United States of America. The page that he had looked at most often was headed *Great Plains*. Whenever he had looked at this page he had seen in his mind plains of grass reaching to the horizons of his mind. When the Volkswagen sedan had been travelling on the plains between Werribee and Little River and when the driver had said that the mother of his girlfriend had travelled with her daughter towards Chicago, the passenger had seen in his mind the war bride and her infant daughter travelling across plains of grass that reached to the horizons of his mind. But when the Volkswagen sedan had almost reached Little River the passenger had heard that the young woman and her daughter had gone on travelling until they had reached the State of Minnesota.

Whenever the passenger in the Volkswagen sedan had looked at the page of his atlas headed *Great Plains* he had seen from the sides of his eyes that the upper right-hand corner of the page was occupied by part of the State of Minnesota. Whenever the passenger had seen this from the sides of his eyes he had seen far out on the plains of grass in his mind a few trees.

While the Volkswagen sedan had been crossing the bridge over Little River, the driver had told the passenger that the war bride and her infant daughter had travelled across the State of Minnesota and had rejoined the American husband of the war bride in the city of Duluth.

Whenever the passenger in the Volkswagen sedan had been looking at the page of his atlas headed *Great Plains* and had seen far out on the plains of grass in his mind a few trees, he had tried not to notice between the trees the pages of his atlas following the page headed *Great Plains*. Whenever he had not been able to avoid noticing in his mind the pages following the page in front of his eyes, he had noticed between the trees in his mind the pale-blue water that he had always seen in his mind whenever he had looked at the page of his atlas headed *Great Lakes*. Whenever he had seen the pale-blue water in his mind he had felt a cold wind blowing from the north-east in his mind and making waves in the pale-blue water and he had heard in his mind the slapping sounds of waves breaking on a shore in his mind.

After the man who is the chief character in this story had travelled over Little River and after he had heard, during the few moments when he had been looking at a clump of rushes or at a pool of water overhung by leaves or at a bed of stones with shallow water trickling between them, that the war bride had rejoined her American husband and had lived with him in the city of Duluth in the state of Minnesota, the man had seen, instead of the image of a clump of rushes or of a pool overhung by leaves or of a bed of stones with shallow water trickling between them that had appeared in his mind whenever he had played in his mind the last part of Water of the Plains, a few trees at the edge of his mind and between the trees the pale-blue water of the Great Lakes in his mind.

The man who was the new owner of six bottles of beer had put his bottles in the refrigerator in the kitchen of the holiday flat. He and his best friend had then lain on their beds and had slept for eight hours. When the two men had wakened, the owner of the beer had taken a bottle of beer and a bottle-opener and two glasses out onto the balcony. The time was about five o'clock and the afternoon was hot and bright. The owner of the beer had invited his best friend to drink beer and to go on talking about his girlfriend and her mother and the United States of America.

The best friend of the owner of the beer had said that he would not drink or talk at that time because he wanted to drive his car into the main street of Lorne and to telephone his girlfriend and to buy some fish and chips.

The owner of the beer had then given his best friend money and had asked him to buy two parcels of fish and chips. The owner of the Volkswagen sedan had then driven his car away from the holiday flats while the owner of the beer had opened the bottle in front of him and had poured some beer into a glass and had tasted the beer.

During the years from 1956 to 1958, when the two men in this story had been young men aged from eighteen to twenty years, they had met beside the lake at Caulfield Racecourse on every fine Sunday morning. In those years the young man who later noticed the girl on the ice at St Moritz was a student for the degree of bachelor of arts with honours in the school of history at the University of Melbourne while the other young man was first a student in the course for the trained primary teacher's certificate at a teachers' college conducted by the Education Department of Victoria in a south-eastern suburb of Melbourne and then a teacher in a primary school in an outer south-eastern suburb of Melbourne.

Each young man had told the other early in 1956 that he no longer believed in the teachings of the Catholic Church, but the young man who was a student at the university still lived with his parents and was afraid to tell them that he no longer wanted to go to mass on Sundays, while the other young man still lived with his mother, who was a widow, and was afraid to tell her that he no longer wanted to go to mass on Sundays. On each Sunday morning from early 1956 until the end of 1958 each young man would ride his bicycle away from his parents' house as though he intended to go to mass. If rain was falling the two young men would meet in a milk bar in a street near the Caulfield Racecourse and would sit on stools and would talk about football or racing while customers came and went. If the weather was fine the two young men would meet beside the lake and would sit on the grass and would talk about young women while they stared at the water.

On every fine Sunday morning the young men had talked about some of the young women that they had seen during the previous week at the university or at the teachers' college or at the primary school. On fine Sunday mornings during the early months of each year each young man would tell the other that they would rent a holiday house at Lorne during the last two weeks of that year and the first week of the following year and would approach young women on the beach and in the streets of Lorne, but during the week before Christmas Day in each year the young man who is the chief character of this story would leave Melbourne and would travel alone by railway train to the district of Allansford in order to spend three weeks with the unmarried brother and the unmarried sisters of his father. During the same week the parents of the other young man would leave Melbourne for Hepburn Springs while their son stayed with his older sister in their parents' house in the suburb adjoining the southern boundary of Caulfield Racecourse.

During the years from 1956 to 1958 neither of the young men in this story had a girlfriend. The young man who was a student at a university had never asked any girl or young woman to go with him to any of the places where young persons went together when they were on the way to becoming girlfriend and boyfriend. The other young man had asked one young woman to go with him to a picture theatre but she had told him that she could not go.

The young man who had once asked a young woman to go with him to a picture theatre had never been alone with a girl or a young woman. The other young man had been alone with a young woman among trees near Spring Creek at Hepburn Springs during the last hour of daylight on an evening during the last week of 1955.

The chief character of this story had asked a young woman to go with him to a picture theatre in May 1957, when he had been aged nineteen years. The young man had first met the young woman in February 1957, when he and she had been in the same class at a teachers' college. The young man had fallen in love with the young woman when he had first met her but he had tried not to appear to have fallen in love.

The chief character of this story had fallen in love continually with girls and with young women since he had first been a schoolboy in the second-last year of the Second World War, but in February 1957 he had no longer believed that most young men fell in love continually with young women and that most young women consented to be loved by young men. By February 1957 he had come to believe that most young men of the south-eastern suburbs of Melbourne took care not to fall in love with young women and that most young women approved of the young men's taking care.

The chief character of this story had decided in February 1957 to ask the young woman that he had fallen in love with to go with him to a picture theatre but he had not wanted to ask her as though he had fallen in love with her and had been preparing for some time to ask her. He had decided to ask the young woman on a Thursday in the future to go with him to a picture theatre on the Friday evening following the Thursday. He wanted the young woman to suppose on the Thursday in the future that he had decided only on that day to go to a picture theatre on the following evening and to take a young woman as a companion.

During the four months while the chief character of this story was preparing to ask the young woman to go with him to a picture theatre in the future, he had decided soon after he had wakened on every Thursday morning that he would ask the young woman on that day. As soon as he had decided this the young man had become afraid that he was about to vomit. Instead of eating breakfast on each of those Thursday mornings, the young man had drunk a few mouthfuls of black tea. Yet even with only a few mouthfuls of black tea in his stomach, the young man had been afraid that he was about to vomit while he travelled in the electric train from the suburb where he lived to the suburb where the teachers' college was.

As soon as the young man had stepped inside the compartment of the train on each Thursday morning, he had become afraid that he would vomit on the clothes of the men and women crowded around him. After one or two minutes the young man had become so afraid that he had decided not to ask the young woman on that Thursday morning to go with him to a picture theatre. After the young man had decided this, he had no longer been afraid that he would vomit in the compartment of the train on that Thursday morning but he had been afraid that he would vomit in the train on the following Thursday morning after he had decided to approach the young woman on that day.

Between Glenhuntly station and Caulfield station the train passed close beside the eastern boundary of Caulfield Racecourse. On each Thursday morning, during the time when the young man was no longer afraid of vomiting on that morning but was afraid of vomiting on the following Thursday morning, he had stared through the window of the compartment at the high dark-green fence along the boundary of the racecourse and had seen in his mind the small lake surrounded by grass near the centre of the racecourse where he would sit with his best friend on the next fine Sunday morning. The young man had then heard in his mind himself confiding to his best friend beside the lake that he, the chief character of this story, no longer intended to ask the young woman at the teachers' college to go with him to a picture theatre in the future. As soon as the young man in the compartment of the train had heard these words in his mind he had no longer been afraid that he would vomit in the train on any Thursday morning in the future but he had been afraid that he would vomit on the beach or in the streets of Lorne during his holidays in the following summer.

While the young man in the train had been afraid that he would vomit at Lorne in the following summer, he had seen in his mind a body of water surrounded by grassy paddocks in the district of Allansford in the south-west of Victoria. The body of water was called Lake Gillear although it had always seemed to the young man a large swamp rather than a lake. The young man and the youngest brother of his father had walked beside the body of water on one afternoon of every January since January 1950, when the young man had been a boy aged eleven years and eight months and when his father had been dead for four months. As soon as the young man in the train had seen Lake Gillear in his mind he had seen in his mind also himself and his unmarried uncle walking beside the water during January of the following year. When the young man had seen this in his mind he had no longer been afraid that he would vomit anywhere in the future.

On a fine Sunday morning in May 1956, beside the lake at Caulfield Racecourse, the chief character of this story had confided to his best friend that he had asked a young woman at the teachers' college on the previous Thursday to go with him to a picture theatre on the Friday following the Thursday but that the young woman had said that she could not go. The chief character of this story had said beside the lake that he had been afraid while he had approached the young woman that he would vomit on the concrete path where he and she were walking. He had then said beside the lake that he had kept himself from vomiting on the path while he had approached the young woman by hearing in his mind the young woman saying that she could not go with him to a picture theatre.

The chief character of this story had said beside the lake that he believed the young woman had not wanted to go with him to a picture theatre because he had seemed to have fallen in love with her. He had then said beside the lake that he believed he had seemed to have fallen in love with the young woman while he had spoken to her because he had seen in his mind while he had spoken to her himself sitting beside the young woman in a picture theatre and vomiting between his knees onto the floor of the picture theatre.

During 1959, when the two men in this story had each become twenty-one years of age, they had no longer met beside the lake at Caulfield Racecourse. During that year the chief character of this story had left his mother's house and had become a boarder in a boarding house in the suburb of Malvern, about one mile north-west of Caulfield Racecourse, and had no longer had to pretend to be going to mass on Sunday mornings. During that year also the other young man had told his parents that he no longer believed in the teachings of the Catholic Church and had no longer had to pretend to be going to mass on Sunday mornings. During that year the two men met each week on Saturday evening at St Moritz ice-skating rink. On each Saturday evening the two men skated on the ice and looked at the girls and the young women around them, or the two men sat beside the ice while the man who still lived with his parents talked with some of the men who played ice hockey with him on Friday evenings.

During 1960, when the two men in this story had each become twenty-two years of age, they had no longer met at weekends or at other times. During that year the man who had noticed the girl with the blonde hair that looked almost white skating on the ice on a Saturday evening in March of the previous year had visited his girlfriend on every Friday and Saturday and Sunday and sometimes on other days as well. Sometimes the man stayed for an afternoon or an evening in the house at the corner of St Kilda Road and Albert Road, watching American films and other programs on a television set or talking to his girlfriend or her mother; sometimes the man took his girlfriend to a picture theatre; sometimes the man and his girlfriend skated together on the ice at St Moritz;

sometimes the man played ice-hockey at St Moritz while his girlfriend sat beside the ice and watched him; sometimes the man took his girlfriend in his Volkswagen sedan to the beach beside the Lower Esplanade at St Kilda or to some other beach beside Port Phillip Bay. During that year also the other man had become a boarder in the house of a widow aged about forty years in the suburb of Elsternwick, about one mile west of Caulfield Racecourse.

The man who is the chief character of this story had thought when he had left his mother's house early in 1959 that he would be free to live as he pleased in the boarding house in Malvern. He had been free in the boarding house not to go to mass on Sunday mornings, but at other times some of the men in the boarding house had knocked on his door and had pressed him to play cards when he had wanted to read and to write in his room.

The man had thought when he had left the boarding house early in 1960 that he would be free to live as he pleased in the widow's house in Elsternwick. He had been free not to go to mass on Sunday morning in the widow's house, but on most evenings when he had gone to his room after the evening meal he had not been free to read and to write as he had wanted to do.

The man's room was next to the lounge room, and during the first two weeks after he had moved into the widow's house the man had heard through the wall while he had been trying to read or to write sounds of music or of men and women shouting at one another or of guns being fired or of cars being driven fast. On every evening during the third and the fourth weeks after he had moved into the widow's house the man had heard, after the sounds from the other side of his wall had been especially loud, the sound of the widow's knocking on the door of his room. After the man had opened his door the widow had told him that something especially interesting was happening on television and that she had thought he might like to watch it.

During the first two weeks after the widow had begun to knock on his door the man had told her whenever she had knocked that he was preparing lessons for his class of primary-school children for the next day and that he would not be able to watch her television set. But during the third week after the widow had begun to knock on his door he had gone into her lounge room for an hour or more during each evening and had watched parts of television programs.

On many evenings when the man had said to the widow that he was preparing lessons for his class, he had been trying to write a script for a film. During 1960 the man had worked each day as a teacher in a primary school but on most evenings he had tried to write a script for a film. The man did not know during that year how scripts for films were written. He wrote with a ball-point pen on lined foolscap pages and he arranged the words on each page in the way that the words had been arranged on the pages of the texts of plays that he had read. The man knew no names or addresses of persons who might have been willing to read his script but he believed that some persons in the future would be willing to read his script and would then be eager to turn his script into a film, and he hoped to earn his living in the future by writing scripts for films. When the man saw in his mind images from the films that might have been made from his scripts in the future, he saw images of plains of grass, or of a few trees beside a shallow stream or a small lake, or of a man and a young woman.

After the man who was writing a script for a film had gone a few times into the lounge room with the widow and had watched her television set he had begun to be absent from her house during many evenings. On some of those evenings the man had left the widow's house soon after the evening meal and had sat alone in a corner of a coffee lounge in Elsternwick and had made notes for his film script until late in the evening. On other days the man had told the widow by telephone from the school where he taught that he would eat his evening meal with friends. At three-thirty, when his classes had ended, the man had gone to a hotel near his school and had drunk beer continually until six o'clock, when the hotel had closed. Just before the hotel had closed the man had bought a flask of vodka and had put it in the inside pocket of his jacket. After the hotel had closed the man had bought a parcel of fish and chips from a fish shop near the hotel. He had then travelled by train to the city of Melbourne and had eaten his fish and chips while he had travelled. In the city of Melbourne he had gone to the Savoy Theatre in Russell Street, where the films shown were always from European countries, or to some other picture theatre where a European film was being shown. Before the program of films had begun and during the interval in the program the man had drunk from his flask of vodka in the toilet of the picture theatre. After the program had ended he had gone by tram back to the widow's house in Elsternwick.

During one evening in the coffee lounge in Elsternwick the man who had not wanted to watch the widow's television set had read part of an issue of *Time* that had on its cover a reproduction of a portrait of a Swedish man who turned scripts into films. After the man in the coffee lounge had read about the Swedish man and about the films that he had made from scripts, the man in the coffee lounge had decided that the Swedish man's films were somewhat like the films that he himself had wanted someone to make in the future from his own scripts. During the days following that evening the man had looked into newspapers for advertisements for the films that he had read about in the issue of *Time*.

During an evening in June 1960 the man who is the chief character of this story had gone to the Camden Theatre in Hawthorn Road, South Caulfield, in order to watch the film *Wild Strawberries*, which was the first Swedish film that he had watched.

When the man had sat down in the Camden Theatre just before the lights had gone out he had looked around and had counted only seven other persons waiting to watch the film. The man had read in newspapers that picture theatres were being closed down or even knocked down in many suburbs of Melbourne because the persons in those suburbs preferred to watch their television sets during the evenings than to go to picture theatres. After the man had counted the seven other persons he had supposed that the Camden Theatre would soon be closed down or even knocked down. In fact, the Camden Theatre was closed down a few weeks after the man had sat in it.

After the man in the Camden Theatre had counted the seven other persons and had thought of the picture theatres being closed down or knocked down in the suburbs of Melbourne, he had thought that his watching *Wild Strawberries* would be his last opportunity for doing in a picture theatre what his best friend had said he had done in the Renown Theatre in Glenhuntly Road, Elsternwick, in 1952. Later, while the man in the Camden Theatre was watching *Wild Strawberries*, he had put his right hand inside his trousers and had tried to do what his best friend had said he had done among the crowd in the Renown Theatre by reaching with his right hand through a hole in the lining of the right-hand pocket of his trousers.

The man walking beside Spring Creek at Hepburn Springs on an evening in the winter of 1987 had never confided to the man walking beside him what he, the chief character of this story, had tried but failed to do in the Camden Theatre in South Caulfield on an evening in the winter of 1960, although the man walking beside him had confided to him on a fine Sunday afternoon in 1952 what he, the boy who became the man who was celebrating his wedding anniversary at Hepburn Springs, had done on the previous Friday evening in the Renown Theatre in Elsternwick.

During the twenty-seven years following the evening when he had sat with seven other persons in the Camden Theatre in South Caulfield, the chief character of this story had sometimes tried to see in his mind an image of the image of the young Swedish female person that he had supposed he must have watched while he had tried but had failed to do what his best friend had done in the Renown Theatre eight years before, but the only images that the chief character of this story had seen in his mind were an image of a man with white hair and a wrinkled face and an image of part of a lake appearing between trees. The man who had seen only these images in his mind had tried to see in his mind the image of the young Swedish female person in order to try to understand why he had failed to do in 1960 what his friend had said he had done in 1952. Whenever he had seen in his mind only the images of the man with white hair and a wrinkled face and of part of a lake appearing between trees, the chief character of this story had supposed that the evening when he had watched *Wild Strawberries* in the Camden Theatre only a few weeks before the theatre had been closed down had been an evening following an afternoon when he had drunk beer continually in the hotel near the school where he taught or in some other hotel in a suburb of Melbourne and had bought a flask of vodka before the hotel had closed.

The man walking beside Spring Creek at Hepburn Springs twenty-seven years after the Camden Theatre had been closed down remembered a joke that he had made four hours before in order to amuse his oldest friend.

At noon on the Saturday at Hepburn Springs the man who had been married for more than twenty-five years had seen that the afternoon would be fine. He had then told the seven other persons that he would lead them beside the creek where he had walked during every day of his holidays in every year when he had been a schoolboy. The man had said that he would lead the seven other persons first upstream along a concrete path among lawns and European trees, then past the springs that he had drunk from in every summer from the end of the Second World War until 1955, then further upstream along a walking track to the furthest spring, which was in the bush, and then back along the walking track and the concrete path downstream to the hotel.

The chief character of this story had drunk water from the

springs at Hepburn Springs only four times. In January of each year from 1946 to 1949, which were the last four years of his father's life and the years when he, the chief character, had been a boy aged from eight years to eleven years, he had travelled with his parents by railway train from Melbourne to Allansford in order to spend his holidays with the unmarried brother and the unmarried sisters of his father. In each of those years, while the boy and his parents had waited at Spencer Street station for the train to leave for the south-west of Victoria the father had taken his son to a milk bar and soda fountain on the concourse of the station. The father had told the boy that the milk bar and soda fountain was the only place in Melbourne where a person could buy what he called genuine Hepburn spa water. The father had then bought two glasses of bubbling water from one of the stern-faced and grey-haired women behind the counter and had given one glass to his son. The son had disliked the taste of the water and had been afraid for a few moments after he had swallowed the first of the water that he would vomit among the crowd of people at the milk bar and soda fountain. After the boy had swallowed a few mouthfuls the father had taken the boy's glass and had drunk the water in the glass even though it was no longer bubbling. Then the father had rebuked the boy in the hearing of the stern-faced and grey-haired women.

When the eight persons had walked upstream along the concrete path to the first spring, the man who had last drunk spring water at Spencer Street station thirty-eight years and five months before had been surprised to see that the water came out of taps protruding from a stone wall with a drain at its base like the drain in a public urinal. The man had expected that the water would have trickled out of a hollow among rocks and ferns or out of a cave as the water had trickled in the pictures that he had seen as a child of Saint Bernadette, who had seen a vision of the Virgin Mary in a cave in the Pyrenees mountains and had dug in the part of the cave where the Virgin had told her to dig and had uncovered a trickling stream that cured illnesses and healed injuries and deformities.

While the seven other persons had crowded around the spring and while the man who had been married for more than twenty-five years had filled mugs of water for the persons, the chief character of this story had hung back. But the man beside the spring had seen his oldest friend hanging back. The man had passed a mug full of spring-water to his wife and had told her in a loud voice to make sure that the man hanging back did not lack for a drink. Then the woman who had been married for more than twenty-five years but whose skin was still clear and pale and whose hair was still blonde and almost white and whose arms and legs were still thin and whose thick woollen sweater still looked almost flat at the front had put the mug of spring water into the hand of the man who had hung back.

The man who had hung back had swallowed a mouthful of the water and had liked the taste. He had then drunk the rest of the water from the mug.

While some of the eight persons had begun to walk along the concrete path towards the next spring, the chief character of this story had hung back again. He had stood beside his oldest friend, who had been pouring a drink for himself from the spring. Then the man hanging back had taken out of his pocket a leaflet with columns of black type and black line drawings on white paper. The man had stared at a certain paragraph of type in the leaflet and had then leaned forward and had looked down at the front of his trousers. The man had then shaken his head and had frowned. When the man frowning had seen that his oldest friend was watching him, he read aloud from the leaflet.

The man reading aloud had taken the leaflet earlier that day from a stack of leaflets in a shop in Hepburn Springs. The man had supposed from the look of the printed words and the line drawings that the leaflet had first been printed about sixty years before and that the shopkeepers of Hepburn Springs had had the leaflet reprinted in order to amuse visitors to the town, although the shopkeeper had not smiled when the man had said that the leaflet looked amusing.

Printed in the leaflet was a list of illnesses and disabilities that had been cured by the waters of Hepburn Springs. The chief character of this story had read aloud to his oldest friend the following items from the list: *fits*, *scrofula*, *quinsy*, *impetigo*. Then he had read aloud the item *sexual impotence* and had looked down again at his trousers and had shaken his head.

When the man had looked down at the front of his trousers he had seen from the sides of his eyes that one of the seven other persons other than his oldest friend was watching him. The man had looked up and had seen that the person watching was the wife of his oldest friend and that she was watching him with an expression of aloofness.

During the first half of the afternoon the four married couples had walked upstream along the concrete path. The couples had stopped at each spring, and the man who had spent his holidays at Hepburn Springs until 1955 had urged the seven other persons to drink the water from the spring. At each spring a few persons had drunk a few mouthfuls. The only persons who had drunk a mug full of water from every spring had been the two men who had been friends for thirty-six years and five months.

During the first half of the afternoon the four married couples had sometimes turned aside from the concrete path and had paused and had talked on the lawns beside the creek. At about the middle of the afternoon the four couples had reached the end of the concrete path and the lawns and the European trees. In order to walk further towards the furthest spring the couples had had to follow a walking track through the bush.

The man who had been married for more than twenty-five years had begun to walk ahead of the seven other persons towards the furthest spring. After the eight persons had walked for a few minutes along the track, the land had become hilly and the track had begun to climb. After the eight persons had followed the track up the first of the hills, two of the women had said that they would prefer to rest beside the track while the other persons went on walking towards the furthest spring. The two women had then sat and had rested on the trunk of a fallen tree. The husbands of the two women had then squatted in the grass beside the track and had waited while their wives had rested. The other four persons had gone on walking towards the furthest spring. The four persons who had gone on walking were the man and the woman who had been married for more than twenty-five years and another couple. The four persons who had waited and had rested were the chief character of this story and his wife and another couple.

After the four persons beside the track had waited and had rested for about fifteen minutes, the other four persons had walked back to them. The other four persons had said that they had walked to the furthest spring and back and that the furthest spring was only a short distance further along the track.

When the chief character of this story had heard what the four persons had said about the furthest spring he had said that he would walk alone to the furthest spring and back so that he could say afterwards that he had drunk from as many springs as his oldest friend had drunk from.

The oldest friend of the chief character had then said that the water from the furthest spring had tasted no differently from the water of some of the other springs.

The chief character of this story had then said that he would not bother to walk to the furthest spring. He had then turned and had walked ahead of the other persons downstream and towards the hotel.

Beside the lake at Caulfield Racecourse, on fine Sunday mornings between May 1956 and December 1958, the chief character of this story had often told the story of his having prepared for three months to ask a young woman that he had fallen in love with to go with him to a picture theatre and of her saying after he had asked her that she could not go. On fine Sunday mornings between January 1956 and December 1958 the other man who sat beside the lake had often told the story of his having been alone with a young woman among trees near Spring Creek at Hepburn Springs on an evening during the last week of 1955.

During the last week before Christmas Day in 1955, when the young man who had spent part of his holidays each year at Hepburn Springs had been aged seventeen years and two months, the young man had arrived with his parents at the guest house where they had arrived each year at Hepburn Springs. On every day afterwards the young man had avoided being with his parents and had played snooker in the guest house or had walked beside Spring Creek or among the trees on the hillside above the creek.

During the last week before New Year's Day in 1956 a young woman had arrived with her parents at the guest house. The young man noticed that the young woman was of about the same age as his age, that she avoided being with her parents, and that she played tennis every day on the courts next to the guest house or walked beside Spring Creek.

When the young man had first seen the young woman walking beside Spring Creek he had been walking among the trees on the hillside above Spring Creek. The young man had wanted at first to walk out from among the trees and to walk with the young woman but then he had become afraid that the young woman would tell him where she lived in one of the suburbs of Melbourne and would ask him to go with her to a picture theatre after she and he had returned to Melbourne and that he would agree to go with her and would be alone with her outside her house after she and he had been to the picture theatre and that the young woman would then learn that he had never previously been alone with a young woman.

On the evening after the young man had watched the young woman from among the trees on the hillside, the young woman had approached the young man at the guest house and had asked him why he had been afraid to come out from among the trees and to approach her while she had been walking beside Spring Creek.

While the young man had been preparing to answer the young woman she had asked him to walk with her beside Spring Creek on the following afternoon. The young man had agreed to walk with her because he had been afraid that she would suspect that he had never been alone with a young woman if he had not agreed.

While the two young persons had walked beside Spring Creek on the following afternoon the young man had drunk from each of the springs that they had passed but the young woman had not drunk from any of the springs. She had told the young man that she was afraid she would have vomited if she had drunk the water from any of the springs. She had told the young man that she came to Hepburn Springs with her parents during part of her holidays each year only because she was afraid of what her parents might have said if she told them that she no longer wanted to spend part of her holidays at Hepburn Springs.

While the two young persons had walked beside Spring Creek during the afternoon, the young woman had asked the young man to walk with her during the evening of that day among the trees on the hillside above the creek. The young man had agreed to walk with her for the same reason that had caused him to agree to walk with her during the afternoon.

While the young man and the young woman had walked together in the evening from the guest house towards Spring Creek and then from beside Spring Creek towards the trees on the hillside overlooking Spring Creek, so the young man had sometimes told his friend on fine Sunday mornings beside the lake at Caulfield Racecourse, the young man had been afraid that he would walk away from the young woman after they had walked in among the trees.

After the two young persons had walked in among the trees on the hillside overlooking Spring Creek the young woman had told the young man to sit on the grass among the trees. After the two young persons had sat on the grass the young woman had put her face close to his face. The young man had then understood, so he had often said afterwards by the lake, that the young woman had wanted him to kiss her in the way that male characters kissed female characters in American films. The young man had then prepared to kiss the young woman in that way.

While the young man had been preparing to kiss the young woman sitting beside him among the trees, the young woman had lain beside him on the grass. The young man had then supposed, so he had often said afterwards by the lake, that the young woman had wanted herself and himself to be naked together as the characters were sometimes naked together in European films.

While the young man had been still preparing to kiss the young woman as though he and she had been characters in an American film, the young woman had got to her feet and had walked quickly away from him. During the first moments while the young man had been sitting alone among the trees and while the young woman had been walking quickly away from him down the hillside towards Spring Creek, so the young man had often said afterwards beside the lake, he had heard the panting noises made by the young woman while she walked quickly away.

Late on the Saturday afternoon in the winter of 1987, when the four married couples had walked almost all the way downstream beside Spring Creek to the place where they had first begun to walk beside the creek and to drink from the springs, the four men had been walking about twenty paces ahead of the four women.

When the men had seen how far ahead of the women they had walked, they had begun to arrange a race in order to prove to one another that their bodies were still fit even though the men were all aged between forty-five and fifty years. The four men had agreed that the race should finish at the spring where they had first drunk earlier in the afternoon, but they had not been able to agree on where the race should start. One of the men had played ice-hockey as a young man and another had played football, and the other two men had claimed that these two men ought to be handicapped by starting behind in the race.

The sun had gone beside a hill and the sky was losing its colour. The four men and the four women were the only people in that part of the valley beside Spring Creek. When the men had stopped talking for a few moments, the chief character of this story had noticed that the only sound in that part of the valley was the sound of the water flowing in Spring Creek. Then the chief character had heard close behind him the sounds of women panting and running towards him.

The chief character of this story and the other men had looked behind them and had seen the four women running towards them. The four women had run past the men and had run towards the spring where the eight persons had first drunk earlier in the afternoon. The men had then supposed that the women had arranged a race among themselves after they had heard the men trying to arrange a race.

The four men had then stopped trying to arrange a race and had gone on walking in the direction that the women had run. After the men had walked about twenty paces they had drawn level with two women who had stopped running in the race. The other two women had continued in the race towards the spring where they had first drunk, but when the leading woman had arrived at the spring, the other woman, who was twenty paces behind, had then stopped running in the race.

The winner of the race towards the spring where the eight persons had first drunk earlier in the afternoon had been the woman who had been married for more than twenty-five years, who was still slim whereas the other women were on the way to being stout.

When the chief character of this story had first heard the panting noises behind him and had turned and had seen the four women running towards him, he had noticed the breasts of the women bobbing while the women ran. The women had been wearing thick sweaters while they had walked beside the creek but each woman had taken off her sweater and had tied it by its sleeves around her waist before the race. The chief character of this story had seen in the shirt of each woman the shapes of her breasts—even the breasts of the woman who was leading in the race and whose breasts were the smallest.

As soon as the women had run past him, and while he had still heard their panting noises but had no longer seen their breasts bobbing, the chief character of this story had heard in his mind part of a piece of music that he had first heard from a radio in 1952 and had heard occasionally from a radio during the years from 1952 to 1987. The man hearing the music in his mind believed that the name of the piece of music was either "Swedish Rhapsody" or "A Swedish Rhapsody" or "The Swedish Rhapsody" and that the music had been heard at times during the film *One Summer of Happiness*, which had been shown in picture theatres in the suburbs of Melbourne during 1952.

The man hearing the music in his mind beside Spring Creek had never seen the film *One Summer of Happiness*. During 1952, when he had been a boy aged fourteen years, his mother had not allowed him to go to picture theatres alone. However, the boy aged fourteen years had seen in a newspaper during 1952 a black and white sketch that had been copied from one of the photographs used in the film, and he had listened on many fine Sunday afternoons during the years from 1952 to 1955 beside the lake at Caulfield Racecourse while his best friend had described some of the images that he had seen on the three evenings when he had watched the film in the Renown Theatre in Elsternwick after having told his parents that he was going to watch another film in another picture theatre.

As a result of his having seen the black and white sketch in 1952 and having listened to his best friend during the years from 1952 to 1955, the man hearing the Swedish music in his mind beside Spring Creek in 1987 had believed during the years following

1952 that the film *One Summer of Happiness* was the story of two young persons who had met at a hotel or a guest house beside a lake in a forest in Sweden where their parents were spending their holidays. On the first fine afternoon of the holidays the young persons had walked together between the trees near the lake. After they had walked for some distance the young persons had sat on the grass among the trees and within sight of the lake and had talked together. After they had talked for some time each young person had confided to the other that he or she had never previously been alone with a person of the opposite sex. After the two young persons had confided this to one another they had stood up and had thrown off their clothes and had run between the trees and towards the lake.

While the two young persons in Sweden had run between the trees the young woman had made panting noises and her breasts had bobbed, but the breasts had been small and their bobbing had not kept the young woman from running ahead of the young man towards the lake.

After the race between the four women had ended and while the four men were walking towards the spring where the race had ended, the chief character of this story had supposed that each of the four men had talked at some time on the previous night about his wedding day in the 1960s. The man supposing this had not remembered any man's having talked about his wedding day in the 1960s in the bed-sitting room of the cabin behind the hotel, but he had remembered that each man had often talked about his wedding day in the 1960s whenever the four men had been drinking and talking together during the 1970s or the 1980s and he had supposed beside Spring Creek on the Saturday afternoon that each man had talked during the last hour of the Friday or the first two hours of the Saturday about his wedding day in the 1960s. The man supposing this had also supposed that he and his oldest friend had each talked about his wedding day in the 1960s more than either of the other two men had talked about his wedding day in the 1960s. Each of the other two men had been married twice, his first wedding having been a church ceremony in the 1960s and his second wedding having been a civil ceremony in the 1970s, and neither man talked for long about either of his weddings. The chief character of this story had supposed also that he and his oldest friend had each told, late on the Friday or early on the Saturday, the same story that he had often told about his wedding day.

Each of the two men who had been married only once had been married in a Catholic church, even though he had not believed the teachings of the Catholic Church since he had left secondary school, and each man had been the other's best man at the wedding. The man who had married the woman that he had first seen skating on ice had been married in January 1962, when he had been aged twenty-three years and three months and his wife had been aged eighteen years. The other man had been married in January 1965, when he had been aged twenty-six years and eight months and his wife had been aged twenty-one years and five months.

The story that the two men had often told was that the first of the two men to be married had arrived with his best man forty-five minutes early at the Catholic church in a south-eastern suburb of Melbourne where the wedding was to take place. While the two men had sat together at the back of the empty church, the man about to be married had said that he was afraid that the priest would look into his eyes at some point during the service and would see into his mind and would then refuse to go on conducting the service.

The man who was about to be best man had then taken out of the inside pocket of his jacket a flask three-quarters full of vodka. The man had shown the flask to his best friend and had said that he, the man about to be best man, had been afraid during the previous week that the priest would look into his eyes at some point during the service and would see into his mind and would then refuse to allow him to continue as best man. The man with the flask in his hand had then said that he had drunk some of the vodka during the past hour, that he intended to drink more of the vodka before the wedding service began, and that he expected not to be afraid during the wedding service.

The man who was about to be married had then said that he would take a sip of the vodka even though he had never previously drunk any alcoholic drink. The owner of the vodka had then offered the flask to his best friend while they had sat at the back of the church, but his best friend had been afraid to drink from the flask while they were sitting there. The two men had then got up from their seat at the back of the church, and the chief character of this story had led the other man to the back corner of the church and had stood with him in the baptistry.

When the man about to be married had seen in the baptistry that he was hidden from the view of anyone who might have entered the church, he had sipped from the flask of vodka, had closed his eyes and shuddered, had swallowed the vodka that he had sipped, and had handed the flask back to its owner. The owner of the flask had then swallowed a mouthful of the vodka, but instead of replacing the lid and putting the flask in his pocket he had put the flask and its lid into the empty font that stood at the centre of the baptistry.

During the next fifteen minutes the two men had stood in the baptistry, each man with one leg crossed in front of the other and one elbow resting on the rim of the white marble font, which reached to the height of the waists of the men, and had talked continually. From time to time while the men had talked, one or another man had lifted the flask out from the font and had drunk or had sipped from the flask. Whenever the man who was about to be married had sipped from the vodka he had closed his eyes and had shuddered, and the man who was about to be best man had begun to be afraid that his best friend would vomit during the wedding service.

The two men had gone on talking and sipping or drinking

until they had heard sounds of people on the steps outside the church. Then the chief character of this story had screwed the lid onto the flask, which by then was no more than quarter-full, and had put the flask into the inside pocket of his jacket. The two men had then walked to the front of the church and had waited for the bride.

The mother of the bride had arranged for the wedding reception to take place in the Domain Hotel, at the corner of St Kilda Road and Park Street. The Domain Hotel no longer exists, but the building where the wedding reception took place has not yet been knocked down.

During the wedding reception the chief character of this story had noticed that the groom sipped beer continually and talked continually. When the bride and the groom had left the Domain Hotel the chief character had been afraid that the groom would vomit later in the evening.

After the bride and the groom had left the wedding reception and while the guests had gone on drinking and talking, the mother of the bride had left her seat and had sat beside the best man. When the best man had seen the woman approaching him he had been afraid that she had suspected him of having persuaded the groom to drink vodka and beer for the first time on his wedding day although he had never previously drunk any alcoholic drink, but the mother of the bride had only said that she was glad that the groom had begun to drink beer at last because she had not wanted to have a son-in-law who was a wowser.

The last part of the story that the two men had often told was that each man had carried a flask of vodka in the inside pocket of his jacket on the Saturday afternoon in January 1965 when they had arrived at the Catholic church in an eastern suburb of Melbourne where the chief character of this story was about to be married.

The two men had arrived at the church forty-five minutes before the service was to begin and had walked to the doors of the church intending to rest their elbows on the baptistry font and to drink some of their vodka together but had turned away from the church when they had heard the sound of the organist's rehearsing the program of music for the wedding and had then walked towards the grounds at the side of the church intending to find a place among shrubs or trees where they could drink some of their vodka together.

The men had looked around the grounds at the side of the church but had seen no place where they might have drunk vodka among shrubs or trees. The only place where they might have drunk vodka without their being seen from the doors of the church was the grotto at the rear of the grounds.

The two men had walked to the mouth of the grotto and had taken out their flasks and had unscrewed the caps. Then the man who was about to be married had looked behind him and had seen that he and the best man were still within view of some of the windows of the presbytery. The two men had then stepped into the grotto, but at the place where they then stood the grotto was too narrow for both men to stand comfortably. The two men had then knelt on the floor of the grotto.

The two men had gone on kneeling in the grotto for ten minutes. During that time the men had talked and had swallowed mouthfuls of vodka. Anyone seeing the men from a distance during that time might have supposed whenever one of the men had tilted his head back that he was looking at the statue that stood at the rear of the grotto or praying to the person represented by the statue, who was Our Lady of Lourdes.

Whenever the chief character of this story had told the story that has been summarised in the previous paragraphs or had heard his oldest friend telling that story, the chief character of this story had remembered certain details that he considered part of that story,

although he had never mentioned those details whenever he had
told that story.

The chief character of this story remembered beside Spring
Creek on the winter afternoon in 1987 his oldest friend's having
said in the church on the summer afternoon in 1962 that he was
afraid that the priest would look into his eyes. The man remembered at Hepburn Springs that he had supposed in the church in
the south-eastern suburb of Melbourne that the man who had
said he was afraid was afraid not only because he no longer believed in the teachings of the Catholic Church but also because he
had done or had tried to do with the young woman who was
about to be married to him some at least of the things that he had
said beside the lake at Caulfield Racecourse on fine Sunday afternoons that he would do in the future with one after another young
woman.

At the time when the chief character of this story had supposed
what is mentioned in the previous paragraph, he had not asked any
young woman to go anywhere with him during the four years and
nine months since he had asked the young woman to go with him
to a picture theatre while he and she had walked on a concrete path
at a teachers' college. During most of his time at weekends during those four years and nine months the chief character of this
story had been alone in his room. On fine Sunday afternoons from
January 1960, when he and his best friend had returned to Melbourne from Lorne, until January 1962, when his best friend had
been about to be married, the chief character of this story had supposed that his best friend had taken his girlfriend or his fiancée in
his Volkswagen sedan to a body of water with trees beside it. On
many fine Sunday afternoons the man supposing this had supposed
that his best friend was alone with the young woman at Hepburn
Springs.

The man who had supposed what is mentioned in the previous paragraph had never seen Hepburn Springs or any place where
water appeared from underground. When he had tried to see Hepburn Springs in his mind he had seen in his mind certain details

from a coloured poster that he had seen sometimes on railway stations in the first years after the Second World War.

The man had seen in the background of his mind plains of green grass crossed by a winding stream of silver water bordered by a few trees with dark-green leaves. He had seen in the foreground of his mind, beneath overhanging leaves, a young woman wearing a sleeveless white robe and holding up a glass goblet. Silvery water bubbled out of the goblet and down to the grass and then away in a stream across the plains of green grass. On the dark green of the leaves above the young woman was printed the word *Schweppervescence*.

The man who had remembered at Hepburn Springs in 1987 the image of Hepburn Springs that had appeared in his mind during 1960 and 1961 had seen only a whitish blur where the face of the young woman should have appeared in his mind. The man who had seen the whitish blur in his mind had not remembered whether he had seen in his mind during 1960 and 1961 a whitish blur or the face of the young woman, but the man seeing the whitish blur in 1987 had remembered that the young woman whose image had appeared in the poster in the years soon after the Second World War had been one of the young women that he had fallen in love with during those years.

During the years 1961 and 1962 the man who had seen in his mind at Hepburn Springs in 1987 a young woman who had caused silvery water to flow across plains of green grass had lived alone in a bungalow of one room behind a house in a suburb twelve miles south-east of Caulfield Racecourse.

In the morning and in the evening of each school day during those years the man had travelled by train between the suburb where he lived and the suburb where he worked as a primary teacher, which was nineteen miles south-east of Caulfield Racecourse. In the morning of each of those days the man had travelled in the same compartment with one or two or three young female teachers from the school where he taught. In the evening of each of those days the man had travelled alone to the suburb where he lived after having drunk beer and talked with a group of male teachers in a hotel in the suburb where he taught in a primary school.

Whenever only one young woman had been travelling with the man, she and he had talked together. Whenever two or three young women had travelled with the man, the young women had talked mostly among themselves while the young man had filled out a crossword puzzle in the *Age*.

Whenever the young women had talked among themselves, each young woman had talked about the American films and the television programs that she had watched recently or about the places in the countryside near Melbourne where her boyfriend had taken her recently in his car or about the parties that she and her boyfriend had attended recently. The man who is the chief character of this story had often listened to the young women while he filled out his crossword puzzle and had noticed that the young women seldom talked about their boyfriends. Whenever a young woman talked about her boyfriend she seemed to the man filling out his crossword to be assuring the other young women that she had not fallen in love with her boyfriend.

Once in every few months the young women had talked with more zest than usual. They had talked with more zest on a morning when one of the young women had told the others that one of her girlfriends had become engaged to be married. They had talked about the ring that the engaged young woman was wearing or about the shower tea or the kitchen tea that would be arranged for her or about the block of land that the engaged couple would buy in an outer suburb or about the wedding day in the future.

When one or another of the young women had been alone in the compartment on a Monday morning with the chief character of this story she had sometimes asked him what he had done during the previous weekend. The man had answered truthfully that he had played cards with a few friends on the Friday evening and had gone to the races on the Saturday and had stayed at home on the Sunday. The man had hoped that the young woman would suppose that he had done some of these things in the company of a young woman.

On one Monday morning in June 1961 the young women had talked with much more zest than usual. The man who was travelling with them had soon learned that one of the young women had announced her engagement to the man who had been her boyfriend for three years. During the next weeks the young women had talked with much zest each morning about the engagement ring that the young woman was wearing or about the shower tea or the kitchen tea that would be arranged for her or about the block of land that she and her fiancé would buy in an outer suburb or about the wedding day in the future.

On one Monday morning in July 1961 the young woman who had recently announced her engagement and the man who is the chief character of this story had travelled alone together on the train. While they had travelled the young woman had asked the man what he had done during the previous weekend.

When the young woman had asked this question, the man had suspected that the young woman knew that he had never had a girlfriend and that he had not asked any young woman to go anywhere with him for more than four years and that the young woman was inviting him to confide to her something that he had not previously confided to any person.

After the young man had suspected these things he had not told the young woman what he had done during the weekend, which had been to play cards with four other men on the Friday evening, to go alone to the races on the Saturday, and to sit alone in his room drinking beer and reading on the Saturday evening and on the Sunday. Instead, the man had told the young woman that he had gone to a picture theatre on the Saturday evening and had seen an interesting Swedish film.

The young woman had asked him the name of the Swedish film.

The man had said that the name of the film was *The Virgin Spring*.

The young woman had seemed not to have heard of the film, but the man had watched the film named *The Virgin Spring* on the previous Wednesday evening after he had first drunk beer with the male teachers in the hotel and had then bought a parcel of fish and chips and a flask of vodka and had travelled by train into the city of Melbourne. During that year the man had gone to a picture theatre in the city of Melbourne once in every two or three weeks, but he had always gone on an evening of a weekday. If the man had gone to a picture theatre on a Saturday evening he would have had to sit alone among couples and groups of friends.

The man had then described to the young woman the few images that had stayed in his mind after he had watched the Swedish film. He had described the image of a girl with blonde hair that had looked almost white who had travelled alone on a path at the edge of a forest in Sweden. He had then described the images of two men and a boy who had watched the girl from among the trees beside the path and who had then run along the path towards the girl and had made panting noises. He had then described the image of the boy's vomiting on the path when he had seen the two men beginning to rape and to kill the girl. The man had then described the image of water bubbling from a spring that had appeared at the place where the girl had been raped and killed.

On a hot evening in January 1964, the eight persons who had later gathered at Hepburn Springs in June 1987 had travelled with fifteen other persons in a boat upstream along the Yarra River to a point about five miles from the centre of Melbourne and then downstream and back to the centre of Melbourne in order to celebrate the second anniversary of the wedding of the man and the woman who had first met on an ice-skating rink in St Kilda.

At about the time when the boat had travelled upstream for as far as it was going to travel before it returned downstream, the man who was celebrating the second anniversary of his wedding had struck a spoon repeatedly against an empty beer bottle until the persons celebrating the anniversary had stopped talking and drinking. The man had then announced to the people the engagement of the man who is the chief character of this story and a young woman.

The chief character of this story had first met the young woman on the morning of the first school day in 1963 when he had been aged twenty-four years and nine months and she had been aged nineteen years and six months and when she had travelled with him on a train beside the shore of Port Phillip Bay towards the outer south-eastern suburb of Melbourne where he had taught for five years in a primary school and where she was about to begin teaching in the same primary school after she had trained for two years at a teachers' college conducted by the Education Department of Victoria. The chief character of this story had not asked the young woman to go anywhere with him until a certain afternoon in June 1963 when he had not gone to the hotel where he drank on most afternoons but had travelled by train to Caulfield in order to drink with a man who was connected with a racing stable. The young woman had been travelling on the same train in order to buy clothes in the city of Melbourne. When the train had been passing the high dark-green fence along the eastern boundary of Caulfield Racecourse the man had told the young woman that he went to the races on every Saturday afternoon. The young woman had then said that she had never been to the races but that she would love to go on some Saturday afternoon. The man had then asked the young woman to go with him to the next race meeting at Caulfield Racecourse. The young woman had then agreed to go with him.

While the boat had been travelling first upstream and then downstream in the Yarra River the chief character of this story had drunk beer continually and had talked continually with his fiancée and with other persons. Sometimes the man had looked out of the boat and across the water towards the lights of houses among the trees overlooking the Yarra River. While he had looked at the lights, the chief character had seen in his mind the quince tree and the boxthorn bushes and the jonquils on the patch of short green grass where the men named Cotter, the bachelor great-uncles of his father, had lived in a house overlooking Lake Gillear in the south-west of Victoria.

On the following morning the man looking out from the boat was going to travel with his fiancée in his cream-coloured Volkswagen sedan to the city of Warrnambool in the south-west of Victoria. The man and his fiancée were going to spend a week of their holidays in the house belonging to the unmarried sisters of his father. When the man looking out from the boat had seen in his mind the place where the brothers Cotter had lived on the hillside overlooking Lake Gillear, he had planned to take his fiancée to that place on a fine afternoon during their holidays and to be alone with her there.

The man seeing in his mind part of the hillside overlooking Lake Gillear had previously been alone with the young woman who had later become his fiancée only during the last hour of each Saturday and the first hour of each Sunday from the first week in November 1963. The man had been alone with the young woman during those hours in his room and had kissed the young woman and had put his right hand inside one or another piece of her underclothing but had not tried to do any more to the young woman because he and she had not yet announced their engagement and because the young woman believed in the teachings of the Catholic Church and the man had been afraid of what she might have said to him if he had tried to do more to her.

The man travelling on the Yarra River and seeing in his mind the grassy paddocks around Lake Gillear had intended to travel on a fine afternoon during the following week in his Volkswagen sedan and with his fiancée beside him five miles from the city of Warrnambool to the grassy paddocks around Lake Gillear. He had intended to tell his fiancée while he and she walked across the paddocks from where he had parked his Volkswagen sedan that he had walked across those paddocks many times during his summer holidays in past years. The man had intended to lead the young woman past tall tussocks and clumps of rushes and to show her patches of green grass where water had lain on the surface of the paddock during winter and where the soil under the grass was still damp. He had intended to confide to the young woman that he had walked past those patches of green grass on fine afternoons during the summer holidays of past years and had wanted to see in his mind himself alone with a young woman on the green grass but had been walking with his unmarried uncle towards the place where the unmarried great-uncles of his uncle had lived on a hillside overlooking Lake Gillear and had not thought of himself alone with a young woman because he had been afraid of what his uncle might have thought if he had guessed what the nephew walking beside him had been thinking.

The man who had intended to do the things mentioned in the previous paragraph had intended next to take the young woman to the place where the house had once stood in a garden overlooking Lake Gillear but where only a quince tree and a few boxthorn bushes and a few clumps of jonquils grew in January 1964 and only a few bricks lay. The man had intended finally to ask the young woman to sit and then to lie beside him on the green grass.

The man walking beside Spring Creek with the woman who had been his wife for twenty-two years and five months and with three other husbands and wives remembered having driven his cream-coloured Volkswagen sedan from Warrnambool towards Lake Gillear with his fiancée sitting beside him early in the afternoon of the last day of their holidays in the south-west of Victoria in January 1964. The man remembered that his fiancée had packed a basket with cakes and fruit and lemonade and had brought a travelling rug after he had told her that he was taking her to a place where they could be alone in the shade of a tree overlooking a lake. The man next remembered that he had turned his Volkswagen aside from the road towards Lake Gillear when he had almost reached Lake Gillear. He had turned the car aside in order to introduce his fiancée to his unmarried uncle, who still lived in a farmhouse near the Hopkins River in the district of Allansford although his two unmarried sisters had recently gone to live in the city of Warrnambool, before he took his fiancée to Lake Gillear.

The man walking towards the hotel in the evening of his last day at Hepburn Springs remembered his fiancée's meeting his uncle and asking him about the history of the house where he lived alone among overgrown gardens and orchards near the Hopkins River. The man remembered his uncle's taking the young woman through the empty rooms of the house towards the room that he called his bedroom-cum-study and unlocking for her the glass doors at the front of the tall bookcase. The man remembered his uncle's lifting out from among the books about history and travel and racehorses and Australian birds and poetry two ledgers with marbled paper on the insides of their covers and his showing the young woman first the ledger where he had written the notes and had drawn the charts for the family history that he had once planned to write and to have published and next the ledger where he had written the notes and drawn the sketches for the book about the birds of his district that he had once planned to write and to have published.

The man remembering the things mentioned in the previous paragraph next remembered that he had frowned at his fiancée for a few moments while she had been looking up from one of his uncle's ledgers and while his uncle had been looking down at the ledger. He had frowned in order to remind her that he still intended to take her to a place overlooking a lake and that she ought to prepare to leave his uncle's house. After he had frowned, his fiancée had looked at him with an expression of aloofness.

The man at Hepburn Springs remembering on a winter evening the summer afternoon in the district of Allansford remembered that he had foreseen after his fiancée had looked at him with an expression of aloofness that she would later ask him to bring the basket from the car so that he and she could share their cakes and fruit and lemonade with his uncle on the veranda of his house before he left for the paddocks in order to call his cows for the afternoon milking. The man remembered that he had foreseen at the same time that he and his fiancée would arrive at the end of the road in the paddocks near Lake Gillear and would begin to walk across the paddocks late in the afternoon and that a cool south-west breeze would be blowing from the Southern Ocean when he and she reached the lake. The man had foreseen also that his fiancée would ask questions about the house that had once stood on the hillside overlooking the lake and about the men who had lived in the house. The man had foreseen also that he would not be able to answer the young woman's questions and that he would then turn and would lead her away from the lake and across the paddocks towards the road.

Early in the evening of the last Saturday before Christmas Day in 1959, the man drinking beer for the first time and looking between the tops of trees towards some of the dark-blue water of the Southern Ocean had heard in his mind his best friend talking from a telephone box in the main street of Lorne to his girlfriend in the house at the corner of St Kilda Road and Albert Road. The man had heard his best friend saying that he had nothing else to do that night but to sit on the balcony of the holiday flat at Lorne and that his friend had nothing else to do than to sit beside him and to drink beer.

While the man on the balcony had heard these words in his mind he had seen in his mind his best friend speaking into the mouthpiece of a telephone in a public telephone booth outside a post office. After the man on the balcony had heard in his mind the words that his friend was reported as saying in the previous paragraph, the sight that the man on the balcony saw in his mind had been divided vertically into two equal parts in the same way that the image on the screen of a picture theatre had sometimes been divided when the man on the balcony had been a young man or a boy watching an American film in which one scene was of a man and a woman speaking by telephone. The man had then seen in the right-hand side of his mind his best friend in the public telephone booth and in the left-hand side of his mind the girlfriend of his best friend standing beside the telephone in the lounge room of the house at the corner of St Kilda Road and Albert Road.

When the man drinking beer alone on the balcony at Lorne had first seen in the left-hand side of his mind the girlfriend of his best friend speaking into her telephone she had been wearing a set of summer pyjamas that left her legs and arms bare. When the man had first seen her in his mind she had had on her face an expression of aloofness, even after she had heard what her boyfriend had said to her from the public telephone box at Lorne. Later, after the man had drunk more beer, the expression on the face of the young woman had changed. Then the man on the balcony had heard in his mind the young woman speaking into the telephone and telling her boyfriend that her mother was going to borrow her best friend's car, that her mother and she were going to set out in a few minutes for Lorne, that her mother was going to bring with her a dozen bottles of beer from the stock remaining after the party and a hamper of food from her kitchen, and that she, the young woman, and her mother would arrive at Lorne at midnight and would have supper with the two men on the balcony and would talk and drink continually with them afterwards.

At some time after the man on the balcony had seen and had heard in his mind the things mentioned in the previous paragraph, he had seen in his mind himself and the mother of the girlfriend of his best friend sitting alone together on the balcony of the holiday

flat and drinking beer continually and talking continually while
his best friend was walking with his girlfriend among the trees on
the hillside. At some time later again the man on the balcony had
heard in his mind himself confiding to the woman aged about
forty who had once been an American war bride something that
he had never previously confided to any other person. The man had
then heard in his mind the woman telling him that her daughter
had a female cousin of the same age as himself in one of the states
of the United States that was mostly plains of grass and that she,
the woman, would write to the girl in America as soon as she had
arrived back in her house at the corner of St Kilda Road and Albert
Road and would invite the girl to travel to Australia.

The man looking forward to drinking beer in the hotel during the
last six hours of the last evening of his holidays at Hepburn Springs
and then during the first two hours of the following morning had
never remembered anything further that he had heard or had seen
in his mind or had said or had done on the first night of his holiday at Lorne. The man remembered, however, that his oldest friend
had often said that he had returned to the holiday flat later that
evening and had found the man who is the chief character of this
story asleep on his bed and still wearing his clothes but had not
learned until he had walked on the concrete path beneath the balcony during the following morning that the chief character of this
story had vomited during the previous evening while he had been
leaning over the balcony in the direction of the trees on the hillside
with a view of part of the Southern Ocean.

During the last two hours of the last Saturday before Christmas
Day in 1959, persons on the footpath below the Lower Esplanade
in St Kilda or on the beach below the wall at the edge of the Lower
Esplanade heard through a set of loudspeakers the program broadcast by one of the commercial radio stations of Melbourne.

The man who walked up and down the footpath of the Lower Esplanade during those two hours and during the following four hours listened while he walked up and down to each of the pieces of recorded music in the program, but during the first four hours of the Sunday morning he heard in his mind only one of those pieces. During those hours he heard continually in his mind the music of what the disc jockey had called an instrumental piece by the name of "Velvet Waters."

When the chief character of this story first heard through the loudspeakers the music of "Velvet Waters," he saw in his mind not musical instruments being played by musicians but water bubbling and flowing over grass on a summer night while the moon was shining. At some time while the chief character in this story heard continually in his mind during the first four hours of the Sunday morning the music of "Velvet Waters," he saw in his mind not only water bubbling and flowing over grass but a few trees around the water, plains of grass around the trees, and a young woman standing beside the water among the trees. The man seeing these things in his mind saw that the young woman was wearing a thin dress and that her arms and legs and feet were bare, but he did not see the face of the young woman because her face was hidden by her blonde hair.

At some time while the chief character of this story saw in his mind the things mentioned in the previous paragraph, the young woman in his mind stepped into the water in his mind and stood while the water bubbled and flowed around her.

At some time during the first four hours of the Sunday, the man seeing the young woman standing in the water in his mind understood that he had previously seen an image of the young woman when he had looked at an illustration in a magazine for women in a year soon after the Second World War. The illustration had been meant to represent a scene from a story with the title "The Pond," by Louis Bromfield.

At another time during the first four hours of the Sunday, the man seeing the page of the magazine in his mind remembered that his mother had been reading "The Pond" when he had first seen the illustration. The man remembered that his mother had told him after she had finished reading "The Pond" that "The Pond" was the most beautiful story that she had read. The man then remembered that he had not read "The Pond" while his mother had been watching him because he had not wanted his mother to guess what was in his mind but that he had read "The Pond" afterwards.

The man who had read "The Pond" at some time during a year soon after the end of the Second World War remembered at some time while he walked up and down the beach at St Kilda and while he looked south-west across Port Phillip Bay that the woman in the story had been born and had lived as a child in a district of forests and streams in America but had married a young man who had been born and had lived as a child in one of the Great Plains states, although his parents had been born and had lived as children in a district of forests and lakes in Sweden. After she had married the young man, the young woman had gone to live on her husband's farm in one of the Great Plains states. Each day she had walked out into the paddocks of grass and had stood among a few trees that had been the only trees on all the plains of grass from her husband's house to the horizon in any direction and had seen in her mind the forests and the streams in the district where she had been born.

One day the husband of the young woman had left his wife in order to fight in the Second World War. After her husband had left, the young woman had continued to walk out into the paddocks of grass each day and to stand among the few trees.

One night while her husband was away, the young woman had gone out into the paddocks of grass while the moon was shining and had stood among a few trees. The day had been a hot day and the night was a warm night, and the woman wore only a thin dress and was barefoot. While she stood among the few trees she had understood that her husband had died during that night. She had understood also that she would later give birth to a child whose father would be the man who had died during that night.

While she had stood among the few trees and had understood these things, the young woman had heard the sound of water bubbling and flowing and had understood that a spring had begun to flow from among the few trees.

The young woman who was the chief character of the story that the man who is the chief character of this story remembered while he walked up and down beside St Kilda Beach had then stepped into the water that was bubbling and flowing and had gone on standing in the water among the few trees on the plains of grass during the hours of the morning.

The White Cattle of Uppington

T he following is a list of descriptions of some of
the details of some of the images in some of the sequences
of images that the chief character of this piece of fiction
foresaw as appearing in his mind whenever during a certain year in the late 1970s he foresaw himself as preparing to write
a certain piece of fiction. Each description is followed by a passage explaining some of the details of some of the images.

*The words "fucked" and "spunk" appear among a throng of other
words on one of the last pages of a second-hand copy of the First
Unlimited Edition, published by John Lane The Bodley Head Ltd,
of* Ulysses, *by James Joyce. The book lies open on the thighs of a
young man whose lower body is clothed in grey sports trousers
with sharp creases at the front. The upper body of the young man
is clothed in a grey-blue sports jacket over an olive-green shirt
and a pale-blue tie. Most of the men in the crowded railway
carriage where the young man sits reading are wearing grey suits*

with white shirts and ties of dark colours. A few of the men are
wearing sports clothes, but all of these men have white or cream
shirts and ties of dark colours.

The men are all on their way to work in office buildings in the
city of Melbourne on one or another morning in a certain year in
the late 1950s. The young man, too, is going to work in an office
building. He has gone to work in the same office building on nearly
every weekday since he finished secondary school three years ago.
But he does not want to go on working in an office building. He
does not want to live for the rest of his life as he supposes the men
around him in the railway carriage live. He does not want to own
a house in a suburb of Melbourne or of any other city. He does
not want to get married, although he wants to have sexual rela-
tions with a woman, and perhaps with more than one woman. He
has read about men who lived lives undreamed of, so he supposes,
by the men around him in the railway carriage; he has read about
D. H. Lawrence and Ernest Hemingway and James Joyce. He wants
to be a writer of the kind that these men were. He wants to live
with a woman in an upstairs flat in an inner suburb of one or another city in Europe or in a cottage deep in the countryside of
Europe. His shirt and tie are the first sign that he has sent to his
fellow workers and his fellow train travellers. He wears the un-
conventional green and blue as a sign that he repudiates the customs and the moral standards of office workers and that he intends
never again to work in an office as from the day when his first work
of fiction is accepted by a publisher. Now, he reads in front of the
nearest office workers a book that was banned in Australia until
only recently. He expects that his own books will be banned in Australia soon after they have been published. He found his copy of
Ulysses in one of the second-hand bookshops where he spends
his lunch-hours. When he takes his seat each morning in a railway
carriage, he looks at the nearest passengers. If a young woman is
nearby, he leaves *Ulysses* in his bag and takes out some other
book; he has no wish to embarrass any young woman. But if the
nearest passengers are men or married women, he spends a few

minutes during each journey running his finger backwards and forwards beneath certain lines in *Ulysses*, hoping that someone from the suburbs of Melbourne will see on the page certain words that he or she has never previously seen in print and will be for long afterwards unsettled.

The partly naked body of a young woman appears in a coloured illustration with two pronounced horizontal creases. The young woman is kneeling on green grass against a background of dense shrubbery. She rests her hands on her hips and holds her head askew and smiles. She is wearing lipstick and probably other kinds of make-up. The skin of her arms and chest and abdomen is a uniform golden-brown, like certain polished woods in coloured advertisements for furniture. Her breasts are thrust forward; the lower parts of each breast are white, and the nipples are prominent. The lower body and the legs of the young woman are clothed in a pair of jeans. The belt in the jeans is unfastened, and the zip fastener at the front of the jeans has been drawn downwards a little way. The picture of the young woman is fastened by tacks to the unpainted plasterboard wall of a bedroom. The bedroom is furnished with a double bed and two chairs. A cord has been strung from nails across each of two corners of the bedroom. Items of a woman's clothing hang from one cord and items of a man's clothing hang from the other cord. The picture of the partly naked young woman is above the centre of the head of the bed. In the wall to the right of the picture is a window without curtains or blinds. In the foreground of the view from the window is a thin forest of second-growth gum trees on a hillside that slopes down and away from the house. The window of the bedroom is closed, but loud clickings and buzzings of insects can be heard from the nearer trees. In the right-hand background of the view from the window is a small conical mountain covered in forest. From the conical mountain, a range of mountains extends to the left for as far as can be seen from the window.

The range of mountains appears as a line of dark blue on the hori-
zon. The season is summer; the time of day is early afternoon; the
weather is fine and hot; the air in the bedroom is very hot. A man
is kneeling on the bed and looking up at the picture of the young
woman. His upper body is naked, and the zip fastener at the front
of his grey sports trousers has been pulled downwards to its full
extent. A double sheet of newspaper has been spread in front of
him on the bed.

The year is the first year of the 1960s. The hillside where the
house stands is in a hilly district just beyond the outer north-eastern
suburbs of Melbourne. The line of mountains visible through the
window is the Kinglake Ranges. The house is owned by a man ten
years older than the man kneeling on the bed. The owner of the
house works on weekdays in an office building in the city of Melbourne and spends four nights of each week in his mother's house
in a suburb of Melbourne, having become separated from his wife
two years before, but lives from early on every Friday evening until
early on every Monday morning in the house on the hillside, which
he bought, together with part of the hillside, one year ago, when
the house had been unoccupied for many years, and which he intends to repair so that he can live in it for the rest of his life, no
longer working in an office building in the city of Melbourne but
painting pictures in the hilly district around his house and in the
Kinglake Ranges. The double bed is shared on every Friday, Saturday, and Sunday night by the owner of the house and a woman
who became separated from her husband one year ago. Sometimes
the owner of the house tells his friends that he and the woman intend to marry as soon as each of them has been divorced, but the
man kneeling on the bed hopes that the man and woman remain
always unmarried. The man kneeling on the bed has never previously met a couple who are living together without having been
married. The man kneeling on the bed first met the owner of the
house on a Saturday afternoon in the last summer of the 1950s, in
the bar of a hotel in the hilly district mentioned above. The man
kneeling on the bed was formerly the young man who wears an

olive-green shirt and a pale-blue tie in the first of the images described in this piece of fiction. During the last years of the 1950s, the man kneeling on the bed went on wearing ties and shirts of colours seldom chosen by office workers and went on wanting to be a writer of published fiction but wrote hardly any pages of fiction. If he had known anyone who might have been interested in hearing about the matter, the man might have explained to that person from time to time that he, the man, was having difficulty in choosing the subject matter and the style of his first work of fiction. Then, in almost the last month of the 1950s, the man read for the first time the book *On the Road*, by Jack Kerouac. From that time onwards, the man supposed he knew what would be the subject-matter and the style of his first published work of fiction. From that time onwards also, the man was anxious to find a group of people among whom he could behave as the narrator of *On the Road* behaved among his friends. The man supposed he would be most likely to find the people he was looking for in the hilly district mentioned above. He had read certain items in the Literary Supplement of the *Age* that caused him to suppose that a few artists and others were following a bohemian way of life in stone or mud-brick houses among the dry hills and straggling forests of a certain district beyond the north-eastern suburbs of Melbourne. Soon after he had finished reading *On the Road*, he bought on hire-purchase a nine-years-old Holden sedan. He went on travelling by train to his work in the office building on weekdays, but every Saturday morning he dressed in his oldest clothes (frayed shirts and trousers that he had formerly worn to work on weekdays) without combing his hair or shaving or showering. Then he drove from the suburb where he lived with his parents to one or another of the few hotels in the district mentioned several times above and sipped beer alone during the afternoon with the Literary Supplement of the *Age* open in front of him, waiting for an opportunity to join one or another of the more interesting groups around him and later, so he hoped, to be invited to a party in the hills. Once during the last month of the 1950s, the man was invited by another solitary man to a party and took bottles of beer to a gathering mostly of solitary men in a partly built house of fibrocement and afterwards slept in his car beside a back road in the hills before returning to the suburbs early on the Sunday morning. Then, in the first month of the 1960s, the owner of the house on the hillside and his girlfriend came up to the man in a hotel and invited him to a party at their house, but the only other persons who attended the party were two solitary men. On the day when such events took place as later gave rise in the mind of the man to the details reported above of the image of a man kneeling in front of an illustration of a partly naked young woman, the owner of the house on the hillside and his girlfriend were still the only persons in the hilly district that the man might have called friends. That day fell in the second month of the 1960s, in the month that is the hottest month of each year in the hilly district and surrounding districts. Early in the second month of the 1960s, the man who has been called "the man" in previous passages of this story began his annual recreation leave of three weeks. On each weekday in the first week of his leave, the man sat for several hours and sipped beer alone or with another solitary man in one or another hotel in the hilly district before returning home to his parents' house in the late afternoon. On the first weekday of the second week of his leave, the man told his mother that he would not be returning home that evening but would be staying with a married couple he was friendly with in the hilly district. Then the man drove his Holden sedan to the hilly district and bought six bottles of beer at a hotel and then drove to the house on the hillside. The owner of the house had told the man during the previous weekend that he was welcome to bring to the house on any weekday during his leave any young woman that he might wish to bring there and had shown the man where the key to the house was hidden from each Monday morning until each Friday evening. When the man arrived at the house with his six bottles of beer, he found the key and let himself into the house and put his beer into the refrigerator. Then he took one of the bottles out onto the veranda of the house and began to drink. For about an hour, the man sat on the veranda, drinking beer and listening to the sounds of insects and looking at the trees around the house or at the line of dark-blue mountains in the distance. Then he walked into the house and into the main bedroom. When he entered the main bedroom, he noticed at once the picture on the wall above the bed. The picture of the half-naked young woman had not been there when he had last looked into the bedroom. The man sat on the bed. He had intended to spend some time in the bedroom studying any item of women's clothing or underclothing that he found there, but he sat on the bed and inspected the picture of the young woman. He learned from a few printed words in the corner of the picture that the picture comprised three pages from the centre of a recent number of *Playboy* magazine. He then remembered that the owner of the house had told him during the previous year that his (the owner's) girlfriend had bought for him as a Christmas present a subscription to *Playboy*, which, so the owner had said, had been banned in Australia until recently. The man sitting on the bed had never seen any copy of *Playboy*. While he sat on the bed and inspected the picture on the wall, he believed he was somewhat nearer to living as the sort of man that he wanted to become and was therefore somewhat nearer to writing the first of the books that he would later write. The man then went to the box in the kitchen where old newspapers were kept. He selected some pages of the largest size in the box. After he had selected the pages, he saw that they were from one or another of the Literary Supplements of the *Age* that he had brought to the house on previous Saturdays. He unfolded the pages and spread them on the double-bed and then knelt on the bed so that he faced the picture of the young woman while the pages covered the bed-clothes in front of him. He then performed a series of acts that is usually summarised as a single act in such expressions as *he then masturbated*.

During the year mentioned in the first sentence of this story, whenever the man mentioned in that sentence foresaw as appearing in his mind the images some of the details of which are explained in the previous paragraph, he observed that the sequence of images that he foresaw as appearing in the mind of the man (or, rather, the image of the man) while he knelt on the bed and performed the acts reported in the previous sentence was such that the man might have been foreseeing himself, while he knelt on the bed, as preparing to write a certain piece of fiction. The man who was the chief character in that piece of fiction might have been alone with a young woman in a clearing in a forest in the USA and might have begun to perform in front of her the acts reported in the previous sentence by way of beginning to explain to her certain details about himself.

A group of about ten cattle stands in long grass with a line of trees behind them. The cattle are at a distance of about a hundred paces from the person perceiving them, but some of the cattle seem aware that a person has begun to approach them. Some of the cattle stand facing in the direction of the person. Each of these animals has long, wide-reaching horns, but none of the cattle stands threateningly. If the person watching were to move closer to the cattle, they would be more likely to run in among the trees than to stand their ground. All of the cattle are white.

The image of the white cattle in the long grass with the trees behind them is an image of an illustration in a book that was given as a Christmas present in one of the last years of the 1940s to the boy who was later the young man who wears an olive-green shirt and a pale-blue tie in the first of the images described in this piece of fiction. On each Christmas Day in the late 1940s, the boy found among his presents a large book chosen by his mother from the children's book section of a department store in the city of Melbourne. Each book had been published in England and contained many illustrated articles on topics that he understood to be subdivisions of the vast subject called General Knowledge, in which subject he was said by several of his teachers to be an expert. On each Christmas Day, he looked at each picture in his book and read each caption underneath. During the summer holidays after each Christmas Day, he read each article in his book once and a few articles many times. After the holidays had ended, he looked into the book only seldom, and only at a certain few pictures and captions. On the Christmas Day when he was in his twelfth year, his new book contained an article about certain old houses in England. He read the article only once. He did not doubt what his father had told him about the so-called great families who lived in the great houses of England: that those families had gained their houses and lands by robbery and murder or by driving pious monks from their monasteries in the age of the Tudors. The image of the white cattle in the long grass with the trees behind them might have appeared in his mind on several occasions during the first two years after he had become the owner of the book containing the picture of the cattle, so he supposed sometimes during the year mentioned in the first sentence of this piece of fiction, but he never afterwards remembered any of those occasions. During the year just mentioned, whenever the man most often mentioned in this piece of fiction foresaw the image of the white cattle and the long grass and the line of trees as appearing in his mind he foresaw that the image would appear just as it had appeared in his mind at a certain moment on a certain evening in the first year of the 1950s, while he was lying in his bed in his parents' house. Three months before that evening, he had performed for the first time the series of acts mentioned in the previous section of this piece of fiction. During the following three months, he had performed the series of acts on many evenings while he foresaw himself as performing the series of acts in the presence of one or another young woman in one or another secluded place out of doors at one or another time in the future by way of beginning to explain to the young woman certain details about himself. On the day before the evening when the image of the white cattle appeared in his mind in such a way that he would remember nearly thirty years later the image's appearing, he had confessed to a priest that he, the boy who became the man most often mentioned in this piece of fiction, had committed a certain sin on many occasions during the previous three months. Before absolving the boy, the priest warned him that he would be in danger of committing again in the future the sin that he had just confessed unless he could learn to take his pleasure from good and holy things. Late in the evening mentioned in the previous sentence, while the boy who had recently been absolved from his sins was lying in his bed, he prepared to cause to appear in his mind images of what he believed to be good and holy things, although he did not expect to be able to take any pleasure from those images. While the boy was thus preparing, there appeared in his mind the image of the white cattle that he remembered nearly thirty years later whenever he foresaw himself as preparing to write a certain piece of fiction.

During the years mentioned in the first sentence of this story, the man mentioned in that sentence was able to remember the caption under the picture of the white cattle in the book mentioned previously: *Survivors of an ancient herd—the wild white cattle of Uppington.* He was able to remember that the article surrounding the picture contained only a brief reference to the white cattle: one or another titled person kept on his estate a small herd of wild cattle of a variety no longer seen elsewhere. The man who remembered this remembered also that he had been reassured as a boy to think of the small and crowded and damaged land of England as containing somewhere inside it a tract of long grass and woodlands large enough for a herd of cattle to run wild in it, and that his feeling of reassurance had been a pleasurable feeling. Yet the man could not remember that he had not performed the series of acts mentioned previously on the same evening when he had tried to take his pleasure from images of good and holy things and when the image of the white cattle had appeared in his mind. The man could readily remember that he had performed the series of acts on many evenings, and sometimes at other times of day, during the years following the evening just mentioned. The man remembered in later years that he had been curious as a boy and afterwards as to where in England was Uppington, with its meadows of long grass and its woods where the white herd hid. The man had never travelled to England, but he might easily have looked into an atlas. Yet he preferred not to look, although he could not have explained why he so preferred until after he had become during the last years of the 1970s a student of a course for a diploma in humanities with a major in creative writing at a college of advanced education in an inner suburb of Melbourne and had enrolled in a unit called Fiction Writing: An Introduction and had heard on one of the evenings when he attended the weekly classes in the subject the lecturer in charge of the subject advising the class that a writer of fiction ought never to consult while writing or preparing to write any piece of fiction any reference book or any map and ought never to visit any library or any other so-called source of so-called facts or knowledge or information.

Certain views of certain valleys and mountains appear as though to a person high up on a mountainside. No road or building appears in any of the views, which are of forests and boulders and sky. The trees in the forests are grey-green in the foreground and dark blue in the background. Above the furthest visible mountain is a narrow band of grey-blue that might be further mountains still or heat-haze or storm clouds.

The mountains are part of the Australian Alps. The views appear to a man as he looks around from where he sits on the veranda of a large guest-house more than a hundred miles north-east of Melbourne. The man was formerly the man who looked for friends in a hilly district just beyond the outer north-eastern suburbs of Melbourne. The season is late summer. The year is in the mid-1960s. A young woman sits near the man on the veranda. The young woman is several years younger than the man and is his wife. She and he have been married for less than a week, after having been for a year engaged to be married. She and he first met in the office building mentioned in the first explanatory section of this piece of fiction, in which office building she has worked for seven years and he has worked for ten years, although the two have always worked on different floors of the building.

While the man stares from the veranda at the mountains and valleys, he foresees himself preparing to enter a clearing among trees. The man on the veranda supposes that the clearing lies about a hundred paces uphill from one or another of the walking paths that lead among the mountains and valleys around the guest house. The man supposes that he and his wife will walk on one or another of the walking paths on each day before they leave the guest-house. The man supposes further that he will persuade his wife, on several occasions if necessary, to leave one or more of the walking paths and to walk uphill in search of a place like the clearing that he has often foreseen himself preparing to enter. When the man on the veranda foresees himself and his wife as having entered the clearing that he has often seen in his mind, he foresees himself as seeing around him only trees and shrubbery and as hearing only loud clickings and buzzings of insects.

The man on the veranda of the guest-house hears in his mind a phrase that he read recently for the first time in a newspaper: *Swinging London*. He believes that persons in England younger than himself are behaving now, in the mid-1960s, somewhat as he had wanted to behave in the late 1950s and had sometimes tried to behave in the early 1960s. The man remembers, on the veranda, a film that he saw six months previously in a cinema in the city of Melbourne in the company of the young woman who would soon become his wife. For a few minutes during the film, he saw on the screen several images of parts of the naked body of a young woman. He had never previously seen such an image as part of any film. The film was set in England. The images of the naked woman appeared against a background that included images of a mansion and of green fields and clumps of trees in the country-side of England. Now, when the man sits on the veranda and hears in his mind the phrase mentioned above, he sees again in his mind the images from the film just mentioned and then he sees in his mind young persons travelling to the countryside of England from London and from other cities of England at weekends and during their recreation leave and doing in rooms of mansions or in corners of extensive gardens or of green fields series of acts such as he foresees himself preparing to do with his wife in the clearing mentioned earlier with all the mountains and valleys and forests of north-eastern Victoria around them while he jeers in his mind at the young persons with only the countryside of England around them.

A view of mostly level grey-green paddocks appears as it would appear to a person standing on the rotting boards of the veranda of a certain weatherboard cottage on a certain dairy-farm in the south-west of Victoria. In most of the view, the mostly level pad-docks reach back to the horizon and are marked only by scattered plantations of cypress trees, by the wooden posts of barbed-wire fences, and by a few weatherboard farmhouses. However, in one quarter of the view the paddocks reach back only a few hundred paces to a line of trees and scrub. In the middle distance of this quarter of the view, a herd of about seventy dairy cows is graz-ing. The cows are of many shades of red or brown, often broken by white.

The weatherboard cottage with the rotting veranda is provided rent-free by the owner of the farm for the share-farmer and his family. The share-farmer milks the cows twice daily on every day of the year and works between milking-times at maintaining the farm—all in return for one-third of the proceeds of the sale of the milk from the cows. The view from the veranda appears to a boy of no more than ten years. The boy, whose father is the share-farmer, will later become the young man who wears a certain shirt and tie in a certain image reported earlier. Whenever the boy looks at the view from the veranda, he looks most often at the line of trees and scrub. The owner of the farm and of two other farms nearby is a man aged about seventy who disregards many of the customs of the district. All the sub-dividing fences on the farm have fallen down, and the herd is free between milking-times to graze in any part of the farm or even to walk in among the trees and scrub. Each of the three farms mentioned above has a patch of bush and scrub left uncleared with a hut of corrugated iron in the thickest part. The owner of the three farms lives for a few months of each year in each of the three huts. The owner lives alone. He is a bachelor, the last alive of a family of which the sons all remained bachelors throughout their lives. The share-farmer and his family look out each morning from the veranda of their house towards the trees and scrub in the distance. If they see smoke rising above the trees, they know that the owner of the farm is living in his hut among the trees and scrub. No matter where the owner happens to be living, he arrives on horseback every few days to talk to the share-farmer about the running of the farm. When the owner leaves at the end of his visit, he often drives ahead of him with the help of his dog a cow that has come into season. The owner keeps his bulls on another of his farms where the fences have been maintained and the bulls can be secured. During his visits, the owner speaks politely to the share-farmer and his wife and children, but the boy mentioned above has heard from his father that the owner is an odd man who prefers his own company. The boy has never seen the owner's hut. One hot afternoon when he went out with the farm dogs to round up the cows and when he found the cows grazing near the line of trees and scrub, he walked a little way in among the trees and listened. He heard only the sounds of insects. While the boy listened, he imagined the old man as sitting on the veranda of his hut and reading from a book or a magazine.

The image of the line of trees and scrub will remind the boy in future not only of the imagined scene reported in the previous sequence but also of certain images connected with the following sequence of events.

In one of the first weeks after the boy and his family had begun to live on the dairy farm, a cow named Stockings was about to calve. The cow had been named for the white legs that contrasted with her red-brown body. On a certain morning, Stockings was not with the herd when the dogs brought the herd towards the milking-shed. After the milking, the boy's father explained to the boy that Stockings would have found a hiding-place in the patch of bush and scrub before she gave birth and would try to keep the calf hidden there until it could run beside her. Later on that day and on the following day, the boy saw the cow Stockings grazing alone near the trees and scrub. Next morning, the boy saw his father driving the cow and her calf in from the paddocks to a small yard near the milking-shed. Later on that day the calf, which was a bull-calf, was taken from the cow Stockings. A few days later, the calf was collected by a butcher's agent. By then, the boy was no longer interested in the calf or the cow, but for as long as the calf had remained hidden among the trees and scrub the boy had supposed that the calf might have become the first of a small herd that would survive out of sight of the paddocks and houses.

Irregular areas of pale shades of brown and pink and gold and green appear as they would appear to a man looking at a certain page of The Times Atlas of the World *and trying to find one or another detail that will enable him to see in his mind one or more images such as might appear to a person looking at one or another landscape in the district of England denoted by the part of the map in front of the man.*

The man looking at the page of the atlas is a mature-age student in an institution known as a college of advanced education in an inner suburb of Melbourne. The man, who was formerly the young man whose shirt and tie were mentioned in the first paragraph of this piece of fiction, has worked for more than twenty years in the same office building. For more than ten years, he has travelled on weekday evenings in a suburban train from the city to the outer south-eastern suburb where he lives with his wife and their two children, but during the past three years he has broken his journey homewards on two evenings of many weeks in order to attend classes at the institution mentioned above. The evening when he consults an atlas in the library of the institution, as reported above, is an evening in a certain year in the late 1970s.

The institution mentioned above was founded in a certain year in the early 1970s. Twenty years afterwards, the man most often mentioned in this piece of fiction would still describe the two years just mentioned and the few years between as the most exciting years of his life. In the year before the first of the years just mentioned, a certain political party was elected to form the federal government of the country where the man had lived throughout his life. This political party had been in opposition for more than twenty years, and the man and most of his friends found the result of the election in itself exciting. The man would recall twenty years afterwards that the policies of the new government had been exciting, especially their policies in education which, as he understood them, offered to adults such as himself a free tertiary education with an emphasis or retraining. He had left school in the second-last year of his secondary education and had never expected to study at a university or any similar institution. In fact, the college where he enrolled in the mid-1970s in no way resembled any of his images of a university. The buildings stood along a side street with no lawns or grounds around them. When he went into the student union building on the day of his enrolment, the person who handed him booklets of information was a woman of about thirty who was breast-feeding a baby, and when he was taken on a guided tour of the college the person who guided him and his party was a man of about thirty who told the new students that he had worked at twelve different jobs, the most recent being as a labourer in a piggery, and that he intended to work as a scriptwriter for a television production company as soon as he had finished his diploma in humanities with a major in creative writing.

The chief character of this piece of fiction, when he enrolled in a course for a diploma in humanities with a major in creative writing, had written no fiction since the year in the late 1960s when his wife had had to give up her job and stay at home to look after the first of his and her two children. Before then, he had taken out one or another of his folders of notes and early drafts on one or another evening each week and had added or emended one or two paragraphs, but after his wife had stopped working he had had to find a second job. He began to work in the early mornings for the newsagency in his suburb, counting out the bundles of newspapers for the delivery boys and then driving parcels of papers to depots on street corners for the boys to pick up on their rounds. He excused himself from writing during the years when he worked at the two jobs, since he had to go to bed early on six evenings of each week. He could not have enrolled as an evening college student while he was working at two jobs, but his children had started at school by the mid-1970s, and his wife had begun to work part-time. Even so, she would not have agreed to his giving up his second job and studying in the evenings if he had not persuaded her that a diploma in humanities would qualify him for more senior positions in the office building mentioned previously.

In his first year as a student of creative writing, the chief character of this piece of fiction had to enrol in units that included short assignments in technical writing, verse writing, scriptwriting, and fiction writing. He completed these units without distinction under a teacher who told his students in the first week that he was not himself a published writer but would prepare them to meet the distinguished writers who would teach them in subsequent years.

The chief character of this piece of fiction enrolled in the second year of his studies in only the two units An Introduction to Fiction Writing A and B. Even before his first classes, he began to make notes for the pieces of short fiction that he would have to write during the year. He believed he might be about to learn at last some technique the lack of which had hindered him as a writer for nearly twenty years. When he opened one of his folders of a morning in the train on his way to work, he had only to add a sentence to one or another paragraph of notes in order to feel somewhat as he had felt as a young man wearing a shirt and tie of provocative colours and reading *Ulysses*. As a young man, however, he had thought of his becoming a writer as leading him to places far from the suburbs of Melbourne: he had seen himself being stared at in cafés in Europe or even in hotels in the hills north-east of Melbourne. As a mature-age student aged nearly forty, he foresaw that he would spend the rest of his working life in an office building in Melbourne and he expected from writing only that it should make him feel somewhat distinguished from other persons in the office building or in the suburb where he lived, as though he had once seen something that the others only wondered about.

The teacher of the units mentioned above was a shabbily dressed man in his fifties. Most of his students were puzzled by him or disliked him and looked forward to taking the third-year units An Advanced Course in Fiction Writing A and B. The teacher of these units was a woman in her thirties whose two books of short stories had each won a literary award and who was often interviewed by the literary editors of newspapers and other journalists. The second-year students had heard from more senior students that the woman began her first class each year with the statement that all writing was a political act and that she continually urged her students to submit their work for publication or to arrange public readings of their work. The shabbily dressed man spoke to his students at their first class as follows. The best service he could perform for them was to persuade them to give up writing fiction as soon as they had finished his course—or even before then. The writing of fiction was something that a certain sort of person had to do in order to explain himself or herself to an imagined parent or an imagined loved one or an imagined god. He himself had

had two novels published more than ten years before but had had nothing published since then and had no intention of writing so much as a sentence of fiction during the remainder of his life. He had stopped writing fiction after having been shown a sign. He had had to write or to prepare to write fiction in order to be shown the sign, but having been shown the sign he no longer wished to write fiction. The shabbily dressed man then said to his class that he had probably said too much to them already and had probably confused them thoroughly. He then said that their first class was over, that their classes for the next month were cancelled, and that they should go away and write their first piece of fiction and deliver it to him three weeks later so that he could prepare photocopies for the workshop classes that would occupy him and them for the rest of the year.

The chief character of this piece of fiction wrote as his first assignment for the shabbily dressed man a piece of fiction whose chief character was a man who lived alone in a hut in a patch of bush in a corner of a dairy farm and had never married or kept company with women or girls. The assignment was returned to the man who had written it with no editorial marks and with no critical annotations but with the outsized inscription 66% in red ink at the foot of the last page.

Talking with classmates in the cafeteria before the first of the workshop classes, the chief character of this piece of fiction learned that the shabbily dressed man was well known for refusing to write comments on his students' assignments. Some students said he was an alcoholic whose hand shook so badly that he could not use it for writing. Others said that he was merely lazy. Still others said that he was afraid of teachers of creative writing in other institutions reading anything that he might have written by way of comment on his students' work.

During the first of the workshop classes, the shabbily dressed man explained to his students that he calculated the mark for each of their assignments by observing what percentage of the text he was able to read before deciding that he wanted to read no more. Yet the man did not actually say that he had not read all the assignments to the end, and when he commented on each assignment in class—after each of the students had taken his or her turn to speak—he said nothing harsh. When the chief character of this piece of fiction heard the shabbily dressed man speaking to the class, he, the chief character, thought the man sounded sorry for his students, as though they were suffering from something that he himself had once suffered from but had long since recovered from.

Before the chief character of this piece of fiction had begun to write his second piece of fiction for the course he had enrolled in, he understood that he had fallen in love with a woman who was one of his classmates. When he decided this, the chief character had never spoken in private to the woman, although he had sat near her sometimes in a small group of students in the cafeteria before class. He knew about her only that she worked in an office building by day and that she spoke with a slight English accent. He guessed that she was five to ten years younger than himself.

What seemed to the chief character the chief cause of his having fallen in love with the woman mentioned above was the piece of short fiction that the woman had written as her first assignment. Most of the class seemed to find the piece better than the average standard of the pieces read in class, but the chief character of this piece of fiction wrote on his copy as a final comment before passing the copy to the author that he was deeply impressed. The person in the class who seemed most in agreement with this opinion was the shabbily dressed man, who said in class that he looked forward to reading the next piece by the same author—something he had never previously said to the class.

The woman mentioned above wore a ring that the chief character of this piece of fiction supposed was a wedding ring, although she had never mentioned a husband or children when she talked in the cafeteria. Yet, even the chief character had lately noticed changes among the people in the office building where he

worked and the suburb where he lived; even he had heard of marriage break-ups and open marriages and of couples moving in together without marrying. A number of the men and women in
his class were separated or divorced, and at least one affair seemed
to have begun among his classmates. But during the time when
the action of this story takes place, the chief character seldom
wondered whether or not he would have with the woman he was
in love with what would be called by other persons an affair or
whether or not he would become estranged from his wife or the
woman from her husband, if she had a husband.

During the time mentioned in the previous sentence, whenever
the chief character thought of the woman he had fallen in love with
he thought often of certain details in the piece of fiction the author of which was the woman and the chief details of which are
as follows.

The chief character is a young woman working at her first job
in an office building in a certain provincial city in England. The
time is the mid-1960s. The young woman spends much of her time
foreseeing herself as a painter of pictures. The young woman spent
her childhood in a small house in a suburb of the city mentioned
above but spent much of her time as a child foreseeing herself as
living in a mansion among certain hills that she saw far away whenever she looked from a certain hill in the suburb where she lived
towards the countryside beyond the suburb. The chief character
meets in the office building where she works a man who has, so he
says, several painters of pictures among his friends. The chief character, who has had few dealings with men, soon believes that she
has fallen in love with the man just mentioned. After the chief character and the man have kept company for several weeks, the man
invites the chief character to a party where, so he says, the guests
will include some of the painters mentioned above. The last paragraph of the story reports the man as driving the chief character
towards the party which, so the man has told her, will take place
in a mansion in the countryside beyond the suburbs of the city
where he and she live. The chief character, who has been looking

out through the windows of the man's car, understands that she is being taken into the hills mentioned earlier. By now, darkness has fallen. The chief character notices that the lights of houses are farther apart than she had expected. She supposes that the countryside is less settled than she had expected. Even the large house or mansion that she and the man approach at last has fewer lights showing than she might have expected in a mansion where a party was taking place with many painters of pictures among the guests.

The piece of fiction summarised above caused the chief character of this piece of fiction, so he believed, to fall in love, but the piece of fiction caused him also to prepare to write as his second piece of fiction for the course that he had enrolled in a piece that would explain certain matters to the woman-author. While he was so preparing, the chief character arrived early one evening at the institution where he was a student and went to the library in order to consult the atlas mentioned earlier. He found on a certain page of the atlas a hatched area denoting a city with the same name as the city mentioned in the previous paragraph. He then looked in widening circles around the hatched area. While he looked, he tried to see in his mind more clearly than he had previously seen them certain details of countryside and of a certain mansion in the countryside. While he looked, he noticed that the areas that he was looking at on the map were marked by fewer names of towns and villages than he might have expected. Then, in an area the colour of which denoted that the area was hilly, he saw a name that is part of the title of this piece of fiction.

Trees can be seen in the foreground. Hills can be seen in the background. Sounds of insects can be heard. A man and a woman sit together. The man talks to the woman.

Sometimes the man who foresees the details above as appearing in his mind foresees himself as leaving the course quietly in the way that several of his classmates have already left. Sometimes he foresees himself as explaining to the shabbily dressed man that his, the chief character's, next piece of fiction will be submitted late because its author is experiencing difficulties of a personal nature. Sometimes he seems about to foresee himself as disregarding all considerations other than that he must write a certain piece of fiction and after that piece many other pieces of fiction. Sometimes he seems about to foresee himself as understanding that he has already written all the fiction that could have been required of him.

In Far Fields

During the years when I earned my living as a teacher of fiction-writing in a university, one or another of my students would sometimes call on me in my office and would claim that she could not write the pieces of fiction that I required her to write and would give as the reason for this that she did not understand what I meant by the word *fiction*. I used the words *her* and *she* in the previous sentence only because three-quarters of my students of fiction-writing were females.

While I was writing the previous sentence, I saw in my mind an image of the view from the chair that I used as my chair in one of the rooms that I used as my office during the years when I was a teacher in a university. The view was of part of the room as it would have appeared to me if ever I had been visited in my office by a certain young woman who was one of my students for two years but never visited me during those years. The young woman never visited me or asked me to explain what I meant by the word *fiction*, but she wrote as the last of her assignments while she was my student a piece of fiction that earned from me the highest numerical mark on a scale of 1 to 100 that I gave to any piece of fiction during the years mentioned above.

While I was writing the previous paragraph, I understood that the young woman mentioned there was listening to the words of a man who was talking about the writing of fiction. I could not see any image of the man, and I could not hear in my mind any words that the man was speaking, but I understood that the man was in the room and that the young woman was listening to the words of the man. I understood these things in the same way that I understand many of the matters that I seem afterwards to have seen and to have heard while dreaming.

While I was writing the previous paragraph, I understood that the young woman mentioned there could not hear any words from the man mentioned there but that she was aware of what the man could well have spoken to her in the same way that I am aware of what could well have been spoken to me by images of persons that I seem afterwards to have been aware of while dreaming.

During the years mentioned in the first paragraph of this piece of fiction, I would sometimes say to one or another of my students in my office that any person who was paid to teach other persons how to write pieces of fiction should be able, in the presence of any number of those other persons, to write the whole of a previously unwritten piece of fiction and to explain at the same time what had seemingly caused each sentence of the piece to be written as it had been written. I would then write a sentence on a sheet of paper. I would then read the sentence aloud to my student. I would then explain to my student that the sentence was a report of a detail of an image in my mind. I would explain further that the image was not an image that I had seen in my mind recently for the first time or an image that I saw in my mind only at long intervals but an image that I saw often in my mind. I would explain that the image I had begun to write about was connected by strong feelings to other images in my mind.

I would then go on to tell my student that my mind consisted only of images and feelings; that I had studied my mind for many years and had found in it nothing but images and feelings; that a diagram of my mind would resemble a vast and intricate map with images for its small towns and with feelings for the roads through the grassy countryside between the towns. Whenever I had seen in my mind the image that I had begun to write about just then, so I would say to my student, I had felt the strong feelings leading from that image far out into the grassy countryside of my mind towards other images, even though I might not yet have seen any of those other images. I did not doubt, so I would tell my student, that one after another detail of one after another of those other images would appear in my mind while I went on writing about the image that I had begun to write about on the sheet of paper that was before me.

Having mentioned the sheet of paper, I would make as though to write a second sentence on it but instead would move the sheet to one side and would place a blank sheet in front of me. I would then write a sentence on the blank sheet. I would then read this sentence aloud to my student. I would then explain to my student that the sentence was a report of a detail of an image distinct from the image whose details I had already begun to report. The second image, so I would explain, had occurred to me while I was writing on the first sheet of paper. A number of images had occurred to me during that time, I would explain, just as they might have occurred to me if I had been performing any other task, but only the one image had caused me to feel that it was connected by feelings to the image that I had already begun to write about.

With the second sheet of paper still in front of me, I would prepare to write a report of another of the details of the second of the images that belonged in my piece of fiction. But then I would tell my student that I had already seen in my mind a third image that seemed to be connected by feelings to the second image or to the first image or to each image by a separate route. In fact, I might not yet have seen such an image, but I would tell my student that I had seen the image so that she would understand that the images belonging in a piece of fiction sometimes appeared so fast and so profusely that the writer of the fiction might despair of being able to report the details of the images before they disappeared again into his or her mind. I would then tell my student that I had sometimes as a younger writer despaired in this way but that I had learned in time that the images and the feelings in my mind were always in their rightful places in my mind and that I would always find my way among them. Sometimes, having told my student this, I would feel for a moment urged to tell her something further. I would feel urged to tell her that the patterns of images and feelings in my mind had become in time more extensive and more intricate whereas the thing that I called my body (or that I should have called, perhaps, the image of my body) had been decaying, causing me to suppose that my mind might go on existing when my body no longer existed. (As to the question whether or not I myself may go on existing after my body no longer exists, the person writing these words cannot answer until he has learned whether or not the entity denoted by the word *I* earlier in this paragraph is in the place denoted by the words *my mind* earlier in this paragraph. As to the question that might have occurred just now to someone reading this piece of fiction: who is the writer of these words if not the entity denoted by the word *I* in the previous sentence?—only a reader of this piece of fiction may answer that question and only after having looked into his or her own mind, which is the only place where the personage exists who is most aptly denoted by the words *the implied author of this piece of fiction*. I learned the term *implied author* from the book *The Rhetoric of Fiction*, by Wayne C. Booth, which was first published by the University of Chicago Press in 1961. Certain parts of that book helped me during the years when I worked as a teacher of fiction. Whenever during those years I used such a term as *implied author* or *implied reader*, I seemed to be explaining to my students what took place in my mind while I wrote or read a piece of fiction. But these matters cannot be explained in so few words, and any reader of these pages who has read certain parts of the book mentioned above will not accept my answer to the question above and will assume that the flesh-and-blood author of this piece must be well aware of at least one implied author who has not been mentioned previously in this text.)

I would never tell my student about the matter mentioned in the previous paragraph, my reason being that I did not know whether or not my student was a person of good will. I cannot decide whether or not a person is of good will by any other means than by reading a piece of fiction written by the person. As to the question: why have I written about the matter mentioned in the previous paragraph when I do not know whether or not the readers of these paragraphs are persons of good will?—these paragraphs are part of a piece of fiction, and the writer of these words is safe forever from readers of ill will. As to the question: what had I to fear from a person of ill will who had learned from me the matter previously mentioned?—I had to fear that my supposing that my mind might go on existing when my body no longer existed would cause my student to suppose that my mind contained an image of a person named God or of a place named heaven or of something called eternity or something called infinity whereas each of these words, whenever I hear it or read it, causes me only to see in my mind the image of grassy countryside that I see whenever I look at the farthest visible parts of my mind.

All the images in my mind were in their rightful places, so I would tell my student, and knowing this, I did not feel panic or despair whenever the details of separate images occurred to me in such a way that I had to write in succession on two or three or more sheets of paper before I had reported more than one or two of the many details that I would have to report of the image that I had begun to write about on the first of my sheets of paper. The images were in their rightful places, and I would find my way in time from image to image, but I did not believe that the order in which the images first occurred to me must be the order in which they were fixed in my mind. I would then remind my student that a diagram of the images in my mind would resemble a cluster of small towns as marked on a map. I would then take from a drawer in my desk six manila folders that I kept there for this sort of occasion. Each folder was of a different colour. I would pick up the nearest at hand of the folders and would place inside it the first of the sheets of paper on which I had begun to report the first of the details of the images mentioned previously. I would then place each of my other sheets of paper into one or another of the other folders. (The reader should suppose that I had by then on my desk six sheets of paper, each with at least a phrase written on it.) The colours of the folders were important, I would tell my student. Like many people, I would tell her, I connected each colour in the world with a different feeling, but unlike many people, perhaps, I saw all the images in my mind as coloured. I was therefore able to decide which of the folders now on my desk was of the most appropriate colour for each of the sheets of paper that I wanted to store in them. I might then change one or more of the sheets from one folder to another, and while doing this, I might write on the front of each coloured folder a word, a phrase, or a sentence.

While I wrote on the front of each folder, I might explain to my student that some of the words that I was then writing might become the title of the whole piece of fiction. I would certainly explain to my student at some time during my instruction that I could hardly begin to write any piece of fiction before I had found its title; that the title of a piece of fiction ought to come from deep inside the piece; that the title of a piece of fiction should have several meanings, and that the reader should not learn these meanings until almost the whole of the piece had been read; that none of the titles of any piece of fiction written by me contained a noun denoting an abstract entity; and that I had not for as long as I had been a teacher of fiction-writing read any published piece of fiction with a title containing a noun denoting an abstract entity.

The piece of fiction of which this paragraph is the twelfth was not written in the presence of any of my students, but if it had been so written, each of the following six passages might have been written on one each of six manila folders before even the first draft of this paragraph had been written. *The far fields of the* Times Literary Supplement*; Books are a load of crap; The man with his chin in his hands; Welcome to Florida; The Homer of the Insects; The man with the coloured folders.* The colours of the six manila folders might have been respectively green, red, blue, orange, yellow, and buff or plain. If I had written in the presence of a student the words mentioned above on the folders mentioned above, I would then have picked up all six folders, holding each so as not to let fall any sheet of paper from inside it, and would have walked about the open space on the carpet at the centre of my office while I placed one after another of the folders at one or another point on the carpet but with no thought as to where I was placing each folder. If I had placed the folders as mentioned, I would then have told my student that the cluster of small towns in the expanse of grassy countryside suggested by the folders as they lay on the carpet might be approached from any of a number of directions, and that a person who had approached the cluster by way of one or another small town might then travel throughout the cluster from one small town to another by any of a number of different routes before he or she reached what had once been for him or her the far side of the cluster and looked towards further grassy countryside. If I had told my student this, I would then have walked away from the folders and would have sat down again at my desk as though I was about to begin writing while the folders and their contents were still lying on the floor behind me. If I had done this, I would have expected my student to understand that I might sometimes write about certain images as though I only remembered having seen them or as though I had only imagined having seen them. Or, instead of leaving all the folders on the floor after I had told my student what is mentioned above, I would have picked up one or another of the folders and would have placed it on my desk. I would then have picked up the remaining folders and would have thrust them into the drawer of my desk where I keep used envelopes and folders. I would then have sat down at my desk as though I was about to begin writing with only the one folder at hand. While I sat there, I would have hoped that my student saw in her mind a small town surrounded by grassy countryside with no end in sight or some other place surrounded by other places with no end in sight and that she saw herself as keeping to that small town or to that other place during the remainder of her life and as reporting detail after detail of image after image that seemed to surround her with no end in sight.

At some time while I wrote or prepared to write in my office, I would remind my student that what I was writing or preparing to write consisted or would consist only of sentences. At some time after I had written a number of sentences, I would point out to my student that the subject of nearly every sentence I had written was a noun or a pronoun or a noun phrase denoting a person. If I had been writing this piece of fiction in the presence of a student, I might have pointed out that this is the eleventh consecutive sentence that has such a subject. If any student had asked me to explain what I had told her about sentences, I would have told her, whether or not I believed her to be a person of good will, that I wrote fiction in order to learn the meaning of certain images in my mind; that I considered a thing to have meaning if the thing seemed to be connected with another thing; that even a simple sentence established a connection between the thing called its subject and the thing called its predicate; that I believed a writer of fiction with a better vantage point than mine could have composed a single far-reaching sentence with clauses to the number of the total of simple sentences and of clauses of all kinds in my published pieces of fiction plus one further clause to establish a connection such as I would never be able to establish, but that I would try to read such a sentence only if the subject of its main clause was a noun or a pronoun or a noun phrase denoting a person.

After my student had watched me writing and had heard me

talking for some time, she would assure me that she had watched and heard enough. Before she left my office, I would tell her, as a last piece of advice, that she need not have learned the meaning of every image reported in a piece of fiction before she had finished writing the final draft. Nearly every piece of my fiction, I would tell her, included a report of an image whose connections I did not discover until long after the piece had been finished. Sometimes these connections had not appeared until I was writing a later piece of fiction, and then I would understand that the image in the earlier piece of fiction was connected with an image in the later piece. If I had ever had in front of me while I talked to a student in my office the first draft of the first five hundred words and more of the piece of fiction of which this paragraph is the fourteenth, I might have told her that the image whose details were reported in the second, third, and fourth paragraphs of that draft, which paragraphs have the same numbering in the final draft, seemed not truly connected with the other images reported in any of the six folders that would have been lying on my desk while I spoke. I might then have told my student that the true meaning of the image just mentioned might still not have appeared to me even while I was writing the final draft of the final paragraph of the report of the images reported in the folder in which that image was first reported, and that if the true meaning had not so appeared, I would report this as the last detail to be reported in the last sentence of that draft.

The far fields of the Times Literary Supplement

On a certain morning in my twenty-third year, when I was writing the first draft of what I hoped would be my first published piece of fiction—a novel of more than 200,000 words—I approached a young man who was only a year or two older than myself, to judge from his looks, but who had seemed to me whenever I had visited Cheshire's Bookshop in Little Collins Street during the previous three years the most knowledgeable of all the sales assistants in

the shop. I spoke to the young man the words that I had been rehearsing for a week. I told him that I was a regular buyer of books,
mostly of fiction and poetry, and that I learned about the latest
published works by reading every Saturday the Literary Supplement in the *Age*, but that I felt isolated from the world of English
and European literature. I then asked the young man if he could
recommend a publication that would keep me well informed about
contemporary fiction and poetry overseas and if he could arrange
through the subscriptions department of his bookshop a subscription for me to the publication.

The young man did not turn me away, and I felt grateful to him
at once. He answered my inquiry, but he spoke as though he was
wearied by having to explain to me something that was common
knowledge among the people he mixed with. At the time, I was
far from supposing that he might have learned his way of speaking from persons who seemed to him as superior as he seemed to
me. Three years later, I enrolled for the first time at the University
of Melbourne as an evening student of first-year English and heard
the same way of speaking among most of the tutors and some of
the lecturers. (Three years later again, when I was enrolled in third-
year English, I saw the man from Cheshire's Bookshop coming
out of an evening tutorial in second-year English.) The young
man looked past me from where he stood behind the counter in
the bookshop while he told me that the premier literary periodical in the world was generally acknowledged to be the *London
Magazine*. I was disappointed to learn that this was only a quar-
terly periodical, but I paid for a subscription and looked forward
to receiving my first copy by surface mail some weeks or months
later.

When my first copy arrived, I saw at once that the *London
Magazine* was not what I needed, but I sat down to read it through.
The first piece was called "The Golden Bowl" and was by a Tony
Tanner. I believed that I was about to read a piece of fiction. I
hardly knew at that time what literary criticism was, and I had
never heard of Henry James or of any of his books. For as long as

I have read, I have been attracted by the promise of certain titles of works and especially by any title containing an adjective denoting a colour. As I began to read, I was imagining the details of an object shaped like a chalice or like the Melbourne Cup and appearing against a background of green fields such as I had seen in illustrations of Glastonbury. I was baffled by the first few paragraphs that I read, and I gave up as soon as I understood that I was reading someone's comments on someone else's book.

I would not have dared to go back to the young man in the bookshop to complain about his choice of a literary periodical, but I set about finding a better. Two years later, I saw in the literary supplement of the *Age* an advertisement for the *Times Literary Supplement*, and I took out a subscription.

For nearly twenty years, I read every page of every issue of the *TLS*. I even read the advertisements for bookshops ("Russica and Slavica bought and sold") and for professorships in West Africa and librarianships in Malta or Singapore. I read the letters to the editor, although I sometimes heard from the prose the same tone of voice that I had first heard from the young man in the bookshop and although I was often unable to understand what was at issue in the many disputes between letter-writers. I admired the intricate addresses of many of the authors who wrote in defence of their books ("The Old Mill Cottage, St John's Lane, Oakover, Shotcombe, near Dudbury, Suffolk") and imagined those persons as living from the royalties of their books in remote green landscapes. For fifteen of the twenty years mentioned above, I cut out book reviews and essays and poems and a few letters, all of which I intended to read again in the future. One day in the late 1970s, when the pieces I had cut out had filled a drawer of one of my filing cabinets and when the residents of the city where I live had not yet been forbidden to burn waste matter in their backyards, I burned all the cuttings that I had kept from the *TLS*, having read none of them since I had filed them, and having decided that I was unlikely to read any of them during the next fifteen years.

During the twenty years or so mentioned above, I bought many thousands of dollars' worth of books, mostly books of fiction, as a result of my having read reviews of the books in the *TLS*. Whenever a parcel of books arrived from my bookseller, I felt that I was a person of exceptional discernment as I opened the parcel and put the books on my shelves. I bought books other than those reviewed in the *TLS*, and each year the number of books that I bought was far greater than the number of books that I read, even though I read part of a book every day, but for most of the twenty years mentioned above I intended to read at least once every book that I owned. During most of those years, I would have said that I remembered some of the books that I had read far more clearly than I remembered others. During most of those years, I would have said that some of the books I had read were inferior or much inferior to others, but I had always read to the last page of any book that I had begun to read. One day in the early 1980s, I decided not to go on reading the book that I was then reading. On the same day, I decided that I would not in future read to the end of any book that I did not wish to go on reading. On the same day, I decided further that I had read in the past to the end of many a book when I ought not to have done so.

The book that I was reading when I made the decisions just mentioned was a book of fiction that had been reviewed most favourably in the *TLS*. The author of the book was an Englishman who was himself a reviewer for the *TLS*. One of his earlier books had been awarded a prize on account of its merit. The book that I had decided not to go on reading had been published by a London publishing house whose distinctive logo was on the spines of many of my books. I had often walked into the room where most of my books were displayed and had tried to look around the room as though I was a visitor seeing it for the first time and had persuaded myself that the first thing such a visitor would notice was the number of books with a certain distinctive logo on their spines.

After I had written the previous paragraph, I went to one of my bookshelves and took down a book bearing the logo mentioned in the previous sentence. As I reached for the book, I was aware that I had supposed for the past thirty years and more that the logo was an image of an object that I called in my mind an urn with leaves and flowers trailing down from the sides of it. While I looked just now at the logo on the spine of my book, I understood that I had seen for the past thirty years and more as details of leaves and flowers two letters of the alphabet.

After I had made the decisions mentioned above, I decided not to put the book by the Englishman back in its place on my shelves. I then decided that I no longer wanted to have the book in my possession. I then decided that the book just mentioned was not the only book of mine that I no longer wanted to possess. I then began to look at the spine of one after another of the books that I had read during a period of nearly twenty years before that day. I found those books with the help of the notebook in which I had listed for nearly twenty years all the books that I read and the dates on which I finished reading the books. While I looked at each spine, I tried to remember one or more words from the book or, failing that, one or more of the images that had appeared in my mind while I read the book or, failing that, one or more of the feelings that I had felt while I read the book or, failing that, one or more of the details that I remembered from the mornings or afternoons or evenings when I read the book or from the places where I had been while I read it. If I could remember while I stared at the spine of a book none of the things mentioned just above, then I removed the book from my shelves.

Some books kept their places on my shelves as a result of my remembering a few words from their texts. For example, I remembered from somewhere in the text of *The Good Soldier Švejk*, by Jaroslav Hašek, which I had read twelve years before, the phrase "on the mournful plains of East Galicia" and also the Serbian curses "Fuck the world!," "Fuck the Virgin Mary!," and "Fuck God!" Some books kept their places on my shelves as a result of my remembering one or more images that had passed through my mind while I read the books. For example, I remembered having seen in my mind sixteen years before, while I read one or another passage in *Nostromo*, by Joseph Conrad, an image of a walled mansion surrounded by grasslands. Some books kept their places on my shelves as a result of my remembering one or another feeling that I had felt while I read them. For example, I remembered having felt seventeen years before, while I read *Auto-da-fé*, by Elias Canetti, a desire to write at some time in the future a piece of fiction about a man who preferred his library to all other places. Some books kept their places on the shelves as a result of my remembering one or more details from the time when I read the book or the place where I read it. For example, I remembered having read twelve years before in *Epitaph of a Small Winner*, by Machado de Assis, a passage reporting the arrival of a butterfly through a window into the room where the writer of the narrative was writing while I was travelling in a train through the suburbs of Melbourne and while the doors and the windows of the train were open because the time was afternoon and the season was summer and while specks of dust were being blown onto the pages of the book in my hands and while I would stop following the narrative from time to time in order to observe the writer's way of interrupting his narrative from time to time in order to report one or another detail from the time when he was writing or the place where he was writing.

The exercise described above occupied for more than two weeks the time that I would otherwise have spent in reading books from my shelves. At the end of the two weeks and more, I calculated that I had stood in front of the spines of more than nine hundred books and that I had removed from my shelves a few more than three hundred. When I had begun the exercise described above, I had intended to remove from my house all of the books that I would have removed from my shelves when I had finished the exercise, but when I saw the three hundred lying all around the floor and the many gaps that they had left on the shelves, I decided to give the three hundred one more chance. During the next few days, I picked up one after another of the three hundred and let it fall open in my hands. I then began to read from one or the other of the pages lying open. I read always from about the middle of the page to the end but never past the end. If, while I read, I felt the least desire to read at some time in the future any page or pages of the book other than the page I was then reading, bearing in mind that I had not yet begun to read for the first time many of the books on my shelves and that I had already been reading books for more years than I would be reading them in the future if I lived a life of average length, I would put the book back in its place on my shelves. If I did not feel such a desire, I would put the book on the floor.

After I had performed the exercise described just above, I counted a few more than a hundred books still on the floor. I then cut my name from where I had written it on the flyleaf of each of these books. I then stacked the hundred and more books in cardboard cartons ready to be removed from the house. I had never previously removed any book from my house. Even duplicate copies were kept in a cupboard to be given in the future to my children.

While I had been performing the exercise described above, I had intended to take the discarded books to one or another second-hand bookshop and to sell as many as the proprietor wanted to buy and to give him or her the remainder. But when the books were in the cardboard cartons, I imagined a certain sort of young person standing in the future in the bookshop where my discarded books would be on the shelves. The young person would be the sort of person that I had been when I bought on the advice of the young man in Cheshire's Bookshop a subscription to the *London Magazine*. After I had imagined the young person in the second-hand bookshop just mentioned, I prepared to take the cartons of books to Fairfield.

During the years when I had lived in the suburb where I lived, I had taken each week a parcel of wastepaper and cardboard in the boot of my car from my house to the nearby suburb of Fairfield. At Fairfield a chute had been installed at the side of a large paper-manufacturing plant. Down this chute the people from many suburbs around threw their wastepaper. As soon as my children were old enough, they used to go with me on Sunday mornings and help me throw our wastepaper down the chute. I would occasionally hear one of the children say of some drawing he or she had abandoned or of some school exercise book that had been filled that it ought to be taken to Fairfield. For many years, the children would have known nothing else about Fairfield than that wastepaper was dumped there.

When I dumped at Fairfield the discarded books mentioned above, my children had reached an age when they no longer cared to travel in my car for pleasure, but even if one or both of them had wanted to come with me on the days when I dumped the books, I would not have allowed it. I had decided that the books deserved to be dumped, but I would still not have wanted my children to see books—many of them hard-covered books with brightly coloured dust-jackets—being thrown down the chute at Fairfield. I wrote the word *days* in the first sentence of this paragraph because I did not dump all of the books together. The chute at Fairfield seems always to have at least one car parked beside it with a person carrying cartons from the car to the dumping-place. I did not want to be seen dumping books. One carton was all that I could safely dump each week without being noticed. I was even wary of the workmen who came from time to time with forklift vehicles to clear away the dumped matter. If I dumped more than one box of books on any one day, so I thought, I increased the chance of my being seen by some workman who would then leap from his seat on his vehicle and hurry to collect the books in some empty dumped carton and who would hail me as though I must have made some terrible mistake.

The discarded books mentioned above were the first books that I removed from my shelves, let alone from my house, but I have dumped other books at Fairfield since my first book-dumping there. During the years since then, I have come to expect more from the books that I begin to read. I buy many fewer books than I used to buy. I seldom buy a book for no other reason than that I have read a favourable review of it, and not since the early 1980s have I bought a book simply as a result of having read a favourable review in the *TLS*. During the last ten years, I have come to expect not only that something of the experience of reading a book should stay with me but that the writing of the book should seem to have cost the writer much effort and that the sentences of the book should seem to have been composed so that the prose is different from the prose of newspapers and magazines.

The books that I have dumped at Fairfield in recent years have included a few that had been on my shelves for some time until I found them wanting. Occasionally, I have judged books for a literary award and have been allowed to keep my copy of each book entered. Most of the books that have been allotted to me on such occasions have been thrown down the chute at Fairfield. As a teacher of writing, I sometimes receive through the mail an unsolicited book from a publisher whose salespersons suppose that I require my students to read certain texts. Sometimes an author himself or herself sends me his or her latest book. Some of the books that I receive in these ways are taken to Fairfield soon afterwards, although I would never be so harsh as to tell the sender of any such book what I had done with it.

Nowadays I read fewer books than in past years, and many that I read are books that I have read at least once previously. Nowadays I do not buy a book until I have first looked into its pages.

I still subscribe to the *TLS*, but I read in each issue only the few pages that interest me, and I seldom read the reviews of books of fiction. As soon as I have read what I have wanted to read in an edition of the *TLS*, I throw it into the carton that my wife and I call the Fairfield box. One day recently, a visitor to our house—a man who is an author of published fiction and who has a room full of books in his house—tried to persuade me that I ought to keep each issue of the *TLS* on some of the empty shelves in the rooms made vacant after my children had left home. After the visitor had left, I tried to remember words that I had read in the *TLS* during the twenty-eight years since I had first become a subscriber or any other details that I remembered in connection with any passage that I had read in any issue. The following paragraphs report all that I remembered.

At some time in the late 1960s or the early 1970s, the front page and part of the second page was given over to a review of an edition in either the French or the English language of the diaries of a parish priest who had lived and died in the eighteenth century in the countryside of France. The man had lived an unexceptional life and was seemingly no different from hundreds of other parish priests in the countryside of France in the years not long before the Revolution. However, he had written a diary that was kept in secret during his lifetime but was made public after his death—as he had almost certainly intended it should be. The diary revealed that the man was an atheist who hated the Church whose minister he was. He hated the Church for being, as it seemed to him, an ally of the oppressive nobility. The man who celebrated mass and prayed for the king each day wrote that he would have spat on the Founder of Christianity if he had existed and that he dreamed of a day when the peasants of France would rise up and kill their tyrannical rulers.

At some time in the late 1970s, I began to read an essay translated from the French language. I had never previously heard of the author, but I have seen his name in print from time to time since the day when I saw his essay in the *TLS*. As I write these words, I cannot recall the first name of the author. His surname is Derrida. I read only a short way into the essay before finding it incomprehensible. And yet, I have always remembered one sentence: *To write is to go in search*.

I cannot remember when I read a certain poem by a poet I had first become interested in during the 1960s: Philip Larkin. The speaker in the poem claimed to work all day and to get half-drunk at night and to wake in the early hours and to understand that he would one day die. I came close to cutting out this poem from the pages of the *TLS* in the way that I had cut out many items years earlier, as mentioned previously. What kept me from cutting out the poem was its title, which I took to be a word in the French language and which I considered pretentious as a title for a poem. I had never previously seen the word and I cannot recall having seen the word since, even though I may have read the word and even an explanation of its meaning in English in the pages of my copy of one or more of *The Collected Poems of Philip Larkin*, *The Selected Letters of Philip Larkin*, or *Philip Larkin: A Writer's Life*.

No more than a year after the death of the critic Lionel Trilling, whenever that event may have taken place, the essay that he had been working on when he died was published on the front page and the second page of the *TLS*. I can remember thinking while I read Lionel Trilling's essay that the prose I was reading was clearer than the prose in any essay that I had ever previously tried to read in the *TLS*. I cannot remember the topic of the essay, but I remember that the writer began by stating that a course he taught at one or another university in the USA was the most popular course among first-year students of literature at the university. The course was on the fiction of Jane Austen, and the writer supposed that the students were attracted to the course because they supposed they would see in their minds while they followed the course the ordered green fields of the English countryside in the late eighteenth century and the early nineteenth century.

I have no way of knowing when I read an essay with the title "Woodbine Willie Lives," by a poet whose surname was Fuller. I remember the article not for its argument but for the details I read in it of an experiment reported in a book I have been too unenterprising ever to find and read, although I have read many references to it: a book by a man named Richards. In the book, so I believe, are accounts of experiments in which undergraduates at Oxford or Cambridge—two places that I have always confused in my mind—preferred from a number of passages of poetry whose authors were not revealed to them the doggerel by the parson nicknamed from the cigarettes that he handed to the troops in the trenches in World War One, even though one of the other authors was William Shakespeare.

I have no way of knowing when I read in the *TLS* a review of a biography of a woman novelist whose books were all best-sellers and earned her large sums of money. The writer herself gained little of pleasure or profit from these earnings. She bought a large house in the English countryside when she was still unmarried, but the bedrooms in the house were soon occupied by relatives who depended on her support. In order to support her large household, she had to write for much of the day and night. When she wrote in her study by night, her relatives complained that the noise of her typing kept them awake. In order to spare her relatives, the writer took to writing by night on a card table set up in a bathroom in a distant wing of the house. When she was no longer a young woman, she was courted by a man who had been an army officer in World War One. She married the man, who then retired from whatever he had been doing beforehand and became one more of her dependents. Soon after the marriage, he, the husband, brought to the country house the man who had been his batman during the war. The husband and his former batman persuaded the writer to buy for them a model railway system, which they installed in the grounds of the house. While the writer oversaw the household or tried to write her next book, her husband rode around the grounds on a model locomotive large enough to carry not only himself but his pillion passenger and former batman, whose name was Gerald.

The man with his chin in his hands

On the Monday of the second week after he had begun the final year of his secondary education, my only son, the elder of my two children, washed and dressed and ate his breakfast as though he intended to go to school but remained in his room for all of the morning. I was surprised and concerned, but I did not knock on my son's door. My son had been a well-behaved child, but for several years he had disliked listening to advice from his parents, and he had politely refused to discuss with his mother or me his choice of subjects for his final year at school or his plans for the future. On the morning just mentioned, I went to the room where I usually did my writing, but I was too anxious about my son to write. For most of that morning I took down from my shelves one or another book and turned a few pages. I had already persuaded myself that my son was going to drop out of school. He had never threatened to do so, and he had obtained high marks in certain subjects throughout his secondary school years, but sometimes a teacher had reported that my son seemed to lack interest in one or another subject, and for some months he had seemed never to have a schoolbook or any other sort of book in his hands. On the Monday mentioned above, my son and I made separate lunches in the kitchen at the same time, but we did not speak. While I was at my desk early in the afternoon, I heard him walking at intervals in and out of the back door. When I believed he was out in the backyard, I looked through the kitchen window and saw him stoking a small fire in the incinerator. I supposed he was burning pages from a diary or letters.

In those days, my wife left for her place of work long before the children left for school and she arrived home long after they had arrived home. When she arrived home on the day mentioned in the previous paragraphs, she had no way of knowing that our son had not been to school that day. Even our daughter did not know. She went to the same school, but she was some years younger than her brother and usually left early for school after her girlfriend and her mother had called for her in their car. On the Monday evening after my son's absence from school, neither he nor I spoke of it to his mother.

My son did not attend school on the Tuesday or any other day of the week mentioned above. On every day while he was at home, he kept to his room and I heard no sound from behind his door. On the Friday, I asked him while we were in the kitchen together at lunchtime whether he had been reading his schoolbooks that morning. He told me that he had not been reading any sort of books that morning. I reminded him that he would have fallen somewhat behind when he returned to school. He told me that he would not be returning to school.

On the Friday evening mentioned above, I told my wife that our son seemed to have decided to give up going to school. She spent much of that evening trying to learn from our son the reason for his decision and to persuade him to change his mind. She telephoned an educational counsellor and made an appointment for our son to consult him, but our son said that he would not keep the appointment. Throughout the weekend, my wife appealed to our son, but he would not relent. On the Sunday morning, when I was preparing to take the family's wastepaper to Fairfield, he told me that he wanted to go with me. He carried out of his room a large cardboard carton that seemed to be filled with newspapers and put it into the boot of the car. While he was carrying his carton from the car to the chute at Fairfield, the wind lifted what I had thought was the topmost of many newspapers in the carton. The newspaper that I had seen was the only newspaper. The rest of the carton was filled with my son's schoolbooks. They were all new books, bought only a few weeks before. Many were hardcovered books, but one on the top layer was a paperback, the cover of which had curled back somewhat. While my son balanced the carton on the sill of the chute, I could see that a corner of the flyleaf of the book had been cut away.

My son was out of the house on many days during the next four months. He would not tell his mother or me the details of what he was doing—only that he had registered for unemployment benefits and was looking for a job. Five years later, he let slip to me that he had been interviewed as an applicant for many jobs after he left school but that most interviewers had been no longer interested in him when he could not show them any of his reports from school, which he had burned in our backyard on the first day after he had stopped attending school.

In June of the year when he left school, my son found a job. At first, he told me few details. I learned only that he was a process worker in an engineering works five kilometres from home. On fine days, he rode his bicycle to and from his place of work. On wet days, I would take him in my car in the morning, and he would travel home on two buses. When he travelled in my car, he would never allow me to drive him to the doors of his place of work; I had to stop around the corner and let him out so that he could walk the rest of the way. He worked in a large industrial estate. Towards seven in the morning, at which time he started work, the footpaths of the estate were crowded with women factory workers walking from bus stops, and the roads were crowded with male workers' cars, most of them early models and scratched or dented.

In the later months of the year when he left school, my son went on working in the same place. He told me that his job was only a semi-skilled job but that he had been told when he began that he might be offered an apprenticeship in one or another skilled trade in the future. I asked him why he had chosen the job he was doing when he might have found a white-collar position, but he would not answer me.

Each night when my son arrived home from work, I resisted the urge to question him. He was always tired and short-tempered when he first arrived home, but I learned that he was more willing to talk after he had showered and eaten a meal. I was eager to learn that someone from the front office, as he called it, had taken him aside one day and had told him he would shortly be offered an apprenticeship in a skilled trade or even some other course the details of which I could not imagine but the result of which would be that he would be qualified for positions in management. My son never told me news of this sort, but he began to tell me each night about the people at his place of work.

According to my son, the owner of the engineering works, who had inherited the business from his father, was too often absent and too easygoing with his staff. Too many people were employed in the place, but no one had been dismissed while my son had been there. My son said he could name several men who ought to have been sacked.

Whenever my son named one of his fellow workers as an idler or simply as the teller of a good joke or the perpetrator of a prank, I struggled to picture the man or to recall anything that my son might have said previously about the man. As my son talked more of an evening, two of his workmates became more distinct in my mind. One was a man of about my own age who was sometimes an adviser and protector to my son. This man will be called from here on the kindly man. The other workmate seemed from my son's descriptions to be a few years younger than myself. This man seemed from my son's first descriptions an idle and malicious man. My son first described the man as small and thin and dark-haired and as spending much of his time on cold days sitting near one of the gas-heaters in a corner of the building and teasing and insulting the apprentices and the youngest of the process workers. When my son first mentioned this man to me, he, my son, told me he could not understand why the owner of the place had not sacked the man long before. My son told me that the owner had seen the man sitting in front of the heater one day but had not seemed to notice anything amiss. The man had been sitting in front of the heater with his chin in his hands, and the owner had walked past the man and had even seemed to greet the man. But a few nights after my son had reported these details to me, he told me that the man had cancer. My son then corrected himself. The man had previously had cancer and had been away from work for many months being treated for the cancer, which was in his jaw. A few weeks before my son had begun to work at the place, the man had returned to work, and word had passed around that the man had been cured of his cancer. But on cold days, the man sat in front of the heater with his chin in his hands and teased or insulted my son and other young workers, and my son had heard some of his workmates saying that the man had not been cured of his cancer. This man will be called from here on the man with his chin in his hands.

During the days after my son had first told me about the man with his chin in his hands, I saw from time to time in my mind one or another image of a small, thin man with dark hair. Sometimes the image was of the man sitting hunched over a heater in a corner of an engineering works. At other times the image was of the man running with long strides through grass that reached to his hips in countryside consisting of grass for as far as I could see.

After I had seen in my mind the images mentioned above, I began to look for opportunities to ask my son about the man with his chin in his hands. By this time, my son was no longer riding his bicycle to and from his place of work. The kindly man, who lived in a suburb adjoining my suburb, would stop in his car each morning to pick up my son from a street corner about a kilometre from my son's and my home. Each afternoon, the kindly man would drive my son to the same corner. On wet mornings or afternoons, the kindly man would often call at my house. My son was less tired and irritable after work, and spoke more willingly about his workmates. I asked him during a succession of evenings such questions about the man with his chin in his hands as whether or not he was married and a father; where he lived; whether or not he owned a car; what interests and hobbies he had; and what details or anecdotes he sometimes reported from his past. I learned from my son that the man with his chin in his hands seemed to be only a few years short of my own age but had never been married; that the man lived with his mother in a rented flat in the suburb of Fairfield; that the man had a sister who lived with her children elsewhere in Fairfield; that the man did not own a car and travelled by bus between his home and his place of work; that the man seemed to spend his evenings and his weekends watching television programmes on his and his mother's television set or watching films by means of their video cassette recorder and that he sometimes boasted to his workmates that his and his mother's television and video recorder were the best available; and that the man never spoke about his past, although my son understood that the man had been employed for many years in the engineering works. When my son first told me that the man lived with his mother, he, my son, went on to say that I should not suppose the man was gay.

My son told me that the man was too ugly and too ill-natured to have had a wife or a girlfriend.

In the last week of August, when the hailstorms that always fall at that time on the suburbs of Melbourne had stripped the pink blossoms from the prunus trees on the nature strips in the suburb where I live, my son told me one evening that the man with his chin in his hands had not been seen at work for several days and that his workmates were saying that the man's cancer had flared up again. On the same evening, my son explained to me why he had arrived home much later than usual on that afternoon, even though he had been driven to his front gate by the kindly man. My son explained the matter as follows. When the kindly man had driven away from their place of work on that afternoon, he had not driven in the usual direction. He had explained to my son that he, the kindly man, was going to call at the home in Fairfield of the man with his chin in his hands. The kindly man used the word *mate* when he spoke of the man with his chin in his hands. The kindly man, so he said, was going to drop in on his mate and lend him a few books to cheer him up and pass the time away while he was laid up at home. The kindly man had pointed his thumb over his left shoulder when he mentioned the books. My son looked over his own shoulder and saw on the back seat of the kindly man's car a cardboard carton almost full of books. In time, the kindly man had stopped his car outside a shabby block of flats between decaying weatherboard houses. The whole of the area surrounding the block of flats was paved with cement and was marked into parking areas for cars. Several cars were parked on the cement and seemed to have been parked there for many hours. This and the shabbiness of the cars suggested to my son that the owners of the cars were unemployed. My son stayed in the kindly man's car while he carried the carton of books to the front door of one of the flats. My son could not see who opened the door of the flats and let the kindly man in. He was inside the flat for about five minutes. He came back to his car without the books. He told my son that the sick man had been pleased to receive a visitor but that he was not at all well.

When I had heard my son's report, I asked him what sort of books had been in the carton. While I asked this question, I kept my face turned away from my son.

My son told me that the books in the carton had been old-looking paperbacks. In my son's words, the books had been westerns and thrillers and a lot of rubbish.

Books are a load of crap

At the time when my son was born, I worked in an office building at the edge of the city of Melbourne. Before my son was born, I used to spend my lunch-hour on each day from Monday to Thursday at my desk, reading the book that I was currently reading. During my lunch-hour on each Friday, I used to look through the books in one or another of several bookshops in the city. In the week after my son was born, I began to spend my lunch-hour reading a book published by the Children's Book Council of Australia. The book contained the publication details and a short description of hundreds of books considered most worthy to be read by children in each of several age groups. As I read the book, I put a mark from time to time beside the title of one or another book. After I had done this for three weeks, I had read every page of the book and had marked the titles of more than a hundred books. These books, many of which were described in the book I had just read as children's classics, I intended to buy at the rate of one each fortnight so that my son would have the beginnings of an impressive library by the time when he began school.

I did not succeed in buying all the books that I had marked in the book mentioned above, but I bought many of them, and I bought as well other books that I saw in bookshops or read about in book reviews (some in the *TLS*). After my daughter was born, I bought books for her also, although I preferred to let my wife choose what would appeal to a girl. I went on buying books each few months for both children, but especially my son, for more than fifteen years. I bought paperback books and hard-covered books in equal numbers, except that each child received several expensive hard-covered books at Christmas and on birthdays. I bought fiction and non-fiction books in about equal numbers, even after both children had told me, when they were aged twelve or thirteen, that they were less interested in fiction. When the children were in the upper years of secondary school, each had a part-time job and each received a weekly allowance from me. By then, I had to pay for music lessons and sports coaching and for most of the children's clothes, and I could hardly afford to go on buying books as I had bought them previously. I told the children one day that I would still buy them books at Christmas and birthdays but that they should use part of their allowance or of their wages to buy any other books that they wished to buy. So far as I was able to observe from that time onwards, neither of my children bought any book.

When the children were in the lower years of secondary school, they and their mother overruled me in the matter of whether or not we should have a television set in the house. Before then, as I used to say, I had kept the house free from spurious imagery. After the day when I was overruled, my wife and children watched dead images from cameras instead of living images from their own minds, as I often told them. To their credit, they seldom watched for more than an hour or two each day, and occasionally the set was left turned off all evening, but from the day when the television set was installed, I never referred to our house as I had often referred to it in the past; I never again told my children that they lived in a house of books.

For many of the years when the house was a house of books, I used to read to my children every night. I began to read to them before they themselves could read. I sat between them on the couch in the lounge-room and read from large picture books and from books in the series that we knew as Ladybird books. I believed from the first that the words and the pictures that came from books would produce in the minds of my children images of such richness and such power that the children would never afterwards be impressed by the contrived images that might come to them from cameras by way of cinema screens or television sets. I expected that the clearest images in my children's minds throughout their lives would be the images produced by the words of the books that I had read to them as children. The images produced in their minds by the illustrations in the books I had read to them would be of lesser power, since those images had come to them by way of the minds of the persons who had made the illustrations. The images that came to my children's minds by way of the screens of cinemas or the tubes of television sets, having come to their minds by way of machinery, would be of hardly any power. So I thought in the house of books.

During the years when I lived in the house of books, reading book after book myself and reading from books each night to my children, I saw an occasional film. Sometimes a friend of my wife would recommend one or another film to us, and if the film was being shown not at a cinema in the city but at one or another cinema in a suburb not more than a half-hour's drive by car from my house, I would sometimes go with my wife to see the film. Because I have seen so few films during my lifetime—fewer in the past fifty years than most persons in the suburbs of Melbourne would have seen during the past year—and because the images on the screen of the cinema are always so large and so brightly lit, I would see often in my mind during the first few days after I had watched one or another film one or another image from the film. I always expected that most of these images would have disappeared from my mind before a few days or weeks had passed. I thought of my mind as passing these images through itself as my body would have passed through its digestive system some pebbles or buttons that I might have swallowed. I was prepared to accept, however, that a few of the images of the film would remain in my mind. I believed that I might not see these images in my mind for so long that I would hardly remember the origins of the images when next I saw them. I believed that some of the images just mentioned might have been so changed during the many years while they stayed out of sight in my mind that I would suppose the images had first come to me while I was reading one or another book.

Soon after I had first seen in my mind, as was reported in the previous section of this story, the image of the man running with long strides through grass, which image I had first seen soon after my son had first told me about the man with his chin in his hands, I understood that the man running with long strides had the face and the body of an actor whose name I had never learned who played the part of a small, thin man with dark hair in a film with the title *Midnight Cowboy* or *The Midnight Cowboy*, which was one of the few films that I had watched during the years when I lived in the house of books. Soon after I had first seen the man running with long strides in the grass in my mind, I remembered that the man in the film had run with long strides along a seashore in his mind, having been cured in his mind of all the ailments that he suffered from. Even after I had remembered this, however, I believed that the man I saw was the soul or shade or spirit of the man running through grass in his mind, the body of the man having already died.

When I had understood that a number of the details of the image in my mind of the man running through the grass had come from my mind rather than from a camera by way of a screen in a cinema, I watched the image whenever it appeared, hoping to learn something of meaning. I learned in time that the grass in the image was connected with another area of grass in my mind, which area of grass was an image of a paddock of grass that I had sometimes walked through during a certain year in the late 1950s. I learned in time also that the grass in the image of the man running was connected with certain feelings that I felt while I watched the film named in the previous paragraph during one or another year in the early 1970s.

During the early 1970s, I earned my living as an editor of

technical publications in what was called in those years a semi-government authority. I had been promoted a number of times in a few years, and my salary was a good deal more than that of the average man of my age. My wife was not employed during the early 1970s but cared full-time for our two children, and yet we lived comfortably from the one income and continued to reduce the mortgage on our house. While I sat in the cinema with my wife beside me and our car in the car park nearby and our two children in the care of a baby-sitter in our neat home, and while I watched certain images of the thin, dark man who lived in an abandoned building and earned no income, I remembered the place where I had lived during certain weekends of a certain year in the late 1950s.

During the year just mentioned, I was in the second year of a course for a bachelor of arts degree and was enjoying free tuition and a living allowance as a bonded student of the Education Department of Victoria. I had only to finish my degree and a year-long diploma of education afterwards in order to become a secondary teacher with a secure career and a comfortable income. At some time during the year just mentioned, I decided that I wanted to be not a secondary teacher but an author of books of fiction. For some time during that year, I had been reading instead of the texts set for my course books of fiction by writers I admired and biographies of writers of fiction who had not earned regular incomes but had lived as bohemians or had worked occasionally at menial jobs. After I had decided to be an author of books of fiction, I no longer attended lectures but wrote fiction each day in the reading room of the State Library. At that time also I began to drink beer, my chief reason being that I wanted to spend each Friday evening in a hotel in Melbourne where, so I had heard, a group of bohemians gathered in a certain bar. One of the men I met in this bar worked in a bookshop by day but wanted to become the owner of a small press and to publish what he called avant-garde writings. This man had bought with a legacy from his dead father a small property north-east of Melbourne in a district that was also, so I had heard, inhabited by groups of bohemians. The property had been at one time a farm and orchard, but when its owner first took me there, the fruit trees were overgrown and the paddocks were full of long grass. The house was dirty and decayed, but the owner slept and ate in the back rooms at weekends and had begun to clean and restore the house and to set up his press in one or another room. On my first visit to the property, I decided to flee from my contract with the Education Department at the end of that year, when my failure as a student would have become known, and to live for the rest of my life in a certain shed that I had noticed a short distance from the house. The shed was full of junk and dirt and cobwebs, but in one wall was a window overlooking several paddocks of grass. I intended to clean and restore the shed and to spend my days there, writing fiction. Until such time as my fiction had been published and was earning money for me, I would support myself by working from time to time as a casual labourer.

During many of the weekends in the later months of the year when I first decided to be a writer of fiction, I worked at cleaning and restoring the shed mentioned above. For some time, I would not tell the owner of the property that I intended to live for the rest of my life in his shed. I believe I was afraid that even he, who often said he wanted the output of his press to shock bourgeois society, would have tried to stop me. Perhaps my not telling the owner of the property was in some way the result of my supposing him to be a homosexual, although he had never seemed interested in me as a sexual partner. I have never been able to remember certain events from the last weeks of that year. Sometimes, when I have to explain to someone the reason for my having been first a university student and then a primary teacher and later a part-time university student and later again a graduate and an editor, I say that I had some kind of crack-up when I first went to university. I speak as though I had merely become exhausted by hard work, but from what I remember, I had decided to give up everything for the sake of being a writer of fiction. During the evening when I watched on a screen in a cinema images of the thin, dark man shivering from cold in an abandoned building, I saw an image of myself in the shed beside the paddocks of long grass. The image of myself was sitting at a crude desk and was writing. I could see nothing else in the image of my surroundings except for shelves of books.

During the years when I worked first as a primary teacher and later as an editor, I went on writing fiction in the evenings and at weekends. On a certain day in a certain year in the early 1970s, which year would have been only one or two years after I had seen in a cinema the image of myself reported in the previous paragraph, I sent for the first time to a publisher a body of fiction that I had finished writing. A few weeks afterwards, an editor telephoned me from the offices of the publisher just mentioned. The editor told me that the body of fiction I had sent to her employers would be published as a book of fiction during the following year. One of a number of things that I did as a result of hearing this message from the editor of fiction was to persuade my wife to become again what she had formerly been: a full-time teacher in a private secondary school. Another thing that I did was to resign from my position with the semi-government authority and to become a full-time writer of fiction. I assured my wife at that time that if I failed to earn enough money in the future from my writing, I could always work as a freelance editor for my former employer and for other similar employers. Soon after I had resigned, the money that I had paid for some years past into a superannuation scheme was refunded to me. I used much of the money to buy a new desk and nearly a hundred books—most for myself but some for my children.

At some time during the late 1980s, after I had begun the practice of dumping at Fairfield books that I considered unfit to be read but when I could still not find a place on my shelves for every book that I wanted to keep, I decided that I owned a number of books not so unfit for reading that I ought to dump them at Fairfield but not of such interest to me that I would read them during my lifetime. I thought of these books as being suitable for me to pass on to someone who might find them more interesting than I found them. When I tried to decide which person or persons I might pass the books on to, I saw an image in my mind of a small, thin boy with a book in his hands. I understood that this was an image of one or another of my grandchildren, although my children were at that time still in the last years of secondary school. From that time on, I thought of a certain sort of book that I owned as deserving to be kept for my grandchildren.

Soon after I had decided that some of my books ought to be set aside for my grandchildren, I decided that I would store those books in the space between the ceiling and the roof of my house. I bought a few cheap planks from a timber yard and placed the planks across the timbers that ran above the ceiling of my house. I understood that the space where I was going to store the books for my grandchildren contained much dust, and so I wrapped each book in a plastic bag. I stacked the wrapped books in a cardboard carton and climbed with the carton up through the manhole in the ceiling of my house. During a period of several weeks, I stored three cartons of books in this way. My son and my daughter noticed me storing the first of the cartons, and I told them that the space above the ceiling was a convenient storage place for the things that they no longer used but did not wish to discard altogether. While I was storing the third of the cartons of books for my grandchildren, I saw three cartons that I had not previously seen in that place. I looked into the cartons and saw in each some of the books that I had bought for my son since the year when he had been born.

The title of this section of this story is part of the last line of a poem by Philip Larkin with the title "A Study of Reading Habits." As each year of my life has passed, I have become more interested in the workings of my mind. In recent years, I have come to believe that I might learn all of meaning that I could ever need to learn if only I could learn why I remember certain images and forget other images. At some time in the past, I would have read a certain poem by Philip Larkin. At some time while I was writing the notes and the early drafts of this story, I would have heard in my mind the words quoted at the head of this section of this story and would then have decided to use those words as the title of this section of this story. Several days ago, while I was preparing to write the final draft of this story, I found in my copy of *The Collected Poems of Philip Larkin*, edited by Anthony Thwaite and published in 1988 by The Marvell Press and Faber and Faber Limited, the complete text of the poem that contains the words that appear at the head of this section of this story. I read the poem slowly and got a certain amount of meaning from it, but a few hours after I had read the poem I could remember nothing of this meaning and none of the words of the poem except for the words at the head of this section of this story.

Welcome to Florida

During a certain year in the early 1980s, when my children were in their earlier years at secondary school, I came to understand that I could no longer go on staying at home by day and writing fiction and working occasionally as a freelance editor. If my children were to complete their secondary education and to go on to tertiary education, so I came to understand, then I would have to go back to working at a full-time job.

I did not want to go back to work as a teacher or an editor and to find myself being supervised by persons who were my juniors when I had last worked full-time. I applied for a position as a security officer at a large private hospital in a nearby suburb. My application had to be accompanied by character references, and one of the persons I asked to write on my behalf was a man who had been my assistant ten years before when I had worked as an editor but who was now himself the chief publications officer in the administration of a college of advanced education. This man told me to tear up my application for the position of

security officer and to apply for the position of lecturer in creative writing that had recently been advertised in the institution
where he worked.

I had learned from books of fiction and from certain references
in articles in the *TLS* that creative writing was taught in universi-
ties in the USA, but I had not supposed that a person might earn
a living as a teacher of creative writing in Australia. And yet, I
earned my living for more than ten years by writing detailed comments in the margins of pages of fiction written by my students,
by conferring with one student after another in my office, and by
acting as chairperson during sessions when a class would read
and then discuss a piece of fiction by someone from that class. In
time, the institution where I worked became part of a university.
As a member of a faculty of a university, I was asked each year to
report on the number of conferences I had attended and the number of keynote addresses I had delivered and the number of research
projects I had obtained funding for and the number of articles I
had had published in refereed journals and the number of con-
sultancies I had engaged in. I answered each such question by
writing NIL in letters of a modest size and I returned each list of
questions promptly to its sender and hoped I might be allowed to
go on for a few more years teaching from February to November
the eighty students who enrolled each year in my course and writing fiction from November to February. I hoped I would be able to
resign from my position soon after my children had finished their
tertiary education and had found secure positions. After the year
in the early 1980s when I began to dump certain books at Fairfield,
I looked forward to undertaking during my retirement the tasks
described in the following paragraph. As a younger man, I had supposed that I would spend my retirement buying and reading new
books and adding them to my collection and erecting new shelves
and dusting the rows of books on the many shelves in the several
rooms that I had filled with shelves of books and sometimes, of
course, reading again a book I had read previously; but after I

had taken my first load of books to Fairfield, I foresaw differently my reading and writing in the future.

After I had retired from full-time work, so I supposed, I would examine continually the power of each of the books on my shelves. I would do this by the means described earlier in this story, but during my retirement I would have time to be more thorough and more stringent.

During my retirement, I would test each book once each year. Once each year, I would stand in front of the spine of each book and wait to see in my mind some of the images that had first appeared there when I had read the book. No other sort of image would save a book as some books had been saved when I had first tested them in the early 1980s. On the other hand, I was not going to dump at Fairfield every book that failed my test. I would simply banish the failed books from my shelves. Many of the banished books would be worth considerable sums of money and, to be fair, some of the books that I had read only once in the early 1960s, when I had first begun to read books continually, were at a disadvantage, having been closed for many years longer than books read in more recent years. (Or, the opposite might have been true if my mind had been more impressionable in early years.) I would keep the failed books wrapped in plastic in cartons in the space above the ceiling or, if that space became crowded, in a spare room of the house.

I looked forward to my retirement whenever I thought of the work I was going to do with my books. If, as I believed, those persons lived longest who had large or never-ending tasks to occupy them, then I was assured of a very long life. I could foresee no end to my task. For as long as I was alive, I would remember something at least from each of a small number of books. My life would have been one continuous experiment as to the worth of books. Of course, I would record in writing the results of the experiment. Readers of what I wrote might learn even before my death the comparative value to me of my best-remembered books or the comparative value of particular passages within one or more book. Or, a reader of my writing might study not the books but the man who partly remembered them. What sort of man, such a reader might ask, would remember this rather than that passage from this or that book? (If I had remembered wrongly, which is to say if I had believed one or more images in my mind to be connected with a book whose text seemed to another reader incapable of giving rise to such an image or images, then a reader of my writing would have a rich subject for study.) I need not write mere reports. I should be able to find connections between some of the images that I connected with separate books. I should be able, perhaps, to write one last book by connecting what I had retained from a life-time of remembering images connected with my books. My last book would be a book of books: a distillation of precious imagery, and if I was able to arrange that the last page or the last paragraph was written on the last day of my life, then I would have advanced an argument that would remain forever indisputable; I would have pointed to my own life as evidence of the supremacy of one or another book.

In certain moods, I foresaw the end of my life as being the op-posite of what is reported above. As a result of one decisive event in my life, or, perhaps, as the end of a long and gradual process, I would turn away from books, never to be reconciled. I might leave the shelves standing in my house and the first editions and other valuable titles in place as part of my legacy for my children, but I would never again open the covers of a book. I would find other tasks to keep from my mind all thought of books or the images they had formerly given rise to. But even if I spent my retirement thus, I would still learn, even against my will, much about the books I had spurned. I could not help but notice, year after year, as I tried to forget whatever I had thought as a result of my read-ing, that some images remained with me long after other images had gone: that some books were harder to forget than other books. And when I thought of this sort of future for myself, I observed something that always surprised me. The act of writing was not so closely linked to the reading of books as I had for long supposed. Even as an aged book-hater, I would still be capable of writing. I might write a book about my efforts to remove all traces of books from my mind. I might even write a book containing no evidence that I had ever remembered having read a single book.

During the first two weeks after my son had told me about the carton of books that had been delivered to the man with the chin in his hands, I waited each afternoon to hear that the man had returned to work and seemed much recovered or that he had been admitted to hospital after having become much more ill or that the kindly man and my son had called again at the flat in Fairfield and had found the man with his chin in his hands no better and no worse than before. If I had heard from my son on any afternoon during the two weeks just mentioned the third of the reports mentioned in the previous sentence, I would have hoped to hear as part of the report that the man with his chin in his hands had returned the carton of books to the kindly man, saying as he returned them that he very much appreciated the loan of the books but that he preferred to watch films and other programmes on his mother's and his television set and video recorder rather than read books.

During the two weeks mentioned in the previous paragraph, I often saw in my mind sequences of images more vivid and more detailed and more apt to recur than any sequence of images that I could remember having seen as a result of any book that I had read recently. Each sequence of images appeared as though on a screen in a cinema in my mind, but while I watched the images I felt as though I was writing certain passages of a book in my mind and as though each passage in the book would drive out of my mind each image from the film in my mind.

On the screen in my mind, the mother of the man with his chin in his hands held her son in her arms on the day when he had been born. The mother admired the body of her son and saw in her mind an image of her son as a tall, strong man.

In the book in my mind, the mother of the man with his chin in his hands held her son as in the film but foresaw that he would be small and thin throughout his life and that he would die while she was still alive.

On the screen in my mind, the mother led her son by the hand towards the school gate on his first day as a schoolboy and foresaw that he would make many friends at school and would learn much and would afterwards earn his living in an office where his fellow workers smiled at him, especially the young women.

In the book in my mind, the mother read one or another school report on her son and foresaw that he would spend his working life as an unskilled labourer and would be disliked by many of his workmates and would never marry.

On the screen in my mind, the man opened one or another book from a carton of books lent to him by one of the few of his workmates who was not unfriendly towards him. The man read a number of pages of the book but then fell asleep or began to watch his television set and afterwards could not remember anything of what he had read about.

In the book in my mind, the man did as reported in the previous paragraph but remembered having seen in his mind while he read one or another of the pages in the book an image of plains of grass reaching to the horizon in his mind.

At the end of the two weeks mentioned above, my son told me when he had returned home from work late that the kindly man had called with him at the home of the man with his chin in his hands. On this occasion, so my son told me, he had gone with the kindly man to the front door of the flat where the man with his chin in his hands lived with his mother. The mother had answered the door. She had been, in my son's words, a fat, hopeless woman. According to my son's report, the kindly man had told the mother that he and my son had called to see how her son was feeling and to collect some books that he, the kindly man, had lent to the son on a previous occasion. According to my son's report, the mother had answered that her son was at that moment asleep, that he had not been at all well, and that she would prefer not to wake him in order to meet his visitors. According to my son's report, he and the kindly man had told the mother to pass on their best regards to her son and had then left.

On a certain afternoon during the second week after the events reported in the previous paragraph, my son told me that he and his workmates had been told during that morning by the owner of the engineering works that the man with his chin in his hands had died. On the following morning, I was about to look through the notices under the heading DEATHS in the *Sun News-Pictorial*, but then I recalled that I knew only the first of the given names of the man who had died, which name was the only name that my son had used of the man. I asked my son as he was leaving for work that morning, but he said he did not know the surname of the man. I then looked through the text of each of the notices in three of the columns headed DEATHS until I had found the notice of the death of the man with his chin in his hands. One notice only had been inserted, the mourners being the man's mother and his sister. I did not look in the columns headed FUNERAL NOTICES.

When my son returned home on the afternoon of the day when I had read the notice mentioned in the previous paragraph, he said in connection with the death of the man with his chin in his hands only that an apprentice at the engineering works had said that he was pleased to have heard that the man had died and would no longer tease or insult him.

On the day following the afternoon mentioned in the previous paragraph, I read among the notices under the heading DEATHS in the *Sun News-Pictorial* only one notice referring to the man with his chin in his hands. In that notice, the dead man was described as a good mate of a man whose first given name was included in the notice. That man has been called in this story the kindly man.

On each of the first few afternoons after I had heard of the death of the man with his chin in his hands, I expected my son to tell me that a party of his workmates, himself perhaps included, had attended during that day the funeral service for the man with his chin in his hands, but my son did not tell me what I had expected him to tell me.

From time to time during the years since the afternoons mentioned in the previous paragraph, I have seen as though on a screen in a cinema in my mind a sequence of images of a fat woman nearly twenty years older than myself looking around a bedroom in a flat in the suburb of Fairfield and preparing to empty the bedroom of most of the belongings of the person who had formerly slept in the bedroom. One of the images in the sequence is of the woman finding under the bed in the bedroom a carton of books.

Sometimes, when I have seen in my mind the image mentioned in the previous paragraph, I have felt as though I was writing in a book in my mind a passage in which the fat woman mentioned above picked up one or another of the books in the carton and opened one or another page of the book and read one or another paragraph on the page and saw in her mind an image of a man surrounded by long grass reaching to the horizon in her mind.

At other times, when I have seen in my mind the image mentioned in the previous paragraph, I have felt as though I was writing a passage in a book in my mind in which the fat woman picked up the carton of books and carried it out through the front door of her flat and left it beside the footpath at the front of the block of flats, knowing that a truck would drive past the block of flats later on that day and that labourers employed by the city in which she lived would collect the carton of books from the footpath and would throw the carton and its contents into the back of the truck, after which the truck would continue on its way towards the waste-paper collection depot only a few hundred metres from the block of flats.

Sometimes, when I have seen in my mind an image of the man with his chin in his hands during the years since I learned that he had died, I see in my mind an image of a line drawing of a famous statue of a man sitting with his chin resting on a fist. The line drawing appeared as a logo on each of the many titles in a series of books with the general title of the Thinker's Library. The series of books was published perhaps as long ago as the 1920s by one or another English publisher whose name I have forgotten. I saw copies of books from the Thinker's Library in second-hand bookshops in the 1950s and the 1960s, and I bought only one title in the series. Whenever I looked at the list of titles in the series, I imagined the books as having been bought by young men in cloth caps. The young men worked by day in factories in the English midlands and read books by night in order to educate themselves. The title that I bought was *The Existence of God*. I remember the surname of the author as McCabe. He was an American and a former priest. His book contained a number of arguments against the existence of God. I have not seen the book for more than thirty years. I bought the book during the year in the late 1950s when I was planning to live as a writer of fiction in a shed at the edge of a grassy paddock. I read the book often during that year. I wanted the arguments in the book to strengthen me whenever I was tempted to believe again in God as I had believed during most of my life until that year. Sometimes, and especially when I was drunk, I would take the book down from my shelves and would read a passage to one or another person and would urge the person to borrow the book from me. Someone who borrowed the book failed to return it, and all I remember of the book today is the drawing of the man with his chin resting on his hand and the claim made by the author somewhere in the book that his children had grown up happily without having been taught about God.

One of the few sequences of images that still remain in my mind from the evening about twenty years ago when I watched in a cinema the film named earlier in this story is a sequence of images showing part of the interior of a bus in which the small, thin man with dark hair sits beside the man who seems to be his only friend. The two men are travelling to the state of Florida, but for some time the small, thin man has been lying back in his seat with his eyes closed. The time is late at night, and the windows of the bus show darkness and the lights of motor traffic. At some time during the night, the bus stops at the border of Florida. While the bus is stopped, a young woman with fair hair who works as an assistant in a shop of some kind just inside the state of Florida or who works as an employee of some kind of the government of Florida says to the passengers in the bus the words at the head of this section of this story. The sequence of images is such that I understand the thin man with dark hair to have already died when the bus reaches the border and when the young woman speaks.

Whenever I have seen in my mind the sequence of images mentioned above, I have then felt urged to begin to write a certain book of fiction which would be a report of a search among the images in my mind for the image or images that suggest most clearly the place where I expect to have arrived when one or another person first observes of me that I have already died.

The Homer of the Insects

Of all the books that I bought for my son as a result of my having read the list of books in the book published by the Children's Book Council of Australia, the book that I most looked forward to his reading was a book of fiction of many pages recommended for children aged from eleven to fourteen years. I cannot remember the title of the book or the name of the author or of the publisher. I remember that the edition I bought for my son was a hardcover edition of more than two hundred closely printed pages. Of all the details on the dust-jacket, I remember only parts of the outline of a line drawing of a boy of about twelve years of age and the outlines of line drawings of tussocks of grass at the feet of the boy.

I cannot remember having read any word of the book mentioned in the previous paragraph. I know that my son has never read the book and that it lies nowadays wrapped in plastic in a carton above the ceiling of my house. And yet, I often see in my mind images of the images that I might have seen if I had read the book.

During the years when I bought many books and when some of those books would stay on my shelves unread for many years while I read the many other books waiting to be read, I would sometimes stand in front of my shelves and look at the spine of a book that I had owned for many years but had not yet read and would see in my mind a sequence of images of the images that I might have seen in my mind if I had read the book and had later remembered having done so. Sometimes, when I stood in front of an unread book, I understood that the images in my mind had arisen as a result of my having previously looked at the dust-jacket of the book and read the words there. At other times, I understood that the images had arisen as a result of my having previously read one or more reviews of the book or essays mentioning the book. At other times again, I would see images in my mind as though I remembered having read a book that I had never read, but I would be unable to understand why those images had arisen in my mind. During the years after I had begun to dump books at Fairfield, one of the plans that I devised for my retirement was as follows. I would go on buying books and keeping them on my shelves, but I would read no more books. I would allow myself to read the dust-jackets of books and to read reviews of books and essays about books, but I would never again look between the covers of any book. After I had retired, I would stare at the spine of one after another of the books that I had never read and while I stared I would study the images that appeared in my mind. I would afterwards describe these images in writing. The written descriptions of all the images would deserve to be considered a book in itself. I might read this book often, observing what images arose in my mind while I read. Or, I might leave the book forever unread but might stand sometimes in front of the book long after I had written it and might observe whatever images might be in my mind.

The most prominent of the images that appear in my mind whenever I remember the hardcover book mentioned in the first paragraph of this section of this story is an image of a man sitting among long grass with his chin in his hands. The man is sitting on a small wooden stool and is staring at something in the long grass just in front of him. I first saw this image in my mind many years before my son told me one afternoon about the man who sat in the engineering works with his chin in his hands. For as long as I have seen this image, I have understood that the man is a famous naturalist who lived for most of his life in the south of France and studied the insects of his native district. For as long as I have understood this, I have supposed that my seeing the image of the famous naturalist is partly the result of my having learned from the dust-jacket of the hardcover book of fiction bought for my son that the book is set in the south of France and that the chief character of the book is a boy who spends much of his time out of doors. On the first occasions when I saw the image of the famous French naturalist, who is always at a distance among the long grass when I first see the image of him, I supposed I was seeing an image of the naturalist as a young man or even as a boy of the age of the chief character of the hardcover book of fiction, but on each of those occasions the image of the person in the long grass subsequently appeared in the foreground of my mind, enabling me to see that he was a man older than myself.

When I was preparing to write this section of this story, I intended to include in the section the name of the famous naturalist. I had read the name several times in the past but had not remembered exactly the spelling of the name. I looked just now into several reference books on my shelves but was unable to find the name of the naturalist. I then looked along my shelves for some time but was unable to see there any book that might have contained the name of the naturalist in a place where I could readily find it.

If I was another sort of man, I would have visited or telephoned one or another library in order to learn the name of the naturalist, but I am a man who has not gone into a library during the past ten years and who intends not to go into any library in the future. If I were to go into a library, I would seem to be acknowledging

that I had failed to acquire all the books necessary for my satisfaction and contentment. If I were to go into a library, I would
seem to be admitting that my own library had failed me. Worse, if
I were to go into a library I would have to talk to one of the persons in charge of the books in the library. I have gone so seldom
into libraries during my lifetime that I have never learned the system or systems according to which the books are arranged on the
shelves of libraries. On my few visits to libraries many years ago,
I was satisfied to walk between the shelves and to wait for the spine
of one or another book to take my eye, but I understand that I
could not hope to find in this way the name of the famous naturalist. I could only find that name after having spoken to one or
another person in charge of part of a library.

More than thirty years ago, before I became a writer of books,
I used to seek out persons who might talk with me about books.
Whenever I was reading a book in those days, I would hear in my
mind the sound of myself talking in the future to someone about
the book. I was careful not to talk about books to persons who
did not value books, but I expected that I would always have in
the future a large number of friends and acquaintances who would
talk about books. After I had become a writer of books, I was more
wary of talking about books. I understood by then that each book
I had written was not the book I had read in my mind before I had
begun to write. I began to suspect that a book, and especially a
book of fiction, is too complicated a thing to be talked about, except by a person talking to himself or herself. I began to suspect
that a book, and especially a book of fiction, ought to be read in
private and then put on the reader's shelves for five or ten or twenty
years, after which time the reader ought to stare at the spine of
the book. After I had begun to suspect these things, I seldom talked
about books. Sometimes I would point out a book to a person or
would place a book in the hands of a person or would leave a book
lying where a person might come across it, but I would seldom talk
about any of these books. Nowadays, I am more likely to hide
books rather than to put them in the way of people. For some years

now, I have not tried to persuade any person to read any book. In future, I will not admit to any person that I have read any book. In future, I will not even reveal to any person the existence of any book that the person has not read unless the person has first persuaded me that he or she has already seen in his or her mind some of the contents of the book. Being nowadays this sort of man, I could hardly bring myself to speak to one or another person in charge of part of a library containing a book I know nothing about.

While I was writing the previous paragraph, I began to understand the place in this story of the image the connections of which I did not understand when I first included details of that image in this story. I have now begun to understand why the young woman whose image in my mind caused me to write the second and third and fourth paragraphs of this story chose never to speak to me about any piece of fiction that she had written or intended to write.

The name of the naturalist who spent most of his life in fields of grass in the south of France studying details of the ways of insects is almost the same word as the name of a famous publishing house in London. The famous publishing house publishes much poetry and fiction, and a number of the books on my shelves at this moment were first published by the famous publishing house. At least one of the books that I dumped at Fairfield in the years when I used to dump books had been first published by the famous publishing house. I can remember of that book only that it was a hardcover edition of a book of prose fiction by a famous writer from the West Indies. One of the books on my shelves from the famous publishing house is a paperback edition of one of my own books of fiction. The design on the cover of this book and the advertisement for the book suggest to me that the persons who prepared these things had not read the contents of the book. Another of the books on my shelves is the hardcover edition of the book mentioned most recently in this paragraph. Whenever I look at the illustration on the front of the dust-jacket of the book just mentioned, I suppose that the illustrator first read every word of the book and then was able to see in his mind every detail of each of the images that he would see in his mind twenty or more years afterwards if he stood at that time in front of the unjacketed spine of the book. The hardcover edition just mentioned was the first of my books of fiction to have been reviewed in the *TLS*. Soon after I had read the review of the book in the *TLS*, I chose not to renew my subscription to the *TLS* when it was next due for renewal, and I did not subscribe to the *TLS* for three years.

From the time when my son was first able to walk around the backyard of our house, I encouraged him to be interested in birds and insects and spiders and plants. I did this partly to safeguard myself from the possible accusation that I was forcing too many books on him, but I genuinely wanted him to take an interest in the natural world. I wanted him to turn to the outdoors whenever he had grown tired for the time being of books. On many fine days when my son was old enough to walk and talk but not yet old enough to read, I would lead him around our backyard, looking for some bird or spider or insect that we could watch.

Whenever I try to remember the days mentioned in the previous sentence, I remember first the image that I have seen often in my mind since I bought for my son the book mentioned earlier in this section of this story. I see in my mind the image of the man sitting with his chin in his hands in the fields of grass. While I watch the man in my mind, he lifts his chin from his hands and picks up from beside him in the grass a pencil and a notebook. In one or another article or essay that I read in one or another publication many years ago, the words at the head of this section of this story were applied to the famous naturalist, who was the author of many books reporting what he saw during his long lifetime in the fields surrounding his home. I watch the man in my mind writing with his pencil in his notebook while he sits in the fields of grass.

Pink Lining

The image that caused me to begin writing this story is an image of a single cloud in a sky filled with heaps or layers of clouds. The single cloud and all the other clouds in the sky are coloured grey, but the single cloud is surrounded by an aureole or nimbus of pink. All the clouds are being driven by wind across the sky, but the single cloud with the aureole or nimbus of pink is moving less swiftly than the other clouds. If the clouds were a group of children being driven past me, then the cloud surrounded by the pinkness would be the one child who is reluctant to be hurried past me: the one child looking back over her shoulder towards me and wanting to tell me something.

All the clouds mentioned in the previous paragraph are details in a picture on the obverse of a card of about the size of the palm of the hand of the man who is holding the card in his hand and looking at the heaps or layers of clouds in the picture that contains the image that caused me to begin writing this story. The card is one of a collection of similar cards that the man keeps in an envelope in a hanging file in a filing cabinet. When the man was a boy he called these cards and other similar cards *holy cards*, but for as long as the cards have been kept in the man's filing cabinet, they have been kept in one of many files labelled *Memorabilia*.

Every card in the collection mentioned in the previous paragraph has on its obverse a picture of Jesus or of his mother or of a male or a female saint and beneath the picture the text of a short prayer of the sort that the man called as a boy a *pious ejaculation*. During the years while the man has kept his cards in the file labelled *Memorabilia*, he has sometimes amused some of his friends by telling them that he was encouraged as a boy by his favourite aunt to ejaculate frequently and piously. The man has always been pleased to amuse some of his friends in this way, but he knows that his friends are amused only because they are somewhat ignorant of the meanings of English words and because they are wholly ignorant of the meanings of words in the Latin language.

Below each of the texts mentioned in the previous paragraph is a statement of the number of days of indulgence that each pious ejaculation earns for the person who utters it. The man who owns the cards has never tried to explain to any of his friends that he not only ejaculated frequently and piously as a boy but that each of his ejaculations earned him an average of three hundred days' measure of the spiritual commodity known as indulgence. The man has never tried to explain this to his friends because he doubts whether even those few of his friends who were eager as children to earn quantities of indulgence understood as children or understand now as adults the doctrine of indulgences.

The man looking at the card in his hand was taught as a boy by his favourite aunt that an indulgence of three hundred days was far from being what non-Catholics of ill will supposed it to be, namely a licence to sin for three hundred days without fear of punishment on earth or elsewhere. The boy was taught also by his favourite aunt that an indulgence of three hundred days was not what many of the Catholic persons who strove to earn indulgences believed it to be, namely an assurance that a person would spend three hundred days fewer than the person would otherwise have been obliged to spend after death in the place of punishment known as purgatory. The man was taught by his favourite aunt that an indulgence of three hundred days was an assurance that a person had earned in the sight of God as much spiritual merit as the person would have earned in the early days of the Church by doing for three hundred days the usual penance of those early days, which was to fast and pray and to wear sackcloth and ashes in public.

After the man looking at the card in his hand had learned as a boy from his favourite aunt what is mentioned in the previous paragraph, he asked his aunt whether she said aloud or read from holy cards prayers that earned her quantities of indulgence. The boy's aunt then told him that she was in the habit of saying each day certain prayers that earned her indulgences to the value of ten thousand days.

The boy mentioned in the previous paragraph often sat near his favourite aunt while she talked to him about the history and the teachings of the Catholic Church. While the boy listened to his favourite aunt, he would sometimes hold the small stack of his holy cards in the palm of his hand, looking at one after another of the cards before moving the card to the bottom of the stack. While the boy looked at one after another of his cards, he looked only briefly at the figure of Jesus or of the holy personage in the foreground of the picture on the obverse of the card before he looked for certain details in the background of the picture. Certain details such as a part of a stone wall or a part of a garden or part of a view of countryside enabled the boy to imagine details of a certain place in his mind.

At some time during every day, the boy-owner of the holy cards mentioned previously imagined details of scenes from the life that he might live in the future. During the years while he learned from his favourite aunt about the history and the teachings of the

Catholic Church, the boy wished to remain in the future what he and his aunt would have called a good Catholic, but he often suspected that he would commit many sins in the future, even as a boy in the future. He would commit many sins in the future, the boy suspected, because he would be eager, even as a boy in the future, to imagine details of scenes in remote countryside in the state of Victoria in which he was a man and about to look at or to touch the naked body of a young woman. Even when he was sitting near his favourite aunt and while she was talking to him about the history and the teachings of the Catholic Church, the boy-owner of the cards would sometimes imagine one or another detail of a scene in remote countryside such as he suspected he would imagine in the future, even while he was still a boy. Whenever the boy-owner of the cards had imagined such a detail while he was sitting near his favourite aunt with his cards in his hand, he would look into the backgrounds of the pictures on his cards for the details mentioned in the last sentence of the previous paragraph.

When the boy-owner of the holy cards looked for details of the place mentioned in the last sentence of the paragraph before the previous paragraph, he supposed that the place was beside a side street of a town of a few thousand people on the inland slopes of the Great Dividing Range in either the state of New South Wales or the state of Queensland. During the years when the boy supposed this, he had lived since the first year that he could remember in a suburb of Melbourne and had travelled no further from Melbourne than to the district in the south-west of Victoria where his favourite aunt lived.

The place mentioned in the previous paragraph was a house of many rooms surrounded first by a veranda and then by a formal garden and then by a high stone wall. Whenever the boy-owner of the holy cards looked for details of this place, he was hoping that the details would enable him to imagine himself as sitting or standing or walking up and down in one or another of the many rooms of the house or on the veranda or in the formal garden. The boy was hoping also that the details would enable him to imagine that he had lived already for many years as a man in the house of many rooms and had sat or had stood or had walked up and down in one or another of the many rooms of the house or on the veranda or in the formal garden during every day of those years and had never travelled outside the high stone wall and that he would live in that place for the rest of his life.

Sometimes the boy-owner of the holy cards supposed that the place mentioned in the previous paragraph was the house where he would live in the future as a bachelor with a library in one of the rooms, a collection of orchids in another room, many tanks stocked with tropical fish in another room, and an elaborate model railway layout in another room. At other times the boy supposed that the place was a monastery for priests or monks.

Whenever the boy-owner of the holy cards supposed that the place mentioned in the previous paragraph was a monastery, he supposed also that he would learn as an older boy from his favourite aunt the whereabouts of every monastery that stood behind a high stone wall in a side street of a town of a few thousand people on the inland slopes of the Great Dividing Range in New South Wales or Queensland; that he would learn also from his favourite aunt the colours and designs of the habits worn by the monks or priests in each of the monasteries as well as the rules followed by the monks or priests and the whereabouts of the sister-houses of the monasteries of the same order of monks or priests in countries other than Australia; and that he would then decide to join an order of monks or priests whose habits were of striking colours, whose rules prevented the monks or priests from travelling outside the high stone wall surrounding their monastery, and whose sister-houses in countries other than Australia were surrounded by remote countryside.

If the boy-owner of the holy cards mentioned previously was looking at one or another card but was not able to see in the picture on the card any detail of a wall or of a garden or of part of a view of countryside, he would look at the sky behind the head of Jesus or Mary or the holy personage in the picture.

If the boy saw that the sky mentioned in the previous paragraph was blue and without clouds, he would not go on looking at the sky but would place the card with the picture that included the blue sky without clouds at the bottom of his stack of cards. If the boy saw in the sky in the picture on a holy card heaps or layers of grey clouds, he would go on looking at that sky.

On a day when the view from the window of the room where the man who was first mentioned in the second paragraph of this story had kept for more than twenty years in a filing cabinet the cards that he had called as a boy holy cards was of a blue sky without clouds, the man was asked by the woman who had been his wife for more than twenty years why he preferred not to look at a blue sky without clouds. On the day mentioned in the previous sentence, the man answered that the blue of a sky without clouds at noon in the only districts where he had lived was also the most noticeable of the colours in each of the two tassels that had sometimes brushed the skin of his arm or his face when his mother had passed close to him each morning in the first year that he could remember, which was a year when she had often worn a dressing-gown of blue and of several other colours that she fastened around her waist with a cord that had at each end a tassel of the same colours.

Whenever the boy-owner of the holy cards mentioned previously looked at heaps or layers of grey clouds in a picture on one or another of his cards, he looked for what he looked for whenever he was walking or was travelling in a motor car or a railway train through the district in the south-west of Victoria where his favourite aunt lived with her parents and her sisters and whenever he noticed that the sky above the mostly level countryside of that district was filled with heaps or layers of grey clouds, which was a single cloud with a ray or rays of light appearing from behind it in such a way that the cloud seemed partly or wholly surrounded by an aureole or nimbus of silver.

Whenever the boy mentioned in the previous paragraph saw the single cloud mentioned in that paragraph, he was reminded of the saying that he sometimes heard from his mother: the saying that every cloud has a silver lining. Whenever the boy saw the single cloud, he was reminded also of the districts surrounding the district where he was then walking or otherwise travelling. He was reminded that the sun might have been shining at that moment over the district of Geelong or the district of the Great Dividing Range or the district on the far side of the South Australian border or the blue district of the Southern Ocean. Whenever the boy saw the single cloud, he was reminded also of the district that surrounded all other districts: namely, the district of heaven.

Whenever the boy mentioned in the previous paragraph was travelling in the district south-west of Melbourne where his favourite aunt lived with her parents and her sisters, he understood that the district came to an end in one direction at the suburbs of a city and in another direction at a range of mountains and in another direction at a vertical line on a map and in another direction at the shore of an ocean, but whenever the boy was reminded of the district of heaven, he understood that the district had no end in any direction. Whenever the boy was reminded of the district of heaven, he understood that each of the houses of heaven was of many rooms and was surrounded by a veranda and then by a formal garden and then by mostly level countryside that had no end in any direction. Whenever the boy understood these things, he understood also that no male person who sat with a female person in one or another of the many rooms of the houses of heaven or who stood or walked with a female person on the veranda or in the formal garden surrounding any of those houses would be eager at any time in the future to imagine any detail of any scene in any remote landscape in which he was an older male person and about to look at or to touch the body of a naked female person.

Whenever the man who was first mentioned in the second paragraph of this story remembered his favourite aunt during the years while she was still alive, he remembered her as resting the weight of her body above the waist on her right elbow while she lay in the bed where she lay by day and by night in her room in a house that was of many rooms and was surrounded first by a veranda and then by a formal garden and then by the mostly level countryside of a district in the south-west of Victoria. Whenever the man remembered his favourite aunt during the years just mentioned, he remembered also other details including some of the following details.

The man's favourite aunt was the eldest sister of the man's father. The man's favourite aunt had three sisters and two brothers. The two brothers each married when he was about thirty-five years of age and later became the father of children. The man's favourite aunt and her three sisters were all unmarried throughout their lives. The four sisters just mentioned lived with their parents until their father had died and then went on living with their mother in the house of many rooms mentioned in the previous paragraph until all four sisters and their mother had died.

The house mentioned in the previous paragraph was of cream-coloured stone that had been dug from a paddock nearby. Most of the work of building the house just mentioned had been done by the father of the father of the man who is looking at a picture on a card in the image that caused me to begin writing this story. During the years when the man just mentioned was a boy who was learning from his favourite aunt, the grandfather of the boy would have been called by his neighbours *comfortably off*. The grandfather's house was furnished with pieces of the sort that are sold for many hundreds of dollars each in antique shops in suburbs of Melbourne nowadays. In the main room of the house was a tall set of bookshelves with glass panels in their doors and several hundred books inside. One of the four sisters who lived in the house had a mechanical gramophone and a collection of a hundred or more records. Another of the sisters owned a piano and listened to music programs from the ABC by means of a battery-powered radio. One of the sisters ordered from time to time items of jewellery or bric-a-brac advertised in mail-order catalogues issued by stores in Melbourne. The sister who was the favourite aunt of one of her nephews subscribed to every periodical issued by every Catholic institution and religious order in every state of Australia.

On a certain morning in his tenth year, the boy-owner of the holy cards mentioned previously got up from the chair where he had been sitting at the bedside of his favourite aunt and left his aunt's room as he was accustomed to leave her room whenever the time was approaching for his aunt's mother to bring into the room the white enamel dish of hot water and the towels and the facewasher and the soap that she brought in each morning.

On the morning mentioned in the previous paragraph, the boy mentioned in that paragraph was spending part of his summer holidays as he was accustomed to spending part of those holidays each year in the house of many rooms where the parents and sisters of his father lived. On every other morning of the many mornings that the boy spent in that house, he would spend the hour while he was out of the room of his favourite aunt reading from the books in the main room of the house or walking in the formal garden surrounding the house.

During the years while the man who was first mentioned in the second paragraph of this story has kept a collection of cards in a file labelled *Memorabilia*, the man has had no occasion to remember any detail from any of the mornings when, as a boy, he left the room of his favourite aunt and did the things mentioned in the previous paragraph. However, the man has sometimes remembered a certain morning in his tenth year when he left the room of his favourite aunt and then walked through the house of many rooms and then across the veranda surrounding the house and then through the formal garden surrounding the house and the veranda and then out into the mostly level countryside surrounding the house and the veranda and the garden. The man has sometimes remembered that the sky on that morning was filled with heaps or layers of grey clouds. The man has sometimes remembered that the boy looked on that morning sometimes in the direction of each of the four districts surrounding the district where he was walking and sometimes in the direction of a certain cloud, which he believed to be the direction of the district that surrounded all other districts.

The man mentioned in the previous paragraph has sometimes remembered that the boy mentioned in that paragraph composed while he walked during the morning mentioned in that paragraph the first line of a poem that he intended to compose. The line of poetry just mentioned is:

O district of my fathers . . .

Whenever the man remembers the line of poetry above, he remembers also that the boy who had composed the line shivered while he first spoke the line aloud after he had composed it. The man supposes that the boy shivered partly because he was proud of having composed the line of poetry and partly because he was afraid.

The man mentioned in the second paragraph of this story as holding a stack of cards in his hand remembers every day one or more details from the years when he used to visit his favourite aunt and her parents and sisters or such of those persons as were still alive after the first of them had died. The following is a summary of the details just mentioned.

The woman who was the favourite aunt mentioned previously was born in one of the first years of the twentieth century and was the eldest of her parents' six children. When she was twelve years of age, her body below her waist became paralysed. The boy who considered the woman his favourite aunt supposed that she had suffered at the age of twelve years from the disease that he knew as *polio*, but when he had become a man he recalled after the death

of the woman who had been his favourite aunt that no one had
ever told him any detail of the story of how the woman had become paralysed below the waist when she was twelve years of age.
Sometimes while the boy's favourite aunt shifted her body in her
bed, the boy looked from the sides of his eyes at the mound made
in the bedclothes by the parts of his aunt's body below her waist.
At such times the boy supposed from the size of the mound that
those parts of his aunt's body were still of the size they had
been when she was twelve years of age. When the boy first became
aware of his partly paralysed aunt, she was a woman of forty or
more years who had spent nearly thirty years in her bed. When the
woman died she was aged about sixty-five years and had spent
more than fifty years in her bed.

The partly paralysed woman mentioned in the previous paragraph rested the weight of her body above the waist on her right
elbow for most of each day while she read or talked or held up a
mirror with a tortoiseshell handle and looked at a reflection of
part of the veranda outside the window of her room or of part
of the formal garden on the far side of the veranda or of part of
the mostly level countryside on the far side of the formal garden
or of part of the sky above the mostly level countryside. The
woman's room was furnished with lounge chairs and was used by
the family as the sitting-room of the house. The many visitors to
the house were shown into this room and were entertained there.
The partly paralysed woman talked and laughed with each of the
many visitors.

The boy who thought of the woman mentioned above as his
favourite aunt preferred to visit the woman when no one else was
in the room and when he could sit in the chair beside her bed and
question her. During the months of each year when the boy was
not on holidays, he would make notes of questions in order to have
a stock of questions that his aunt would spend many hours in answering when he next visited her. The boy might notice, for example, among the embroidered designs on the altar cloths of the

church in his parish the figure of a parent-bird with a long beak together with several infant-birds whose beaks were pointed up-wards towards the parent-bird. The boy might ask his favourite aunt when he next visited her to explain this design. The boy's favourite aunt might tell him that the birds in the design were pelicans and that the parent-bird of the pelican was traditionally supposed to pierce its own breast with its beak so that its young could feed on the blood that flowed.

The card mentioned in the second paragraph of this story has on its obverse an image of the head and the body above the waist of a female saint of the Catholic Church. Behind the image just men-tioned is the image of a sky filled with heaps or layers of clouds, one of which is described in the first paragraph of this story as being surrounded by an aureole or nimbus of pink. On the re-verse of the card just mentioned are words printed with black ink in bold typefaces. Some of these words are *Of your charity, pray for the repose of the soul of* . . . followed by the name of the woman who was once the favourite aunt of one of her nephews. Others of the words just mentioned are *May perpetual light shine upon her* . . . Other words and numerals nearby denote a date in one of the first years of the twentieth century and also a date in the seventh decade of the same century.

Whenever the man who owns the card mentioned in the previ-ous paragraph looks at the reverse of the card, he remembers a day during the week before the second of the dates mentioned in that paragraph. On the day just mentioned the man visited for the first time in several years the house of many rooms where three of his father's sisters still lived with their mother. When the man entered the room that was used as the sitting-room of the house, he no-ticed that the woman in the bed in the room was lying not on her right side but on her left side. He noticed also that the woman was not resting the weight of her body above the waist on her left elbow but was lying in the bed in such a position that if her eyes had been open she would have seen through the window in front of her no part of the veranda on the far side of the window or of the formal garden on the far side of the veranda or of the mostly level countryside on the far side of the formal garden and only a part of the sky above the countryside.

On the day mentioned in the previous paragraph, the man mentioned in that paragraph spoke to the woman in the bed, but the woman spoke in return only the man's given name. On that day the man learned from the sisters and the mother of the woman in the bed that the woman had not told them at any time recently that she was ill but that she had told them several times recently that she was afraid.

On a certain day when the boy-owner of a collection of holy cards was questioning his favourite aunt about the teachings of the Catholic Church in the matter of heaven, hell, purgatory, and the fate of the soul after death, the boy asked his aunt whether any of the saints of the Church would have known during his or her life on earth that he or she would reach heaven after he or she had died. The boy's aunt then told him that even the most pious of the saints could not have known before they had died how God would deal with them after they had died. The boy then asked his aunt whether any person living on earth could know whether any of the person's friends or relatives who had died had reached heaven. The boy's aunt then told the boy a story.

The story mentioned in the previous paragraph was about a nun who had lived for most of her life in a convent of many rooms surrounded first by a formal garden and then by a high stone wall and then by countryside in a country of Europe. Many years after she had died, the nun had been proclaimed a saint by the Church, which meant that any Catholic could be certain that the nun had reached heaven and could pray to the nun, but the events in the story told by the aunt to her favourite nephew took place soon after the death of the nun and at a time when no one on earth could be certain of what had happened to the nun after she had died. While the aunt told the story to her nephew, the nephew did not know that the card that the mother of his favourite aunt and her two surviving sisters would cause to be printed and distributed soon after her death would have on its obverse a picture of the head and of the body above the waist of the nun in the story.

The story mentioned in the previous paragraph may be summarised as follows. During her lifetime, the nun had as a friend a woman who was not a nun but who visited the nun from time to time. The nun and her friend often agreed on how hard it was for persons living on earth that they could not know whether any of their friends and relatives who had died had reached heaven. One day the nun told her friend that if she, the nun, died and reached heaven while her friend was still alive, she, the nun, would send to her friend as a sign that she, the nun, had reached heaven a rose from one of the formal gardens of heaven. In time, the nun died while her friend was still alive. A few days after the nun had died, her friend visited the convent where the nun had lived. The friend talked to the head nun of the convent about the nun who had died. While they were talking, the head nun invited the friend of the dead nun to walk in the formal garden surrounding the convent. While the two persons were walking in the formal garden, the head nun walked over to one of the rose bushes and cut one of the roses from the bush and gave it to the friend of the nun who had died.

On a certain morning in his fifth year, when the boy who later became the owner of the holy cards mentioned previously had not yet become accustomed to spending part of his summer holidays in the house of many rooms mentioned previously, he walked in from the formal garden surrounding the house in order to sit beside the bed of the woman who had already become his favourite aunt. In the hallway of the house, the boy found that the door leading to the room of his favourite aunt was closed. The boy then reached up to the handle of the door and turned the handle and opened the door.

At certain times during the years following his twenty-fifth year, the man who was first mentioned in the second paragraph of this story believed that he had never looked at or touched the naked body of any woman before his twenty-fifth year. At other times during the years just mentioned, the man believed that he had looked at the naked body above the waist of a certain woman during his fifth year. Whenever the man believed what is mentioned in the previous sentence, he believed that he had seen, after he had opened the door mentioned in the previous paragraph, the naked body above the waist of his favourite aunt while she leaned over a dish of white enamel filled with water and on that body two breasts, each with a nipple surrounded by a zone of pink. Whenever the man believed what is mentioned in the sentence before the sentence mentioned in the previous sentence, he believed that he had seen, after he had opened the door just mentioned, the naked body above the waist just mentioned and the dish filled with water just mentioned and on the body the nipples of a girl whose breasts had not yet begun to grow.

On a day when the view from the window of the room where the man who was first mentioned in the second paragraph of this story had kept for more than twenty years in a filing cabinet the cards that he had called as a boy holy cards was of a sky filled with heaps or layers of grey clouds, the man was asked by the woman who had been his wife for more than twenty years why he called such a sky his favourite sky. On that day, the man answered that the sky on the first day that he remembered had been a sky filled with heaps or layers of grey clouds.

On the earlier of the two days mentioned in the previous paragraph, the boy mentioned in that paragraph was a boy in his third year and living with his parents and his younger brother in a suburb of Geelong. On that day the boy had stood alone in the formal garden surrounding the house where he then lived and had looked up at the heaps or layers of grey clouds in the sky and had imagined for the first time that he afterwards remembered certain details of a district other than the district where he then lived.

On a certain day in the twenty-first year of the man who was first mentioned in the second paragraph of this story, the man moved from the house in a suburb of Melbourne where he had lived for most of the time that he could remember with his parents and his younger brother and began to live alone in a room in a house in another suburb of Melbourne. On the day before the day just mentioned, the man told his father that he, the man, no longer believed in the teachings of the Catholic Church in the matter of heaven, hell, purgatory, and the fate of the soul after death or in any other matter.

On a certain day three months after the day mentioned in the previous paragraph, the man mentioned in that paragraph received from his mother a letter telling him that she and his father and his younger brother had moved from the suburb of Melbourne where they had previously lived to a suburb of Geelong. The mother of the man did not mention in the letter the reason for her and her husband's having moved, but the man believed three months later that he understood the reason. The mother of the man wrote also in her letter about some of the families who lived in the suburb of Geelong where she then lived. A certain member of one of those families will be mentioned in a later section of this story.

During a certain hour before daylight on a certain morning

three months after the man mentioned in the previous paragraph had received from his mother the letter mentioned in that paragraph, and while the man was sitting beside the bed where his father was lying in a room of a hospital in the city of Geelong, the man believed that he understood why his father had recently moved from a suburb of Melbourne to a suburb of Geelong. The man believed that his father had moved because he understood, even though he was a man in his fifty-sixth year who had not been ill since the years of his childhood, that he would soon die, and because he wanted to move before he died as near as he could move to the district in the south-west of Victoria where he had been born and where his four unmarried sisters still lived with their mother.

During the hour mentioned in the previous paragraph, the younger of the two men mentioned in that paragraph looked into a small cupboard of steel that stood beside the bed where his father appeared to be asleep in the room mentioned in the same paragraph. Among the things that the younger man saw in the cupboard just mentioned was a man's dressing-gown rolled into a bundle with the cord of the dressing-gown tied loosely around the bundle. While the man just mentioned was looking at the tassels on the ends of the cord just mentioned, he supposed for the first time in his life that the dressing-gown mentioned earlier in this story as having been worn often by the mother of the man in the first year that he afterwards remembered had belonged not to his mother but to his father; that the dressing-gown just mentioned had been bought by his father during one of the many years when he had been a bachelor; and that the mother of the man had worn the dressing gown often during a number of years because she and her husband and their two sons had been poor during those years.

During the hour following the hour mentioned in the previous paragraph, the younger of the two men mentioned in that paragraph understood that his father was about to die. At some time during that hour, the younger man remembered his father's having described to him more than ten years earlier certain details from the first day that he, the father, afterwards remembered. The father had said that he had run on that day along the veranda and through the garden surrounding the house that stood in the early years of the twentieth century where a house of cream-coloured stone of many rooms was later built. The father had also said that he had run to escape from his father and that his father had then run after him.

When the man who was mentioned in the previous paragraph as having understood that his father was about to die had first heard from his father the details of the father's running to escape from his father, the man asked his father whether he had been taking part in a game of chasing with his father. The father of the man who asked the question just mentioned had then said that he, the father, had not been taking part in a game and that he had been, on the first day that he afterwards remembered, afraid.

Late on a certain morning in the first summer after the death of the father of the man who was first mentioned in the second paragraph of this story, the man travelled alone in a motor car from the suburb of Melbourne where he lived alone in a room of a house to the city of Geelong. While the man was travelling on the road that led south-west from Melbourne across mostly level countryside on the way to Geelong, he heard in his mind from time to time certain words from a song that he had first heard from a radio during the previous year. While the man was travelling, he looked from time to time at the sky over the district of Geelong and over the beginnings of the district south-west of that district. The sky that the man looked at was filled with heaps or layers of grey clouds. While the man was travelling, he imagined from time to time details of scenes in remote countryside.

The morning mentioned in the previous paragraph was the first morning of the man's summer holidays. The man was on his way to spend the first day and the first night of his holidays in the house in the suburb of Geelong where his mother lived with her younger son. The man intended to leave his mother's house on the second morning of his holidays and to travel during the remainder of his holidays through districts in New South Wales and Queensland.

When the man mentioned in the previous paragraph had first arrived in the suburb of Geelong where his mother lived, he stopped his car in a street of shops and went into a shop with the sign NEWSAGENCY STATIONERY. The man intended to buy in the shop a map of the nearest districts of New South Wales and a writing pad and a pen that he would use for writing some of the poems that he intended to compose during his summer holidays.

While the man mentioned in the previous paragraph was looking at maps in the shop mentioned in that paragraph, he saw behind the counter of the shop a young woman whose age he supposed to be about eighteen years. After the man had seen the face of the young woman, he began to imagine details of remote countryside in the district of Geelong where he and the young woman would be alone together in the future.

While the man was beginning to imagine the details mentioned in the previous paragraph, he remembered a detail of a letter that he had received from his mother on a certain day three months after he had first moved from his parents' house and had begun to live alone in a room of another house.

One of the last paragraphs of the letter mentioned in the previous paragraph may be summarised as follows.

In the suburb of Geelong where the letter was written, some of the families were poor. Some of the children of the poor families attended the same Catholic primary school that the younger son of the writer of the letter attended. The writer of the letter had first begun to learn how poor were some of these families when the annual fête was soon to be held in the Catholic parish where she and her younger son lived and when the nuns who taught at the primary school had urged their pupils each day to bring from their homes donations of goods that might be sold at the fête. Many of the children had brought to school such items as a tin of fish paste or of baked beans. A few children had brought toys that were scratched or chipped or even broken. And a child who must have come, so the writer of the letter supposed, from the very poorest of families brought to school one morning what the writer of the letter described as a toothbrush holder: an object of pinkish plastic that looked as though it had been taken down a few hours earlier from the hook where it had been hanging for many years on the wall of the bathroom in a house occupied by a poor family of many persons.

When the elder son of the writer of the letter mentioned in the previous paragraph had first read the letter, he had seen in his mind an image of a girl of about twelve years of age holding in her hands and close to the front of her body a pinkish object. On many occasions during the years after he had first seen in his mind the image just mentioned, the elder son of the writer of the letter remembered that he had not seen in his mind when he first read the letter any detail of the face of the girl just mentioned or any detail of the pinkish object just mentioned. On the many occasions just mentioned, the elder son of the writer of the letter remembered that he had first seen some of the details of the face of the girl and of the pinkish object on a certain morning in the first summer after his father had died, when he, the elder son of his father, had been standing in a shop in a suburb of Geelong. On the many occasions just mentioned, the elder son of the father just mentioned remembered what may be summarised as follows.

The man who was described in the previous paragraph as the elder son of his parents and in the second paragraph of this story as the owner of a file labelled *Memorabilia* was standing among displays of writing pads and pens and road maps and other items of stationery and was imagining details of remote countryside. At a certain moment while he was imagining those details, the man saw in his mind an image of a girl of about twelve years of age who was holding close to the front of her body a pinkish object that she was about to offer for sale for the benefit of a parish of the Catholic Church. At the moment just mentioned, the man saw that the details of the face of the girl were the details of the face of a young woman who was standing behind the counter of the shop that he was standing in at that moment. At the moment just mentioned, the man saw also that the pinkish object was an object that had hung on the wall of the bedroom of the favourite aunt of the man during all the years when he had spent part of his summer holidays each year in the house where his favourite aunt lived with others of her family.

The pinkish object mentioned in the previous paragraph was of a kind of object known as a holy water font. The man mentioned in the previous paragraph was used to seeing as a boy large fonts of stone or marble standing inside the doorways of Catholic churches and to dipping his fingers in the holy water in each font as he entered or left the church and then making the sign of the cross on himself with his wet fingers. The man understood as a boy that any person was free to buy from any shop selling Catholic devotional objects one or more of the small fonts of porcelain for sale and then to hang the font or fonts inside one or more of the doors of his or her house, but the only house where the man had seen as a boy a small font of porcelain was the house of many rooms where his favourite aunt lived with others of her family, and the only room in that house that had a font hanging inside its doorway was the room where his favourite aunt lay by day and by night in her bed.

The holy water font mentioned in the previous paragraph was of fine porcelain in the shape of the body above the waist of a person with long hair and with the upper parts of a pair of wings visible at the person's back. The person wore a loose robe over a close-fitting tunic. The arms of the person appeared as though they supported in front of the person the bowl that was the receptacle for the holy water. The bowl occupied part of the space where the body below the waist of the person would otherwise have been. The colour of the face and hands and wings and hair and robe of the person was white. The colour of the tunic was pink.

The boy whose favourite aunt was the owner of the holy water font mentioned in the previous paragraph was accustomed to dipping the ends of two or three of his fingers in the bowl of the font whenever he passed the font during the years when he spent part of his summer holidays in the house where the font was hung. On many of the occasions when the boy dipped the ends of his fingers in the bowl of the font, he looked at the front of the close-fitting pink tunic worn by the person who held the bowl of the font where the parts of the body below the waist of the person would otherwise have been. During the years mentioned in the sentence before the previous sentence, the boy looked on many occasions also at the front of the tunic of each statue of a person with long hair and a robe and a pair of wings that he saw in any schoolroom or church. During the years just mentioned, the boy looked on many occasions also at the front of each tunic in each picture that he saw of a person with long hair and a robe and a pair of wings in any book or in any schoolroom or church.

The boy mentioned in the previous paragraph understood that the statues and pictures that he looked at were representations of the creatures known as angels. The boy understood also the teachings and traditions of the Catholic Church concerning angels. He understood that the angels lived in the district of heaven. He understood also that the angels were spiritual beings who were without bodies and were, therefore, neither male nor female. Yet the boy expected that at some time in the future while he looked at one or another of the tunics that he would look at in the future, he would learn that the wearer of the tunic was a female person.

After the man who was first mentioned in the second paragraph of this story had seen in his mind on a certain morning during his twenty-first year and soon after his father had died an image of a girl of about twelve years of age holding close to the front of her body a pinkish object, the man took the map and the writing pad and the pen that he intended to buy to a man behind the counter of the shop mentioned previously and then bought the goods and left the shop. The man then continued to travel towards the house where his mother lived with his younger brother. While the man travelled, he looked from time to time at the sky, which was filled with heaps or layers of grey clouds, and he heard in his mind from time to time certain words from a song that was mentioned earlier in this story and he saw in his mind from time to time details of scenes in remote countryside on the inland slopes of the Great Dividing Range in either New South Wales or Queensland.

The image that caused me to begin writing this story is an image of a single cloud in a picture on the obverse of a card in the hand of a man. The cloud just mentioned is one of many clouds in a sky filled with heaps or layers of clouds. The sky just mentioned is behind the head and the body above the waist of a saint of the Catholic Church: a female person wearing the habit of an order of nuns.

The single cloud in the image mentioned in the previous paragraph is surrounded by an aureole or nimbus of pink. The man looking at the card mentioned in the previous paragraph has not yet seen the aureole or nimbus just mentioned. The man takes the card into his hand once in each few years and then reads the printed words on the reverse of the card and then remembers the woman who was once his favourite aunt and then calculates in round figures what quantity of indulgence a person would have amassed if the person had earned ten thousand days of indulgence every day for fifty years and then remembers certain teachings that he has not believed since his twenty-first year and then looks at the sky in the picture on the obverse of the card.

The man mentioned in the previous paragraph has not yet seen the aureole or nimbus mentioned in that paragraph. I first saw the aureole or nimbus on the day when I began to write this story, and I have seen the aureole or nimbus whenever I have looked since that day at the image in my mind of the clouds in the sky in the picture in the hand of the man.

I first saw the aureole or nimbus mentioned in the previous paragraph while I was hearing in my mind some of the words of a song that was mentioned earlier in this story. The man mentioned in the previous paragraph has heard in his mind from time to time the words of the song just mentioned, but he has never heard the words in such a way that they have caused him to see in his mind what the same words have caused me to see in my mind.

The song mentioned in the previous paragraph is one of a sort of song known in the late 1950s and the early 1960s among many of the people who listened to radio programmes as a folk song. The title of the song is either "The Sloop John B" or "The Sloop John V." The previous sentence may be untrue. Whenever the man mentioned in the previous paragraph hears in his mind some of the words of the song just mentioned, he notices words reporting that the narrator has travelled on the sloop named *John B* or *John V* around Nassau Town and has stayed awake all night and has got into a fight. Whenever the man hears these words in his mind, he remembers certain events from the years when he used to spend part of his summer holidays each year travelling in his motor car through New South Wales and Queensland. When I heard the words of the song just mentioned in such a way that they caused me to see in my mind the image that caused me to begin writing this story, I noticed words reporting that the narrator was travelling with his grandfather and that he, the narrator, felt so broken up that he wanted to go home.

Boy Blue

A few weeks ago, the person writing this story read aloud to a gathering of persons another story that he had written. The chief character of the story that was read aloud was a man who was referred to throughout the story as the chief character of the story. After the person writing this story had read aloud the story mentioned in the previous sentence, the persons listening were invited by the organiser of the gathering to ask questions of the person who had read. The gathering was what some persons might have called a distinguished gathering, and the first person to ask a question was what some persons might have called a most distinguished person, she being the author of a number of books. The first person to ask a question asked the person who had just read whether the chief character of his story might have been a more interesting character if he had been given a name. The person who had just read the story whose chief character was referred to as the chief character of the story had been asked many times previously why the characters in his stories lacked names. The person who wrote stories about characters lacking names understood why his characters could have no names and tried always to explain to his questioners why his characters lacked names. However, the person whose characters lacked names suspected that he had seldom conveyed to any questioner the reason why his characters lacked names, and at the gathering mentioned previously he suspected that his answer to the author who questioned him failed to convey to her the reason for the lack just mentioned. Soon after the gathering just mentioned, the person writing this story decided that he would begin the next story that he wrote by explaining why the characters in that story lacked names. Soon after the person just mentioned had made the decision just mentioned, he began to write this story, "Boy Blue."

This is a story about a man and his son and the mother of the man. The man just mentioned will be called in this story *the man* or *the father*; the son just mentioned will be called in this story *the son* or *the son of the man*; the mother just mentioned will be called *the mother* or *the mother of the man*. Other characters will be mentioned in this story, and each of those characters will be distinguished from the other characters, but none of the characters will have what could be considered by any person reading or hearing the story a name. Any person who reads these words or hears these words read aloud and wishes that the characters in the story each had a name is invited to consider the following explanation but to remember at the same time that the words of the explanation are also part of this story.

I am writing these words in the place that is called by many persons the real world. Almost every person who lives or has lived in this place has or has had a name. Whenever a person tells me that he or she prefers the characters in a story to have names, I suppose that the person likes to pretend, while reading a story, that the characters in the story are living or have lived in the place where the person is reading. Other persons may pretend whatever they choose to pretend, but I cannot pretend that any character in any story written by me or by any other person is a person who lives or has lived in the place where I sit writing these words. I see the characters in stories, including the story of which this sentence is a part, as being in the invisible place that I often call my mind. I would like the reader or the listener to notice that I wrote the word *being* and not the word *living* in the previous sentence.

The man who is the chief character of this story was sitting in the dining area of his and his wife's house at the end of the first hour of a certain morning at the time of the year when the first pink flowers appeared on the branches of the prunus trees in the suburb where he lived with his wife and his son and his daughter in a city in the invisible place mentioned in the previous paragraph.

At the time mentioned in the previous sentence, the son of the man was sitting in the kitchen adjoining the dining area of his parents' house after having eaten a plate of curry and rice that had been put into the oven by his mother during the last hour of the previous evening. At the time mentioned in the previous sentence, the father had in front of him the book *Woodbrook*, by David Thomson, published in 1991 by Vintage, and was pretending to read while he listened for any words that his son might speak. At the time mentioned in the previous sentence, the son had recently returned to his parents' house from the factory where he worked on four days of each week from mid-afternoon until midnight as the operator of a machine. The son worked on only four days of each week because the workers at the factory just mentioned had chosen during the previous week to work for fewer days of each week rather than to have some of themselves dismissed.

Early in the second hour of the morning mentioned in the previous paragraph, the son told his father that the manager of the factory where the son worked had told the workers on the previous evening that one or more of them might have to be dismissed in the near future because fewer orders were being placed at the factory for the parts of the motor car engines and of other machinery that were made there. During the hour just mentioned, the son told his father also that he, the son, believed that the worker in most danger of being dismissed from the factory just mentioned was either himself or a certain man who will be called during the rest of this story the workmate of the son. The son did not have to tell his father why he, the son, was in danger of being dismissed. The father knew that his son had begun to work at the factory more recently than any other worker at the factory. But the son had to explain to the father why the workmate of the son was in danger of being dismissed. Before explaining to his father the matter just mentioned, the son told his father the following details that he, the son, had learned from his workmate or from other workers in the factory.

The workmate of the son was a man a year older than the father of the son. The workmate lived with his wife, his son aged sixteen, and his daughter aged fourteen in a rented house in the suburb where the factory mentioned previously stood, which suburb was often said to be the poorest of all the suburbs in the quarter of the city mentioned previously. The workmate's wife had recently been dismissed from her job in another factory and was looking out for another job of any kind. The workmate and his wife owned only their clothing and the few pieces of furniture in the house that they rented. The workmate owned also a motor car that he had bought during the previous year for seven hundred dollars, but the motor car was in faulty order, and the workmate lacked the money to pay for repairs to the motor car. The television set in the house was also in faulty order, but neither the workmate nor his wife had the money needed to repair the set.

After having told his father the details mentioned in the previous paragraph, the son explained to his father why his, the son's, workmate was in danger of being dismissed from the factory where he worked. His workmate, so the son said, often failed to adjust correctly or to check the settings of his machine, and many of the metal objects that were cut or ground by the machine were found afterwards to be faulty. The workmate wore spectacles with thick lenses, and the son sometimes supposed that the workmate was unable to read the tiny numerals or to see the fine markings on his machine. At other times, the son supposed that his workmate hurried at his work so that he could gain the time for smoking one or more of the many cigarettes that he smoked while he was in the factory.

When the father heard what is reported in the previous paragraph, he wanted to learn more about his son's workmate, but the father did not ask the son to tell him more. The workmate who was in danger of being dismissed was the first person that the son had talked about from among the many persons he had worked with. During the five years before the first morning to have been reported in this story, the only persons that the son and his father had talked about were persons mentioned in the newspapers and magazines that the son read in his room on most evenings. Before he had begun to work at the factory mentioned previously, the son had had no job for more than a year. During the year just mentioned, the son had visited a number of factories as an applicant for one or another job but had not talked to his father afterwards about any of the visits. During the three years before the year when the son had had no job, he had worked at different times in five factories but had not talked to his father about any of the persons he had worked with. During the year before the three years just mentioned, the son had been at first a student in the final year of secondary school but had later stopped going to school and had spent most of each day and evening watching in his room a television set that he had repaired after having found it on a nature strip where it had been left among household rubbish because it was in faulty order. During the year just mentioned, the son had not talked to his father about any matter.

In the first hour of the morning after the first morning to have been mentioned in this story, the man was sitting in the dining area mentioned previously and reading the book mentioned previously when his son arrived home from the factory where he worked. Among the pages that the man had read from the book just mentioned during the hours just mentioned were pages 159 and 160, where the following words are printed inside quotation marks: *a greater amount of urgent and pressing destitution . . . than in*

any other part of Ireland I have visited, as in addition to want of
food which exists to as great an extent as in any other part of
Ireland, want of shelter from the inclemency of the seasons exists
to a far greater extent . . . vast numbers of families have been un-
housed and their houses destroyed. You cannot admit them to the
workhouse, there is no room; you cannot give them outdoor re-
lief, they have no houses . . . their cries may be heard all night in
the streets of this town; and since my arrival here I have con-
stantly been obliged to procure shelter in the stables in the neigh-
bourhood for persons I have found perishing in the streets at 12
o'clock at night. While the son was taking out of the oven mentioned previously the meal that his mother had left for him, which
was a plate of chops and rice, he told his father the first of the
details in the following paragraph. After the son had eaten the
meal just mentioned, he told his father the remainder of the following details just mentioned.

The son had noticed late on the previous afternoon that the
metal objects leaving his workmate's machine had been wrongly
finished. The son had then left his own machine and had offered
to help his workmate check the settings on his machine and to put
again through the machine the objects that had been wrongly finished. The workmate had agreed with the son that the objects
leaving his, the workmate's, machine had been wrongly finished,
but the workmate had not agreed to let the son check the settings on the machine. The workmate had said that he himself had
checked the settings earlier in the afternoon. The workmate had
then said that the machine itself was at fault. The workmate
had then walked away from his machine and had lit a cigarette
and had begun to smoke the cigarette.

After the son had taken out of the oven mentioned previously the plate of chops and rice mentioned previously, he first
carried the plate and the chops and the rice to the bench between the kitchen and the dining area, then carried back to the
oven door the tea-towel that he had used to protect his hands from
the heated plate, then took out a knife and a fork from the drawer

of cutlery in the kitchen, then put the knife on one side and the fork on the other side of the plate of chops and rice, then took out from the food cupboard in the kitchen a salt shaker and a pepper mill and a bottle of sauce with the word *Cornwell* and the words *Father's Favourite* on the label, and then shook salt from the cellar and ground out pepper from the mill over the chops on his plate. During some of the time while the son did the things just mentioned, he was facing in a direction such that his father could have seen his face if he, the father, had looked up from where he was sitting with the book named previously open in front of him, but the father did not look up.

During the first hour of each of the three mornings following the morning most recently mentioned, the father was sitting in the position mentioned previously with the book named previously open in front of him when the son returned from the factory where he worked. On the first two of the mornings just mentioned, the father waited for the son to speak while he took his meal from the oven mentioned previously and again after he had eaten his meal, but the son did not speak. On the third of the mornings just mentioned, while the son was taking out of the oven just mentioned the plate of curry and rice that his mother had left for him he told his father that the workmate who had been in danger of being dismissed had not been at his machine when the workers on the evening shift had begun work on the previous afternoon; that he, the son, had asked the foreman of the evening shift where the workmate was; that the foreman had answered that the workmate had been dismissed; that the son had then asked what the workmate had said after he had been told that he had been dismissed; that the foreman had then said that no one had told the workmate that he had been dismissed and that the management of the factory dismissed a person by employing a courier to take to the address of the person a letter telling the person that he or she had been dismissed and a sum of money equal to his or her pay for two weeks plus any money owing to the person for leave not taken. During some of the time while the son told the father what is reported in the previous sentence, the son was facing in a direction such that the father could have seen the son's face if he, the father, had looked up from where he was sitting with the book named previously in front of him, but the father did not look up.

During the second hour of the morning most recently mentioned, while the man was lying in his and his wife's bed beside his wife, who was asleep, and while the man was waiting to fall asleep, he saw in his mind a scene in a house that was furnished with only a few pieces of furniture. In the scene just mentioned, a man one year older than the man in whose mind the scene appeared was sitting at a table in the kitchen of the house and smoking a cigarette while the wife and the son and the daughter of the man were sitting in the adjoining lounge-room and watching a television set that was in faulty order. The man who saw the scene just mentioned in his mind did not look in the direction of the face of any of the persons in the scene.

During the hour mentioned in the previous paragraph, whenever the man saw in his mind the scene mentioned in that paragraph he told himself that the scene was in his mind and not in the place that was called by many persons the real world. During the hour just mentioned, the man told himself further that the scene in his mind was of the kind of scene that appeared in his mind while he read from a book of fiction or even from the kind of book that reported events believed to have happened or even agreed to have happened in the place that was called by many persons the real world.

During the first hour of the day following the day mentioned in the previous paragraph, the man was sitting in the dining area mentioned previously with the book named previously open in front of him when his son arrived home from the factory where he worked. When the son walked into the kitchen of his parents' house during the hour just mentioned, the father greeted the son but did not look up from the book named previously. After the father had greeted the son as mentioned in the previous sentence, the son greeted the father and then took out of the oven mentioned previously the plate of chicken and rice that had been left for him by his mother and then prepared to eat the meal.

On a certain day in the year when the son was aged five years and had recently begun to go to school and when the father and the son were alone together in the dining area mentioned previously, the father began to tell the son what was likely to happen to him in the future. The son would go to secondary school for six years. Then, so the father said, the son would go to a university and would learn there to be a scientist or an engineer. Then, so the father said, the son would work for five days of each week as a scientist or an engineer. The son would be paid much money for his work, so the father then said, and he, the son, would use some of the money to buy a motor car and a house and furniture and books and a television set. At some time in the future, so the father then said, the son would marry, and at some time afterwards he would become the father of a son and a daughter. Late on a certain evening after he, the son, had been living for many years in his house with his wife and his son and his daughter and his furniture and his books and his television set and with his motor car and his wife's motor car in a garage beside the house, so the father said, a visitor would arrive at the son's house. The visitor would knock at the front door of the house, so the father then said, and the son would open the door and would see an old man standing in front of him. The old man would be wearing shabby clothes, so the father then said, and he would say while he stood at the front door that he owned no house or furniture or television set or motor car and that he had no money in his pockets. The old man would then ask, so the father then said, whether he, the old man, might take shelter for the night in his, the son's, house. The son would then look at the face of the old man, so the father then said, and would discover that the old man was his father.

After the father had told his son what is reported in the previous paragraph, the father asked his son what he would say or do after the old man had asked for shelter. The son then said that he would invite his father to come into his, the son's, house and to rest on his, the son's, furniture.

While the son said what is reported in the previous paragraph, the father looked at the son's face. The father then put an arm around the shoulders of his son and said that the scene that he, the father, had been describing was only a scene in a story told by the father.

In the house where the father lived when he was aged from five to seven years, his mother would sometimes ask him whether he would like to hear the poem "Boy Blue." The mother would ask the question just mentioned most often in the late afternoon of a cloudy and windy day, when she had not yet turned on the light in the kitchen of the house just mentioned and when the wind was rattling the windowpanes and the loose weatherboards of the house. Whenever the mother had asked the question just mentioned, the boy would answer that he wanted to hear the poem. The mother, who had stopped going to school when she was twelve years of age, would first recite the words *Little Boy Blue, by Eugene Field* and would then recite from memory all six stanzas of a poem that she had learned when she was eight years of age from the *Third Book of the Victorian Readers*, published by the Education Department of Victoria.

While the mother recited the poem mentioned in the previous paragraph, her son, the person referred to elsewhere in this story as the man or the father, saw in his mind an image of a room containing a chair on which was a toy dog covered with dust and a toy soldier red with rust, each of which, the toy dog and the toy soldier, was wondering as he waited the long years through what had become of the person known as Little Boy Blue since he had kissed them and put them there and had told them to wait until he came and to make no noise. While the father saw in his mind the image of the room just mentioned, he pretended that the room was not part of an image in the invisible place that he often called his mind but a room in the place that he and others called the real

329

world. The father as a boy pretended that the room in his mind was a room in the place called the real world so that he could further pretend that a person who lived in the place just mentioned would come into the room at some time in the future and would explain to the dog and the soldier mentioned previously why they had to wait and to wonder for so long and so that he could further pretend that he would never again begin to weep while his mother read the poem and would never again pretend to be comforted after his mother had read to the end of the poem and had then looked at his face and had then told him that the dog and the soldier and the room where they were waiting were only details in a story.

Emerald Blue

In the Gippsland Forest

For most of his lifetime, he had kept in his mind certain details from pictures he had seen, but he had hardly ever been interested in art. He had never gone voluntarily into an art gallery and he felt no regret that he had never seen the art of Europe. One day when he was aged more than forty and was walking past the National Gallery of Victoria, he asked himself what images, if any, he could call to mind from the few occasions when he had been obliged to accompany someone through that building. He recalled two images: a distant view of a winding river in a painting called, so he thought, *Still Flows the Stream and Shall For Ever Flow*, by an Australian painter whose name he had never learned; and in the foreground of a crowded painting called, so he believed, *Cleopatra's Banquet*, a dog resembling one of the whippets that had contested a race reserved for their kind on each of the weekly programmes of races for greyhounds at the track called Napier Park, which had been covered

over for nearly thirty years by certain streets of houses in the suburb of Strathmore in the north-west of Melbourne.

In his last year at secondary school, some of his teachers had
told him that he should go to university. At the end of that year he
passed the matriculation examination, but then he joined the state
public service as a clerical officer of a lowly grade. He was afraid
of the university. He had looked into the handbook for the faculty
of arts—the only faculty he was qualified for—and had been repelled by the lists of books to be read. He did not want to read the
same books that were read and discussed by all the other students
and by the lecturers and tutors. There was much that he wanted
to learn, but he could not believe that he would learn it as other
people learned what they learned. He believed in something that
he called to himself precious knowledge. As a child, he had hoped
to find some of that knowledge in some discarded or forgotten
book. Later, he came to understand that such knowledge as he
was looking for was not readily passed from one person to another. Sometimes he thought of precious knowledge as lying on
the other side of the pages of one or another book whose title
and author he had yet to hear of. In order to obtain the precious
knowledge, he would have had to get inside the book itself and to
live in the places where the characters lived. Looking out from
those places, he would see such things (knowledge being to him
always something visible) as only the characters in the book were
privileged to see, whereas readers and even the author of the
book could only speculate about them.

In the first year after he left school, he bought and began to
read many blue-and-white-covered Pelican books: histories of
places and periods not studied at the University of Melbourne;
summaries of the works of certain philosophers; books of popular
psychology. At some time during that year, he bought the Pelican
book *Landscape into Art*, by Kenneth Clark, first published in
1949 and published as a Pelican Book in 1956. If the title had
been *The Art of the Landscape* or *Landscape as Art*, he might not
have bought the book, but he was taken by the force of the prep-

osition *into*. The phrase *landscape into art* seemed to promise him precious knowledge. He was going to see, perhaps, into the mind of some man who had landscapes passing through him. Green fields and blue or grey skies drifted into him from the one side; mysterious things happened in the depths of him; and then a painted landscape of vistas and perspectives drifted out of the other side of him.

Before he had begun to read the text of *Landscape into Art*, he looked at the series of black and white illustrations in the middle pages. Of the landscapes or details of landscapes reproduced in those pages, one image lodged in his mind and was never afterwards dislodged. More than thirty years later, he could still see in his mind an image of certain ruts filled with water beside a road in the painted landscape *February Fill Dyke*, by B. W. Leader, whereas he could remember no detail of any of the other illustrations in *Landscape into Art*. The first pages that he read in the book were the pages listed in the index beside the entry *Leader, B. W.* He learned from these pages that the painting that had so impressed him had been included in the book only as an example of the least praiseworthy sort of painted landscape. *February Fill Dyke* was, according to Kenneth Clark, by far the worst painting of all those illustrated.

The image of the water-filled ruts had been in his mind for thirty-three years before he began to understand how that image had come to be there. He had never learned where or when the painter Leader had lived. He had never read any other reference to Leader apart from the disparaging passage in Clark's book. In the first few years after he had first taken the image of the ruts to heart, he regretted sometimes that he still knew nothing about the person who had painted the ruts or about the place where certain water-filled ruts beside a country road in England (if it *was* England) had been changed into a painted image of water-filled ruts. When he was aged in his twenties and thirties and keeping a journal with long entries explaining what he called his world-view, he would have said that the so-called original ruts and country road existed only in his imagination, while the real ruts and road existed only in the illustration that he had seen long ago in a book. In his fifties, he could have said no more than that an endless series of images of water-filled ruts beside country roads existed in a part of himself. He had come to believe that he was made up mostly of images. He was aware only of images and feelings. The feelings connected him to the images and connected the images to one another. The connected images made up a vast network. He was never able to imagine this network as having a boundary in any direction. He called the network, for convenience, his mind.

The image most often visible of the images of water-filled ruts, so he discovered one day in his early fifties, was connected with an image of a road in a picture called *In the Gippsland Forest*. All of the images just mentioned were connected also with certain images that he had seen more than forty years before the day just mentioned but had not seen since.

When he was seven years old, someone had passed on to him a small collection of foreign postage stamps in an album. He read the names of the countries named on the stamps. He knew where some of those countries were in the image that he had of the world. No one in his house had an atlas, but he understood that the world was in the shape of a globe and that England and America, as he called the USA, were the two most important countries in the world and were, appropriately, on the upper half of the globe and far away from his own country. One stamp was from Helvetia. The stamp was blue-grey, and the image on the stamp was of the head and shoulders of a man with a high collar and thick, dark hair and a hint of sorrow in his looks. He, the owner of the stamp, wanted to know where Helvetia was, but no one he asked had heard of any country of that name.

More than forty years afterwards, he still remembered that he had seen in his mind from time to time for several years images of a place he supposed to be Helvetia. He had seen some of the citizens of Helvetia going about their business. He had even watched for a few minutes the man with the high collar and the dark hair and had learned something that might have explained the hint of sorrow about the man. He, the owner of the stamp collection, asked his teachers and a few other adults from time to time where Helvetia was, but no one could tell him. As soon as he was able to use an atlas, he searched for Helvetia. When he could find no part of the world with the same name as the country in his mind, he felt for a few moments as awed and delighted as he would ever afterwards feel before the strangeness of things. He soon explained the mystery to himself by supposing that Helvetia was the former name of a country now named differently, and in time he met a boy whose stamp album included pages of information including the equivalent names in the English language for Suomi, Sverige, Helvetia, and a long list of many other names that he, the chief character of this story, might have used all his life instead of Helvetia to denote a certain place in his mind if he had seen any of them on the first few of his postage stamps.

As a young man, he had sometimes regretted that he had never seen again the country that had appeared in answer to his need. Later, he had come to understand that the landscape of Helvetia was not the only such landscape he had seen. Whenever he was invited to a house that he had not previously visited, he would see in his mind at once the house as it looked from the front gate, the interior of the main room, the view of the back garden from the kitchen window. Then he would visit the house, and the other house would have followed Helvetia into oblivion. Sometimes, while he read a certain letter or answered a certain telephone call, the writer or the caller would become surrounded by rooms and gardens and streets that were doomed to disappear. Whenever he read a work of fiction, he looked past the characters in his mind to the landscapes that reached far back in the direction of Helvetia.

He had proved to his own satisfaction that his sighting unfamiliar rooms and vistas was not merely an inferior sort of remembering: that his imagining—to use that word—was not merely a calling to mind of details he had previously seen but had then forgotten (and would forget again). He had never been able to believe in something called his unconscious mind. The term *unconscious mind* seemed to him self-contradictory. Words such as *imagination* and *memory* and *person* and *self* and even *real* and *unreal* he found vague and misleading, and all the theories of psychology that he had read about as a young man begged the question of *where* the mind was. For him, the first of all premises was that his mind was a place or, rather, a vast arrangement of places. Everything he had ever seen in his mind was in a particular place. He did not know how far in any direction the places extended in his mind. He could not even deny that some of the furthest places in his mind might have adjoined the furthest places in some other mind. He had no wish to deny that the furthest places in his mind or in the furthest mind from his mind might have adjoined the furthest places in a Place of Places, which term denoted for him what is denoted for some other persons by the word *God*.

Between the ages of about four and fourteen, he visited often with his mother and his younger brother a certain house in an eastern suburb of Melbourne. On one of the walls of that house was a picture with the title *In the Gippsland Forest*. If he had ever mentioned the picture to anyone in his lifetime, he would have been able to use no more precise word than *picture* for the object whose details were still in his mind forty years after he had last looked at them. The object may have been an oil painting or a pastel drawing or a water colour or a reproduction or one or another of those three or one of a series of prints or, what he thought more likely, one of an unnumbered series of reproductions of an illustration by an unnamed person who drew or painted subjects suitable for framing behind glass and for being sold during the 1920s and the 1930s in shops in the eastern suburbs of Melbourne to young married couples who were furnishing their newly bought houses in those suburbs during those years. If he had stopped to think about the matter, he would have had to admit that the pictures sold to young married couples in the 1920s and the 1930s would have been the same in most suburbs of Melbourne, but whenever he thought of a young couple choosing *In the Gippsland Forest* for a wall in their new house, he thought of them as being in a shop in an eastern suburb with a view of the blue-black ridge of Mount Dandenong visible from the street outside the shop.

He had been born in a western suburb of Melbourne and had lived in that suburb with his parents and his younger brother until his thirteenth year. In that year, the family moved to a house that the father had bought in an outer south-eastern suburb of Melbourne. He, the chief character of this story, lived in the house just mentioned until his twenty-ninth year, when he married a young woman who will be mentioned later in this story and moved with her into a rented flat in an inner-northern suburb of Melbourne. In his thirty-third year, he and his wife moved to a house that he and she had bought in an outer northern suburb of Melbourne.

The house where the picture hung on a wall belonged to one of his mother's sisters and her husband. These two lived in the house with their three daughters and their son. The youngest of the daughters was five years older than the chief character of this story, but the boy, their brother, was nearly five years younger than the chief character. In the early years of his visiting the house, the girls would sometimes lend him some of their comics to look through, but in later years the girls seemed to be always out of the house, and the doors to their rooms were kept shut. He seldom played with his boy-cousin and in later years would bring a book with him to the house and would sit reading it in the front room. After he had turned fourteen and was allowed to choose not to accompany his mother on her visits, he no longer visited his aunt's and his uncle's house. On the day of his uncle's funeral in the mid-1980s, he spent an hour in the house, which had been enlarged and redecorated. He did not see the picture on any wall.

During the years when he no longer visited the house in the eastern suburb, whenever he remembered the picture he remembered one or more of the following details: a man is walking alone on a narrow road of red gravel or closely packed red soil; on either side of the road, tussocks of grass grow and long, narrow puddles of water lie and blackened stumps of trees stand; on either side of the tussocks and stumps, tall trees grow closely together with thick scrub between their trunks; the man is walking towards the background of the picture; ahead of the man, the road turns aside and out of his view, but no detail in the picture suggests that the man will see ahead of him, when he reaches the place where the road turns aside, a different sight from the sight he now sees ahead; the light is dull, as though the time is early evening and as though some of the upper branches of the trees meet above the road and the man walking.

During the years when he sometimes remembered one or more of the details mentioned above, he would sometimes remember also one or more of the following.

In the years when he lived in the western suburb and visited the house in the eastern suburb, the street where the house stood was the easternmost place he had ever visited. During those years, the easternmost place he had ever seen was the summit of Mount Dandenong, which he saw against the sky whenever he looked eastwards from any of the hills in the eastern suburb. He had believed as a boy that the word *Gippsland* denoted all that part of Victoria east and south-east of Mount Dandenong. He had believed as a boy that the region of Gippsland had been from the time of the creation of the world until the year in the nineteenth century when the first persons from England or Ireland or Scotland arrived in the region wholly forest; that most of Gippsland had been turned from forest into green paddocks and towns and roads and railway lines during the hundred years between the year just mentioned and the year when he himself had been born; that the few patches of forest still standing in Gippsland had burned away during the week before his birth when, so his father had often told him, the worst bushfires in the history of their country had been burning and the suburbs all around Melbourne had been overhung by smoke; that one of the chief reasons for the picture's having stayed in his mind was the article *the* in the title of the picture, which word caused him to think of the one forest that had formerly covered all of Gippsland as appearing still in the mind of the man who was walking between the puddles and the stumps and in the mind of the man who had painted the picture; that the man in the picture was walking in an easterly direction, with Mount Dandenong and much of Gippsland behind him; that the man walking from Mount Dandenong towards the far side of Gippsland had lived for most of his life alone.

Sometimes, when he remembered the house where *In the Gippsland Forest* had hung, he supposed that he might never have noticed the picture if he had found during his early visits to the house one or another book of fiction that he could have read. His father had once told his mother in a mocking tone that her sister in the western suburb lived in a house without books. (The man who said this owned no books himself, although he borrowed and read three books of fiction each week from a circulating library.) He, the son, always believed his father's dislike of his wife's relatives was the result of their being Protestants. The son himself always preferred his father's relatives and thought of his mother as being less than a true Catholic because she had only been converted shortly before her marriage. During most of his first visits to the house in the eastern suburb, the son had been left to stare at the plants in the garden or at the ornaments in the lounge-room, but he had once heard words from a book and had remembered them for long afterwards.

The time had been late afternoon. He and his mother and his brother had been about to leave on their long trip by tram and suburban train to the western suburb where they lived. One of his female cousins had brought a girlfriend to the house, and the two girls were amusing the young boy-cousin of the chief character of this story. The girls would have been about thirteen years of age, and the boy about four. The girl-visitor was reading to the boy. The chief character of this story had been listening through a half-closed door but had heard only a few of the words being read. Then, while his mother was saying goodbye to her sister and while he was expecting to be urged at any moment out of the house, the girl who was reading began to raise her voice and to speak with overmuch expression. At the time, he had supposed that the story being read was approaching its climax. Whenever he remembered the voice of the girl during the forty and more years afterwards, he supposed that she had become aware that he was listening to her from behind the door. Before he left the house, he heard words that he remembered afterwards as ". . . and then he saw the river winding far away into the distance like a blue ribbon through the green hills . . ." Having spoken these words, the girl-reader paused as though she was showing to her boy-listener the picture that accompanied the words.

In the firs by the lattice

When he first read the book of fiction *Wuthering Heights*, he was in his eighteenth year and living with his parents and his younger brother in the house mentioned previously in the outer south-eastern suburb of Melbourne. At that time he had been travelling for four years and more in suburban electric trains on weekdays to and from an inner south-eastern suburb, where he attended a secondary school for boys on a hillside with a distant view of Mount Dandenong. On each afternoon when he travelled from his school towards his home, the train that he travelled in displayed at its front the word DANDENONG. When he first read *Wuthering Heights*, he had never travelled to the place denoted by the word on the front of the train. He understood, however, that the place was not the blue-black mountain that he looked at through the windows of his schoolroom but a town built on mostly level land ten miles south-west of the mountain.

At some time ten years or more after he had first read *Wuthering Heights*, he understood that the place named Dandenong had become an outer south-eastern suburb of Melbourne, but during the year when he first read the book, he thought of Dandenong as the nearest to Melbourne of the towns of Gippsland. During that year, he had been no nearer to Gippsland than in the suburb where he then lived, but he was reminded of Gippsland every day whenever a country passenger train pulled by a blue and gold diesel-electric locomotive sped along the suburban line, running express through station after station on its way to Warragul or Sale or Bairnsdale. His father had told him more than once, and without smiling, that the people of Gippsland were inbred and degenerate and that the girls and women of Gippsland had goitres hanging out from under their chins because the soil of Gippsland was lacking in essential minerals. The man who said these things had been no nearer to Gippsland than his son had been. The man had been born in the south-west of Victoria, had moved to Melbourne during what he always called the Great Oppression, had married a young woman who was also from the south-west, had lived during the first fifteen years of his marriage in rented houses in the western suburbs of Melbourne, and had then moved to the house mentioned previously in an outer south-eastern suburb, having chosen that suburb only because a certain man who was a racecourse acquaintance and who was on his way to making a fortune from what was then called spec-building had offered to arrange for him a loan through what was called a private building society so that he could begin to buy, without having paid any deposit, a weatherboard house on an unfenced rectangle of scrub beside a street consisting of two wheel-ruts, often deep under water, winding among tussocks of grass and outcrops of scrub.

Whenever the chief character of this story had begun to read any book of fiction in all the time before he had begun to read *Wuthering Heights* for the first time, he had hoped that the book he was beginning to read would be the last book of fiction that he would have to read. He had hoped of each book that it would cause to appear in his mind an image of a certain young woman and an image of a certain place, after which event in his mind he would need to read no more books of fiction. While he was reading the early chapters of *Wuthering Heights*, certain sentences caused him to suppose that he was reading the last book of fiction that he would have to read. The first of those sentences is this from Chapter 6: *But it was one of their chief amusements to run away to the moors in the morning and remain there all day and the after punishment grew a mere thing to laugh at.* Other such sentences are the following from Chapter 12. *"This feather was picked up from the heath, the bird was not shot—we saw its nest in the winter, full of little skeletons. Heathcliff set a trap over it, and the old ones dare not come. I made him promise he'd never shoot a lapwing, after that, and he didn't."* The remainder of the sentences are the following from Chapter 12: *"Oh, if I were but in my own bed in the old house!" she went on bitterly, wringing her hands. "And that wind sounding in the firs by the lattice. Do let me feel it—it comes straight down the moor—do let me have one breath!"*

After he had finished reading *Wuthering Heights* for the first time, and while he was reading for the first time the next of the list of books that he was obliged to read as a student of the subject English Literature in the syllabus for the matriculation examination for the University of Melbourne, he began to notice often in his mind an image of the face of one of the young women in school uniform who travelled on weekday afternoons on the train that ran through the outer eastern suburbs to the place that he thought of as the nearest of the towns of Gippsland. He understood from this that he was about to go through once again a series of states of feeling such as he had gone through many times before.

Whenever, as an adult, he heard people recalling their childhood or he read the first chapters of an autobiography or passages about childhood in a convincing piece of fiction, he supposed that he had been an extraordinary oddity as a child. Throughout his life, he could remember clearly occasions from as early as his fifth year when he saw in his mind an image of a woman or of a girl and felt for that image a feeling for which he knew no better name than love. The word *occasions* in the previous sentence applies only to the first two or three years of his falling in love. From about his eighth year, one or another image was continually in his mind for weeks at a time.

At some time during the year in the late 1960s which was the last year before he became a married man, he read in the *Times Literary Supplement*, in a short review of a certain book of autobiography, that the author of the book had been an extraordinary oddity as a child in that he had felt, from his very early years, a passionate affection for numbers of girls and young women. He, the chief character of this story, believed he was about to learn at last that he was not the only man of his kind. He placed a special order with his bookseller for the book, which was *Monsieur Nicolas, or The Human Heart Laid Bare*, by Restif de la Bretonne, translated by Robert Baldick and published in London by Barrie and Rockliff, but when his copy had arrived he learned from the first chapter that the narrator and he had little in common and he went back to believing that he had grown up differently from all other men.

The narrator of *Monsieur Nicolas* had been strongly attracted to girls and young women from about his tenth year, but they were persons from his neighbourhood, some of whom actually kissed and petted him, and he felt towards them a sexual desire that seemed to the chief character of this story undistinguished, especially after he had read of how the narrator of the book had been taught by a young woman how to satisfy that desire. This lesson had taken place when the narrator was still not twelve years of age and was reported on page 27 of the book. The remaining four hundred and more pages of the book contained mostly reports of the narrator's first desiring and soon afterwards enjoying one after another girl or young woman or woman. The chief character of *this* story, from the age of four, would often find in his mind when he was alone, and especially when he was in sight of paddocks of grass or stands of trees or even a corner of a garden, an image of the face of a woman or a girl. Some of the faces were of images of persons in photographs or other illustrations; a few of the faces were of images of persons from films he had seen; and sometimes a face appeared to him, so far as he could surmise, from the same source that had given rise to the images of Helvetia.

The faces of this last sort interested him more than the others whenever during his later life he studied his memories of what he had come to call the female presences. Each face was never less than beautiful, according to his notion of beauty, but a presence would often appear at first with an expression of sternness or aloofness. He got much pleasure from knowing that this expression was only to keep secret from outsiders the warmth of the feelings that he felt continually from the presence. He understood that each presence was eager for him to confide in her, even though he suspected at the same time that she knew already what he most wanted to confide. He understood also that if he were to report to any presence some of the worst and most shameful things that he had done or said or thought—things that he knew to be sins according to his religion—she would be no more than curious to learn what his motives had been or what queerer things he could get up to.

Usually, the female presence seemed to be his wife or the person who would become his wife in the future. The man who remembered these matters up to fifty years afterwards did not find it strange that the boy from the age of four had talked to a wife-in-his-mind rather than to a friend-in-his-mind of either sex. Until he was nine years old and able to read passages from the books of popular fiction that his parents read, the boy believed that the only persons who took part in sexual behaviour were husbands with their wives, and for many years after that he believed that he himself could never so much as speak about sexual matters with any female person who was not his wife or his betrothed. He spoke about such matters often with the female presences in his mind and he did with them in his mind certain things, but only after having warned the presences of what to expect. No matter how perceptive and knowledgeable a female presence might be and how much about him she knew without his having to tell her, she would always be quite innocent in sexual matters and would wait to learn from him.

Whenever he saw himself with his wife-in-his-mind, he and she were in a particular place. Husband and wife lived together without children in a house set far back from the road on a farm of several hundred acres. The details of the farmhouse changed as often as he saw in one of the women's magazines that his mother read an illustration of one or another house described as ultra-modern or luxurious, but the farm always appeared in his mind as a rectangle of green paddocks with a road of red gravel at its front and with thick forest at its sides and its rear. The boy who saw this farm in his mind did not learn until he was a man aged more than fifty years which farm in the place that is called for convenience the real world most nearly resembled the farm with forest on three sides. For most of his life, he had taken pleasure from seeing in his mind images of grassy countryside with a line of trees in the distance. These images resembled, as he well knew, landscapes that he had seen when he had looked from the windows of country trains between the western suburbs of Melbourne and the district in the south-west of Victoria where the parents of his parents lived. This district was mostly grassy countryside, but in certain parts of the district a line of trees was visible in the distance, and for most of his life the chief character of this story would have said that a broad expanse of grass and a distant line of trees was his ideal landscape except that he sometimes remembered that he and his wife-in-his-mind had always lived in a place where the grassy paddocks seemed no more than a large clearing in a far-reaching forest.

Late in his life, the man discovered that certain details of certain images in his mind would begin to flicker or waver while he looked at them and that this flickering or wavering was often a sign that a surprising image or cluster of images would soon appear from behind the wavering or flickering detail or details. One of the first details that had wavered or flickered in this way was the line in his mind where the green paddocks of the farm mentioned in the previous paragraph came to an end and the thick forest surrounding the farm began. The man remembered many years afterwards that the boy would sometimes want to see himself and his wife-in-his-mind as talking together or being naked together in their modern and luxurious house but would find himself instead looking at the wavering or flickering boundaries of his and her farm.

After his eighth year, the female that he considered his wife-in-his-mind was sometimes a version of a girl of his own age from his own school or neighbourhood. Each of these girls had what he considered a beautiful face and kept herself aloof from himself and other boys. He never deliberately chose one or another of these girls. One day when he found himself growing tired of the face of his wife-in-his-mind, he would notice that her face had become in a moment a version of the face of a girl that he knew. At first he might protest to himself (knowing that the female presence was listening, even though she was faceless for the time being) that he had never considered the girl's face beautiful. But he would be gradually won over. Against the background of the farm with the forest around its boundaries, the face would become the face of his wife. He would become impatient to be in his schoolroom again or on a certain street in his neighbourhood, so that he could see the face-in-his-mind as it had now been revealed to him.

When the appearance of a girl from his school had settled in his mind in this way, he was not at first eager to have the girl know that he and she were now connected. He preferred to watch the girl when he thought she was unaware of him. His watching was meant only to make more vivid in his mind afterwards the face of the female presence. When the details of a face were quite clear in his mind, so he had learned long before, the female presence was more likely to surprise him by what she said and did and so to reassure him that she existed apart from himself. At such times, the husband of the female presence seemed not the boy as he might have become in the future but the boy as he might have been at that moment if only he could have been living in the world where one of the countries was Helvetia. Soon, however, the man and the woman in his mind would become almost wholly himself and the girl in the future, and soon after that, the face-in-his-mind would have become the face of the schoolgirl that he saw each day, and he would have begun to be unhappy.

The man read the book of fiction *Remembrance of Things Past*, translated by C. K. Scott Moncrieff from the French of Marcel Proust and published in London in 1969 by Chatto and Windus, when he was a few more than thirty years old. The passages reporting the unhappiness of Swann over Odette and of the Narrator over Gilberte and Albertine were the first accounts he had read of a state of mind similar to his own whenever during the years from his ninth year to his twenty-ninth year he felt towards a female person what is most conveniently denoted by the word *love*. (Until he had read those passages, the most nearly accurate accounts that he had read of his state of mind when in love had been accounts of the states of mind of female characters in fiction.) During much of the period of twenty years just mentioned, he would be continually unhappy while he was out of sight of the girl whose face was in his mind, but no less unhappy when he was in sight of her. Away from her, he was unhappy to think of her talking or laughing among people he had never met and doing a thousand small things that he would never know about. But at such times, he could at least talk with her image in his mind. When he was in sight of her, he was made aware that she was not thinking continually and anxiously about him. He was able to remember forty years afterwards what he had seen and felt one Monday morning in his tenth year when he had turned in his seat in a classroom and had looked for the first time in three days at a girl whose image had been in his mind for much of that time and had been almost certain that she was aware of him looking at her but had seen her looking deliberately past him at the blackboard and copying one after another of the details there into her exercise book.

Sometimes his looking so often at a particular girl led some female friend of the girl to challenge him to deny that the girl he looked at so often was his girlfriend. He would have liked to make this denial and so to save himself from being teased in the schoolground, but he was always aware that the girl he so often looked at might herself have caused him to be questioned and might be hurt if he denied that he was interested in her, and so he would admit that he considered the girl in question his girlfriend. The end of the matter would follow after a few days. Now that he had confessed, he was no longer free to look at the girl. Whatever the girl might have felt towards him, she and he had to make a show of disliking the mere sight of one another for a few days before the other children would leave off tormenting them. Sometimes, his few days of having to avoid the girl would cure him of thinking about her. At other times, he would go on loving her in secret for months, and her face would continue to be the face of his wife-in-his-mind.

At some time during his ninth year, when he was trying to remove from his mind the image of the face of one or another schoolgirl and so to be free from his latest mood of unhappiness, he found a way of breaking out of the cycle of feelings reported in the previous paragraphs. Two of his father's brothers and four of his father's sisters had never married. One of the unmarried sisters had died, and one of the unmarried brothers had gone to live in Queensland, but the other four unmarried persons had gone on living in their parents' house in a large town in the south-west of Victoria. Each of the three women had a room or a sleepout in the house, but the man—called from now on the bachelor-uncle of the chief character—lived mostly in the garden behind the house, in what was always called the bungalow: a small room with a bed, a wardrobe, a desk, a bookshelf, a chair for sitting at the desk, and a chair for a visitor. The bachelor-uncle ate most of his meals in the house and sat for a half-hour each evening with his parents and sisters (and with his sisters alone after their parents had died), but he spent most evenings and many afternoons in the bungalow, sitting at his desk or lying on his back on his bed while he read from books or listened to radio programmes on the ABC or to broadcasts of horse-races. He earned his living by breeding and fattening cattle in a few paddocks of grazing land that he leased in the countryside that surrounded the town where he lived. He spent only three or four mornings each week with his cattle. Every Saturday he drove his car to the nearest race meeting. Every Sunday he went to mass in his Catholic parish church. The chief character of this story had heard as a boy that his bachelor-uncle had had as a young man several girlfriends who would have made excellent wives, but he, the chief character, hoped as a boy that his parents and others were predicting rightly when they said that his uncle would always be a bachelor. And at some time during his ninth year, the boy decided that he himself would be a bachelor and not a husband when he became a man.

He could not remember, years afterwards, the first occasion when he turned away from the wife-in-his-mind and became a bachelor in his mind, but he remembered later occasions when he had felt suddenly relieved that he would never again be preoccupied with girls or young women whose faces had become fixed in his mind: that he would never have to find a wife in the future. As soon as he had become a bachelor in his mind, he would see himself in the future not on the farm with the forest at three sides but in a bachelor's bungalow or looking out across grazing land or arriving alone at a race meeting. Years later, when he came across the word *heartwhole* in his reading, that word seemed especially apt for describing the feeling of strength and soundness that he had got from thinking of himself as a boy-bachelor. And yet, he had never thoroughly rid his mind of female presences in his bachelor-days; nor did he try to do so. He would sometimes feel as a bachelor that he was being watched from a distance by one or another female presence: someone who resembled no girl he had ever seen; someone who was almost a stranger to him. She was, perhaps, the wife he would never know: the woman he might have married if he had not been a lifelong bachelor. He would never have behaved cruelly towards her, but her quiet sadness did not move him.

During each of his bachelor-moods, he would become interested again in things he had ignored while he was preoccupied with women- or girls-in-his-mind. As a boy-bachelor, he took pains with his schoolwork and with his prayers in church, and he helped his mother with housework and his father with gardening. After a few weeks, however, he would find himself again thinking often of a female person watching him, and then the cycle would begin again.

Quite apart from all the female persons mentioned so far in this story is another group that the chief character sometimes called in his mind the women of the scrub.

During the first few years when the chief character lived with his parents and his younger brother in the south-eastern suburb, he, the chief character, knew of no other young person of his own age who lived within walking distance of his house in any direction. Every house that he knew of among the sandy tracks and the clumps of scrub contained a young married couple and as many as three or four small children. A few of the wives-in-his-mind in earlier years had had the faces of young married women that he had seen outside his mind, but as from this thirteenth year the young married women of his neighbourhood in the south-eastern suburb did in his mind what no wife had ever done or would ever do there.

On a very hot day in January in his thirteenth year, he decided to endure for no longer a sensation that he had endured at intervals on every hot day of that summer. He walked in among the grey-green scrub that had not yet been cleared from behind his house. Because the land around the house had not yet been fenced, he was able to continue walking in an easterly or south-easterly direction through the scrub until he was out of sight of his house. In a thick part of the scrub, he knelt and set about relieving himself of the sensation that had been troubling him. The scrub grew so closely around him that his forearms and his thighs were prickled continually. When he had still not yet fully relieved himself but had almost done so, he began to imagine that a certain few young women of his neighbourhood had followed him into the scrub and were watching him. While they watched, they jeered at him or rebuked him or commanded him to stop what he was doing.

In his eighteenth year, when he first noticed in his mind an image of the young woman in school uniform mentioned earlier, the scrub had for long been cleared away from his neighbourhood, and the land was covered over by houses and fences and backyards. One day, soon after the scrub had been cleared, he had supposed that if tracts of scrub had still been growing in all the outlying parts of all the suburbs between his suburb and Dandenong during the year when he had first come to live in his suburb, then he could think of himself and his family as having lived for a short while at the westernmost edge of an outlying district of Gippsland. After the very hot day mentioned in the previous paragraph, he had gone into the scrub once in about every week and had relieved himself in the same way until the hot weather had ended in late March and he was no longer wearing summer clothes and able to feel the scrub prickling his bare skin. From that time onwards, he relieved himself from time to time in his bed. Before the following summer had begun his house had been fenced and much of the scrub cleared. He relieved himself less often during the following years, and sometimes not for a month or more while he was in love with an image of a face in his mind. But his way of relieving himself was almost always the same. He would have gone alone into scrub or forest in his mind in order to relieve himself but he would have been followed in his mind by young married women. As he grew older, the behaviour of the young married women in the scrub in his mind became more subtly provoking, but the sting of their taunting and teasing always felt in his mind like the prickling on his bare skin of the scrub that had grown in the past almost to the walls of his parents' house.

His school uniform was mostly grey, with trimmings of royal blue and gold. Her uniform had white and pale-blue trimmings on a colour that seemed to him at first black but proved to be a dark navy-blue. He had been in love for some weeks with the image of her face in his mind and had looked often at her face of an afternoon when they were travelling in the same compartment of a train in the direction of Dandenong and had satisfied himself that she was aware of his looking at her before he first spoke to her. Her voice when he first heard it seemed to have a faint English accent, and he learned during the many afternoons when they talked to each other in the train that she had been born and had spent her first five years in a south-western county of England before her parents had moved with her and her two older sisters from England to Australia and had settled in a newly built house in an outlying street of Dandenong.

During the weeks when he talked with the young woman in the blue-black uniform, he had cause for believing that she was pleased to be talking with him and even that she might have seen an image of himself in her mind from time to time before he had first spoken to her. And yet, he sometimes regretted that he had spoken to the girl so soon. During the first weeks after he had first read *Wuthering Heights* and when the image of her face had first appeared in his mind, she had seemed, more than any previous wife-in-his-mind, to be as full of images of him as he was of her. If he had not spoken so soon to the girl on the train, so he sometimes thought, he would have begun to live, with the image of her in his mind, a life more rich and complicated than any life he had yet lived in his mind. He would have lived that life among landscapes more varied and inviting than any view he had yet had of the farm in the forest. But those landscapes were now, so he understood, where Helvetia was in his mind, and the people who lived among those landscapes were with the grey-blue man of the slightly sorrowful look.

He had first seen her image in his mind late in the summer and had first spoken to her in mid-autumn. One afternoon in the first week of winter, after having given much thought to the matter and having prepared his words beforehand, he asked her whether she would like to go with him to a football match at the Melbourne

Cricket Ground on a certain Saturday afternoon in the near future. She answered that she had been preparing for some time to ask him whether he would like to have afternoon tea with her at her parents' house on a certain Sunday afternoon in the near future. After she had talked to her parents, it was decided that he should meet her family over afternoon tea before he and she went to a football match or on any other outing together.

During the days before the Sunday of the afternoon tea, he felt at times proud to have acquired a girlfriend in whose house he was welcome but he felt at other times unhappy. He had already imagined himself leaving school at the end of the year and joining the state public service. She was two years younger than he, but she too would be leaving school at the end of the year, so she had told him, and would go to work in a bank, as her parents had advised her to do. He had already imagined himself going with her to a picture theatre or a party every Saturday night and calling on her at her parents' house every Sunday afternoon for several years until he had saved enough money to buy a small second-hand car, after which time he and she would travel in the car every Sunday afternoon around the outer south-eastern suburbs in search of a block of land to buy. He had already imagined the house that would be built in time on the block of land and details of the life that he and she would live in the house as husband and wife. What made him unhappy was that he could not imagine what images he would have in his mind during all the years that he had already imagined.

Of the events of the Sunday afternoon when he visited her house for afternoon tea, only the following belong in this story.

While he walked from Dandenong railway station to her house, he saw often a view of Mount Dandenong so unlike the only view that he had previously seen that he sometimes lost his bearings and supposed that he was looking at the mountain from a position on what had always previously been to him the far side of the mountain and had therefore travelled a considerable distance into the region of Gippsland.

About half an hour after he had arrived at the house, and while he and his girlfriend were sitting together in the living-room, someone let into the house one of the two or three dogs that the family owned. These dogs were of a breed that was very rare in the suburbs of Melbourne: the bull-terrier breed. The dog that had been let into the house had come at once into the living-room and before he had even learned its name or its sex it had risen onto its hind legs, had clasped its forelegs around one of his knees, and had thrust its haunches again and again at the lower part of his leg. In the first moments after the dog had mounted his leg, he could think only of pretending to be unaware of what was happening. Then his girlfriend reached out and slapped at the dog and drove it away from him.

At some time while he and all her family were taking afternoon tea, he became aware that he and his girlfriend were the youngest persons at the table and he became concerned that her parents and even her older sisters might be alarmed or angry or even merely amused if they surmised that he had already imagined himself buying a block of land and marrying this girlfriend in the future. In order to prevent them from so surmising, he told her family, when the conversation had next turned to him, that he often foresaw himself living as a bachelor all his life and buying and racing horses with the money that he would have saved by not having married.

After someone had mentioned the family photograph album, and after he had begged to be allowed to look at it, and after his girlfriend had sat beside him and had shown him what she said were the only pages he would be interested in and had closed the book and had put it aside, he had watched for an opportunity to pick up the book as though idly and to find again without anyone's noticing his eagerness the page with the photographs of the house where his girlfriend had lived during all the time she had lived in England, which was a house of two storeys at the edge of a village, and to stare without anyone's noticing his concern at the background of each photograph in turn in order to see more clearly what he had previously taken to be clumps of woodland.

In far-off, smoke-hued hills

The words just above were written by the chief character of this story on a line near the foot of a page of ruled paper while he sat in his room in his parents' house on a certain evening early in the winter of the first year after he had finished his last year of secondary school. At the time when the words were written, no other words had yet been written on the page. During the first hour after the words had been written, the writer of the words wrote and then crossed out many other words on many of the lines above the first words. Soon after the end of that hour, the writer of the words put the sheet of paper in a manila folder containing a number of sheets of ruled paper with no words written on them and then placed the folder under a pile of books and magazines on the floor beside the small table where he sat. At the time when the folder was put away, the words at the head of this paragraph were the only words that had not been crossed out on the page that the writer of the words had been writing on.

At the beginning of that year, he had started work as a clerical officer in a department of the state government. His first job was to check the details of the application forms filled out by persons wanting to be granted in return for a small fee the right to set up beehives or to distil eucalyptus oil from the branches of gum trees in forests on public lands in the north of Victoria, which was a region where he had never been. Before he started work, he had imagined the north of Victoria as a district of arid paddocks and of mullock heaps left behind by gold-miners, with a few pockets of stunted trees at intervals along the trickling creeks that flowed towards the inland from the Great Dividing Range. But each day at his desk, as he read one after another of the applications from apiarists and eucalyptus distillers, the north of

Victoria in his mind became more of a forest and less of a parched grassland.

From the time when he began to work as a public servant until the evening mentioned in the first section of this story, he travelled in the morning of each weekday by suburban train from the south-eastern suburb where he lived with his parents into the central city. In the late afternoon of every weekday he travelled out of the city in a train with the word DANDENONG at its front. One of the many stations that he passed on his way to and from the city was the station where he had formerly left the train each weekday morning to walk to his secondary school and where he had formerly waited each afternoon for the train with the word DANDE-NONG at its front. During the evenings of weekdays, he stayed in his room and read books or magazines or listened to what he called classical music on his radio. Each Saturday, he went to the races. Each Sunday morning, he went to mass. On three Saturday evenings out of every four, he travelled to his girlfriend's house in an outlying street of Dandenong. During the previous year, her parents had allowed him to take their daughter only twice to a football match and to visit her only once each month at their house. Now, he was allowed to visit her more often.

On two of the three Saturday evenings mentioned above, he travelled with his girlfriend in the so-called picture bus from her home to the main street of Dandenong, where they attended a cinema before returning to her home in the same bus. On the third Saturday evening of those three, he had a meal with his girlfriend and her family and afterwards went with her and one of her sisters and the boyfriend of that sister to the dance that was held once a month in the hall beside his girlfriend's parish church. (On this Saturday evening and on many others, his girlfriend's other sister stayed at home and watched television with her parents and her fiancé in order to save money for the house that he and she intended to build on a block of land that they were buying by instalments in a grassy paddock that they said would be the next part of Dandenong to go ahead.) On the Sunday following the one

Saturday in each four when he did not visit his girlfriend, he visited her home in the afternoon, sometimes walking with her through the streets around her home, sometimes attending with her the ceremony of benediction in her parish church, and sometimes having afternoon tea in her home with her parents. He travelled to and from his own home and his girlfriend's home mostly by bicycle. Even when the weather was cold, he had to pedal slowly on his way from his home to Dandenong so as not to sweat. If the weather was in the least warm, he carried a small towel in a haversack on his back so that he could wash his face and his underarms when he arrived. On most of his journeys to Dandenong, he carried in his haversack what his mother called a respectable shirt and a tie and a jacket.

He was pleased to mention his girlfriend to his workmates or to any of his former schoolfellows that he met in the city, but he never spoke of her as his girlfriend or of himself as her boyfriend when he was speaking to her or to any of her family. He suspected that her parents thought he was much too serious about their youngest daughter, who had only recently turned sixteen and left school. And he suspected that her parents and her sisters thought he was somewhat crazy.

He supposed that his girlfriend's family thought him odd because he talked too much. He talked continually when he was in their house, and not only to his girlfriend but often to her parents and sisters. Someone in the family would sometimes comment on his talking, but he always assumed the comment was made in fun. He talked, so he understood many years later, because he mistook his girlfriend for the person with the same face who had been his wife-in-his-mind since the days soon after he had first read *Wuthering Heights*. He did not make the opposite mistake. At least once in every waking hour when he was away from his girlfriend, he confided one or more matters to the female presence in his mind who was clearly not his girlfriend, the sixteen-year-old bank clerk, even though the two faces were almost identical. And he did not expect that the young woman he talked to for a few hours each week in her home or in the picture bus or on the way to the parish dance would give any sign of her having been entrusted with his confidences for days past. But during the few hours each week when he was with his girlfriend, he talked to her as though she had been listening to him for years past and as though she would go on listening until he had told her every word that he could tell about himself and would then interpret for him the whole of what he had told her.

Much of his talk was about things he had learned from books. He had told his girlfriend and her family on one of his first visits to their house that he had earned higher marks in his last year at school than some of his former classmates who were now at university; that he was going to teach himself from the books he chose in future to read far more than a person could learn at university; that he read each week three or more books from cover to cover and many other books by looking into various pages that had taken his interest. He had announced during an early visit that he preferred not to read popular or well-known books or books that were regarded as authoritative in a particular subject. He suspected, so he had said at the time, any theories or beliefs subscribed to by large numbers of people. (When he had said this, he had gone on at once to say that he did not question the teachings of the Catholic Church, which, as everyone knew, had millions of followers. But he had sometimes recently thought for a moment that he might one day read some book that would persuade him to become an agnostic or an atheist. He had thought this only for a moment on each such occasion and had then felt giddy and afraid. He had glimpsed himself-the-agnostic-or-atheist as a man walking alone in a grey or black borderland far from the places he knew.) He quoted the first two lines of the poem "On First Looking into Chapman's Homer," by John Keats, and then said that he, like Keats, thought of reading as travel. He said that the best sort of books made him feel as though he was exploring the borderlands of the landscape of knowledge.

He talked in his girlfriend's house about such things as the haunting of Borley Rectory; the experiments in extra-sensory perception by Professor Rhine of Duke University in the United States; the life-story of Shaka Zulu and of Hannibal the Carthaginian; the man Ishi, who had lived for several years alone in the forests of California as the last survivor of his people; the Australians who had settled in Paraguay in the nineteenth century; and many other matters. Her parents asked him sometimes of what use his knowledge was to him. He answered that he would find before long a particular branch of knowledge which interested him more than any other and would study it until he became an expert in it, after which he would write a book on his chosen subject, after which he would be rewarded in some way by some person or some organisation. To keep the parents from thinking him too irresponsible to be the boyfriend of their daughter, he added that he would never give up his job in the public service unless he had first secured a better job and that he would do all his studying and even the writing of his book in the evenings.

When he wondered what his field of expertise would be, he sometimes found himself thinking about his bachelor-uncle in the bungalow in the south-west of Victoria. His uncle had read a great many books and had put together as a result of his reading what his nephew thought of as a private history of the world. Many years later, the nephew looked into the book *The Everlasting Man*, by G. K. Chesterton, and recognised that the uncle had borrowed much from that one book, but even then the nephew admired the uncle's creation. It seemed like a long, winding pathway that the uncle had followed in and out among the shadows of the cities and the mountains and the forests of the world towards the bungalow, with its single bed and its desk and bookshelf in the backyard of the house in a side street of a country town on the lower side of the world. In the uncle's view of things, the first human beings had been created by God only a few thousand years before the birth of Jesus. The people that others called cave-men the uncle called pre-Adamites; they were a race of creatures who may or may not have been human but who were not among the people redeemed by the Son of God made Man. The history of the Christian era had been distorted by English Protestant historians. The so-called Dark Ages had actually been the true Golden Age. The Spanish had been far less blameworthy as colonisers than the ruthless English. Sir Francis Drake and Sir Walter Raleigh had committed crimes that cried out to heaven for vengeance. Elizabeth the First of England had been a man in disguise. The Catholic Portuguese had discovered Australia, and one of the first places they had come ashore was in the south-west of Victoria where they must surely have celebrated mass and taken possession of the land later known as Australia. The people known as the Aborigines had arrived in the land only a few hundred years before the Portuguese. The Aborigines were close relatives of the gypsies and had set out, like the gypsies, from India but at a later date and in a different direction. Among the most misguided of persons had been the Protestant do-gooders of the nineteenth century who had brought into being in England and Australia the cruel and wasteful institution of free, compulsory, and secular education. Most children were better off unschooled. The brightest boy in each parish should be taken in hand by the priest and given the run of his library; the other boys should be apprenticed as tradesmen or farmers or craftsmen. These and many other details made up the view of the world that the bachelor-uncle saw from the bungalow, and the nephew of the bachelor not only thought often about his uncle's view but reported many details of it and elaborated on those details to the family that he visited in Dandenong and even told them that he, their visitor, considered his uncle an expert of a kind and would be proud if he, the visitor, could become an expert in his own way at some time in the future.

In the past, he had been constantly unhappy not to be able to see the girl whose face was always in his mind and constantly jealous of those who were in sight of her. With his girlfriend from Dandenong (his first true girlfriend, as he called her to himself), matters were reversed. For as long as he was away from her, he felt as though a version of her was watching him in his daily life and smiling at his many odd little ways. When he was with her, however, he was uneasy and, at times, jealous. Being with her reminded him of how little he knew about her. If she said something about her work in the bank, he remembered that he had never once supposed during the previous week that he was looking down through her mind into the Dandenong branch of the English, Scottish and Australasian Bank and sharing in her moment of perplexity or being touched by her pretty frown as she stood in her green and gold uniform and hesitated over the files she was searching through. (During the rest of his life, whenever he thought of the few months during which he had visited his girlfriend at Dandenong, he felt as though he could have written page after page about his own feelings at the time but no more than a few sentences reporting anything that she had said or done.)

If he was talking to her or to some member of her family and if she seemed to be listening to him, then, at least, he was not unhappy, although he might have been concerned that she had not understood his latest narrative or argument as he had wanted her to understand it. But if he was compelled to be silent with her, as he was when they sat in the cinema nearly every week, or if he and she were merely two young persons among a crowd of young persons, as they were at the parish dance each month, then he would become afraid of seeming to her nothing more than a public service clerk of a lowly grade and he would expect that she would soon grow tired of his company. He believed he was distinguished only by what he saw in his mind. In the eyes of anyone who had been told nothing about the numerous landscapes and vistas that he was continually aware of, he was of no interest. He knew that he dressed drably, even shabbily. He played no sport. He did not listen to rock-and-roll music. He did not go to the beach in summer. He knew nothing about motor cars. Although he sometimes watched television, the images moved too fast for him, or his mind wandered, and he seldom remembered afterwards what he had seen.

He was never able to take in the plots of the films that he and his girlfriend watched each week. Either he was thinking of something he had said to her recently and of how she might have misinterpreted it, or he was thinking of something he would have to say to her when they had left the cinema. Or, again, he was dreading the appearance on the screen of the first scene in which a male character and a female character expressed in words their love for one another or embraced and kissed.

Whenever he and she walked the last few hundred paces from the bus stop to the front gate of her house after they had alighted from the picture bus, and whenever they walked the same distance on their way home from the parish dance, he would hold one of her hands in one of his hands. In all his later life, he never laughed or even smiled at any spoken or written comment that seemed intended to mock or belittle the feelings of young persons for one another. If ever he had become a writer of fiction, he would never have written about any young person as though to suggest that his or her love, as he or she called it, for one or another young person was of any less account than any state of mind of any person who was no longer young. In short, he believed for the rest of his life that his reaching out for his girlfriend's hand on certain evenings as he and she picked their way along a gravel footpath in an outlying street of Dandenong, which was at that time in the way of changing from being the nearest to Melbourne of the towns of Gippsland to the furthest suburb from Melbourne in the direction of Gippsland, and her letting his hand find her hand and her letting her hand lie in his hand until they reached her front gate were, at the very least, equal in meaning to any other events that occurred in the lives of any other persons in the world during his and her lifetime. While he was sitting beside her in the cinema, he was preparing himself for the moment later that evening when he would reach out for her hand. Their holding hands was one of a few subjects that he would never have spoken about to her, although he did talk to her about other subjects while they walked hand in hand. He would be hoping, in the cinema, that she, while she sat beside him, was looking forward to his taking her hand later that evening and was hoping that he understood that she understood that they had come to the cinema that evening only because a visit to the cinema was one of the few outings possible for a young man who owned no motor car and a young woman whose parents wanted her to be always in a crowd of young persons whenever she went out with her boyfriend on a Saturday evening in a place that was changing from being a town in the countryside to a suburb of a capital city. And while he was so hoping, he would see on the screen in the cinema the first of the scenes that he had been dreading.

Throughout each of the many love scenes that he watched with his girlfriend seated close beside him (he never offered to hold her hand in the cinema), he wished that he could have had the courage to tell her afterwards that he would never expect her to fall into his arms when she had hardly got to know him, as American women were expected to do; that he would not give in to his passions (to use the term favoured by Catholic philosophers and theologians) before he had explained himself to her down to the last detail. He was bothered even by the gestures of the men and women in the love scenes: their sighs, the staring of their eyes, the clutching of their hands. He would have liked the young woman beside him to know that his regard for her was so complex and that he was so distinctive a person that he could never express himself by such means as gasps and moaning sounds.

On the shady side of the house where he sometimes looked at the picture of the man in the Gippsland forest, a treefern grew under a roof of dark-green lattice. At some time during each of his visits to the house, he would stand under the shade of the lattice, touching the fronds of the fern or stroking the hairy trunk. One day he was halfway along the side of the house on his way to the treefern before he saw the oldest of his girl-cousins (she was about nineteen at that time) standing in the shade of the treefern and staring up into the face of the young man who had recently become her fiancé. The year was the last year of the 1940s, and few young men owned motor cars. He had often seen young couples with arms around one another in laneways or in parks but always in darkness. His cousin and her young man were standing only a few paces from him in the light of afternoon, shaded only by the lattice and the fronds of the treefern, and they did not know he was watching them. He stood there, expecting to learn in the next few moments more about the behaviour in private of men and women than he had learned from all his reading and speculating. The two persons in their shady corner then hugged and kissed, but only, so he saw, in imitation of what they had seen in American films, and he tiptoed away, feeling embarrassed for them.

Even a few months after he had seen for the last time the person who had been his girlfriend for a few months, he could remember no more than some of the names of the films they had watched together. He remembered for the rest of his life much of what had passed through his mind in the cinema, but almost everything that had passed in front of his eyes was lost to him. Likewise, from the hours that he spent at the parish dance on one evening each month he recalled for the rest of his life only his feelings of unrelieved misery and embarrassment.

He and his girlfriend, together with her sister who was still unengaged and her boyfriend, would set out from his girlfriend's house. Her mother would stand at the front door until they were out of the front gate. She would call out to them to have fun and to enjoy themselves. He still hoped, until the moment when she had stepped back inside and closed the door, that she might call out to him that she had noticed during the past hour that he had not looked well; that his girlfriend might say to him that she had noticed the very same thing; and that his girlfriend and her mother might together urge him not to go to the dance that evening but to stay with his girlfriend's parents in their lounge-room, watching television and talking. Every month, as the date of the dance drew nearer, he rehearsed a speech to his girlfriend in which he told her that he did not want to monopolise her company and to keep her from meeting other young people of her own age; that he intended in the future to take her to the doors of the parish hall on the evening of the dance and to call for her after the dance had finished but to spend the intervening time with her parents. What kept him from delivering this speech was his believing that he did not deserve the exquisite pleasure of walking back to her house with her hand lying in his hand unless he had first endured the torture of attending the dance.

When he and his girlfriend had still been meeting on the train from school and when she had mentioned that she liked dancing, he had quietly begun a course of dancing lessons in a large upstairs room in the shopping centre near his school. He had continued the lessons for nearly six months and had paid much money to the middle-aged woman who taught him for half an hour for week after week. She seemed to be the only teacher in the studio, as she called it, and he seemed to be her only pupil. She did not require him to hold her in the usual dancer's hold; he and she kept at a little distance from one another with hands on one another's shoulders. She seemed to be in her forties or fifties, and he was able to relax somewhat with her, although she told him several times that he was a difficult pupil. When he told her at the end of one of his lessons that he was going with his girlfriend to a dance for the first time on the following Saturday evening, she told him to have fun and enjoy himself.

During the first ten minutes at the first parish dance he attended, he understood that his lessons had been a waste of time and money. The press of people left only an oval space for dancing instead of a rectangle, so that he forgot at once all he had been taught about half-turns and quarter-turns. He was even more confused by having to stand so close to his partner and by not being able to look down at his feet or hers. None of the music played by the band had the simple rhythms of the tunes that his teacher had played for him on her portable record-player. On his first night at the dance, he danced only with his girlfriend and her sister and with a friend of each of them, and he danced only one dance with each of those four, and he sensed that each of his partners was doing her best to help him, but he knew that what he was doing did not deserve to be called dancing. He talked ceaselessly to each of his partners to distract her and himself from what was happening below the level of their waists. When the progressive barn dance was announced, and he understood that he would be required to dance with dozens of strange young women, he left the hall and walked in the darkness outside for ten minutes.

He could hardly believe in later years that he had stayed to the end of not only the first dance but five others. At the last dance he attended, he was no less incompetent than he had been at the beginning. He danced nearly always with the same few partners, stumbling or shuffling around in a trance of embarrassment and babbling at them all the while. He always went outside before the barn dance began, and he was always grateful to his girlfriend and her sister for never having remarked to him afterwards that they had missed him during the progressive barn dance. Even the long periods that he spent at the side of the hall were of little relief. He felt obliged to look always as though he was quietly contented, in case his girlfriend or her sister should look at him from out of the crowd. When either of them stood or sat with him for a short while, he suspected that she was only feeling sorry for him or he felt guilty at keeping her from the enjoyment that he supposed a person got from being actually able to dance.

At the fifth dance he attended, he danced for the first time with a new partner. In each of the back corners of the hall was one of two groups that he called in his mind the Bachelors and the Spinsters. Members of each group were older than the average person in the hall, some bachelors or spinsters seeming to be in their late twenties. He envied the bachelors, most of whom seemed to know one another and to have much to talk about. Some bachelors seemed never to dance and yet not to be ashamed of this. Even more noticeable than the age of the spinsters was their plainness in appearance. He had thought at first that the spinsters would have been clumsy dancers also, but when one of them was asked to dance, as sometimes happened, she seemed no less skilful than any of the regular dancers. He was often touched by the sight of the spinsters. While he stood watching the dancers, shifting from foot to foot and trying to keep a half-smile on his face for the sake of his girlfriend, he could at least pretend that he did not feel inclined to dance. No one was likely to believe that the spinsters preferred not to dance and had recently declined invitations from would-be partners. Many of them had the same awkward half-smile that he could feel on his own face. He tried not to catch the eye of any spinster. He thought it would have been cruel to give her some hope that he was going to ask her to dance. But at the fifth dance, and again at the sixth, he danced several times with one of the spinsters.

His girlfriend knew many of the persons in the hall. She was talking to a young woman who might have been twenty-five or even older, and he was standing beside the pair of them, when the band began to play and his girlfriend went to dance with someone she had promised to dance with. He and the woman went on standing together. He hoped she would walk back to the spinsters' corner where he had seen her often, but she asked him to dance and he was too afraid to refuse. Stupid as he was in many matters, he did not suppose that the spinster was interested in any romantic way in an eighteen-year-old boy. She seemed like a youthful aunt, and he understood that she presented herself as a sort of adviser and wise older sister to his girlfriend and a few other young women. He should have felt at ease with her after she had said to him, when they had only just begun to dance, that the hall was much too crowded for dancing proper steps and had thereafter moved her feet in such a way that he was able to move around the floor in whatever gait he chose without so much as touching a toe of her shoes, whereas he had never previously tried more than three or four steps without having trodden on a toe or an instep of his partner. He should have felt at ease, but he did not like her way of calling his girlfriend a sweet young kid; the spinster seemed to be hinting that his girlfriend was too young and sweet to be pestered by such an odd person as himself.

He danced twice with the spinster on the night when she first asked him to dance, and he sat with her for a little while in a seat halfway between the bachelors and the spinsters. At the next dance, a month later, he asked her to dance soon after he had danced the first dance, as he always did, with his girlfriend. He still did not like the spinster. He still believed she was preparing to give him some unpleasant advice. He had even thought several times that his girlfriend might have arranged for the spinster to become friendly with him so that she could deliver to him some message that his girlfriend could not bring herself to deliver. And yet, he was much more comfortable shuffling around the floor with her than standing foolishly at the side of the hall. He had even begun to be silent for short periods while he and the spinster were moving around together. And in the periods of silence, he had even begun to think some of the thoughts about the future such as he usually thought when he was near his girlfriend: such a thought as that he would ask his girlfriend after she had become engaged to him never to require him to attend any place where the chief activity was dancing, or, perhaps, that he would ask her after they had become engaged to spend a few hours alone with him in the lounge-room of her home when no one else was in the house and to teach him the beginnings of the baffling art of dancing.

At every dance he had attended, one or more couples had fallen to the floor. Some subtle change would take place in the slow eddying movement of the dense throng of dancers; two or three young women would cry out; couples would stop dancing all around the hall and would look in the direction of the commotion. Only those nearest the fallen would know how many had gone down or who they were. He, the chief character, since he was hardly ever one of the throng of dancers, had seen only a few couples struggling to their feet or being helped up. When the first fall had taken place at the first dance he attended, he had expected to hear howls of laughter, but onlookers seldom laughed. On the contrary, the people around the fallen were sympathetic and solemn and even, so he believed, rather embarrassed. He himself had always been troubled by the resemblances between dancing and sexual intercourse, and when he first noticed a couple disentangling themselves on the dancefloor and then getting to their feet with flushed faces among onlookers who seemed anxious to put out of their minds what they had just witnessed, he had prayed that he would never be seen lying on top of some young woman on the floor of the crowded hall in his girlfriend's parish.

He was always sure that the fall had been caused by someone far ahead of him and the spinster, but no one had ever mentioned the matter afterwards, and he never knew whether or not his girlfriend had thought he was in any way responsible for the fall. He had not fallen far. Some other couple already down had broken the fall of the spinster, and she, being his partner and directly in front of him when those ahead fell, in turn broke his own fall. He had seemed to fall a very short distance and to have been soon upright again. And yet, he seemed to remember having leaned forward for a long time with his hands, which, of course, he had flung out in front of him, each neatly in place and cupped a little around the mound of each of the breasts of the spinster.

On the second Saturday evening after the events reported in the previous paragraph, he stayed at home before rising early on the Sunday and riding his bike to his girlfriend's house in time for eight o'clock mass. He and his girlfriend and her sister and her boyfriend walked to mass carrying a picnic hamper and wearing casual clothes with thick sweaters and scarves over their arms. After mass, they and fifty and more young persons from the parish seated themselves in two buses in the churchyard. The young persons were going on what had been advertised as *a picnic to the snow (we hope!!!) at Donna Buang*. He, the chief character of this story, had had to learn from a map that Mount Donna Buang was east-north-east of the city of Melbourne whereas Mount Dandenong was almost due east; that Donna Buang was almost exactly twice as far from Melbourne as Mount Dandenong; and that Donna Buang was only fifty feet short of being twice as high as Mount Dandenong.

On either side of the aisle in the bus that he and his girlfriend travelled in were seats that each held two persons. Most of those seats were occupied by established couples, with the girl sitting nearer the window and her boyfriend nearer the aisle. At the rear were several long seats, each with room for half a dozen persons. On these seats sat four or five unattached females and more than twice that number of unattached males. In the bus, as in the parish hall on dance-night, he thought of these groups as spinsters and bachelors.

His girlfriend had sat down at once in one of the window seats, and he sat down beside her, but he believed that this would be the last occasion he could consider the young woman beside him his girlfriend. He was prepared to hear her say when they arrived back at her home from the trip to Donna Buang that he should visit her less often; that he was becoming too serious. He had already heard her say that morning, in the first show of irritation she had ever made towards him, that he sometimes talked too much. He felt sick and foolish as he sat beside her during the first hour of the trip. He was trying to call to mind images that would enable him to see himself once again as a bachelor—not as one of the guffawing bachelors at the rear of the bus who were looking out for the next attractive female who had broken with her boyfriend, but the sort of bachelor he had formerly dreamed of becoming. In the past, whenever he had been sick with anxiety over some girl, he had had a sudden glimpse of himself as a bachelor and had become strong at once.

Even at the risk of irritating her, he wanted to tell her one last thing about himself. When the bus had left the outer suburbs behind, and the road ran between farms with forested hills in the background, he set out to tell her that he was now further east than he had ever been and that he was now entering a region that he had often seen in his mind since his mother had told him

as a child about the fires that had burned in the week before he had
been born.

She half-turned towards him several times and nodded, but
mostly she stared out of the window or looked over her shoulder,
waiting for a chance to join in talking with the couple in the seat
behind. He soon stopped talking.

He had wanted to tell her that his father and mother had been
born in the far south-west of Victoria, in the region that he always
thought of as consisting of grassy countryside with a line of trees
in the distance. Even when they had moved to Melbourne, they had
stayed on the western side, which was mostly treeless and grassy,
as distinct from the eastern side, where forests and scrub still grew
in places. In the week before he was born, his mother had been
afraid that the world would end before she had given birth to her
first child.

The department where he was employed, he might have told
his girlfriend as the bus carried them further in among the mountains of the Upper Yarra district, was concerned with Crown lands,
whether grassy or forested. In the library of the department, he
had gone looking for and had found the report of the Royal Commission into the causes of the bushfires and other matters. He
might have impressed her, if he had not already repelled her
with all his talking, by quoting to her in the bus some of the passages that he had copied out and memorised from the introduction to the report. *Seventy-one lives were lost. Sixty-nine mills
were burned. Millions of acres of fine forest, of almost incalcu-
lable value, were destroyed or badly damaged. Townships were
obliterated in a few minutes. On that day it appeared that the
whole state was alight. At midday in many places it was dark as
night. Travellers on the highways were trapped by fires or blaz-
ing fallen trees, and perished . . .* These and several other passages he might have quoted to her, but even while he was thinking
of what he might have said to her, he was noticing the thick forests on either side of the road. In his mind, he had always thought

of the eastern half of Victoria as blackened by fire. He had known that the image in his mind was a child's simple image, but he had expected to see on the trip to Donna Buang some evidence still remaining of the day, fewer than twenty years before, when the whole of Victoria had appeared to be alight.

His girlfriend and the couple behind were playing a version of the child's game of Bags. Each person in turn would call out that she or he bagged some desirable object or person through the windows. When his girlfriend took her first turn, she bagged a whole farm. She said she would love to live in the white-painted farmhouse that they were passing and to own the green paddocks around it for as far back as the forest in the background. The young woman in the seat behind told his girlfriend that she could hardly live in the house alone. No one spoke for a moment, and then they went on with their game.

The bus stopped at a place that the driver called the turntable. More than twenty other buses were stopped nearby, some with groups of young persons gathered around. Those from his own bus who had been to Donna Buang in previous years explained that lunch was to be eaten at the turntable, after which everyone was free to climb to the summit.

His girlfriend and her sister had packed a large hamper for their boyfriends and themselves. He forced himself to eat a sandwich and a cake while the others ate the rest of the lunch, saying how hungry they felt in the cold air.

On the way to the summit, the bachelors from the rear seats of the bus began to make snowballs from the few patches of hard snow lying about. With the snowballs in their hands, the bachelors changed from being the awkward outcasts of the parish dance or the rear of the bus. A pair of them would single out a pretty young woman—even though her boyfriend might have been beside her—and would try to drag the collar of her pullover away from the back of her neck and to force snow down against her bare skin. Some unspoken rule prevented the boyfriend from trying seriously to protect the girl. He would smile while his girlfriend was squealing and struggling against the bachelors, but the only help he would offer her would be to shake the snow from her clothing afterwards or to wipe her neck with his scarf. Other girls might leave their boyfriends and try to help a threatened girl, but this would only bring the whole pack of bachelors, and the outnumbered girls would all go back to their boyfriends squirming and squealing and dragging at the snow under their clothing.

He knew what was coming, and his girlfriend seemed also to know. The whole pack approached her. She shrugged and looked at her sister and tried to hold her collar close around her neck. They had something different in mind for her, as he had known they would. They hardly bothered to force any snow down the neck of her clothing. Instead, two of the bachelors leaned towards each other and locked hands to make a seat for her. Two others hoisted her onto this seat. She teetered and had to fling an arm around the shoulders of each of the bachelors whose hands she was sitting on. When she was seated securely, the pack of bachelors escorted her to the side of the track. They stopped a few paces short of a patch of deep snow. When she saw the snow, she began to squeal. While she squealed, the two bachelors who were carrying her began to swing her backwards and forwards and to count aloud. Several times they counted down to zero, and each time she shrieked and pleaded, but each time they went on swinging while she kept her grip around their shoulders.

Even he, watching from a distance and grinning, had not expected the bachelors to throw her into the snow. He foresaw that they would release her in their own good time and that she would come back to the group where he was standing and would smile at her sister and her boyfriend but not at himself. But he foresaw more than this. While the bachelors had been seizing her and carrying her off, he had noticed something in the way that a certain bachelor had behaved towards her. He, watching, had been surprised and stung, but she, so he had noticed, seemed not to have been even surprised.

The bachelor mentioned in the previous paragraph had been

one of the two who had made a seat for her with his hands. He, the chief character, had thought while he watched the bachelors of how they had become emboldened as soon as they had set foot on the mountain. On Donna Buang, the bachelors had taken liberties that they would never have attempted at any dance or party or even in the bus on the way to the mountain, and the boyfriends had deferred to the bachelors. He had watched especially his girlfriend's hand clutching at the shoulder and the neck of the bachelor who had behaved in a certain way towards her. He, the chief character, had watched even more the hands of the bachelor taking through a mere layer of the grey cloth of her slacks the weight of her thighs and buttocks.

While he watched, he foresaw a number of events, most of which later took place as he had foreseen. He foresaw himself moving gradually away from his girlfriend and her sister and her boyfriend as they approached the summit of Donna Buang—not to join the pack of bachelors but to walk as a solitary bachelor and to stand conspicuously alone looking out at the view from the summit. He foresaw himself joining up with his girlfriend's party again for a few minutes when they arrived back at the turntable. The vacuum-flasks in the hamper would still have enough warm tea for all four in the party to take a last drink together, and he would thank his girlfriend and her sister for all the trouble they had taken in preparing lunch. (The bachelor who had behaved in a certain way towards his girlfriend would have been by her side when her party had reached the summit, but he would have broken away as they approached the turntable again and would have stood with the pack of bachelors while he took the last drink that he would take with them as a bachelor.) As the various parties filed into the bus for the trip homewards, he, the chief character, would walk down the aisle and would choose a seat at the very edge of the bachelors' seats. His girlfriend, who would be by then no longer his girlfriend, would sit in the same window-seat that she had sat in on the way to Donna Buang, and the bachelor who had looked at her in a certain way while they were climbing the mountain, and who would be by then no longer a bachelor, would sit beside her. He, the chief character, would not talk to the bachelors and certainly not to the spinsters on the return journey but would look out through the window towards the dark shapes of mountains and forests and the lights of farmhouses and townships beside the road leading back to Melbourne from the easternmost place that he had yet visited. He foresaw himself getting down from the bus in the churchyard and then walking to the house of the young woman who had formerly been his girlfriend in the company of that young woman and her sister. While they walked, he would carry the empty hamper and would talk cheerfully with the young women. He would not be merely pretending to be cheerful. He would be a bachelor again and would no longer have to endure the misery and the anxiety that he had endured while he had been in love. He would be somewhat proud of himself for having conducted himself with dignity while he had been changing earlier that day from a boyfriend to a bachelor. While he prepared to say goodbye politely to the young women outside their house and then to ride away on the bicycle that he had left in the morning in their backyard, so he foresaw, he foresaw that he would live as a bachelor for several months, after which he would fall in love with one image after another in his mind until the next occasion when he noticed that the image in his mind was an image of a person from outside his mind. At the same time, he foresaw that he would see by chance from time to time in the future on some train travelling between Melbourne and Dandenong the young woman from Dandenong who had once been his girlfriend and would talk with her easily as a bachelor to a woman content with her boyfriend or fiancé or husband. He did not foresee that he would remain a bachelor for most of the next ten years; that he would not have seen the young woman or have heard of her for more than thirty-five years on a certain afternoon in the future when he learned from a woman who had formerly lived in Dandenong that the young woman had married many years before and was by then a grandmother and that she had lived for much of her life in a place that had been when she first lived there one of the nearer towns of Gippsland but had later become one of the outermost south-eastern suburbs of Melbourne. He did not foresee that he would learn also from the same woman who had told him these things that the mother of his girlfriend of more than thirty-five years before had died while her daughters were still young married women and that the father of those women, after he had been a widower for several years, had become a lay-brother in the monastery of the Cistercian order between Yarra Glen and Healesville, which monastery he, the chief character, had once visited and which he remembered afterwards as a pale-coloured building surrounded first by green paddocks through some of which the Yarra River wound and then, on three sides, by mountains covered with forest.

When he had first got down from the bus and for almost all the time while he and the others had climbed towards the summit of Donna Buang, they had been surrounded by what they thought was mist or fog, but just as they approached the summit they saw blue sky above them and they stepped into bright sunshine. He stood alone, just as he had foreseen, while he looked out at the view from the summit. The summit was a grassy and mostly level place, and he walked at once to what he judged to be the eastern side of the summit. He had not foreseen the view that he saw to the east of the summit.

The poems that had interested him most at school had been those that brought to his mind images of places. When he took out a sheet of ruled paper and prepared to write on it during an evening in the week after the events reported in the previous paragraphs, he had never previously tried to write a poem but he supposed that a poem was the sort of writing that would most clearly record the details of the place that had been in his mind for much of the time since he had come down from the summit of Mount Donna Buang on the previous Sunday. At some time before he sat down in front of the sheet of ruled paper, he had begun to hear in his mind the words at the head of this section of this story, and at some time soon afterwards he had decided that the words should be the last line of his poem.

If he had been able to write the earlier lines of his poem, those lines would have reported first the details of the place that he had seen in his mind whenever during the years before he had first travelled to Mount Donna Buang he had imagined the eastern half of Victoria, which details would have included a large area of green in the foreground being the region of Gippsland and a narrow zone of blue-black at the left-hand side being the mountains, many of them damaged by fire, at the northern edge of Gippsland. The lines would have reported next the details he had seen in his mind whenever during the days since he had travelled to Mount Donna Buang he had imagined himself as putting his face close to the narrow zone of blue-black as though it was a detail in a picture in his mind, which details would have included a large area of blue in the foreground being ranges of mountains covered with forests that had grown in place of the forests burned in the past and a narrow zone of the colour of smoke at the horizon, which zone he was not yet able to imagine as being close to his face.

In the Blue Dandenongs

The words above were the caption of a coloured illustration on a calendar that his mother received from one or another shopkeeper in one or another year during the late 1940s when she and her husband and their two sons were living in a rented house in a western suburb of Melbourne. The calendar hung for a year in the kitchen of the rented house and was designed so that the numbered spaces denoting the days of one or another month were torn away at the end of that month while the illustration above the numbered spaces remained visible throughout the year. After he had looked several times at the illustration on the calendar during the first days after it had been hung, he resolved not to look again at the illustration during the remainder of the year, but he went against his resolution many times.

In later years, whenever he remembered the illustration on the calendar, he remembered the following details. In the foreground, two children are standing in green grass that reaches halfway to their knees. Near the children, a horse has lifted its head from the grass and is looking towards them. The girl holds out a hand towards the horse. In her hand is a carrot with the green top still growing from the red root. From where the children and the horse are standing, the grassy paddock slopes downwards through the middle ground of the illustration towards a fence. On the other side of the fence, a mountain rises from an unseen gully. The side of the mountain is covered with forest. Behind this mountain, in the far background, is part of another mountain. The forest on this mountain is blue-grey. The mellow light suggests that the time of day is late afternoon.

The children had at first reminded him of children in illustrations in the books for English boys and girls that his unmarried aunts lent to him to read during his summer holidays. Those books, so his aunts would remind him, had belonged to his father and his brothers when they were boys. The girls in those illustrations were as tall as women but had the innocent faces and the hips and chests of children of nine or ten. The boys had the chests and shoulders of men, but they wore short trousers and had the guileless faces and tousled hair of choir-boys on a Christmas card. The boys and girls in the books that he read from his aunts' collections defended themselves against burglars and spies and smugglers and were spoken to respectfully by detectives but were never troubled by even the thought that they might fall in love.

The children on the calendar had reminded him at first of child-men and child-women in English storybooks, but the illustration on the calendar was a photograph, and so the children were not distortions or caricatures. He was able to estimate from the bodies and the faces that the children were about eleven years of age. But he tried for most of the time not to look at the children. Their air of innocence annoyed him.

He was not so angry with the girl. She was trying to coax the horse towards her and could have been excused for her look of preoccupation. If he could have seen more than her profile, he might even have found that her face was of the sort that appeared in his mind from time to time and caused him to fall in love. The boy might have been looking at the face of the girl or at the carrot in her hand or at the horse or even at something that had distracted him from beyond the range of the camera. His curly hair and his vacant grin seemed meant to make adults think of him as a likeable young rascal who was preparing, even while he posed for the photographer, to put a caterpillar on the girl's skirt in order to make her squeal.

If, in spite of himself, he looked at the picture on the calendar, he tried to look past the boy and the girl who had never fallen in love or felt jealous or anxious in connection with a person whose image stayed in his or her mind. He tried to see, behind the forested mountain in the background, one of the many other pairs of children who would have been in the Dandenongs on the day when the photograph was taken.

That boy and that girl lived in the same neighbourhood in an eastern suburb of Melbourne, and their parents often visited one another and arranged family outings together. Each family owned a motor car, and at least once in each month the two cars followed each other through the outer eastern suburbs and then through grassy countryside and then into the foothills of the Dandenongs and then along the red-gravel roads through the forested gullies and between the mountainsides. On hot days in summer, the children paddled among mossy stones in creeks with treeferns on their banks. Late in summer, they picked blackberries. In autumn, they scooped up armfuls of coloured leaves among stands of European trees. In the coldest days of winter, when the fathers had fixed chains to the car-tyres, the children played in shallow drifts of snow. In late winter, they picked sprays of wattle-bloom. In spring, they visited the camellia and rhododendron gardens. On wet days in any season, they drank soft drinks in cafés while their parents were served Devonshire teas. At a certain hour late on many a Sunday afternoon, he had felt, even as a child in his first years at school, that some other male person of exactly his own age was living, perhaps only a few miles away, the life that he himself ought to have been living. When he had felt this on certain Sundays as he was waiting with his mother and his younger brother at a tram-stop near the home of his aunt who lived in an inner eastern suburb, before returning to his home in a western suburb, he had some-times seen in the rear seat of a motor car passing the tramstop a young person returning with his family from a place that must surely have been in the Dandenong Ranges, so he, the chief char-acter, supposed on some day during the year when he looked for pairs of children in the background of the picture on the calendar.

Something else about the children on the calendar unsettled him. Some detail such as the bagginess of the boy's trousers or the shapes of the bows in the ribbons in the girl's hair made him, the chief character, often suppose that the photograph had been taken ten or more years earlier. He was not unfamiliar with what had been worn in the late 1930s. He had once found under sheets of linoleum torn up from the floors of the rented house many sheets of newspapers from the year before he had been born and had studied the drawings in the advertisements, especially the draw-ings of children. He had been curious about the children who had seen the sky over Melbourne dark with smoke on the day when his mother had thought the world was about to end but whose lives had not then ended. He could hardly blame the grinning boy or the girl whose eyes were on the horse if they were unaware that the place where they were playing would be soon destroyed by fire. But he expected that one at least of those couples outside the boundaries of the illustration on the calendar—one of those couples who had fallen in love, although their parents had never suspected it—would sometimes imagine a blue-grey mountain on the horizon to be smoke moving towards them.

On a certain Saturday afternoon in the early autumn in his twenty-third year, the chief character of this story sat for several hours beside a young woman in one of a number of enclosures of green canvas in the upper deck of the public grandstand at the racecourse in Caulfield, a south-eastern suburb of Melbourne. Each of the enclosures of green canvas was described in advertisements authorised by the club that conducted race meetings at Caulfield Racecourse as a luxuriously appointed private box, with drink waiters in attendance, available for hire to members of the public on race days. He, the chief character, had paid for the hire of a box for two persons a sum of money equal to one quarter of his weekly earnings after tax.

From time to time during the past three years, he had fallen in love with one or another face in his mind, but he had always gone back to thinking of himself as a bachelor before he had begun to feel unduly anxious or unhappy about the person whose face kept appearing in his mind. During his twenty-first year, he had enrolled in a subject for which evening classes were offered at the university and had obtained a pass as his final result. He had become somewhat tired of reading out-of-the-way books in his room by night but having to spend his days among persons who had not opened a book since they had left school. On a few evenings, he had tried to write poetry but had given up and instead had read some of the poems that had most impressed him at school, especially "The Lotos-Eaters," by Tennyson, and "The Scholar-Gipsy," by Matthew Arnold. While he read certain lines of "The Lotos-Eaters" and watched images of places drifting into his mind, he would feel as he believed he would have felt when he had formerly looked at landscapes of Helvetia in his mind. While he read certain lines of "The Scholar-Gipsy," he felt as he supposed his bachelor-uncle must sometimes have felt in his bungalow.

At the time of his outing with the young woman to Caulfield

Racecourse, he had begun to study a second subject at university and had been promoted at work to a more responsible position in which he was required to proofread some of the contents of booklets and leaflets informing the public about certain forests and foreshores and parks. When he had taken up this position, he had moved to a higher floor of the building. The face of one of the young women that he met on the higher floor had entered his mind at once. She was only a few months younger than he. She was well-mannered and popular, but she was quick-witted and was not afraid to join in the debates that began among several men in her office—all of them senior to her—whenever one or the other man made a comment on something he had read in the morning newspaper. He, the chief character, understood from her arguments at these times that she was a fervent Catholic. He himself no longer went to church, but the face of the young woman in his mind persuaded him to believe that he could live as a Catholic in the future with her as his wife. As a Catholic, she would not want to practise what she would call artificial birth control, and he and she might become the parents of four or five or six children. He could accept this, but he could not foresee himself providing for such a number of children and also buying a house in an outer suburb of Melbourne. He foresaw himself instead settling with her in the future in one of the large country towns where his department had branch offices. In each of those towns, the senior officers paid a small rent for modest but comfortable houses built by the Housing Commission of Victoria. When he tried to foresee which large country town he and his wife would settle in, he understood that the town would not be in Gippsland. He had learned from maps published by his department that the word *Gippsland* denoted a region larger than he had once supposed and that the region contained much forest. But ever since the day when he had looked eastwards from the summit of Mount Donna Buang, he had seen Gippsland in his mind as a narrow green margin along one side of an extensive zone that appeared sometimes blue-black and sometimes blue-grey and sometimes pure blue. The town where

382

he and she settled would not be in the south-west of the state. He believed that the young woman was the ideal Catholic wife that his bachelor-uncle had never found, and he, the chief character, who had so often thought of becoming himself a bachelor in a place like a bungalow, did not want to seem to be boasting in front of his uncle. The town would have to be in the north of the state, in the region where he had never been: the region of old goldfields and box-tree forests that he had never yet visited.

He did not own a car, and he called in a taxi at the address that she had given him. She lived in her parents' house in an eastern suburb of the sort that journalists called *comfortable* or *middle-class*, in a street of the sort that they called *leafy* or *tree-lined*, but the house was built of weatherboards, and when he was approaching the front porch he thought that her house was no more spacious and solid than his own parents' house, except that it had been built in an outer suburb with few trees and with many of its streets still rutted and swampy. She answered his ring at the doorbell. She was dressed for the races, with her handbag on her arm, and she stepped outside and closed the door behind her.

She was as much a talker as himself. On the way from her home to the racecourse, he told her that he had always envied the people of the eastern suburbs for having lived ordered lives among pleasant surroundings. She then asked him to name the particular families that he envied. He then told her that he had visited an aunt in a house with paintings on the wall in an inner eastern suburb for many years when he was a boy, but he knew while he told her this that he had never envied his aunt and her family in their house without books. He then told the young woman that he had grown up in a suburb with no persons of his own age. She then told him that every Catholic parish in the suburbs of Melbourne had at least one organisation for young persons to meet one another.

A few miles short of the racecourse, she pointed out her old school. It was a cluster of brick buildings no larger than his own school, but the hill where her school stood seemed to offer a wider view around. She reminded him that his and her schools were in neighbouring suburbs and that senior boys from his school had sometimes been invited to social evenings at her school. He then told her that he had been anti-social and eccentric when he was at school.

Soon after they had been shown to their private box at the race-course, he told her that Caulfield Racecourse had been called many years before the Heath, and that the grassy racecourse in their view had been cleared from an expanse of dense scrub. She then told him that the racecourse had been used during the Second World War as an army camp and that her father had spent much time in a tent somewhere in the grassy expanse in front of them.

He had brought with him the pair of powerful binoculars that he always took to the races, and he began to point out to her what he called his landmarks and then to invite her to look at the landmarks through the binoculars. He showed her first the roof of his parish church, four miles away to the south-east. He then showed her the treetops on the golf course where he had worked as a caddy while he was at secondary school. His own street, he told her, was somewhere just beyond the far side of those trees. She then said that the trees made it seem as though he lived in a clearing in a forest. He would have liked to let her look through his binoculars at Mount Dandenong, but the grandstand at the racecourse faced south, and the mountain was somewhat to their rear and out of view. He showed her instead the dark-blue ridges of the Lysterfield Hills, which were halfway between Dandenong and Mount Dandenong and which he had thought were the southern aspect of Mount Dandenong itself on his first few visits to his girlfriend at Dandenong. The young woman beside him at the racecourse said she had lived all her life in Melbourne, but she still thought it strange that Mount Dandenong and Dandenong were two quite separate places far apart. He asked her how often she and her family had been to the Dandenong Ranges during her childhood. He wanted her to say that hardly a Sunday had passed without their going deep among the mountain-ash forests and the treefern-gullies and the waterfalls and all the sights he had never seen, but she only answered that she had been there often enough.

She aimed his binoculars to the south and asked him what was the low blue ridge far away in that direction. He told her it was Mount Eliza, with all of the Mornington Peninsula lying behind it. He wanted her to say that she and her family had gone for three weeks during every Christmas holiday to the camping-ground beside the beach at Rosebud or Rye or Dromana on the peninsula, but she only recited to herself the names *Rosebud*, *Rye*, and several other names of places where families from the suburbs spent their summer holidays.

He had wanted to hear that she had gone often to the Dandenongs or to the beaches on the Mornington Peninsula. He believed already that he had been deluded to suppose that the young woman was interested in him in the way that he was interested in her. He intended to ask her, when he said goodbye to her outside her house later that afternoon, to go with him to a cinema on the following Friday or Saturday evening, but he believed already, while they sat together in their private box before the first race at Caulfield, that she would politely decline to go with him on any further outing. He expected that he and she would go on talking pleasantly for the rest of the afternoon, but he had become again a bachelor in his mind before the first race had been run, and he expected to remain a bachelor for longer than he had ever previously been. He wanted to remember as a bachelor that the last young woman who had allowed him to keep her company had been one of the many persons who had spent their childhood dreaming of places no further than the Dandenong Ranges or the Mornington Peninsula.

He did not consider himself superior to such persons. He had always seen Melbourne and its suburbs as a resting-place that his father had found on his way from the grassy countryside of the south-west of Victoria to some place much further afield. He, the son, had never supposed that his father had been travelling eastwards with only the map of Victoria in mind, so that his goal was no further than Gippsland in his mind. He, the son, had sometimes supposed that his father was travelling from west to east in his mind on a map of Helvetia in his mind. Whenever the son tried to imagine the place that his father supposed he was travelling towards, he, the son, saw the place as peopled by the tall girl-women and boy-men from the books that his aunts had kept all their lives. When he had thought of these personages only as characters in his aunts' books, he had been angered by the innocence of the personages, but when they appeared to him as the inhabitants of the eastern region of Helvetia, with their untroubled faces and their sexless bodies, he would have liked to stand with them on the verandas of their farmhouses or at the edges of their small townships in that region where no one fell in love or married in his or her mind and to look out across the grassy country-side that reached to the horizon in every direction.

At the time when the chief character sat with the young woman overlooking Caulfield Racecourse, his father had travelled as far to the east as he would travel, although he, the chief character, did not know this. (His father died in the south-west of Victoria only a few months after his elder son had married and had gone to live in a northern suburb of Melbourne.) At the time when the chief character sat at the racecourse, his father had been for as long as the chief character could remember what most people would have called a good father, but the chief character decided soon after his father had died that he ought not to have married and become a father. His father, so the chief character believed in the last part of his life, had been better fitted to live as a bachelor than as a husband and father and ought never to have left the district of grassy countryside where he had been born and ought to have lived there as a bachelor throughout his life.

He, the chief character, had been born in a suburb of a city that had been built on a bank of a river near its entrance into a large bay, but throughout his life he seldom noticed the river and he always avoided the bay. He always thought of Melbourne as an inland city with one or another range of mountains or hills visible from every suburb. In his later life, he looked out for published ac-

counts of the childhoods of persons who had been born in the suburbs of Melbourne and had lived there during the ten years and
more before his own birth. When he was nearly forty years old,
he found and read the books *Goodbye Melbourne Town* and *The
Road to Gundagai*, both by Graham McInnes and both published
in London during the 1960s by Hamish Hamilton. The author of
the books had been born in England, had arrived in Melbourne
as a boy, had lived there during the 1920s and part of the 1930s,
his home for much of that time being in an eastern suburb with
views of Mount Dandenong (the same suburb in which the chief
character of this story attended secondary school), had left for
Canada as a young man just out of university, and had written the
books mentioned while he remembered Melbourne from far away
and thirty years later. Somewhere in one of those books, he, the
chief character of this story, read a passage in which the author
named all the mountains or hills that he always remembered as
having appeared in the distance around Melbourne.

He, the young man sitting beside the young woman in the
grandstand at Caulfield Racecourse, was far from despising anyone who remembered as the sites of their falling in love with certain faces in their minds places with views of mountains or hills to
the south-east or the east or the north-east or the north. He believed that he himself would have been such a person if he had
not been born and had not spent his early years on the level and
grassy side of Melbourne and if he had not thought of that place
as the eastern edge of the countryside where his father had been
born and where he, the father, ought to have lived as a bachelor
throughout his life.

At some time in mid-afternoon, when he had assured himself
that the young woman beside him in the enclosure of green canvas would fall in love at some time in the future with one or another young man who had spent many a Sunday afternoon in the
Dandenong Ranges and would later marry that man and would
live with him after their marriage in one or another outer eastern
suburb of Melbourne, he, the chief character of this story, having

decided that he would be a bachelor for the remainder of his life, began to relax and to tell the young woman things that he would not have told her if he had still been in love with the image of her face in his mind.

He told her that he had sometimes dreamed of owning a race-horse. Being a public servant on a modest salary, he could not afford to be the sole owner of a horse during the foreseeable future, so he told her, but after about his fortieth year, when he had been promoted several times, as he could reasonably expect to be, he should be able to spend on a racehorse what another man of his age would spend on his wife and children. He spoke as though she did not need to be told that he was going to be a bachelor for the remainder of his life, and she did not interject that he should have been married and a father by his fortieth year. He supposed that she was as well aware as he was of the unspoken rule binding young persons of the suburbs of Melbourne at that time while they were together on outings as a result of the young man's having, in the words used at the time, *asked out* the young woman: the rule that neither young person should use the word *marriage* except in such a way as to suggest that the speaker had never once in his or her lifetime entertained the least possibility that he or she would, in the words used at the time, *become serious* about another person (least of all the person he or she was, in the words used at the time, *going out with*), much less consider marrying. He told her that he often foresaw an afternoon far into the future when he would stand in the mounting yard of a racecourse in a suburb of Melbourne and would watch his horse walking or cantering onto the course proper ten minutes before the start of a certain race. He did not name the racecourse when he told her this. None of the three racecourses then in use in the suburbs of Melbourne had ever seemed to him to be the racecourse that was the site in his mind of the race far into the future. That race had always seemed to be about to take place on one of the racecourses at which his father had attended meetings during the years before his, the chief character's, birth, but which had long since closed.

The racecourse was Sandown Park, which had been halfway between the suburb where he had lived from his thirteenth year to
his twenty-ninth year, and Dandenong, the place that had for
long been a town at the western edge of Gippsland but had later
become an outer south-eastern suburb of Melbourne. The old
Sandown Park racecourse, so his father had told him, had seemed
to be surrounded by scrub, and from the grandstand a person
could look out at the Dandenong Ranges. He, the chief character,
told the young woman at Caulfield Racecourse that the sunlight
on the afternoon that he foresaw had a peculiar mellowness such
as he noticed each year in the light over the suburbs of Melbourne
on certain afternoons in the last week of February or the first
weeks of March. (The day when he told her this was a day in early
March, but the sky was cloudy and a breeze was blowing from the
south-west.) He told her that the sight of this mellow light each
year caused him to forget for a few moments that he was in one or
another suburb of Melbourne and to suppose that he was in one
or another region of a country that he had imagined as the boy-
owner of a collection of stamps from places whose whereabouts
he did not know. (He did not name Helvetia when he told her this.)
He told the young woman that the first occasion when he had seen
the peculiar mellowness in the sunlight had been, so he believed,
in midsummer rather than in autumn. This occasion had been
one or another of the afternoons during the first weeks of his life
when his mother had lain him in a bassinette in a shaded part of
the backyard of the boarding house in the western suburb where
his parents had lived when he had been born. He told the young
woman that he had been born while the smoke still hung in the
upper atmosphere after the terrible Black Friday bushfires that
she must surely have heard about from her own parents; that he
had seen a photograph of himself lying in his bassinette between
two trees with the back door of a weatherboard house in the
background but that the photograph was, of course, in black and
white although the date in his mother's handwriting on the back
was a date only three weeks after Black Friday. He told the young

woman that the sight of the peculiar mellowness in the sunlight caused him sometimes as a young man to suppose not that he was in an imagined country but that fires were burning throughout some region far away and that the smoke from the fires still hung in the upper atmosphere.

He told the young woman that the owner of a racehorse could know that his horse was supremely fit before a particular race and could bet large sums of money on his horse but could never be sure that his horse would not be narrowly beaten in the race by a horse whose owner had known about his horse and had bet as the first owner had known and bet. He told her that on the afternoon far into the future, the owner that he would be at that time would have known several times in the recent past that his horse had been supremely fit and would have bet several times large sums of money on the horse but would have seen the horse narrowly beaten. But on the afternoon that he foresaw, so he told her, with a certain mellow light in the air and a view of the Dandenong Ranges on the far side of the racecourse, his run of losses would come to an end at last. He did not tell the young woman that he always foresaw that he would understand on that afternoon in the far future that a certain woman of a few years less than his own age would be among the crowd who would watch him standing beside the winner's stall in the mounting yard as his horse returned to scale; that he would not know the name of the woman or any detail of her history, although he would have recognised the woman at once if he had happened to see her face at any time during the afternoon; that the woman would have wondered for a few moments about him when she saw him standing with no wife or child beside him and only the trainer of his horse for company but would not have known what he would have known if ever he had seen her face, namely, that she was the woman he would have met and married if his life had taken the course it would have taken if he had not decided as a young man to be in the future a bachelor and the owner of a racehorse.

At some time during the afternoon while they sat together in the canvas enclosure, he told the young woman that the colours carried by the horse that he had foreseen himself as owning would be one or another combination of pale green and dark blue. When the young woman had asked him why he had named those particular colours, he did not answer truthfully. He told her that his chosen colours were the most striking of the many colours in the main window of stained glass above the altar in the Catholic church in the large town in the south-west of Victoria where he had often spent his summer holidays. This much of what he told her was true. One Sunday morning during his summer holidays five years before, while he had been kneeling in the church beside one of his unmarried aunts, he had noticed the prominence in the window above the altar of the colours that he had already adopted as his racing colours: the dark blue in the mantle of the Blessed Virgin Mary and the pale green in what he supposed to be a shower of divine grace or some other spiritual emanation reaching down to the Virgin from on high. But he had decided on his colours at some time during the previous year while he had been in his room in his parents' house one evening. He wanted colours that were seldom used by other owners, and he wanted his colours to suggest what was most distinctive about him. He knew already that he would never be able to become the owner of a racehorse unless he remained a bachelor throughout his life, and he believed that his bachelorhood would be what most clearly defined him. When he asked himself what colours best suggested bachelorhood, he thought at once of his bachelor-uncle in his paddocks in the south-west of Victoria. He, the chief character, then saw those paddocks as pale green and the line of trees that seemed always in the distance as dark blue. Even while those colours were occurring to him, he was aware that the combination of pale green and dark blue hardly ever appeared on the racecourses of Melbourne or the country districts of Victoria.

Few sentences in this piece of fiction are of the kind that might be verified by reference to other publications in the world where the book containing this piece of fiction will later be published, but the sentences in this paragraph are of that kind. On almost every Saturday during the years of the late 1950s and early 1960s, the racebook containing, among many other details, the details of the colours worn by the riders of all the horses entered at the race meeting in one or another suburb of Melbourne on that day contained no details of any jacket and cap of only pale green and dark blue. On some Saturdays, the colours *green, blue spots, red cap* were listed in the racebook. One of the few horses that raced under those colours, the green of which appeared as pale green on the silk of the actual jacket so that the colours could be imagined as consisting only of pale green and dark blue when the jockey wearing the colours stood in the mounting yard with his cap not yet on his head, was named Grassland, and the sire of this horse was a horse imported from England with the name Black Pampas.

After the race meeting at Caulfield, the young woman insisted that the chief character of this story must not go to the expense of taking her to her home in a taxi, even though he and she would otherwise have to travel by train and then by tram to the end of her street. He was pleased to travel by train and tram because this would give him much more time for talking to her, but the train was too crowded for talking privately, and as soon as they were alone together at the tram stop, she began talking to him. She told him that she had very much enjoyed his company but that she would very probably not be able to go out with him again. She told him that she had been going out regularly for some time with a man who had proposed marriage to her; that if she were to accept the man's proposal, he and she would have to be engaged for several years at least, since the man had taken on certain financial commitments that would not allow him to marry at present; that she sometimes seriously doubted whether it would be morally advisable for herself and the man to enter into such a long engagement as they would have to enter into; that she had gone out with him, the chief character, because he was an interesting person, because the man who wanted to marry her was often unable to get to Melbourne from the country district where he lived, and because she did not consider in any case that she should go out exclusively with him until they had become engaged, if that should happen; but that he, the chief character, should understand that she could not consider becoming interested in anyone else until she had made up her mind about the man she had told him about.

Having become a confirmed bachelor in his mind some hours before, he was not made unhappy or anxious by her speech, but he was curious to know what commitments the man mentioned had entered into and what the young woman had been thinking of when she said that a long engagement might not be morally advisable. He, the chief character, assumed that the man who had proposed marriage must have been at least as fervent a Catholic as the young woman. He, the chief character, found himself thinking of the man as being a member of one of a few Catholic cooperative settlements that he, the chief character, knew about. One of the settlements was in remote mountain country in the northeast of Victoria, which was a region that he could only imagine as a blue haze of mountains. Another settlement was in the foothills of the mountains to the north of Gippsland, which settlement he imagined as a clearing in a forest, with log cabins for houses. The third settlement that he knew of, and the one where he imagined the proposer of marriage to be living, was in the next range of mountains on the far side of the Dandenong Ranges. He, the chief character, had heard that these cooperative settlements, which had been founded ten or fifteen years previously when many Catholics from Melbourne had wanted to live a simple life away from the evils of city life, were struggling to survive. He supposed that the man who wanted to marry the young woman beside him at the tram stop in an eastern suburb in the late afternoon of a day in the early autumn was at that moment milking cows by hand or weeding a potato paddock or felling a tree with a crosscut saw in order to add to the meagre wealth of the cooperative so that it could pay him back in cash for the cash that he had invested in it some years previously, which cash had been his life-savings. But then he, the chief character, supposed that the man was toiling at the cooperative not because he wanted to leave it and return to Melbourne but because he wanted to earn enough units of credit according to the system of exchange that operated in the cooperative so that the other members would help him at some time in the future to clear and to fence a small area and to build a simple cottage in the area and so to be able to provide a home for his bride after their marriage.

As for the question why a young Catholic woman would wonder whether a long engagement was morally advisable, he, the chief character, had tried to answer this to himself from the moment when the young woman had used the words that had caused the question to occur to him, even postulating answers in his mind while he and the young woman went on talking about trivial matters in the tram that would take them to the end of her street. What seemed to him the most likely answer was as follows. The proposer of marriage had somehow conveyed to the young woman by hints and murmurings that he would be likely to commit regular if not frequent mortal sins alone and in both thought and deed if his and the young woman's engagement should be unduly prolonged. He, the chief character of this story, supposed that the young woman was unable to imagine in any detail how such sins might be committed, but he imagined the sinner as being compelled from time to time to walk alone into the forest surrounding the cooperative settlement and to relieve himself there while the undergrowth prickled his bare forearms and while he imagined certain young married women of the cooperative rebuking him or commanding him to stop.

After he and she had got down from the tram, she took his hand and squeezed it for a moment and thanked him for a very pleasant day and asked him not to bother to walk with her to her house. He said goodbye to her and stood waiting for a tram to take him back the way he had come. The place where he stood was on the western side of a slight hill, so that he could not see Mount Dandenong, but he could see, on the next hillside towards the city, what he believed to be part of one of the buildings of her old school, and he wished that he had asked her whether she had been able to see Mount Dandenong from any of her classrooms when she had been a schoolgirl. A few more than thirty years later, he would be passing her school one day and would notice an estate agent's noticeboard stating that a large number of apartments would soon be for sale on the site, most with splendid views of the Blue Dandenongs.

In the Bois de Boulogne

The words just above came into his mind one day during the mid-1980s when he was trying to remember from the English translation of the book of fiction À la recherche du temps perdu, by Marcel Proust, which he had read ten years earlier, a certain phrase that he believed had first brought to his mind when he read it in the book an image that had occurred to him often during the following ten years, which image seemed sometimes connected with his feelings when he remembered certain events on a certain afternoon in the autumn of a certain year in the mid-1960s and also with his feelings when he remembered a certain passage at the beginning of the section of the book with the title "Cities of the Plain."

During much of his life, whenever he heard or read another person's account of his or her having read one or another book of fiction, he supposed that he was the only person who remembered having read fiction in the way that he remembered it. Whenever he remembered his having read one or another passage in one or another book, he remembered not the words of the passage but the weather during the hour when he had read the passage, the sights or sounds that he had seen or heard around him from time to time while he read, the textures of the cushions or curtains or walls or grasses or leaves that he had reached for and had touched from time to time while he read, the look of the cover of the book containing the passage and of the page or pages where the passage had been printed, and especially the images that had appeared in his mind while he had read the passage and the feelings that he had felt while he had read.

Whenever he remembered having read the passage of fiction mentioned in the first paragraph of this section of this story, he remembered himself as sitting on a patch of green lawn among green shrubs in the yard behind the house in the outer northern suburb of Melbourne where he lived with his wife and their two children and as seeing in his mind among many other images an image of grey-blue roofs of houses, each of several storeys, which image he understood to be an image of a certain suburb of the city of Paris, which he had never visited, and an image of a margin of green around part of the area of grey-blue, which image he understood to be an image of part of the forest that surrounded part of the suburb of Paris. Whenever he remembered having read the passage of fiction just mentioned, he remembered himself as believing while he read the passage that the insect that was needed to bring to the flower of the rare plant exposed in a certain courtyard in the suburb just mentioned a certain grain of pollen kept mostly to the forest just mentioned but would bring the grain of pollen on some day in the future from deep inside the forest and so would cause to be fertilised the plant that had remained for so long unfertilised.

(The writer of this piece of fiction has just now looked through the early pages of the section with the title "Cities of the Plain" in each of the two English translations that he has read of *À la recherche du temps perdu* but has found no reference to any view of any part of any forest seen or remembered or imagined by the narrator of the section.)

Whenever he remembered having read the passage of fiction mentioned several times above, he remembered himself also as having seen in his mind soon after he had seen the margin of green an image of a photograph he had once seen of part of the green grass and the white railings of the racecourse of Longchamps and a caption explaining among other things that the racecourse was in the Bois de Boulogne.

Whenever he remembered having read the passage of fiction mentioned several times above, he remembered himself also as having remembered whenever he read in that passage the references to the character mostly referred to as M. de Charlus the notions that he, the chief character, had had as a boy and later as a young man about the men referred to as bachelors. One of these notions was that each of these men had wanted as a young man to marry a certain young woman but that she had not wanted to marry him and that this had brought so much unhappiness to the young man that he had never afterwards approached a young woman. Another of these notions was that each of these men had fallen in love as a young man with an image of a young woman in his mind but had never met an actual young woman who was sufficiently like the young woman in his mind for him to want to approach her.

Whenever he remembered having read the passage of fiction mentioned several times above, he remembered himself also as having remembered while he read that he had often supposed as a boy and as a young man that he would be a bachelor throughout his life.

Whenever he remembered having read the passage of fiction mentioned several times above, he remembered himself also as having remembered while he read certain events that had led to his learning on a certain afternoon in a certain clearing on a hillside covered with forest that he would not be a bachelor in the future, which events may be summarised as follows.

During his twenty-seventh year, when he had passed more than half of the subjects of a degree of bachelor of arts, he was promoted in the department where he worked to an editorial position on a publication with the title *Our Forests*. His duties were wholly editorial; he was not required to visit any of the places that were the subjects of articles or illustrations in *Our Forests*. However, he now worked on a higher floor of the building where he had worked for nearly ten years, and his desk was near a window with a view to the north and the north-west, and on clear days he could see the blue-black ridge of Mount Macedon.

During one of the first mornings that he spent at his new workplace, he overheard a young woman he had never previously seen explaining to a young woman at a desk near his desk that she, the young woman he had never previously seen, would not be able to attend a party she had been invited to on the forthcoming Saturday evening because she would be doing during the following weekend what she did on many another weekend, which was to travel by train to the district in Gippsland where she had formerly lived and to spend the weekend on the dairy farm in that district where her parents lived with her three younger sisters.

During the days following the morning just mentioned, he learned the name of the young woman just mentioned and the whereabouts of the desk where she worked and he found opportunities for observing her and for listening to her conversations with other young women. The young woman did not resemble any image of any young woman that he had fallen in love with in his mind during his lifetime, but an image of her face had begun to appear in his mind soon after he had first seen her, and he supposed that he was about to experience once again the series of states of feeling that he had not experienced during the four years and more since he had gone with the young woman mentioned previously to a race-meeting at Caulfield.

He was no longer interested in his studies at the university but he intended to finish his degree for the sake of his career, as he had begun to call what he had previously called his job. When he had joined the state public service fewer than ten years before, most of his seniors had seemed to be grey-haired men, but younger men and even a few women had lately been promoted to responsible positions. Some of these people dressed and conducted themselves as though they wanted to be mistaken for persons in private enterprise, which was the name that public servants used for the world outside their office buildings. He, the chief character, knew he would never want to go along with anything that his workmates considered fashionable—he was already known among them as an eccentric—but he was confident that his degree and his thoroughness with paperwork would earn him promotions up to a certain level. He did not want to reach a position in which, to use the language of his place of work, he would be expected to formulate policy; he wanted to make his career at the highest level at which, to use the same language, policy was implemented. In his most frequent daydream of himself in his mid-thirties and later, he was the editor of publications in the department where he had worked for six of his eight years as a public servant. In that position, he would choose and edit for publication reports and articles and photographs and diagrams from foresters and technical officers and scientists all over Victoria. He would commission staff from his own office sometimes to travel far from Melbourne. He himself would hardly ever leave Melbourne. Years would pass, and the glass display case in his office would be filled with sample copies of the issues he had edited of *Our Forests*, each cover showing an aerial view of forested hills or mountains or a glade or a clearing or a track or a road in a forest or, sometimes, a single tree. One cover would surely show blackened trees after a fire. He would enjoy correcting a visitor sometimes when the visitor had said that he, the editor, must have seen a good few forests in his time. He would take pride in being the sort of expert who understood his subject from a distance.

One reason for his not wanting to be a formulator of policy was that he supposed such a person would use by day the energy that he, the chief character, used of an evening and wanted to go on using. Whenever he was not reading or writing in order to achieve a safe pass in the subject he was currently studying at the university, he was trying to be a Helvetian, which task he expected would take up most of his time away from work during the rest of his working life. Even as a child, he had ceased to hope that he would see again in his mind the scenery of the place that he afterwards thought of as True Helvetia, and he had still been a child when he learned in which country of the actual world a postage stamp had once been issued with the word *Helvetia* on it. Yet, the word *Helvetia* was often in his mind during his later life. Even though he sometimes saw behind the word a vague outline of steep, forested mountains with grassy valleys deep among them, he meant by *Helvetia* at different times many other kinds of place. Until a certain evening, which will be mentioned in the following paragraph, his trying to be a Helvetian was no more than his going on with his search for what he had earlier called precious knowledge. He carried on this search mostly by looking into books but sometimes by trying to write poems.

During the evening mentioned above, he had reached, as he often did, the point of admitting that he would never write a poem likely to be found suitable for publication in any of the periodicals that he sometimes sent a poem to. The words in which he admitted this to himself included an expression to the effect that there was no place where his poems might be published. The word *place* stayed in his mind for a few moments, and its staying there seemed to him afterwards the nearest thing to an explanation for his deciding at the end of those few moments that he would have been a published poet if he had lived in Helvetia.

Soon after he had made the decision just mentioned, he decided that he was an inhabitant of Helvetia (and, of course, a published poet of that country) for as long as he was at his desk and writing poetry. Soon afterwards again, he decided that he was a Helvetian for as long as he happened to be thinking of himself as a writer of poems or thinking of any word or phrase from his poetry. Soon afterwards again, he decided that any image appearing in his mind while he wrote any word or phrase of a poem or while he read afterwards any such word or phrase was an image of a person or a place or a thing in Helvetia.

He began to write poetry every evening. He took even more care with his poems than previously, being aware that every line, as soon as he had thought of it as finished, became part of the latest volume from one of the foremost poets in Helvetia.

He was writing his Helvetian poetry during the evenings of the days when he was observing the young woman mentioned earlier, but he sometimes put aside his poetry to study maps borrowed from the collection in the library of the department where he worked. The maps were detailed maps of the district where the parents of the young woman lived, so she had told him one day when he had spoken to her as one workmate to another. The district seemed to consist of plains, with hills to the south—the same hills that covered much of Gippsland—and to the north the first of the mountains that covered most of eastern and northeastern Victoria.

On a certain Saturday afternoon in the winter of his twenty-seventh year, he sat with the young woman mentioned in the previous paragraph in an enclosure of green canvas called a private box at Moonee Valley Racecourse. From where they sat, he and she could see across a wide valley through which the Monee Ponds Creek flowed, although it was out of their sight at the far side of the racecourse. Except for the large green rectangle of the racecourse, most of the floor of the valley and all that they could see of its sides were closely covered by the older sorts of houses of the inner northern suburbs of Melbourne. When he and the young woman looked out across the racecourse from their private box, they were looking in the direction of Mount Dandenong, far to the east, but they could see no further in that direction than the far side of the valley where the creek flowed and the racecourse lay.

For several weeks past, he had been sitting or walking with her for a few minutes on each fine day in the gardens near their office building. He was puzzled at how calm he was in her company. He thought this might have been because he himself had grown older by five years since he had last approached a young woman. But he thought of other possible reasons: he had not yet fallen in love with the image of her face in his mind, although he often saw the image in his mind; she was five years younger than he; he thought of himself from time to time as a poet of Helvetia.

He had at first asked her to go with him to a race meeting at Sandown Racecourse, which had recently been built on a site near the site of the racecourse of the same name mentioned earlier, but she had told him that she was already obliged to return to her parents' house on the weekend of the meeting at Sandown. He had not been troubled at having to put off their first outing. Her returning so often to her parents' farm told him that she had no boyfriend in Melbourne, and he imagined her spending her weekends on the dairy-farm in Gippsland with only her parents and sisters for company.

More than six months later, she told him that she had, in her words, gone out with a man nearly ten years older than herself on some of the weekends when she was staying in Gippsland. The man was managing and would later inherit his father's farm. The man and his parents had been friends of her parents for many years. The man had been interested in her since she had left school four years previously and had asked her out whenever he had broken off with a girlfriend. She, the young woman who told this later to the chief character, had never been seriously interested in the farmer. She had always hoped that she would meet in Melbourne a man who could talk to her about many more things than a farmer could talk about. She had stopped going out with the farmer as soon as she had been sure that he, the chief character, had been seriously interested in her. When she had told the farmer that she would not be going out with him again, he had told her that he had been preparing to ask her in the near future to marry him, but this had not changed her mind.

During the afternoon in the private box at Moonee Valley, he told her that his father and his mother had both been the children of farmers in the district of mostly level grassy paddocks that covered most of the south-west of Victoria and reached all the way to some places where the western suburbs of Melbourne had long since been built and might be said to have reached as far as the Moonee Ponds Creek, so that he, the chief character, and she, the young woman, might have been sitting at that moment at the easternmost extremity of his native plains and looking towards the creek where they finally ended. She told him that the district of Gippsland where her father owned a dairy farm was mostly level and grassy but that she could remember having lived as a young child among steep and bare green hills in a district in the south of Gippsland, which district had been covered in forests until the first settlers had arrived and had cut down every tree. She told him further that her father had settled in the mostly level district where he now lived in the early 1950s, when that district had been turned into what was then called a soldier-settlement area, with large estates being divided into small farms watered by irrigation channels.

During the six months following the afternoon mentioned in the previous paragraph, he and the young woman went together to a number of restaurants and cinemas and theatres and race meetings and football matches and cricket matches on Saturday afternoons or evenings and afterwards sat alone together in the front seat of the late-model Chrysler Valiant that he had recently bought, which was the first motor car that he had owned. When they sat alone together in the car just mentioned, it was parked in the street outside the block of flats where the young woman shared with three other young women from country districts of Victoria a flat with two bedrooms. The flat was in the eastern suburb of Melbourne that was mentioned in the first section of this piece of fiction and was only a few blocks to the west of a house mentioned earlier: the house where an aunt and an uncle of the chief character had a certain picture hanging on one of the walls of their house. During the six months mentioned above, he took the young woman several times to visit his parents on a Sunday afternoon, but he did not take her to visit his mother's sister in the house that he himself had visited on many Sundays between the ages of about four and fourteen. As he had grown older, he had felt more sure that he was the son of his father and of his father's people rather than of his mother and her people. Even though he no longer considered himself a Catholic and stayed in his room on

Sunday mornings while his parents and his younger brother went to mass, he still spent a week of his holidays each year in the south-western town where his unmarried aunts and his bachelor-uncle lived and he called on them every day during that week. His aunts and his uncle were Catholics, not so much from intellectual conviction, so he thought, as from their concern for the past. Their parents had died before he, the chief character, was twenty years of age, but the house was still furnished as the parents had furnished it, and most of the books and ornaments had either belonged to the parents or been acquired by the aunts and the uncle when they were children. He, the chief character, found all of this interesting, whenever he visited the house, but he never forgot that the house was only a sort of reconstruction of what was always spoken of as the old house. They had left the old house and had moved to the house in the town when he was only five years old, but he had several clear memories from his visits to the old place. He often remembered part of an afternoon when he had sat beside one of his aunts while she read to him extracts from the book *Bevis*, by Richard Jefferies. He and his aunt sat on a cane couch on the side veranda of the house. Beyond the veranda was a lawn of buffalo grass with a mauve-flowered veronica bush in a circular bed. Beyond the lawn was a hedge of wormwood. While he sat beside his aunt he was unable to see over the hedge, but from time to time he had stood on the seat of the couch and had looked again across the mostly level grassy paddocks towards the line of trees in the distance. And yet, he would not have felt comfortable visiting his uncle and his aunts with the young woman. In the past, he had not felt comfortable in their house whenever he was in love, even if only with an image in his mind.

On each evening when he sat alone with the young woman in the parked car outside her flat, he had asked her beforehand how many of the young women she called her flatmates were at that time in the flat and he had always been told that one or more of the young women was there. Towards the end of the six months mentioned in the previous paragraph, when he believed that he was in love with the young woman and when he suspected that the young woman was in love with him, and when he had become more bold with the young woman than he had previously become or had expected to become with any young woman, and when he wanted to be alone with her in a place more private and comfortable than a parked car in a street of an inner suburb, he asked her whether he and she could visit her family in Gippsland at some weekend in the future and whether he and she could go together on an outing on the Saturday or the Sunday of the weekend to some clearing in a forest.

At the desk where he worked during each week, he had looked over large-scale maps of every district of Victoria; had noted the areas covered by forest in each district; and had even noted the roads and tracks leading into those forests and the places beside the roads and tracks where persons were permitted to light fires for picnics or to camp overnight. He had even, as mentioned earlier in this section of this story, studied on a map the part of Gippsland where the parents of the young woman lived on their dairy farm. And yet, whenever he talked to the young woman during the six months mentioned above, he saw again in his mind one or another of the images that he had seen in his mind as a boy whenever he had tried to see Gippsland in his mind. And whether he saw Gippsland as the one forest with only a few tracks or roads leading into it or whether he saw it as bare green hills with isolated stands of blackened trunks of trees, he still sometimes saw as part of the image in his mind a few blue-grey ridges of mountains in the far background.

On a certain Friday evening in his twenty-seventh year, he drove his Chrysler Valiant with the young woman sitting beside him through the outer south-eastern suburb of Dandenong and into Gippsland, which he had never previously entered. The sun was already going down when he saw the first green countryside between Hallam and Narre Warren, and the sky was dark before he had reached Drouin, but he learned during his first hour in the region that Gippsland contained among its green hills many more stands of timber and patches of forest than he had supposed. He arrived at the young woman's home long after dark. Her parents were wary of him. She whispered to him afterwards that they would have preferred him to be a farmer rather than an office worker. He wished that he could have stood on his dignity with her parents—perhaps by reminding himself that he was one of the outstanding young poets of Helvetia—but he smiled and spoke politely in their presence before they went into the front room to watch television and left him and the young woman to have a late meal in the kitchen.

He slept in the tiny bedroom that belonged to the young woman, while she slept in the room that was shared by her younger sisters, one of whom was away from home while she trained to become a nursing sister. He woke up early, at the time when the young woman's father was moving around before he went out to do the milking. He, the chief character, stepped to the window and saw in the distance a line of mountains still grey-black in the light before sunrise. He supposed that he was looking north-west and that the mountains were among the many folds of mountains that had been out of his sight in the far distance when he had looked eastwards from Mount Donna Buang nearly ten years before.

On that Saturday and on several of the remaining Saturdays before the end of his twenty-seventh year, he and the young woman set out in his motor car late in the morning on what she told her parents and her sisters was a picnic. On each of those Saturdays, he and she travelled during the middle of the day across mostly level grassy countryside and then between farms bordered by stands of timber or even by what seemed the edges of the same forest that covered the mountains far ahead of them. On each of those Saturdays he steered his motor car to one or another place that she had described to him beforehand as a peaceful and unfrequented place on the outskirts of the mountains, and he and she ate and drank and were alone together and surrounded by thick stands of timber on land that sloped upwards on either side, but he did not seem afterwards to have travelled into the blue-grey mountains that were visible from all over the mostly level and grassy district where the young woman lived and also, so she told him, from certain other districts of Gippsland.

During much of the time while he and she travelled to and from the places mentioned in the previous paragraph and while they were alone together in those places, he told her such things as that he had once tried to write a poem as a result of his having seen from a great distance certain blue-grey mountains in a district that he had believed at the time to be a part of Gippsland, which mountains, so he now understood, were among the folds of mountains that would surely have been visible from a great distance if he and she were able to stand on the summit of the tallest of the blue-grey mountains visible from her district and to look in the direction of the mountains visible from the eastern suburbs of Melbourne. During much of the time mentioned in the previous sentence, she told him such things as that she had written a number of poems and stories when she was in her thirteenth year, which poems and stories were intended to report and to interpret certain events in the lives of certain husbands and wives and children whom she imagined as living for the most part contentedly among the folds of bare green hills that she imagined as extending far away in every direction from the bare green hills of the district of Gippsland where she lived at that time.

On a certain Saturday soon after the beginning of his twenty-eighth year, when the weather was so dry and so hot that the newspapers and the news bulletins on radio and television contained warnings that bushfires might break out in any district of Victoria, he and she set out in his motor car in mid-morning along a route that he had chosen without consulting her, which route had seemed likely, when he had studied it previously on a large-scale map used by the senior officers at his place of work, to lead him far into a district that was unquestionably part of the mountains that seemed always blue-grey from a distance. At about midday, he steered his motor car away from a certain red-gravel road that he had already followed for some distance away from a certain main road and began to steer the motor car along a track marked only by two wheel-ruts leading in among dense forest. At a certain point along the track just mentioned, he stopped his motor car a little to one side of the track, in the clearing that was mentioned in the eighth paragraph of this section of this story. The land was so steep on either side of the clearing and the trees around were so dense and so tall and he had travelled for such a distance from the nearest main road that he could not doubt that he was in a place that would have appeared from a distance as part of a range of blue-grey mountains. He and she ate and drank in that place and were alone together there, but the writer of this story will report no more of what passed between them than the writer of the book of fiction mentioned earlier in this section of this story would have reported of what passed between the characters known mostly as M. de Charlus and M. Jupien if he, the writer, had not contrived a means for himself, in the person of the narrator, to listen through a wall of the room where they were alone together in rooms opening off the courtyard where the orchid mentioned previously had been for so long exposed, which courtyard appeared in the mind of the chief character of this story, whenever he remembered his having read the first paragraphs of "Cities of the Plain," as a clearing surrounded by ridges and slopes and valleys of blue-grey partly surrounded by a margin of green.

On a certain Saturday morning in the autumn of the year mentioned in the previous paragraph, he and she went together into a jewellery shop in a city in the region of Gippsland and were met by appointment by a young woman who called herself the manageress and who was a stranger to him, the chief character, but who had been a schoolfriend of the young woman beside him. While she and he were in the jewellery shop, they accepted the congratulations of the manageress on having become engaged to be married and then chose one of the rings from a tray of engagement rings that the manageress had put in front of them, which rings she said she had set aside for the young woman because the stone in each ring was an emerald and because she, the manageress, had always considered that the young woman's special gem should have been the emerald.

More than twenty years after the events reported in the previous paragraph, when he was employed in a position such as he had looked forward as a young man to occupying, although he was in a different building and in a different department from those in which he had expected to remain and spent his days supervising publications to do with the restoring of salty soils by means including the planting of many thousands of trees in parts of inland Victoria, and when he went to a race meeting every Saturday and tidied the garden around his house every Sunday morning, he would spend most Sunday afternoons sitting in front of his bookshelves and trying to see in his mind the titles and the authors' names and even some of the contents of the books that would have comprised his library if he had been sitting at that moment in his home on the grasslands of Helvetia. He was not an unhappy or a disappointed man, but he believed his wife, who often went with him to the races and who always worked with him in the garden, and their son and daughter, who were successful as students and seemed stable and contented persons, would have been surprised to know what he thought about on Sunday afternoons.

Even to his wife and children he had sometimes said that Sunday afternoon was the saddest time of the week: the time when you had to admit that you were no more than the person you were. To himself he would have added that Sunday afternoon was the time when he tried to understand how he had come to be who he was and where he was rather than someone else in some other place. And to himself he might have added further that Sunday afternoon was the time when he was sometimes for a moment, and despite everything that had happened to him in the course of what he called his life, a much published and much renowned poet in Helvetia.

Many a child had learned the trick, so he supposed, of saying his name aloud again and again until it seemed no longer his and he wondered what his true name was. The same child had surely also stared at his image in a mirror in order to confuse himself, he thought. And he believed he was only one of many who could hardly recognise their own drab backyards when they looked at the ordered greenery in a corner of the backyard of some family snapshot. But not so many people, he thought, might have learned his trick of bringing to the foreground of his mind an image that had been for long in the background of his mind but had often taken his notice and of then watching the image until it became another image, which other image was often of something Helvetian and might have been for long in the foreground of his mind if he had lived in Helvetia. One of the first images that he watched in this way was the image in his mind of the green stone in the engagement ring that his wife sometimes wore and sometimes kept in her wardrobe, which image would always become, as it approached the foreground of his mind, an image of a zone of green surrounded by a broad margin of grey-blue.

In the Heytesbury Forest

All around the large town in the south-west of Victoria where his unmarried aunts and his bachelor-uncle lived and where he visited them every year as a boy and as a young man and occasionally during later years before the last of them had died, the countryside was mostly level and grassy. In any view of paddocks or farms from a road or a railway line, one or more plantations of cypress would appear as a green-black stripe or stripes against the yellow-green of the grass, but he often travelled for several miles without seeing a gum tree. All through his childhood, he supposed that the countryside where his father claimed to belong had been hardly less bare of trees when the first Europeans had arrived there a hundred and a few more years before. His father often said that he preferred his native district to all others, but he never spoke as though the grassiness or the levelness had sometimes moved him; he seemed to be attached to that district only because his grandfather had chosen to settle there in the 1870s. He, the chief character, from the first years that he could remember until he was almost in his middle age, felt attached to his father's district, but he, the chief character, believed he had loved the sight of the level and mostly grassy countryside since the time when he had visited as a small child the so-called old house, which had been on a treeless plain with the cliffs of the Southern Ocean as one horizon and a horizon of grass in every other direction except for a quarter in the south-east, where a distant line of trees was visible.

First his father and then his mother died while he was still not fifty years of age. He felt as though he knew much about his father's childhood from having seen the house surrounded by grassy paddocks where his father had lived until he was twenty years of age and from hearing from his, the chief character's, unmarried aunts and bachelor-uncle accounts of his father as a boy. But after his, the chief character's, mother had died, he began to reflect on how little he knew of her early years. He knew that she had been born and had spent her first twelve years in a small town surrounded by grassy countryside on the main road leading inland from the large town mentioned several times previously in this story. She had occasionally told him, when he was a child himself, of something that had happened to her at home or at school in the small town, and even though he had only once travelled through the small town in his bachelor-uncle's utility truck, he, the chief character, had easily imagined the small town in the wide, bare countryside while his mother was talking to him. But whenever he tried to think of his mother from the age of twelve onwards, he became aware of a strange fault in the image that he had in his mind of the south-west of Victoria.

In every image in his mind of the grassy countryside that extended far around the large town mentioned earlier, he saw the countryside as a topographical map with the viewer looking from west to east, or from the vicinity of the large town towards Melbourne, which was, however, some 250 kilometres away. In every such image, the grassy countryside ended in the far background at a line of trees, and these trees seemed always as far away from the viewer as the line of trees had seemed far away from him, the chief character, in the view that he remembered having seen from the so-called old house of his father's family. He understood that these trees were the nearest to view of the trees of a huge expanse of forest. He understood that he had heard this forest talked about often when he had visited his father's relatives—they called it mostly the Bush, although his father sometimes called it the Heytesbury. He, the chief character, understood that the forest was far larger than the expanse of grassy countryside that he considered to be the surroundings of the large town mentioned previously or to be his father's native district. He, the chief character, understood that he had often seen in his mind an image of the western half of Victoria as though he was looking at it from a point in the upper air above Bass Strait, and that the forest in this image was a huge zone of a blue-black colour whereas the grassy countryside was a narrow margin of yellow-green on the far side of the blue-black. He understood that he had visited several places in the forest on several different occasions while he was a boy and that he had kept in his mind ever since a number of images of meaning. He understood all these matters, but he could never remember anything of the several journeys that he must have made from the grassy countryside into the forest. He would have been interested to remember how the forest had appeared from the nearest grassy paddocks or how he had felt as he passed from countryside into forest or out again from the forest afterwards but he could only remember being far inside the forest or far out in the grassy countryside. And in his memories of being far inside the forest, he seemed unaware that the forest gave way in certain quarters to grassy countryside, just as in his memories of being out in the grassy countryside the forest was no more than a line of trees on the horizon.

In his middle age, and at a time later than the last of the events that will be reported in this section of this story, he remembered that he had seen, while he travelled through the forest, paddocks and whole farms cleared of trees and scrub and sown with grass and that he had passed through several small towns in the forest but that he had always remembered the farms and the towns afterwards as mere glades. He remembered likewise that he had sometimes seen in the grassy countryside a patch of scrub along a roadside or a stand of trees in a corner of a paddock, but that he had never thought of these as remnants of larger areas, preferring to suppose that seeds from the forest were sometimes spread by the wind or by birds. At the time when he remembered that he had thought thus, he remembered also one of the few remarks that his bachelor-uncle had ever made to him on the subject of sexual morality. His uncle had said something such as that if he had not been lucky enough to have had a Catholic upbringing, he would have dashed into the nearest scrub with one or another young woman as soon as he had become old enough, just as the other young men of the district were doing. When he, the chief character, remembered this remark at the time mentioned in the previous sentence, he wondered why he had not wondered at the time of his hearing the remark why his uncle had spoken as though a patch of scrub grew conveniently close to the homes of each young couple who wanted to dash into it whereas according to his, the chief character's, image of the countryside, any such couple might have had to travel for many miles in search of the scrub they needed unless they had used for their purposes what he had always supposed were used for such purposes, namely the places where the grass of the countryside grew longest.

From the age of twelve, his mother had lived in the forest. Her father, who had been until then a share-farmer or a farm labourer, had obtained in the year 1930 a block, as it was called, of several hundred acres from the Government of Victoria, together with a grant of money to buy stock and tools and a simple house as soon as he had cleared the first of his land, which had at first been covered by scrub and timber. He was expected to pay for the land and to pay back in the future the grant of money, but no repayments were due for the first ten years. He, the chief character, learned none of these details from his mother. All that she had told him was that she had lived for some years from the age of twelve on a bush block at a place that she named, which place he had learned from a map was deep inside the forest mentioned earlier. He did not learn the details of the obtaining of the block until he read a few months after the death of his mother a book that he had bought fifteen years earlier but had only looked into during those fifteen years, which book will be mentioned again before the end of this story.

He had never known how long his mother had lived in the forest. He had never learned where or when his parents had first met. This event could have taken place in the forest, since his father had sometimes worked there as a young man, as will be mentioned later in this story. Or, they could have met in the large town surrounded by grassy countryside, where both his father and his mother stayed from time to time as young persons with uncles and aunts. Or, his mother and his father might not have met until two or three years before he was born, in which event they would have met in a certain inner western suburb of Melbourne where each of them worked in one or more factories during the late 1930s.

One or another reader may have been surprised not to read any reference in the previous sentence to the marriage of the parents of the chief character of this story. The wife of the chief character and one or another of his friends had sometimes been surprised when he told them that he had never been told by either of his parents when or where they had met or any details of their courtship or when or where they had been married. He had never doubted for a moment that his parents, who had been faithful Catholics for as long as he had known them, had been married in a Catholic church. And he had understood for most of his life that he could have obtained from the appropriate office of the Government of Victoria a copy of his parents' certificate of marriage. But he had decided as a young man that he was not going to pay a group of strangers to impart to him information that his parents should have been able to impart to him free of charge. He had decided further that he was not going to ask either of his parents to impart to him information that most parents, so he believed, would have been pleased to impart to a child without having first to be asked. And so, he was able to say after he had seen to the burial of both his parents before he had reached his fiftieth year, that he had still not learned how those two had become his parents and that he expected to know no more of the matter before one or both of his own children or his widow, as she would then be, saw to his own burial.

He had sometimes speculated that his parents might have been ashamed of the poverty of their wedding, but his mother had not been reluctant to talk about her poverty as a young woman: about how she had bought second-hand shoes and dresses during the first years after she had arrived in the inner western suburb from the south-west. His father had told him, the chief character, of how he, the father, had worked for two years without pay on his father's farm when the price of butter fell to sixpence per pound during the Depression and of how the trousers of his only suit of clothes had been so short around his ankles and the sleeves of his jacket so short around his wrists at that time that he had kept away from the dances in his district and had slunk into the back seat of the church each Sunday. Both parents had told him, the chief character, that they had been renting a room with a double bed in a boarding house when he had been born and for six months afterwards. After his parents had died, he thought of their silence about their courtship and marriage as something he would never be able to explain to himself any more than he could explain why he could never remember having approached the forest from the grassy countryside or the grassy countryside from the forest or having passed from one into the other.

His mother had told him a few things about her life in the Bush, as she had called it. She had been taken away from school at the age of thirteen, even though she was required by law to attend until she had turned fourteen. The school had been so remote and the teacher so careless of his duties that several children had left early to work on their parents' blocks. His mother had worked for six days each week and for some years doing what was regarded by the settlers on the blocks as the lighter clearing tasks; her job was to search the cleared paddocks for seedlings of trees or for young shrubs and the outer margins of those paddocks for roots of bracken that had crept through from the forest on the other side and then to grub out the intruding plants with a pick and to make heaps of them in certain places and later, when the heaps had dried, to set fire to them. His mother's only recreation as a girl and a young woman, so it seemed to him from the little that she told him, was to attend a dance that was held on many a Saturday evening in the school that she had formerly attended. On the evening of a dance, she and her brothers and sisters would walk together to the school, which was three miles from their home. They would take turns to carry a lantern and a sack containing each person's shoes and socks and some rags. They walked barefoot along the roads, some of which were mere ruts filled sometimes with dust and at other times with water. Outside the school, they would wipe their feet with the rags and would then put on their socks and shoes for the dance. What troubled the young persons most on their way to and from the dance were leeches and prickly Moses. Sometimes the lantern would be blown out by the wind, or the person holding the lantern would hold it so that it failed to shine on the road. At such times his mother had more than once cut her feet on the sharp vine that they called prickly Moses or had stepped into a rut filled with water and had had a leech fasten itself to her skin without her knowing it.

He had never seen the farm that his mother had helped to clear in the forest. Since her father had worked in later years as a labourer in the large town mentioned often previously, he, the chief character, had supposed that his mother's father had given up after a time his effort to clear his block in the forest. He, the chief character, had further supposed that some other person had later undertaken to clear, with the help of his family, the same block and to meet the conditions laid down by the Government of Victoria. But despite his supposing this, he, the chief character, had throughout his life imagined the bracken that his mother had grubbed out of the edges of paddocks as having later spread unchecked and the scrub as having taken the place of the grass in the paddocks, and saplings as having grown up among the scrub, and the whole of the so-called block that was required to have been cleared as having become again forest before the end of his mother's life.

He had never seen the place that his mother had helped to clear in the forest, but he had seen as a child two other partly cleared blocks in the forest. One of his mother's married sisters lived for a few years in the 1940s with her husband and their children on a small farm in the forest. He, the chief character of this story, remembered this farm for the first time in many years on a certain day in the early 1990s, which day will be mentioned before the end of this section of this story. On many a day after the day just mentioned, he remembered many details of the farm and of the persons who lived there, but he could not remember his having travelled to the farm from the grassy countryside further southwest, as he knew he must have travelled; nor could he remember his having travelled from the farm back to the grassy countryside, as he knew he must have travelled. The farm was surrounded by forest, but he could not remember in the early 1990s whether his uncle, the husband of his mother's sister, was renting the farm or on his way to owning the farm. What he chiefly remembered in the early 1990s are the details listed in the following four paragraphs.

The farm had been surrounded by forest. He had asked his cousins several times to take him a short distance into the forest, but none of them had been willing to do so. This and other matters had confirmed him in his thinking that his mother's relatives were dull by comparison with his father's people. One of the other matters just mentioned was the bareness of the house in the forest. He understood, of course, in the 1990s that his mother's sister and her husband had been too poor even to furnish their house, which lacked such things as window-blinds and floor-coverings, but when he had visited their house as a child, he had been annoyed to find no books or toys such as he always found in the home of his father's unmarried sisters and brother. He found, however, in the shabby house in the forest one thing that kept his interest for much of the time of his visit. He never learned from where his cousin had got the thing, but his girl-cousins kept on the front veranda a two-storey doll's house. He seemed to remember forty and more years afterwards that the exterior was somewhat damaged and that some of the fittings were missing from outside the house, but he remembered in the 1990s the upper bedrooms that he had peered into and a certain single bed in one of the upper rooms. He had complained to his girl-cousins that a young female doll should have been sleeping in the bed, and he had even come back to the toy house several times during the day of his visit, hoping to see through the tiny unglazed windows that a girl-doll had turned back the quilt on the bed and had lain her head on the smooth, white pillow and was resting in safety.

At some time during the day of his visit to the farm in the forest, his uncle had invited him to watch while he, the uncle, fired his rifle at a small flock of eastern rosellas that he had seen in a tree at the edge of the forest. The birds were waiting, so his uncle had said, to fly down into the few fruit trees beside the house and to eat the fruit from the trees. He, the chief character, had watched while his uncle had fired the rifle. The uncle had announced that he had brought down a bird, although the chief character had not seen any bird fall from any tree. The uncle had then led him across the narrow paddock between the fruit trees and the edge of the forest. As he walked across the paddock the uncle had kicked at ankle-high clusters of green growth that was clearly not grass. He had explained to the chief character that the farm would never be properly cleared for as long as seeds and suckers from the forest could get into the paddock. He, the chief character, thought of the clusters of shoots and suckers and seed-

lings as stands of regrowth forest or of tall scrub in grassy countryside in the eyes of persons small enough to live in the house of
two-storeys whose upper windows he had looked through.

The rosellas had been perched in a tree that grew just outside
the boundary of the farm, but the body of the dead bird had fallen
just inside the boundary-fence. His uncle had turned the body over
with the toe of his boot. When his uncle was looking elsewhere,
he, the chief character, had crouched beside the body and had
stroked with a fingertip the place low on the belly of the bird
where a zone of bright green feathers adjoined a zone of dark-blue
feathers.

One of his girl-cousins had a face of the kind that he had fallen
in love with often in the later years of his childhood, but he understood, even as a young child, that he ought not to think of a
first-cousin as even a wife-in-his-mind. And even if he had not understood this, he would have supposed that he could not have seen
the face of his cousin in his mind for long before he perceived about
her the dullness that he found in most of the people of his mother's
family.

The second of the two partly cleared blocks mentioned earlier
he had seen when he was so young that he was never able in later
years to connect his memories of the place. He could not remember how he got to the block or how he left the block. He could not
remember any sequence of events from the time while he was
at the block, which time he suspected to have been about a week.
After his father and his mother had died, he recalled that he had
never asked them to explain to him why they and he and his
younger brother had lived for a week on the partly cleared block
in the forest. One day after both their parents had died, he asked
his younger brother whether he remembered having lived for a
week in a hut with walls and roof of corrugated iron on a partly
cleared block in a certain forest. His brother had thought that he,
the chief character, was joking, but the brother was three years
younger and presumably remembered nothing of their stay in the
forest. After he had spoken to his brother, the chief character

understood that he, the chief character, was the only person alive who remembered the partly cleared block in the forest as it had appeared during the few days nearly fifty years before when he had lived there.

The family had lived in the hut during a week of mostly hot weather in January. Every year, they spent a week of holidays with his father's parents and unmarried sisters and brother. His, the chief character's, few memories of the so-called old house were of an early holiday there, but later holidays were always spent in the house in the large town. Since his father had never owned a motor car, he, the chief character, saw the countryside only occasionally, when his bachelor-uncle drove one or two of the family out of the town in his utility truck. And yet, in one or another year of the 1940s, someone had driven him and his brother and his parents and, surely, some bedding and a suitcase of clothes and a few days' supply of food away from the old house and across the grassy countryside towards the line of trees in the distance and then among the trees of the forest and then to the partly cleared block far inside the forest. (He supposed they had travelled from the old house. Since he remembered little of the trip and only a few details from the week in the forest, he supposed he was remembering a time before his grandfather had died and the old house was sold. If so, then he, the chief character, might have travelled to the block in the forest in the back seat of the huge Dodge sedan owned by his grandfather, with the gas-producer attached to the back to provide fuel during the years of petrol rationing.)

He did not know why his parents had chosen to spend their holiday in a hut with a dirt floor, hessian screens for windows, an open fireplace for cooking and no sink or wash-trough or bath or ice-chest or radio. He remembered that the block had belonged to his father's father, but this explained nothing. Seemingly, the block had not been bought under the same conditions that applied to purchasers such as his mother's father in 1930; the hut had been built, and the trees had been cleared for fifty yards around the hut, but no pasture had been sown, no animals grazed, and no fences had been built. And yet, his father had worked from early morning until late afternoon on every day of his stay, felling trees in the farthest part of the block, sawing the trunks and trimming the branches away, and then dragging and manhandling the logs into stacks as tall as himself. Perhaps, so the chief character supposed, his father had done all this work in the heat of January merely for the love of it. In later years, his father had seldom talked about the bush, but he, the chief character, was always able to remember the sound of his father's voice on the day when they had been driven into the forest. His father had been pointing out to the driver or to his, the chief character's, mother, or to both the stretches of the red gravel roads that he remembered having worked on during the year when he had worked as a young man with one of the gangs making roads through the forest. Perhaps, so the chief character supposed, his father had often dreamed of going back to the forest again. Perhaps the forest was the place where his, the chief character's, father had met the young woman who later became his wife, he being at the time a farmer's son working on a road gang and she being the daughter of a settler on a block in the forest.

Any of the preceding explanations was possible, he sometimes thought, but the most likely explanation had to do with the debts that his father owed throughout his life. He, the chief character, had never understood the details of his father's loans from his father and some of his brothers and sisters but he, the chief character, knew that his father had paid back during his lifetime little of the money that he had borrowed. He had got into debt even before he was married. The western suburb where he lived when he first came to Melbourne was near Flemington Racecourse, and he had got to know several track-work riders and strappers and even a man who made his living as a commission agent for several trainers. He, the father, told little to his wife and children, but his son, the chief character, understood that his father had always bet beyond his means, that he had often bet on credit, that he had several times borrowed large sums against his share of his father's estate, and that he had paid back none of this money before his father's death. He, the chief character, supposed as the most likely explanation for his father's cutting timber for a week on his own father's block in the forest that he, the man who had got into debt, wanted to show his father that he was not an idler and, at the same time, to remit through his unpaid woodcutting and clearing some of the interest on his debts.

He, the chief character, sometimes entertained another possible explanation for his father's having chopped wood for a week. His father, throughout his life, had devised impractical schemes for starting afresh. Even in his fifties, he made enquiries about a scheme for establishing farmers on a so-called land reclamation project near Esperance, in Western Australia. When he remembered his father standing beside the stacks of timber he had built and looking around the large clearing he had made in the forest, he, the chief character, supposed his father might have intended to turn the whole block into a farm and to settle there with his wife and his sons.

Each morning while they lived in the hut, his father left soon after breakfast. He walked away between the trees in the direction of the rear of the block, following a track that was wide enough for a motor vehicle. He, the chief character, understood that a truck had been driven into the forest from time to time in the past in order to collect timber from trees that had been felled. He was not allowed to walk along the track into the trees. On the one day when he had seen his father at work and the stacks of timber, he and his brother had been led along the track by their mother. He, the chief character, spent much of his time laying out a network of toy farms on the outer edge of the clearing around the hut. In order to make the ground smooth for his toy roads and fences and farmhouses, he had to pull out of the ground some of the smaller grasses, but he left in the soil the larger clumps. He had learned on his first day on the block that one at least of the common plants there could slice through the skin of his hand and could draw blood.

Whenever he remembered his games during the years when he remembered the hut in the forest often after having seldom remembered it for many years, which years—the years of his remembering—followed an event that will be reported in the paragraph following the next paragraph, he supposed that he imagined himself during all of his games as living with one or another wife-in-his-mind on one of the toy farms that he had cleared near the toy forests that he had left uncleared. At some time during one of the years mentioned in the previous sentence, the chief character remembered having seen for a moment of the one day mentioned in the fifth sentence of the previous paragraph some of the blue or green feathers on the breast of a bird that flew through a shaft of sunlight in a place of dense timber and undergrowth beyond the clearing that his father had made in the forest. He, the chief character, remembered his father telling him that the bird was one or another kind of kingfisher. After he had remembered these matters, the chief character sometimes saw in his mind as though they were details that he remembered images of a stream of water flowing through parts of the forest where his father had not yet gone.

On one of his last days in the hut, the weather was so hot that his mother told his father before he left that she was afraid a bush-fire might break out somewhere in the forest that day. He, the chief character, watched the sky all day. In mid-afternoon, the sky to the south-east became filled with dark-grey clouds, but they were the clouds of a thunderstorm that broke over the forest soon afterwards. The sky was dark for half an hour during the storm, and the rain was so loud on the iron roof of the hut that he and his mother had to shout their words. He was afraid for his father, who was still out in the forest, and who might have been struck by lightning. But the storm ended suddenly, and the sky became a clear pale blue, and his mother led him and his brother a short way along the track while they looked out for their father. They saw him before he saw them. He looked old and dejected, but only because his hat and his clothes were wet and dripping and because he was looking downwards to avoid stepping into the pools of water in the wheel-ruts on the track between the trees.

At some time during the mid-1980s, he, the chief character, calculated that thirty years had passed since he had left school. He had never joined any organisation for old boys of his school, nor had he made any effort to stay in touch with any of his schoolfellows, but at the time just mentioned he decided that he would begin reading each day in the newspaper the column headed DEATHS, keeping his eye out for the first one or two of his contemporaries to have died in their early middle age. On a certain morning soon after the time just mentioned, his eyes were drawn towards a certain entry in one of the columns headed DEATHS, which entry had brought to his mind an impression first of what he called to himself afterwards prickliness and second of what he called to himself afterwards blackness. Each of these impressions was caused by a cluster of full points and upper-case letters in the entry. Both the full points and the upper-case letters had been used in the abbreviations placed after the names of members of religious orders of the Catholic Church. The entry was a report of the death of a man whose four sons had all become members of one or another religious order. The surname at the head of the entry was a most unusual surname, and he, the chief character, had suspected at once what he verified a moment later when he read through the whole text of the entry. The man who had died had been the father of four sons and two daughters. Each of the sons had become a member of a religious order of the Catholic Church, but each of the daughters had married and had become the mother of at least four children. One of the daughters had been, more than twenty-five years before, the young woman who had sat with the chief character in a private box at Caulfield Racecourse, as was reported in the section of this story headed with the words "In the Blue Dandenongs."

After he had said goodbye to the young woman just mentioned, on a hillside in the eastern suburbs of Melbourne on a day in autumn more than twenty-five years before he would read the notice in the newspaper of the death of her father and in the circumstances reported earlier in this story, he and she merely nodded or murmured to one another if they happened to pass in the building where they both worked. Some months after they had gone together to Caulfield Racecourse, she was transferred to another department on another floor of the building where they both worked. A year or more later, he read in the publication that reported appointments and vacancies and such matters that she had resigned from the State Public Service. He learned soon afterwards from one of the young women in his office that the young woman who had resigned had done so because she had been recently married and because her husband was a farmer in a country district of Victoria. The young woman who gave him this information did not know which country district the married couple were now living in. However, the compiler of the notice of death mentioned earlier had followed the custom of inserting in parentheses after the given name of each of the daughters of the dead person both the married name of the daughter and the place where the daughter lived.

The married woman in early middle age who was the mother of at least four children but who had once been a young woman whose face had been the face of one of the wives-in-his-mind lived in a small town in the south-west of Victoria. He had never seen the small town. During the first fifteen years and more of his life, when he and his family used to travel each year to the south-west of Victoria for a week of holidays, the small town just mentioned did not exist. At that time, the place where the small town later stood was part of what he had thought of during his childhood as the forest—the only forest that he had known and the only forest that he had ever lived in.

At a certain moment on the day when he had been with his father in the place on the bush block where his father was felling trees, his father had looked all around him and had said that they were surrounded by miles of virgin forest. He, the chief character, had not known what his father had been thinking at that moment, and his father had soon afterwards begun to fell the next tree that he wanted to fell, but he, the chief character, had sometimes remembered during the following forty years and more of his life that he had only twice been in a place surrounded by virgin forest.

At different times during the years from the early 1960s onwards, he had read in newspapers or magazines or he had learned by other means that almost all of the Heytesbury Forest had been cleared and that grassy countryside and small towns had taken the place of what he had called as a child the forest or the bush. He had taken promotions in the State Public Service to branches unconnected with forests and Crown lands, and so he had nothing officially to do with the work of the Rural Finance and Settlement Commission. When he learned during the years mentioned above some further detail of the changing of the forest into grassy countryside, he had tried to remember the few details that he could remember of the forest, as he called it, and he had felt, while he had tried to remember those details, just as he had felt many times during his life whenever he had tried to see in his mind some detail of a landscape in Helvetia.

On a certain day in the early 1990s, several years after the latest event reported in this section or in any other section of this story, he attended the funeral of a cousin: the man who had been the boy-cousin mentioned in the first section of this story. During the 1980s and the 1990s, he, the chief character, had almost given up visiting his relatives on both his mother's and his father's side and had failed to attend the funeral of many an aunt or uncle or cousin. If anyone had asked him the reason for his seeming thus to have turned away from his relatives, he would have answered that he had become unable to travel. He could have justified this answer by pointing out that he had never travelled further than to Sydney and Adelaide, each of which cities he had visited only twice and many years ago; that he had never been in an aeroplane or a sea-going vessel; that he had not owned a motor car for many years; and that he had not left the suburbs of Melbourne since he had attended his mother's funeral in the far south-west of Victoria and that he did not expect to leave them again. He kept to the suburbs of Melbourne, however, because he chose to do so. He was hoping to take early retirement from the State Public Service and afterwards to spend his days in writing the book that would confirm his reputation as the leading man of letters in Helvetia. He had come to recognise that the only subject he was able to write about was his own mind—and only in such a way that the only place where his writing might be found suitable for publication was Helvetia. In that country of paradoxes and enigmas and lacunae was his true readership. He had been preparing for many years to write the definitive work on his mind. At the time of the funeral mentioned in the first sentence of this paragraph, what he called his notes filled several hanging files in a filing cabinet. The notes did not consist of consecutive paragraphs or pages of prose. He had done much writing, but it was all in the form of labels or detailed annotations for a series of more than a hundred maps. Each of these maps was itself an enlargement of one or another detail on an earlier map in the series, and the first map, from which all the other maps and all the text arose, was a simple representation looking more like a coat of arms than a map of any place on earth. The first map was an area of land roughly square in shape and divided *per bend sinister* into two triangles. The upper triangle was coloured a light green and the lower triangle was coloured a dark blue. Later maps were almost covered with paragraph after paragraph of his handwriting, but on the first map only four words were written. Beside the area of light green were the words GRASSY COUNTRYSIDE, and beside the area of dark blue were the words VIRGIN FOREST. He expected the literary critics of Helvetia to place many interpretations on his book and to find many themes running through it, but no reader could fail to understand, so he thought, that the chief character of the book often thought of his father's family as being, among other things, bachelors and spinsters in their minds if not in their lives whereas he often thought of his mother's family as being, among other things, early marriers and prolific breeders. He attended the funeral mentioned earlier in this paragraph because the church and the cemetery were both in an outer eastern suburb of Melbourne and because he had visited his cousin's home often as a child.

After the funeral, he spent an hour in his cousin's house in the outer eastern suburb mentioned above, which was in the foothills of the Dandenong Ranges. The house was filled with mourners, but he recognised few of them. Some of the middle-aged persons around him, he knew, would have been among the many first cousins on his mother's side that he had not seen for forty and more years. He was able to identify the men and women who had been the boys and girls when he had visited the farm in the forest mentioned earlier in this section of this story. The cousins recognised him, and each of them spoke a few polite words to him, but only one of them was willing to talk at length with him. He, the chief character, learned from this cousin, who had been a boy of about his own age on the day in the 1940s when he had visited the farm in the forest, that he, the cousin, could remember that his father had shot many rosellas and other birds that had come out of the forest and had eaten the fruit on his trees although he, the cousin, could not remember any doll's house that his sisters had played with on the veranda of their house. In answer to a question from the chief character, the cousin said he and all but one of his brothers and sisters had married and had become the parents of at least four children each, although several of those who had married had since become separated or divorced. The exception was one of his sisters, a woman of about the same age as the chief character, who had never married or had a child but had lived with her parents while they were alive and now lived alone in the house where they had lived during their last years, which house was in a small town not previously mentioned in this story, which town was in the south-west of Victoria and far inland from the large town mentioned often previously.

In the Plenty Ranges

In a certain year in the late 1980s, the bachelor-uncle of the chief character died in a hospital in the large town where he had lived for the last forty years and more of his life. The chief character of this story did not attend the funeral of his uncle, which began in the Catholic church with the stained glass window containing the areas of blue and green mentioned earlier, but he had travelled by train to and from the large town two weeks before his uncle had died and had visited his uncle for an hour and more in the hospital where he was dying. During his visit, his uncle said that he, the chief character, had seemed like a son to him years earlier, when they had sat together in the bungalow and had talked about racing.

During the year after his bachelor-uncle had died, he, the chief character, received a legacy of several thousand dollars from his uncle's estate. He, the chief character, paid half of this money into his and his wife's joint account at the branch of a certain bank in their nearest shopping centre, which branch was the place where he and she had all of their bank accounts, after having told his wife that the value of his uncle's legacy was half of the sum mentioned above. The other half of the legacy he hid as cash between the pages of one of the books on his shelves before he did with it what he is reported in the next paragraph as having done.

For many years, he and his fellow-workers in the State Public Service had been working according to a system whereby a person might work, for example, long hours on four days and then be free to work for only half of the fifth day. This was what he himself did every week. On his free half-day he was often alone in his house while his wife was at work and his children were at school. At such times he would sit in the room that he used as his office and would pull down the blinds and would put on a pair of ear-muffs and would stare at the spine of some book the title of which he could not make out in the dim light and would try to think of himself as sitting in the library of his country estate in Helvetia. Soon after the events reported in the previous paragraph, he began to take his free half-day on each Friday afternoon. On the first such afternoon, he took the bank-notes mentioned earlier out of his book, put the notes in his pocket, and walked eastwards for two kilometres to the shopping centre in the suburb adjoining his own suburb. There, he went into the branch of the same bank that he had used for their own banking. He stood at the counter under the sign NEW ACCOUNTS. On the other side of the counter, a young woman wearing the grey-blue uniform of the bank got to her feet from behind her desk and walked towards him. What he thought when he saw the young woman's face will be reported in the next paragraph. What happened between him and the young woman at the counter just mentioned was that he opened a new savings account, using his correct name and address and paying into the account all but a few hundred dollars of the cash from his uncle's legacy, which he took out from his pocket in front of the young woman and counted in front of her. When the young woman asked him whether or not he had any other account with that bank, he told her the details of an account in his name alone at the branch in the suburb where he lived, but he did not tell her that he had two joint accounts with his wife at that branch.

He had kept up his interest in horse-racing, although he had stopped betting during his son's and his daughter's school days, when the family had often been short of money. During those years, he had devised a way of betting that he believed would return him a regular profit if ever he could acquire the thousand dollars and more that he needed for a betting bank. On the Friday afternoon when he walked to his neighbouring suburb, he intended only to use his uncle's money to test the way of betting just mentioned without his wife's protesting that the money could be put to a better use. Any profit that he made he intended to put back into his betting bank so that he could increase his stakes. If he continued to make a profit and to increase his stakes in this way, he would reveal to his wife what he had been doing and would retire early from the public service, using his income from racing to supplement his superannuation pension. When he saw the young woman who came to attend to him in the bank, he fell in love with her face at once and hoped while she was setting up his new account that she had taken him for a bachelor who had recently moved to that suburb, perhaps to live with his ageing parents, and whose chief interest was horse-racing. He watched her from under his eyebrows while she leaned forward to write and he decided that if she was working as a teller on any Friday afternoon when he came into the bank he would withdraw a large amount so that she would think of him as a fearless punter. He foresaw himself as keeping always in his pocket when he left for the bank on each Friday afternoon a large sum from his household account—not that he would use his or his wife's salary for betting but so that he could deposit a large sum in his private account if he happened to find himself at the teller's window where the young woman in front of him was working, and so that she would think of him as having won that money from betting. The things that he foresaw at the time just mentioned and the things that he decided at the same time to do in the future—these things he did from time to time during the next two years until he had failed to see the young woman mentioned above on so many consecutive Fridays that he had to conclude that she could not be merely on leave but must have left that branch. (He did not think of her as having transferred to another branch. He had not failed to notice that she had been promoted during the two years while he had watched her; he supposed that she had gone into the head office of the bank in Melbourne.) His way of betting proved neither profitable nor unprofitable; he would win for several weeks and would then lose what he had won before the cycle began again. But on the day in every month or more when he happened to meet at the teller's station the young woman whose face he was

431

in love with, he made either a large withdrawal or a large deposit. He had always assumed that a young female bank employee of ambition would never have set foot on any racecourse, and so he assumed that the racecourses where she sometimes saw him in her mind were imaginary. He felt entitled, therefore, whenever he was in her presence, to consider himself a professional punter of Helvetia.

He had never intended that the young woman mentioned in the previous two paragraphs should be in the least aware of any thought that he entertained in connection with her. When he first saw her and fell in love with her face, he felt as though he was no older than she and perhaps even a few years younger, but when he had recollected himself a few moments later, he was well aware that he was a man of almost fifty years while she was in her early twenties and not much older than his own daughter. During all the times when he was within sight of her, he tried never to have her catch him looking at her, but she sometimes seemed to know what he was about. He was afraid at first that her knowing he admired her would make her angry or embarrassed, but she seemed always calm when he was near her and watching her sur-reptitiously. Sometimes, when she was the teller who happened to serve him, she seemed to go out of her way to give him some extra piece of information about the symbols in the entry in his pass-book or to explain to him some recent change in the routine of the bank. While she told him such things, she would look him in the eye and he would look at her as though this was one more dull moment in the business of his day, but in his mind he would be in Helvetia and listening to his wife-to-be while she declared herself to him.

Even when he was approaching the main street of the neigh-bouring suburb on the Friday afternoon mentioned previously, he had felt alert. He had travelled by motor car through the neigh-bouring suburb a few times previously, but he had never approached the suburb on foot. Both his suburb and the suburb he was ap-proaching were filled with streets of houses and would have looked to many people indistinguishable. But as he walked he was aware that the land was rising. And when he reached the main street mentioned above, he saw that the street followed a slight ridge running from north to south. He stopped and looked around. He was still very much in a northern suburb of Melbourne, but when he faced north he seemed to be on the dividing line between two sorts of country. All around him to his right were valleys and hills, and even though suburbs whose names he knew covered both hills and valleys, the trees in the streets and the gardens of those suburbs and on the still unoccupied land were so thick that the whole landscape seemed more forest than suburbs. Across the horizon ahead of him was a steep blue line of mountains and hills that he had seen on nearly every day since he had come to live in the northern suburbs more than twenty years before—the Kinglake Ranges. Away to his right he saw a mountain that he had hardly ever seen from the suburbs of Melbourne. He had not known it was so clear to view from so near to his own home. Mount Dandenong was also clearly visible almost behind him to his right, but the mountain to his right was longer and higher and more impressive than Mount Dandenong, even though it was further away and its colour more grey-blue than the rich, dark blue of Mount Dandenong. The mountain to his right was Donna Buang. When he had looked all around him from the main street in his neighbouring suburb, he said in his mind the words at the head of this section of this story.

The four words just mentioned are from a note by the author at the front of the book *An Afternoon of Time*, by D. E. Charlwood, first published in 1966 by Angus and Robertson. He, the chief character of this story, had read the book soon after it was first published but had forgotten soon afterwards all of the experience of reading it except that he remembered for long afterwards that certain passages in the book had described the forests of the Otway Ranges and the countryside of the far west of Victoria. The forests of the Otway Ranges are the continuation of the east of the Heytesbury Forest, and the countryside of the far west of

Victoria is the continuation to the west of the countryside in the south-west of Victoria. The only other words that the chief character of this story remembered afterwards from the book mentioned above are the four words quoted at the head of this section of this story. Soon after he had first read the words, the chief character looked at a number of maps of Victoria but could not see in any of those maps the words just mentioned. For many years afterwards, the chief character would look into any map of Victoria that he had not previously seen and would try to find the words just mentioned but would never find them. And yet, he remembered those words on the afternoon in the late 1980s when he stood for the first time in the main street of his neighbouring suburb and looked all around him.

In the note at the front of the book mentioned in the previous paragraph, the author of that book explains that he began to think of writing that book on a day in the mid-1950s when the temperature was 108 degrees on the Fahrenheit scale and when he was playing cricket in the Plenty Ranges. The heat of the day together with other circumstances reminded the author, so he explained, of other days in the 1930s when he had lived in the far west of Victoria. When the chief character of this story said in his mind the words at the head of this section of this story, he supposed, among other things, that the cricket ground where the author of the book mentioned above had been reminded of his earlier life must have seemed in the 1950s to be a clearing in a vast forest.

While he stood on the Friday afternoon mentioned previously in the main street mentioned previously, he, the chief character, saw that he had been living for the past twenty years in the northern suburb that was the easternmost part of the grassy countryside that might be thought of as covering most of the western and south-western parts of Victoria. He saw also that he had been living for the past twenty years in the northern suburb that was the nearest place to the forest that might be thought of as covering most of the eastern and south-eastern parts of Victoria.

After he had stepped out for the first time from the branch of the bank where he had seen for the first time the young woman mentioned above, he, the chief character, saw that the face of the young woman, which face was then in his mind, resembled most of the faces of the young women mentioned previously in this story. When he tried to find a word or words to denote or to suggest the most obvious quality of those faces, he could think only of the words *sharpness* and *prickliness*.

We had first smelled the acrid smoke from a great distance

The words just above are from Chapter 8 of the book *Death of a Forest*, by Rosamund Duruz, published in 1974 by Lowden Publishing Company, Kilmore. The town of Kilmore is described on the dust-jacket of the book as being Victoria's oldest inland town.

The chief character of this story had understood for many years before he read the book mentioned above what he should have been told by his father when he first showed his son, the chief character, the farm where he, the father, had been a boy and the grassy countryside all around the farm: that the farm and the grassy countryside around it and the district of mostly level grasslands that comprised much of the south-west of Victoria had previously been covered by forest.

The chief character of this story had learned at some time before he began to read the book mentioned above that the village or town of Heytesbury in England is in the south-west of that country and is at the edge of the Salisbury Plain. He has never seen the Salisbury Plain, but he imagines it as mostly level grassland.

The book mentioned above is one of many books that he, the chief character of this story, bought during the 1970s but did not read until many years afterwards, if at all. When he finally read the book in the late 1980s, he learned that the author was an English woman who had arrived with her husband in the Heytesbury Forest in the early 1950s, in the very year when he had moved with his family from the western suburbs of Melbourne to an outer south-eastern suburb which was mostly scrub. Much of the book was a history of the Heytesbury Forest, which history was of some interest to him, although he never read it a second time. The chapter of the book that he read a number of times after he had first read it was Chapter 8, which was headed "Forest Memories: 1950–60." From that section he learned, among other things, that the farmers who lived in clearings of the Heytesbury Forest or at the edges of the forest used to burn large parts of the forests in the 1950s on the pretext that they were preventing the spread of bushfires in the future.

Of the sections of the book mentioned above that he read only once, the section that he most often remembered was Chapter 7, which was headed "Progress and Destruction: Modern Times." Much of this section reported the work of the Rural Finance and Settlement Commission from 1954 until the mid-1960s.

Of the illustrations in the book mentioned above, all of them reproductions of black and white photographs, the illustration that he most often looked at afterwards was the illustration facing page 17 of the text. Part of the caption beneath the illustration reads: *This land was all forest-clad twenty-five years ago.* The illustration is of grassy countryside with what seems to be a line of trees in the distance and in the foreground what seem to be scattered outgrowths of scrub in a paddock of grass.

The Interior of Gaaldine

A true account of certain events recalled on the evening when I decided to write no more fiction.

For a long time, I used to dream at night that I had gone to live in Tasmania. After the first few dreams, I would spend my last waking hour each evening at my desk, looking at a map of Tasmania or at one or another leaflet for tourists who might be persuaded to visit Tasmania. (I had no books about Tasmania.) I was hoping either to lengthen the sequences or images in my dreams or to introduce into my dreams details that I would afterwards mistake for memories of an actual place I had left many years before but would return to in the future, but I only succeeded in dreaming of myself at my desk in Tasmania.

I was nearly fifty years of age before I visited Tasmania, although I almost went to live in Tasmania at the age of ten. Before I had reached that age, I had lived in six different houses in Victoria. Like many families at that time, we lived in rented houses, but unlike many fathers of families, my father did not intend to live in his own home in the future. One of his many unusual beliefs was that a working man was entitled to a house at the expense of his employer. My father, who was skilled as a farmer and a gardener, read continually the columns headed SITUATIONS VACANT in several daily and weekly newspapers. He looked forward to becoming one day a head gardener or farm manager at some prison or mental hospital in a provincial city with a rent-free house provided on the premises. At one time, he even applied for several positions as a lighthouse keeper on capes of southern Victoria or islands in Bass Strait. He often spoke of the many hours each week that a man would have for his private pursuits if he could live at the place where he worked and if he was free from the burden of paying for his own house, although he seemed to do no more in his spare time than to read books from the Crime Fiction and General Fiction shelves of the nearest circulating library.

One day when I was ten years of age, my father announced that he had applied for the position of assistant gardener at the mental hospital at New Norfolk in Tasmania and that he was confident of being awarded the position. After he had obtained the position at New Norfolk, so my father told my mother and my brother and me, we would all live together in a six-roomed stone house that was more than a hundred years old and had been built by convicts. While he was waiting for a reply to his application, my father called at the office of the Tasmanian Tourist Bureau in Melbourne and brought home and showed us a publication whose pages contained coloured photographs of Tasmania together with short paragraphs of text. I studied the illustrations and prepared to think of myself as a Tasmanian.

My father was seriously considered for the position at New Norfolk. In the jargon of these days, he was short-listed. The persons making the appointment arranged for my father to travel at their expense by aeroplane from Essendon Airport to Hobart and then to New Norfolk and, of course, back to Essendon. These events took place nearly forty years ago. Few people travelled by aeroplane in those times, and my father was so afraid of taking his first air journey that he made his will beforehand. He travelled safely to Tasmania and back in a Douglas DC-2 but would never speak of his experience in the air and never again stepped into an aeroplane. Soon after he had returned from Tasmania, he learned that he had not been appointed to the position he had applied for. He soon became interested in some other advertised position and never again mentioned the mental hospital and the stone house at New Norfolk. I kept for several years the book with the coloured illustrations of Tasmania but lost it during one of my family's later moves from one rented house to another. During the thirty-five years and more since I last saw the coloured illustrations, I have forgotten all but a few of the many details in the illustrations. Those few are some of the details of an illustration showing a young woman with a basket of apples from the trees of the Huon Valley, of an illustration showing a view from an aeroplane of Elwick Racecourse, which lies beside the estuary of the River Derwent, and of an illustration showing the front of a large house built in a style that I have since learned is called the Georgian style and surrounded by level grassy countryside.

On a certain day in a certain year in the late 1980s, when I had not dreamed for many months about Tasmania, a man who was a stranger to me telephoned me from Hobart and invited me to take part with two other writers in a week-long tour of Tasmania arranged by a writers' organisation of which he was an office-holder. This was the first invitation I had ever received to take part in an event outside the state of Victoria. The man who telephoned me was the first person who had ever spoken or written to me from Tasmania. I wanted to accept the man's invitation, but I had never stepped into an aeroplane and I intended never to do so, and I explained to the man in Hobart that I could only accept his invitation if he could arrange for me to travel to and from Tasmania by sea. The man told me that he was surprised by my request and that he would have to look at the budgetary ramifications. The following day, the man told me that I was welcome to join the tour and that I could travel to and from Tasmania in the ferry *Abel Tasman* but that I would have to spend a weekend in Tasmania before the tour proper began. The first engagement of the tour was in Devonport on a Monday evening, so the man told me, and the other two writers would, in his words, fly in to Devonport on the Monday afternoon, but the *Abel Tasman* arrived in Devonport only on Tuesday mornings, Thursday mornings, and Saturday mornings, so that I would have to amuse myself, so he said, in Devonport from the Saturday morning until the Monday afternoon when the other writers arrived, although his organisation would book me into a comfortable hotel in Devonport for the Saturday night and the Sunday night.

The tickets for my journey to Tasmania arrived in the post together with a note from the man in Hobart telling me that he had paid in advance for my accommodation for two nights at the Elimatta Hotel and that all other matters would be looked after by a woman from his organisation who would call for me at the hotel on the Monday afternoon and would accompany me and the other two writers on the tour.

I calculated that I was one year younger than my father had been when he travelled by air to Hobart nearly forty years before. For all my years, I had hardly ever travelled outside Victoria and had only once stayed in a hotel. The nine days that I was going to spend in Tasmania would be my first absence from my family since I had become a married man twenty years before. I packed at one end of my suitcase a bowl and a spoon and nine small plastic bags each containing the measured amount of wheat germ and raisins and walnut pieces and honey that I intended to eat in my room each morning for breakfast after having added water from the bathroom tap. I packed also a bundle of blank pages and the few finished pages of a piece of short fiction that I had been trying to write for several months. I packed also two books. The first book—*The Seven Mountains of Thomas Merton*, by Michael Mott, published in Boston by the Houghton Mifflin Company in 1984—I had owned for several years but had not yet read. The second book—*A Life of Emily Brontë*, by Edward Chitham, published at Oxford by Basil Blackwell in 1987—I had owned for only a few days; I had ordered the book from my bookseller as soon as I had read a notice of its publication, and my copy had arrived from England by surface mail only a few days before my departure for Tasmania.

I was due aboard the *Abel Tasman* late on a Friday afternoon. I ate my usual breakfast on the Friday morning, but I could not eat lunch. For most of the afternoon, I paced up and down the lounge-room and the hall of my house while my suitcase stood packed and locked at the front door. I was afraid of missing my train into Melbourne or the train from Melbourne to Station Pier, even though the trains I planned to take would bring me to Port Melbourne more than an hour before the first passengers were permitted aboard. At the same time, I was afraid of travelling so far from home. I had always been afraid that if I were to travel out of what I thought of as my native territory, I would become a different person and would forget the person that I had been. Only a year before I was invited to Tasmania, I had read somewhere of a belief among certain North American Indians that a person who travelled faster than a person could travel on horseback would leave his or her soul behind. I would have had to admit that I had held a driver's licence and had travelled by motor car for nearly thirty years and that I had often travelled in trains, but I could have argued that I had hardly ever travelled out of what I thought of as my native territory. If I had left my soul behind me when I travelled by train to Sydney in 1964 or by car to Murray Bridge in 1962, then I had joined up with my soul soon afterwards when I hurried back to my native districts.

As the time for my leaving my house became closer, I began to sweat, and the muscles in my legs felt weak. I knew that I could have kept myself calm if I had drunk something alcoholic, and I had six stubbies of beer and two flasks of vodka in my suitcase, but I was afraid that if I drank even a glass of water during the afternoon I would vomit as soon as I stepped on board the *Abel*

Tasman and felt the movement of the sea. I had never been in any vessel larger than a rowing-boat, but I had seen cut-away illustrations of ocean-liners in books I had read as a child, and I supposed that the gangplank of the *Abel Tasman* would lead onto a vast upper deck and that my vomiting would take place in front of numerous promenading passengers.

I have never since remembered anything that might have happened to me between the time when I left the train at Port Melbourne and the time when I unlocked the door to my cabin deep down among the many corridors inside the *Abel Tasman*.

The first thing I saw when I had locked the door of my cabin behind me was that I was sealed off from the world. This made me afraid again. I had expected my cabin to have a porthole with a view of sea and sky, but all I could see was the interior of my cabin and all I could hear were faint mechanical noises. I spent the first few minutes in my cabin trying to learn whether or not I was above the waterline. I listened through the wall that I believed was nearest the hull, but I heard only voices, and I began to understand that I was deep inside a honeycomb of cabins and that I would not know whether I was above or below the surface of the sea for as long as I could not remember how many sets of stairs I had descended on the way down to my cabin or how far above the sea I had been when I crossed the gangplank.

A life-jacket was fixed to the inside of my cabin door. Behind the jacket was a notice with instructions for putting on the jacket and following a certain route through the corridors and up the stairways if the ship's alarm sounded. I took down the jacket and began to fasten it around me. I got the jacket into what I thought was the correct position, but then I saw from the diagram on the door that I had fastened the jacket wrongly. I tried to get the jacket off me, but I could not get it off. I was sweating and trembling. I sat on the bed with the life-jacket still tied around me. I imagined a steward knocking on the cabin door and then entering by means of his master key to welcome me aboard and finding me already in a life-jacket. I imagined myself trying to sleep with the jacket still fastened around me.

I opened my suitcase and took out one of my stubbies and drank. The beer was still cool, and I drank it all in a few minutes and began to feel less anxious. I opened another stubby and began to work at getting the life-jacket off. I remembered the fruit-knife that I had packed in my bag for quartering the apples and scraping the carrots that I intended to eat whenever I could avoid having to sit down in dining-rooms or motels or wherever the writers were going to be fed on tour. I took out the knife and hacked with it at the fastenings of my life-jacket.

The captain's voice spoke from just behind me, and I dropped the knife. His voice was coming through a sound system into the cabin. He welcomed all the passengers on board and gave us a few items of information and then let us hear the sound of the alarm and reminded us of what to do if we heard the sound during the voyage. While he was talking, I went on fiddling with my life-jacket, and something gave way and enabled me to struggle free. But I was not able to put the jacket back on the door in the way I had found it, and I thought I could see signs of damage where I had hacked at one of the straps with my knife.

While I was drinking my third stubby, the vessel began to move. The noise of the engines was loud in my cabin, but I was surprised at how little movement I noticed. When I had finished the stubby, I left my cabin in search of a bar.

I found a bar and drank beer alone there until nine. For most of the time, I leaned against a window with a hand cupped around my eyes and stared out into the darkness. I was still surprised at how calm the sea was, considering that the season was winter. For most of the time, I could see a few lights in the distance, but I did not know where I was.

When I was back in my cabin, I did not feel sleepy. I had eaten nothing since breakfast, but I did not feel hungry. I opened another stubby and took out the two books I had brought. Since I had become the owner of the book about Thomas Merton, I had looked forward to learning the circumstances of his death. Merton had travelled widely as a young man, but after he had become a Cistercian monk he had observed what was called his vow of stability and had never left his monastery in Kentucky. In his early middle age, when he had for long been a well-known writer and had corresponded with people in many countries, he began to ask his abbot for permission to travel to conferences. The abbot refused his permission for some years, but finally allowed Merton to attend a conference in Thailand of persons from different religions interested in meditation. On the first day of the conference, Merton was found dead in his hotel bathroom, having been electrocuted by faulty wires. This was as much as I had learned from magazine articles, and I wanted to learn more. But I expected to learn more also about Merton's life as a monk and a writer. I had been interested in Merton for more than thirty years, as the following paragraph will explain.

While I sat in my cabin during the first sea journey I had ever undertaken, I was aware that the two books I had brought with me were about the two writers who had most influenced me during the first of many years in my life when I spent much of my time wavering between what I saw as the only two courses that my life could take. During the last year of my secondary education, I had read, among other books, *Elected Silence* and *Wuthering Heights*. Soon after the examinations at the end of that year, I forgot the experience of having read every book except the two mentioned just now. I never afterwards forgot my foreseeing while I read *Elected Silence* that I would become a solitary and a writer as Merton had become. (Sometimes the term *solitary* seemed to mean that I would become a priest in a religious order or a monk in a monastery; at other times the term meant that I would become a bachelor living alone among books.) Nor did I afterwards forget my foreseeing while I read *Wuthering Heights* that I would fall in love with one or another young woman who would seem to me to resemble the image in my mind of Catherine Earnshaw before she had first thought of becoming the wife of Edgar Linton. (In order to meet such a young woman, so I supposed, I would have to live the opposite of a solitary life.)

I did not want to begin reading either book at the beginning. I looked at the pages of illustrations in both books and then at the indexes. I read from each book by turns—a page or two from the one, a chapter or so from the other. I remember myself lying back on my bed at some time towards midnight and drinking the last of my sixth stubby and promising myself that I would never again feel obliged to read the pages or the chapters of any book in the order decided on by the author or the editor and regretting that I had read too many books of fiction during my lifetime and too few biographies of writers of fiction. I remember myself at about the same time taking a pen and paper from my suitcase and making a note to remind myself in the future to consider writing a piece of fiction which would be published as though it was a biography, with an index, illustrations, and whatever else might be needed to complete the illusion.

At about the time mentioned in the previous paragraph, so I remember, I decided that I had been mistaken as a young man to think of Thomas Merton as a solitary. I read in my cabin that Merton as a monk had been continually visited by friends. I read that he had fallen in love, as a man in early middle age, with a young woman he had met when she was a nurse in a hospital where he had been admitted as a patient and that he and the young woman sometimes had picnic lunches together in the woods near the monastery when he had left the hospital and gone back to the monastic life. In my cabin I decided that Thomas Merton had posed as a solitary but that Emily Brontë had been a true solitary.

At about the time mentioned in the previous paragraph, I decided that I had been mistaken as a young man when I thought of finding in the future one or another young woman resembling the young Catherine Earnshaw. What I read in my copy of the book by Edward Chitham persuaded me that Catherine Earnshaw had seemed to the woman who wrote about her to be an inhabitant of the place called Gondal, which was a place in the mind of Emily Brontë. When I had expected as a young man to fall in love with a young woman resembling Catherine Earnshaw, so I recall having decided in my cabin, I ought to have understood that such a young woman could be met with only in the place called Gondal.

After I had finished the last of my stubbies, I set aside my books and put on my jacket. I put my flasks of vodka in the pockets of the jacket and walked to the highest and foremost part of the upper deck. The time was soon after midnight and the weather was fine but cold. The barman who had served me earlier had told me we would not come into sight of the lights of Tasmania until early daylight, but I sat on a seat on the deck and stared ahead of the ship. I sipped from my flask and began at last to feel what I usually felt after drinking, which was a feeling that I need no longer trouble myself with reading or writing, since I would shortly see as a result of my drinking what I had for so long been trying to see as a result of my reading and writing.

Even at that time, a few people still sat or walked on the upper deck, but an hour or so later I seemed to be the only person there. I went on sipping from my flask. I have been a drinker for most of my adult life but never what is called a seasoned drinker. I have never been able to keep pace with men who drink regularly in hotels, and I have often vomited in the toilet of some hotel while my drinking companions were talking quietly and with no appearance of drunkenness in the bar. I have always preferred to drink alone, sipping from stubbies of beer and trying to maintain in myself the feeling I described in the previous paragraph. I have always disliked wine and spirits, but in situations where I could not have at hand a half-dozen stubbies I have usually had a flask of vodka in a pocket. On the upper deck of the *Abel Tasman*, in the early hours of the morning, I began to sing to myself.

Among the many songs that I must have sung, several stay in my mind. I sang what I knew of "My Old Kentucky Home," if that is its title, as a result of having read earlier of Thomas Merton in the monastery in Kentucky. I sang what I knew of "The

Camptown Races," if that is its title, as a result of my having re-membered that Merton's monastery was in the district of Kentucky celebrated for its racecourses and stud farms. I sang what I thought of as a song about Gondal. The tune and all the words but one were from a song I had heard sung by the American group the Weavers. I sang as I crossed Bass Strait that Gondal was a dread-ful place where the whalefish did go and the north wind did blow and the daylight was seldom seen. I sang as though I wanted to warn the curious away from travelling towards Gondal so that I might be one of the few to enjoy its pleasures.

Not long before daylight, as the barman had foretold, a tiny light appeared far ahead in the darkness. I sat watching the light. By now I had almost finished my second flask of vodka. While I watched, a few persons came up onto the deck and watched also, but I felt confident that I was the only person who could see the single sign in the darkness of the land ahead.

When the sky began to lighten, I drank the last of my vodka and then went back to my cabin and packed my books into my suitcases. The books were the only things I had unpacked. I was still wearing the clothes I had put on nearly twenty-four hours ear-lier in Melbourne. I did not clean my teeth or wash any part of myself. I looked at my face in the mirror and told myself that I was not drunk, but I felt strange. In all my life, I had never gone for so long without food or sleep.

I carried my suitcase up to a coffee shop on an upper level and sipped two cups of black coffee and watched the mountains of Tas-mania becoming clearer to view. A few other people sat around me, but I believed they could not see me. When the vessel was en-tering the Mersey River, I stood in a crowd near the purser's office and was surprised when people did not blunder into me.

I walked down the gangplank. The persons waiting all looked through me. I took a taxi to the Elimatta Hotel. I told the driver I was a bad traveller and had not slept all night, and he left me alone. I intended to talk to no one for the whole weekend. I believed I was about to resolve some momentous matter if only I could be left alone. I did not want to sleep or eat. I wondered how soon I might buy a six-pack of stubbies from my hotel.

The young woman who came to the reception desk in the hotel after I had pressed the bell several times told me that my booking was in order but that I could not occupy my room before eleven.

I have always preferred to disguise my feelings in the presence of others. I was dismayed by what the young woman had told me, and having stayed only once in all my life at a hotel, I could not understand the reason for my being shut out, as it seemed to me, from my own room. But I behaved as though I had only called at that hour to confirm my booking and to leave my suitcase in her care. I put my suitcase behind her desk and strolled out of the hotel as though I had friends outside waiting to drive me to their home for a shower and a shave and a substantial breakfast. I turned towards the main streets of Devonport. The time was about eight-thirty.

I walked for fifteen minutes and reached the commercial centre of Devonport. I was not unaware that I would be mostly confined to my hotel room for the next two days, and I bought a bag of apples, a few bananas, and a bunch of carrots, but I went on walking with the fruit and the carrots swinging in a bag from my hand. I did not want to eat. I was almost afraid to eat. I felt as though my body no longer needed food: as though my body could be sustained by the powerful thoughts about to enter my mind. Such a feeling was invigorating, but I thought occasionally that if I ate so much as a mouthful I would fall to my knees in the street and would crawl to the gutter and would begin to vomit. The police would be called. I would be taken back to my hotel. My suitcase would be searched. Something in my baggage would enrage the police. It might be my books or something I had scribbled during the previous night. I would be escorted to the *Abel Tasman* and left in the care of the captain until the vessel sailed for Melbourne on Sunday evening.

I went on walking. I walked for more than two hours, very slowly and with frequent pauses. I walked through streets of houses at first, and later I walked back to the river and then along a path that took me to the headland where the Mersey enters Bass Strait. I believe I walked for ten minutes or more along the ocean before I turned back. But I remember hardly anything of what I saw while I walked. The one detail I remember is the spur-winged plovers. I noticed the plovers first while I walked along the grassy bank of the river from the Elimatta Hotel towards the main streets. Every twenty or thirty paces, I passed a pair of plovers walking up and down the grass and listening or watching for their prey. I had always been interested in plovers. In the early mornings in the suburb of Melbourne where I lived, I would sometimes hear the cry of a plover and would suppose that I was receiving some kind of message. In the streets of Devonport, I would stand at a few paces from a plover, trying to see the eye of the bird. I remember one bird that turned away and would not meet my eye on a neat lawn that I learned a few moments later was part of the surrounds of the library of Devonport.

I cannot remember having arrived back at my hotel. I assume that I arrived towards midday and was shown to my room. Perhaps I ate soon afterwards in my room one or more of the carrots or apples or bananas that I had been carrying for so long, but I suspect that I lay on the bed in my room and slept for a few hours. My room was part of a block of rooms across a courtyard from the main building of the hotel. The first thing that I can recall from the Saturday afternoon is my walking across the courtyard to the drive-in bottle shop and buying a dozen stubbies of Tasmanian beer and two or three flasks of vodka and then taking them back to my room. I can recall from that same afternoon a few minutes when I was drinking from a stubby of beer and when the sunlight was bright on the other side of the curtains of my room (I had not opened them since I had first entered the room) and when I noticed a radio near the bed that I was lying on. I turned the radio on. I heard part of the description of a football match between two Tasmanian teams. The broadcast was interrupted by a broadcast of a race from Elwick. I listened to the broadcast, but I had never previously heard the name of any of the horses in the race. (I did not often listen to broadcasts of races in Melbourne, but when I listened I would always recognise the name of one or another horse.) I got up from the bed and walked into the bathroom attached to the bedroom. I looked into the mirror and told myself that I should no longer doubt that I had crossed the sea and had arrived in Tasmania.

I can recall also from the late afternoon or the early evening of the Saturday a period of about fifteen minutes when I awoke on my bed, still fully clothed, and supposed the time to be the morning of one or another day. I took out of my suitcase one of the parcels meant for my breakfast on each day of my tour. I emptied the oats and other things into my bowl and added water and ate. The first mouthful was hard to swallow, and I supposed I was about to vomit it up again. I stood at the door to the bathroom and toilet with my food in my hand. I went on eating but I was ready to vomit if I had to do so. After each mouthful, I felt less uncomfortable. I nudged with my foot the plastic lid of the toilet. The lid fell over the bowl of the toilet. I sat on the plastic lid and ate the remainder of my breakfast food.

I can recall a few minutes from a time that I suppose to have been soon after dark on the Saturday evening. I had woken again on the bed that I considered my bed. I was still wearing the underclothes and shirt and trousers that I had put on in my home in Melbourne at least thirty-six hours before. I walked to the small refrigerator in the corner of my room. I opened the door of the refrigerator and looked at the supply of beer and vodka inside. I seem to recall that I saw an unopened flask of vodka and more than six stubbies, but this must have seemed not enough to keep me contented throughout the Sunday. I seem not to have supposed that a guest of the hotel might order drinks on Sunday, since I remember walking across from my room through darkness and buying another six stubbies and another flask of vodka from the bottle shop.

I must have slept soundly at last during the late evening of the

Saturday. What I next remember is my hearing while I slept a sound that seemed to me a sound in a dream. I seemed to be dreaming that a branch of a tree was knocking against the window of my room. As I awoke, I understood that someone was knocking at my door.

I got up from the bed. I had covered myself with the bedspread, but I was still dressed in the shirt and trousers and underclothes that I had worn when I left Melbourne. I supposed the person knocking was one of the staff of the hotel. I opened the door. A youngish woman asked me if she could come in and then stepped forward as though I had already invited her to enter.

I stepped back. The woman walked into the middle of the room and then stood and looked around for the best place to seat herself. She walked to an armchair near the head of my bed, as I thought of it, and sat in the chair. She had been carrying in her right hand a bulky briefcase of the sort that men had carried on suburban trains when I had worked as a public servant in Melbourne twenty-five years before. Having sat, she rested the briefcase across her thighs.

I closed the door to my room. The only places where I could have sat were the bed and the other of the two chairs, which was on the opposite side of the bed from the chair where the woman was sitting. I sat in the chair, and the woman and I looked at one another across the bed.

Even before the woman had spoken at the door, she had seemed to give off a certain warmth and friendliness towards me. As she had walked into my room, I thought she must have mistaken it for some other room. She had arrived at the hotel to visit someone she had never seen but had corresponded with for a long time, but she had knocked at the wrong door—that explanation would have fitted exactly.

We looked at one another by the light of the bedlamp. I cannot report that she smiled at me, but her face was composed and her look was friendly. I was sure by now that she took me for someone else.

451

Every year, I am less able to estimate the ages of persons much younger than myself. The woman in my room might have been any age from thirty to forty. How did she look to me? My instinctive reaction whenever I meet a female person for the first time is to find her either sexually attractive or sexually unattractive. I did not react instinctively when I first met the woman I am writing about. I seem to have noted few details of her appearance. I remember that her hair was neither dark nor fair, but I do not remember that it was brownish or gingery. Her eyes, her skin, her body—none of these I could describe. What I recall continually is an impression I got from her voice and her posture and her manner towards me. I understood from the first that she thought of me as a friend or an ally of some kind. When she looked at me or spoke to me, it seemed understood between us that we had dealt with one another previously and had long since set aside such petty matters as love and passion. Now, we were together once more in order to deal with things that truly mattered.

When I had sat down, she told me her name. I heard it as Alice. She told me that she knew my name already but not as a result of her having read anything I had written. She was interested in writing, she said, but not in the sort of writing that she understood me to have written. She knew my name, she told me, because a man she knew—the owner of the briefcase in her lap—had pointed out my name to her in a paragraph in a newspaper. My name had been printed in a paragraph reporting that three writers were going to take part in a tour of Tasmania. The man her friend, so she said, seemed to know something about me or to have read some of the articles or poems or novels or plays that I had written. Her friend had asked her to telephone the newspaper and to ask who had supplied the details of the paragraph about the writers' tour. She had telephoned and had been told the name of the organisation that had arranged the tour. She had telephoned the organisation for several days afterwards before she had finally spoken to someone. She had asked for details of the itinerary of the writers, including the names of the hotels and motels where they would be staying. She had had to pretend to be a devoted reader of all my writings before the person from the writers' organisation would give her any details. The person was a man, so she told me, and she believed he would not have given her the details if she had not been a woman and had not spoken pleadingly. When she had reported to her man-friend that I would be staying for two nights alone in the Elimatta Hotel in Devonport before the tour began, he had been pleased. He had then arranged for the visit that she was making at the time of her telling me this.

I wanted at first to ask her why her man-friend himself had not come to show me whatever was in the briefcase. But then I supposed that the briefcase contained a typescript of the same sort of writing that I had had published during the past fifteen years and that I had come to Tasmania to talk about. If I was right, then the friend of the woman was a writer who had not yet been published and who wanted me to read some of his writing and to help him to get the writing published. For as long as I had been a published writer, I had been approached, after I had talked or read to one or another group of people, by unpublished writers wanting me to read their writing and to help them to get their writing published. And for the first few minutes while the woman was talking to me in my room, I supposed that she had been sent by her friend to persuade me to read his writing. For as long as I supposed this, I tried to think of a polite way of refusing to accept from her the contents of the briefcase in her lap.

I can hardly believe, as I write this account, that I was able while the woman talked to me not only to hear her out calmly but to put one after another interpretations on her words. And yet, I recall that I soon decided while listening to the woman that her story of her man-friend was untrue and that she had brought me some of her own writing to read. After I had begun to believe this, I expected that I would not be able to refuse her when she handed her writing to me and asked me to read it. However, as tired and as dazed as I might have been, I was still determined, so I recall, to carry on the pretence that the writing I had been asked to read was the work of a man who was an admirer of my own writing but was unknown to me. This pretence, so I thought, would save me from having to tell the woman to her face that I had not thought highly of her writing. (I had never thought highly of any writing that had been shown to me by unpublished writers of the kind I have been describing.)

She asked me, as I had expected, to read the contents of the briefcase. In a few graceful movements, she got up from her chair, opened the briefcase, let the bundle of pages fall onto my bed so that the uppermost page was conveniently placed in front of me, and then let herself out of my room. The previous sentence may not be an accurate report of events. I cannot remember her leaving her chair or the room, but certainly a time arrived when she was no longer in the room, and she is not in the room with me now, although she will surely return to this room, or to some other room that had already been reserved for me in some other city in Tasmania, in order to collect the briefcase and its contents and to learn my comments on what I might have read.

More strange than my not remembering the woman's leaving my room is my not remembering her having imparted to me the information I am about to record, which information is a summary of the life of the man said by the woman to have been the author of the pages left in my keeping.

He had lived all his life in Tasmania. He was of about my own age but he had never once travelled the few hundred kilometres by sea that I had finally travelled between Tasmania and the mainland. He had been born in Hobart but had lived as a child for an equal number of years in both Hobart and Launceston and had never afterwards been sure of how to answer persons who asked him where he came from. During his years at secondary school, he had been at least an average student in most subjects but among the best few in English and geography. At the age of fifteen he had had a poem published in his school magazine and had confided to one of his teachers that he wanted to be a poet, but no evidence survives of his having written any other poem or any other piece of literary writing, and in his last year of school his teachers commented in his reports that he seemed to lack ambition. After secondary school, he obtained a place in the training college for primary teachers in schools in the government system. He followed the course for the required two years and earned his trained teacher's certificate. At that time, in the late 1950s, teachers were in short supply. His certificate entitled him to a permanent place in the employment of the state government. At the time when his briefcase was delivered to my room in the Elimatta Hotel in Devonport, he had been a teacher in primary schools in Tasmania for thirty years.

In his early years as a teacher, his junior rank had obliged him to teach in schools unpopular among his colleagues: schools in industrial towns or in government housing estates. As he became more senior, he was more able to teach where he chose, and he chose always to be an assistant teacher in a school in a middle-class suburb of a city. He never sought promotion to any position of responsibility, much less to any head teacher's position. Most of his colleagues were driven at sometime during their careers to study by night for qualifications entitling them to enter the higher-paid grades of the teaching service, but the author of the pages at my elbow, who was close to fifty years of age, had been for fifteen years the most senior teacher in the lowest grade in the system of classification used in Tasmania.

The author of the contents of the briefcase had never married. According to the woman who had brought the briefcase to me, the author, as I intend to call him from now on, had never been seen in the company of any person to whom he might have been linked romantically. Most young teachers in the 1950s lived in boarding houses or as boarders in family homes when they were living away from their own homes. The author as a young man would share a bathroom or a toilet with other persons but would always live in a detached or self-contained room with at least a gas-ring and a sink so that he need not observe the mealtimes of others. As his income increased, he began to live in small rented flats. He saved money each year. Most he put aside for a small house for his retirement; some he used to buy cheap furniture and fittings for the rented flats that he began to occupy after about his thirtieth year; the rest he put towards the cost of buying and maintaining the second-hand cars that he began to buy and to maintain after about his thirtieth year.

He had stayed for no more than five years in any one place during his career. The life he lived was simple and blameless, and yet his colleagues and his neighbours could not leave him alone, and their questions and their scrutiny had always caused him to move on. The population of Tasmania had been never more than a few hundred thousands throughout his career, but he had been able to move seven times during his career to a place where he was scarcely known. At the time when I first heard of him, he was planning to make one further move at about the age of fifty and then to take advantage of a scheme for early retirement and to live for the rest of his life in a village more than thirty kilometres from any place where he had taught. He had lived at two different periods of his life in each of Launceston and Hobart, once at Burnie, once at Devonport, once in Wynyard, and once in New Norfolk. In each place, his routine was as reported in the following paragraph.

He arrived an hour early at school and prepared the lessons for the day. He taught his class conscientiously throughout the day and did whatever other duties his head teacher assigned to him. He ate his cut lunch in the staffroom and took morning and afternoon tea in the same place and exchanged small talk there with his colleagues. After school, he shopped for his supplies and then went to his lodgings. On one afternoon each week, he would call at the local library to borrow and return several books, and on Friday afternoons, if any of his colleagues were in the habit of drinking at a hotel near the school, he would join them for an hour. After he had arrived home each evening, he remained indoors; he was never seen at any meeting or gathering by night. On Saturday, if a race meeting was held in the town or the city where he lived, he would always attend. Sometimes, in the winter, he was seen at a football match. On other Saturdays, he would walk for an hour in the late afternoon. He attended no church on Sunday or on any other day. His only outing on Sunday was a short walk late in the day. Each year while one or both of his parents was alive, he spent Christmas Day in their house. When his parents had died, he ate Christmas dinner at the home of his married sister, who was his only sibling. On Boxing Day each year, he arrived in one or another unfashionable hotel in one or another seaside town and stayed for a week. He took his short holiday partly so that he would be able to satisfy the questions of his colleagues in the first weeks of the new school year but also as a genuine break in his routine. In the hotel, he went to his room only to sleep. Each morning he walked, always in sports trousers and long-sleeved shirt, along the streets nearest the sea, or he sat on the foreshore and looked at the beach. In the afternoons, he sat in the bar of his hotel, drinking beer slowly and listening to radio broadcasts of cricket or tennis or golf or horse-races or watching televised reports of those events or talking with any other drinker who might have begun a conversation with him. In the evenings, he watched television programmes with other guests in the hotel lounge, again drinking slowly and talking with anyone who offered to talk to him. At the end of this week, he returned to his home and stayed indoors all day for most of the days until school resumed.

The author sometimes invited to his home one or another of his colleagues. On perhaps one Friday each year, when the author was drinking with colleagues (always males), he would invite to his home some young man whose wife was staying with a sick parent or was in hospital after having given birth to her first child or (as often happened in later years) had recently separated from her husband. The two men would buy a few bottles of beer and a meal of fish and chips and would sit in the author's lounge-room for three or four hours before the visitor would return to his home.

Whatever odd sights the visitor might have expected to see in the rooms of the bachelor who had invited him home, he saw little worth reporting back to anyone who might have questioned him later. The furnishings would have struck most observers as drab and tasteless. There was a portable television set at least fifteen years old, a cheap mantel radio, and an old record-player with a dozen or so records. A few shelves of books were in a corner— mostly books about horse-racing in Europe and the USA. The rooms were bare of pictures. There were no vases or ornaments. The only unexpected item in the lounge-room might have been the filing cabinets. (There would have been only one cabinet during the first seven years of the author's teaching career, but the number increased by one every seven years.) The author was never uncomfortable if his visitor stared at the filing cabinets or asked about them. In fact, these casual-seeming invitations to his home were part of a deliberate policy by the author. He hoped his visitor would tell his colleagues afterwards how little of note he had seen in the bachelor's quarters. This, so the author hoped, would bring an end to any gossip that might have circulated about him. Whenever a visitor seemed curious about the filing cabinets, the author would say offhandedly that he did a bit of writing for a hobby. The author then gave one or another brief account of his hobby depending on how much the visitor seemed to be aware of all that might have been denoted by the word *writing*. To someone who had seemingly never opened a book since his years at the training college, when he had been compelled to read a novel, a play, and an anthology of poetry for his literature course, the author would say that he had been taking correspondence courses in the hope of learning how to write a best-selling crime novel so that he could give up teaching. To someone who might have had on his own shelves some of the *Reader's Digest* condensed books, the author would say that he had had a poem published when he was at school and a poem or two published in obscure places over the years since then and that he had been trying for years to get together a small collection of poems that might one day be published. To the one man of the twenty and more who had heard that the owner of the filing cabinets was some sort of writer and who had then asked such questions as revealed that he sometimes read a novel or even a book of poetry or even that he may once have tried or thought of trying himself to write a novel or a book of poetry or even a single poem—to that man the author said that each of his poems had been published under a different name and that he preferred not to disclose these names, since he believed that the enterprise known as literature had taken a wrong course from the time when pieces of writing first began to be published with the true name of the author attached. From that time, so the author believed, critics and reviewers and commentators and all other persons who claimed to be able to distinguish good writing from bad writing had never had their skills fairly tested. The author wished that all writers of all texts that might have deserved to be considered as literature had either refused to put a name to any of their texts or had put to every text a different name. If the world had been as he wished, the author said to the one man mentioned earlier in this paragraph, readers would have been able to learn about the author of any text only what the text itself seemed to tell them, and persons claiming to be skilled at commenting on texts would have had to spend much effort in trying to establish which of the many texts published each year came from one or another previously published author. In that world, the author had said to the man mentioned above, no person claiming to be skilled at commenting on texts would be able to praise or to denigrate any piece of writing safe in the knowledge that he or she knew who was the author of that piece and knew that other texts by the same author had been praised or denigrated by other persons claiming to be skilled at commenting.

Thus the author had lived for about thirty years. Now, he was within a few years of retiring under an early retirement scheme that allowed teachers employed by the government to leave work in their fifties. He expected to be left alone by his neighbours after he had retired. Anyone who heard that he was some kind of writer would suppose him to be one more middle-aged man trying to do in his retirement what he had dreamed of doing while he had worked for a living. As a retired man, he would be largely free from having to pretend. And yet he intended, as an extra safeguard of his privacy, to tell none of his former colleagues where he intended to live after his retirement. He had been on good terms with many of his colleagues during his career, but he considered none of them a friend. He had no friend, although the woman who had called at my room was somewhat close to him. He had known for many years where he wanted to spend his retirement, and he had made his last move as a teacher to a place far from the place he was going to retire to. When he left his last school, he would tell his colleagues that he intended to take a long holiday before deciding what next to do. In fact, he would use his savings to buy a cottage in the tiny township of N— on the river of the same name. (I had learned only the first letter of this name.)

The man has given much thought to his choice of the place where he would live for the remainder of his life. He knows that Tasmania is considered a place of mountains and forests, but the township of N— is near the centre of the largest district of mostly level pastureland in the whole island. After his retirement, the author will see mountains and forests in the distance, but he will be surrounded near at hand by mostly level and grassy countryside.

In the briefcase that the woman left with me are nearly two thousand pages. In the upper right-hand corner of each page is a date. The earliest of these dates is from the late 1950s; the most recent date is from this year. (In the text on many pages are other dates, but these are from a different calendar.) If the pages comprised a work of literature, I might report that the first thousand or so comprise an introduction to the work while the other pages are samples chosen at intervals from the narrative proper. If the pages comprised a work of literature, I might describe that work as a novel with many thousands of characters and a plot of infinite complications.

The author of the pages in the briefcase has imagined an island-country of approximately the same shape as Tasmania but with about twice its area and twice its population. The name of the country is New Arcadia.

The island-country of New Arcadia is situated with its midpoint at the intersection of the 145th meridian east of Greenwich and the line of latitude forty degrees south of the equator of a planet whose geography and history are similar to those of Earth except that the imagined planet contains no country corresponding to the country Australia. I have not yet learned from the pages I have read whether or not New Arcadia is a member of the British Commonwealth of Nations or the system by which the country is governed. The people of New Arcadia have similar racial origins to the people of Tasmania as it was in the 1950s, except that New Arcadia has considerably fewer people of Irish or Scots or Welsh origin. A less noticeable difference appeared to me as I looked through the pages. The persons in New Arcadia who own racehorses (a slightly larger proportion of the population than in Tasmania) often choose names for their horses such as few Tasmanians would have the knowledge or the wit to devise. A note in one of the early pages explains that the author got many of the names of New Arcadian racehorses from the books that he borrowed continually from libraries. Yet, when I read in the pages such names as Scholar-Gipsy, Laurids Brigge, La Ginistra, Clunbury, Das Glasperlenspiel, and Into The Millennium, I found myself thinking not of a primary teacher sitting alone of an evening in a shabby lounge-room but of men—and a few women—leafing through books in the libraries or on the verandas of sprawling houses set among clumps of trees and wide lawns in far-reaching expanses of mostly level countryside.

The reader should have guessed from the contents of the previous paragraph that the pages I have been looking at or writing about for most of this evening and of the day that preceded it and of the morning that preceded the day are part of a detailed chronicle of horse-racing in New Arcadia from the late 1950s until almost the present day. An introduction to the chronicle contains, among many other matters, maps of the racecourses of New

Arcadia, lists of all owners and trainers and jockeys in the country, details of all the principal breeding studs, summaries of the annual balance sheets of all the racing clubs . . . By far the bulk of the pages left with me are filled with details of particular race meetings, but throughout the chronicle I found notes written by the author to explain his methods of devising his imagined world. (He seems to have intended from the first that one or another reader would one day see his text.) In addition to all these contents, the pages also include sample pages from a vast index of all the horses that have raced in New Arcadia during the past thirty years, with each race that each horse contested being listed by serial number beside the name of the horse.

About 1,400 races are run in New Arcadia each year. I have learned from a note that the author has always fallen short of his ultimate aim, which is to report for every race every detail that is capable of being decided by the method he has devised for running races. (This is the term he uses. One of his notes begins: *I have run three races every night for the past week . . .*) Such details include the betting fluctuations for every runner; the amount, if any, invested on the horse by the owner(s), the trainer, and the proxy bettor for the jockey; and—what took the most time by far—the position of each horse after each two or three furlongs of each race.

The author runs a race by consulting a passage of prose chosen at random from one or another of the same library books that he scans for the names of New Arcadian horses. After many months of experiment, he decided as a young man in the 1950s that each letter of the alphabet would have a certain numerical value. Before the running of a race, the names of the starters are listed vertically at the left-hand side of a page. The words of the chosen passage of prose are then written in vertical columns adjoining the list of names in such a way that each name soon has beside it a horizontal array of letters. When this array is of a certain number, the numerical value of the array is calculated and the total is written beside the last of the letters. A comparison of the totals determines the progress of each horse up to a certain point of the race; roughly speaking, the horse with the highest total is the leader at that point.

The description in the previous paragraph grossly simplifies the author's method of running a race. A race run by the method described above would scarcely resemble any race in the world where I sit reporting on the author's pages. In a race run by the method as described above, the lead would change constantly, as would most other positions. In a series of races run thus, rank outsiders and short-priced favourites would win with equal frequency. In the short time remaining to me, I can only report that the author foresaw from the beginning the need for corrective devices that would be combined with the evaluation of scrambled texts. The chief of these is a banking system that allows him to hold in reserve for any horse a sudden addition to its total. Thus, a horse running fifth halfway through a race and suddenly earning a large score from the letters allotted to it—such a horse may hold its position for some distance further until it needs to draw on its bank. The author also provides each starter before the race with a bank in proportion to its odds in the betting ring, with favourites receiving much more than outsiders. This is done, of course, so that favourites and outsiders will win about the same percentage of races that they win in the world where I am writing this sentence.

The author has a name for his method of deciding races by consulting books borrowed from libraries. Whenever he runs a race by the detailed method reported in the previous paragraphs, he thinks of himself as *decoding* a certain text. In the years when he was running the first few thousand races in New Arcadia, he would sometimes become interested in one or another book whose pages he was opening at random and decoding and would sometimes begin to read passages from the book. He found in time that he could get little meaning from reading such a book. Instead of reading in the accepted sense of the word, he was decoding the book in his mind: seeing the letters of word after word listed vertically and imagining the forward rush of a field of horses. I believe that the author has not read any book for nearly thirty years. He still scans certain books or consults the indexes of certain books in search of names for the latest crop of two-year-olds in New Arcadia, but when he walks out of a library nowadays holding in his hand a book that he intends to decode, the pleasure he feels as he closes his fingers around the bulk of the book comes from his thinking of it as the source of the stringing out of the field on the far side of the course in a steeplechase of two and a half miles at Leamington (population 40,000; chief city of the north-west of New Arcadia) or of the bunching of the field on the turn into the straight in a mile weight-for-age race at Killeaton Park in Bassett (population 300,000; capital city of New Arcadia).

The author has always lived close to a library, but when he has retired and has gone to live in N—, he will no longer be able to stroll home with an armful of books each week. He has already begun to prepare for his retirement by buying books. New books would be too expensive, even if he wanted to buy them, and so he looks through the shelves of second-hand booksellers. The books that I would call novels of the Victorian period are what he most prizes. He loves these books, as I can readily understand, for the sheer mass of their texts. A few chapters from a novel by George Meredith or Anthony Trollope can bring to his mind a whole race meeting somewhere in New Arcadia, together with such consequences as that a certain horse will show signs of injury on the following day or that a certain owner will have been enabled by his success to buy a costly yearling for racing in the future.

But the author loves more than the mere wordiness of these books some quality that he claims to find in the prose itself. In a note that I cannot claim to have understood, he seems to state (I have, as it were, translated his note; he uses no grammatical or literary terms, decodable books being for him mere agglomerations of words) that the profusion of realistic detail in Victorian novels gives to the images of horse-racing that they cause to arise in his mind an unsurpassed richness and vividness. If my interpretation of his note is correct, then his method of decoding a text must surely be more complicated than I have so far described it. If he merely converts letters of the alphabet into numbers in accordance with a fixed scale, how could the details of his races be in any way affected by what most readers would call the subject matter of the texts he decodes?

Nor is this the only mystery about the author's methods. In another note, he seems to state something similar to Gustave Flaubert's claim that he could hear the rhythms of his unwritten sentences for pages ahead. The author seems in this note to state that he can hear the multiple thudding of horses' hoofs in any text he looks at, and that of all the various kinds of prose (I translate him again), the Victorian novel is best able to generate the slow rising towards the frantic climax appropriate to a horse-race. Again, I suspect that his decoding, as he calls it, is more complex than I have so far understood it to be.

When the author has retired, he will be able to run in detail every race in New Arcadia and to keep the calendar of that place aligned with the calendar of the world that contains the township of N—, but until then, he will have to go on running certain races in detail and merely determining the results of all other races. He determines the result only of a race by a method that he calls *gutting* a text. The method of gutting a text is much more straightforward than decoding. He begins to gut a text by looking only at what most people would call the passages of quoted speech. His term for these passages is *junk-mail*. As with decoding, the words to be gutted are written vertically beside the names of the horses in the race. The scale of numerical equivalents consulted when gutting is different from the scale consulted when decoding. I have not yet understood the difference between the two scales, but I suspect that the scale for the method of gutting might be called crude and unsubtle. Its only purpose is to determine the finishing order at the end of a race. It is not required to suggest any of the gradual unfoldings or the multiple possibilities suggested by the method of decoding. In this matter, as in many others, I suspect the author of hiding behind a show of bluff simple-mindedness. His using quoted speech in this way seems to mock the purpose of the authors who use it in their fiction. Such writers, he seems to be saying, suppose that the best fiction is the most lifelike; that the best prose is speech. (The Victorians used quoted speech as much as any later writers, but he seems more tolerant of them for some reason—perhaps because the speech in Victorian novels seems to readers nowadays too formal or too elaborate to be lifelike.)

A different sort of writer from myself might have wondered why the author of the pages in the briefcase had gone to such trouble to invent a duplication of what was already available to him: why he should have invented the racecourses of New Arcadia when he could have bought a racehorse for himself and watched it of a Saturday at Mowbray or Elwick. I have always been interested in what is usually called the world but only insofar as it provides me with evidence for the existence of another world. I have never written any piece of fiction with the simple purpose of understanding what I might call the real world. I have always written fiction in order to suggest to myself that another world exists. And whenever I have read a piece of fiction that seemed to me worthy to be read, whether the author of that fiction was myself or another person, I have always read with the purpose of suggesting to myself that a world might exist beyond the world suggested by the fiction, even if that further world was suggested only by such passages in the fiction as a report of the narrator's reading a text that he could not understand or of a character's dreaming a dream that was not reported in the text.

The author of the pages in the briefcase might have been making a declaration similar to my declaration in the previous paragraph when he made such notes in the margins of his pages as he made after his detailed report of the running, in a certain year, of the Rosalind Park Stakes (1 mile, 7 furlongs; weight for age; run in the autumn at Killeaton Park). In that race, Psalmus Hungaricus (owner/trainer S. T. Juhasz; rider M. L. Quayle) beat Lavengro after having been beaten by that horse by a margin of three lengths at their previous meeting under somewhat similar conditions. The author in his note asked, and was, of course, unable to answer, the question whether the trainer and the rider of Psalmus Hungaricus had agreed not to let the horse run on its merits in the race in which it was beaten.

While I was writing certain passages in the earlier pages of this piece of writing, I fell into one of my ways of writing fiction, which is to write as though I am looking at one or another detail in my mind and reflecting on that detail at my leisure. Certain passages in the earlier parts of this narrative may have suggested that I have been and will continue to be at leisure to imagine what ought next to be reported of the imagined narrator. I beg the reader to be under no misapprehension. While I have been writing this and the previous paragraph, I have felt less and less able to pretend that I am writing one more piece of fiction of the kinds that I have written in the past. My time is short. In a few hours, the woman representing the writers' organisation will call at the reception desk of this hotel, and my tour of Tasmania will begin. (If any reader of these words should wonder about my health, let that person be assured that I have largely recovered. In order to have finished this narrative before I leave the hotel, I have omitted many a paragraph that I might have written to report my having slept for a few hours or eaten a bowl of oatmeal and other things or drunk a few stubbies of beer.) What I intend to do in the time remaining is to pack my suitcase and to be ready for the writers' tour and then to write a last few paragraphs in an effort to answer certain questions in my mind. (The briefcase is already packed, with its contents in the same order that they occupied when I first looked at them. If the woman who left the briefcase has not returned before I leave this room, I intend to put the briefcase inside my suitcase and to lug it around Tasmania until I am confronted by either the woman or the author, as will surely happen if no one calls on me during the next few hours.)

Why did the woman bring me the briefcase? Who is the woman

and what is her connection with the author of the contents of the briefcase?

I list my answers to these questions in the order in which they occur to me and not in the order of their likely accuracy.

The author of the pages sent them to me out of gratitude. One or another of my books of fiction, when decoded, had caused the three-year-old colt World Light to come from last on the turn and to win the renowned Stanley Plate, run over nine furlongs at set weights on the Merlynston Racecourse at Inverbervie (second city of New Arcadia; population 200,000).

The author of the pages sent them to me because he wanted to meet me. He had come to believe that I was ready to be converted to his own way of life. Something that I had written or something that I had said in one or another interview had persuaded him that I would be happier decoding and gutting texts than writing them.

The author of the pages wanted to meet me in order to persuade me to write a different sort of fiction in the future. He would never dare to think of interfering in the multitude of possibilities that might affect the running of any race in New Arcadia in the future, but he had observed certain things in all the years while he had been decoding and gutting texts. He would like to suggest to me that a few changes to my way of writing the texts that would later be published as books might one day result in a few more races in New Arcadia ending with what are called by race commentators blanket finishes.

The author of the pages in the briefcase is not a man of my own age, a bachelor who had worked all his life as a teacher in primary schools. The author of the pages is the woman who brought the briefcase to my room for some purpose that I cannot as yet divine.

I have read many texts during my lifetime: many more texts than I have written. Whenever I have read any text, I have had in my mind an image of the personage who caused the text to come into existence: the implied author, as I call him or her. The ghostly outline of this personage has arisen in my mind as a result of my having read certain details in the text. While reading many a text, I have begun to mistrust and to dislike the implied author. As soon as I have begun to do this, I have stopped reading the text. While reading other texts, I have begun to like and to trust the implied author. When I have begun to do this, I have gone on reading and have sometimes felt so close to the implied author that I seem to have understood why he or she wrote the text that I was reading. While I was reading the pages in the briefcase, I seemed to understand that the implied author of the pages—the person in my mind who had written the pages—had written the pages in order to cause to arise in the mind of one or another reader of the pages one or another image of a personage who would seem to the reader more likeable and more trustworthy than any person in the place where the reader was reading.

I have trusted for many years that I will remember from every text that I read the few words or phrases that I need to remember. I remember now the names of the owners and the trainer of the winner of a maiden race in a certain year at Cleveland (population 60,000; chief city of the midlands district of New Arcadia). The colours carried by the horse were an unusual combination: grey and white. The owners were J. Brenzaida and F. de Samara. The trainer was Ms A. G. Almeida.

The text ends at this point.

Invisible Yet Enduring Lilacs

I first read part of the novel *À la recherche du temps perdu*, translated into English by C. K. Scott Moncrieff, in January 1961, when I was aged a few weeks less than twenty-two years. What I read at that time was a single paperback volume with the title *Swann's Way*. I suspect today that I did not know in 1961 that the volume I was reading was part of a much larger book.

As I write these words in June 1989, I cannot cite the publication details of the paperback volume of *Swann's Way*. I have not seen the volume for at least six years, although it lies only a few metres above my head, in the space between the ceiling and the tiled roof of my house, where I store in black plastic bags the unwanted books of the household.

I first read the whole of *À la recherche du temps perdu*, in the Scott Moncrieff translation, during the months from February to May in 1973, when I was thirty-four years old. What I read at that time was the twelve-volume hardcover edition published by Chatto and Windus in 1969. As I write these words, the twelve volumes of that edition rest on one of the bookshelves of my house.

I read a second time the same twelve-volume edition during the months from October to December 1982, when I was forty-three years old. Since December 1982, I have not read any volume by Marcel Proust.

Although I cannot remember the publication details of the volume of *Swann's Way* that I read in 1961, I seem to remember from the colours of the cover a peculiar brown with a hint of underlying gold.

Somewhere in the novel, the narrator writes that a book is a jar of precious essences recalling the hour when we first handled its cover. I had better explain that a jar of essences, precious or otherwise, would be of small interest to me. I happen to have been born without a sense of smell. That sense which is said by many persons to be the most strongly linked to memory is a sense that I have never been able to use. However, I do have a rudimentary sense of taste, and when I see in my mind today the cover of the paperback of *Swann's Way* that I read in 1961, I taste in my mind tinned sardines, the product of Portugal.

In January 1961, I lived alone in a rented room in Wheatland Road, Malvern. The room had a gas ring and a sink but no refrigerator. Whenever I shopped, I looked for foods that were sold in tins, needed no preparation, and could be stored at room temperature. When I began to read the first pages of Proust's fiction, I had just opened the first tin of sardines that I had bought—a product of Portugal—and had emptied the contents over two slices of dry bread. Being hungry and anxious not to waste anything that had cost me money, I ate all of this meal while I read from the book propped open in front of me.

For an hour after I had eaten my meal, I felt a growing but still bearable discomfort. But as I read on, my stomach became more and more offended by what I had forced into it. At about the time when I was reading of how the narrator had tasted a mouthful of cake mixed with tea and had been overcome by an exquisite sensation, the taste of the dry bread mixed with the sardine oil was so strong in my mouth that I was overcome by nausea.

During the twenty or so years from 1961 until my paperback *Swann's Way* was enclosed in black plastic and stored above my ceiling, I would feel in my mind at least a mild flatulence whenever I handled the book, and I would see again in my mind, whenever I noticed the hint of gold in the brown, the light from the electric globe above me glinting in the film of oil left behind after I had rubbed my crusts around my dinner plate in my rented room in Malvern on a summer evening in 1961.

While I was writing the previous sentence, I saw in my mind an image of a bed of tall flowers near a stone wall which is the wall of a house on its shaded side.

I would like to be sure that the image of the tall flowers and the stone wall first appeared in my mind while I was reading *Swann's Way* in 1961, but I can be sure of no more than that I see those flowers and that wall in my mind whenever I try to remember myself first reading the prose fiction of Marcel Proust. I am not writing today about a book or even about my reading of a book. I am writing about images that appear in my mind whenever I try to remember my having read that book.

The image of the flowers is an image of the blooms of the Russell lupins that I saw in an illustration on a packet of seeds in 1948, when I was nine years old. I had asked my mother to buy the seeds because I wanted to make a flower-bed among the patches of dust and gravel and the clumps of spear grass around the rented weatherboard house at 244 Neale Street, Bendigo, which I used to see in my mind continually during the years from 1966 to 1971, while I was writing about the house at 42 Leslie Street, Bassett, in my book of fiction *Tamarisk Row*.

I planted the seeds in the spring of 1948. I watered the bed and tended the green plants that grew from the seeds. However, the spring of 1948 was the season when my father decided suddenly to move from Bendigo and when I was taken across the Great Divide and the Western Plains to a rented weatherboard cottage near the Southern Ocean in the district of Allansford before I could compare whatever flowers might have appeared on my plants with the coloured illustration on the packet of seeds.

While I was writing the previous paragraph, a further detail appeared in the image of the garden beside the wall in my mind. I now see in the garden in my mind an image of a small boy with dark hair. The boy is staring and listening. I understand today that the image of the boy would first have appeared in my mind at some time during the five months before January 1961 and soon after I had looked for the first time at a photograph taken in the year 1910 in the grounds of a State school near the Southern Ocean in the district of Allansford. The district of Allansford is the district where my father was born and where my father's parents lived for forty years until the death of my father's father in 1949 and where I spent my holidays as a child.

The photograph is of the pupils of the school assembled in rows beside a garden bed where the taller plants might be delphiniums or even Russell lupins. Among the smallest children in the front row, a dark-haired boy aged six years stares towards the camera and turns his head slightly as though afraid of missing some word or some signal from his elders and his betters. The staring and listening boy of 1910 became in time the man who became my father twenty-nine years after the photograph had been taken and who died in August 1960, two weeks before I looked for the first time at the photograph, which my father's mother had kept for fifty years in her collection of photographs, and five months before I read for the first time the volume *Swann's Way* in the paperback edition with the brownish cover.

During his lifetime my father read a number of books, but even if my father had been alive in January 1961, I would not have talked to him about *Swann's Way*. Whenever my father and I had talked about books during the last five years of his life, we had quarrelled. If my father had been alive in January 1961 and if he had seen me reading *Swann's Way*, he would have asked me first what sort of man the author was.

Whenever my father had asked me such a question in the five years before he died in 1960, I had answered him in the way that I thought would be most likely to annoy him. In January 1961, when I was reading *Swann's Way* for the first time, I knew hardly anything about the author. Since 1961, however, I have read two biographies of Marcel Proust, one by André Maurois and one by George D. Painter. Today, Monday 3 July 1989, I am able to compose the answer that would have been most likely to annoy my father if he had asked me his question in January 1961.

My father's question: What sort of man was the author of that book? My answer: The author of this book was an effeminate, hypochondriac Frenchman who mixed mostly with the upper classes, who spent most of his life indoors, and who was never obliged to work for his living.

My father is now annoyed, but he has a second question: What do I hope to gain from reading a book by such a man?

In order to answer this question truthfully, I would have to speak to my father about the thing that has always mattered most to me. I would never have spoken about this thing to my father during his lifetime, partly because I did not understand at that time what the thing is that has always mattered most to me and partly because I preferred not to speak to my father about things that mattered to me. However, I am going to answer my father truthfully today.

I believe today, Monday 3 July 1989, that the thing that has always mattered most to me is a place. Occasionally during my life I may have seemed to believe that I might arrive at this place by travelling to one or another district of the country in which I was born or even to some other country, but for most of my life I have supposed that the place that matters most to me is a place in my mind and that I ought to think not of myself arriving in the future at the place but of myself in the future seeing the place more clearly than I can see any other image in my mind and seeing also that all the other images that matter to me are arranged around that image of a place like an arrangement of townships on a map.

My father might be disappointed to learn that the place that matters most to me is a district of my mind rather than a district of the country where he and I were born, but he might be pleased to learn that I have often supposed that the place in my mind is grassy countryside with a few trees in the distance.

From the time when I first began as a child to read books of fiction, I looked forward to seeing places in my mind as a result of my reading. On a hot afternoon in January 1961, I read in *Swann's Way* a certain place-name. I remember today, Tuesday 4 July 1989, my feeling when I read that place-name more than twenty-eight years ago, something of the joy that the narrator of *Swann's Way* describes himself as having felt whenever he discovered part of the truth underlying the surface of his life. I will come back to that place-name later and by a different route.

If my father could tell me what mattered most to him during his lifetime, he would probably tell me about two dreams that he dreamed often during his lifetime. The first was a dream of himself owning a sheep or cattle property; the second was a dream of his winning regularly large sums of money from bookmakers at race meetings. My father might even tell me about a single dream that arose out of the other two dreams. This was a dream of his setting out one morning from his sheep or cattle property with his own racehorse and with a trusted friend and of his travelling a hundred miles and more to a racecourse on the edge of an unfamiliar town and there backing his horse with large sums of money and soon afterwards watching his horse win the race that he had been backed to win.

If I could ask my father whether the dreams that mattered to him were connected with any images that appeared in his mind as a result of his reading books of fiction, my father might remind me that he had once told me that his favourite book of fiction was a book by a South African writer, Stuart Cloete, about a farmer and his sons who drove their herds of cattle and flocks of sheep out of the settled districts of southern Africa and north-west into what seemed to them endless unclaimed grazing lands.

One of my feelings while I read certain pages of *Swann's Way* in January 1961 was a feeling that my father would have agreed with. I resented the characters' having so much leisure for talking about such things as painting and the architecture of churches.

Although January 1961 was part of my summer holidays, I was already preparing to teach a class of forty-eight primary-school children as from February and to study two subjects at university during my evenings. The characters in *Swann's Way* mostly seemed to lead idle lives or even to enjoy the earnings of inherited wealth. I would have liked to frogmarch the idle characters out of their salons and to confine them each to a room with only a sink and a gas ring and a few pieces of cheap furniture. I would then have enjoyed hearing the idlers calling in vain for their servants.

I heard myself jeering at the idlers. What? Not talking about the Dutch Masters, or about little churches in Normandy with something of the Persian about them?

Sometimes while I read the early pages of *Swann's Way* in 1961, and when I still thought the book was partly a fictional memoir, I took a strong dislike to the pampered boy who had been the narrator as a child. I saw myself dragging him out of the arms of his mother and away from his aunts and his grandmother and then thrusting him into the backyard of the tumbledown farm-workers' cottage where my family lived after we had left Bendigo, putting an axe into his hand, pointing out to him one of the heaps of timber that I had split into kindling wood for the kitchen stove, and then hearing the namby-pamby bleating for his mama.

In 1961, whenever I heard in my mind the adult characters of *Swann's Way* talking about art or literature or architecture I heard them talking in the language used by the gentlemen and lady members of the Metropolitan Golf Club in North Road, Oakleigh, where I had worked as a caddy and an assistant barman from 1954 to 1956.

In the 1950s, there were still people in Melbourne who seemed to want you to believe that they had been born or educated in England or that they had visited England often or that they thought and behaved as English people did. These people in Melbourne spoke with what I would call a world-weary drawl. I heard that drawl by day from men in plus-four trousers while I trudged behind them down fairways on Saturday and Sunday afternoons. In the evenings of those days, I heard the same drawl in the bar of the golf club where the same men, now dressed in slacks and blazers, drank Scotch whisky or gin-and-tonic.

One day soon after I had first begun working at the Metropolitan Golf Club, I looked into a telephone directory for the addresses of some of the most outrageous drawlers. I found not only that most of them lived in the suburb of Toorak, but that most of this majority lived in the same neighbourhood, which consisted of St Georges Road, Lansell Road, and a few adjoining streets.

Six years after I learned this, and only a few months before I first read *Swann's Way*, I travelled a little out of my way one afternoon between the city and Malvern. On that fine spring afternoon, I looked from a window of a tram down each of St Georges Road and Lansell Road, Toorak. I got an impression of tall, pale-coloured houses surrounded by walled gardens in which the trees were just coming into flower.

While I read *Swann's Way* in 1961, any reference to Paris caused me to see in my mind the pale-coloured walls and mansions of St Georges Road and Lansell Road. When I first read the word *faubourg*, which I had never previously read but the meaning of which I guessed, I saw the upper half of a prunus tree appearing from behind a tall wall of cream-coloured stone. The first syllable of the word *faubourg* was linked with the abundant frothiness of the pink flowers on the tree, while the second syllable suggested the solid, forbidding wall. If I read a reference to some public garden or some woods in Paris, I saw in my mind the landscape that I connected with the world-weary drawlers of Melbourne: the view through the plate-glass windows of the dining room and bar in the clubhouse of the Metropolitan Golf Club—the view of the undulating, velvety eighteenth green and the close-mown fairway of cushiony couch grass reaching back between stands of gum trees and wattle trees to the point where the trees almost converged behind the eighteenth tee, leaving a gap past which the hazy seventeenth fairway formed the further part of the twofold vista.

My father despised the drawlers of Melbourne, and if ever he had read about such a character as Monsieur Swann, my father would have despised him also as a drawler. I found myself, at the Metropolitan Golf Club in the 1950s, wanting to distinguish between the drawlers that I could readily despise and a sort of drawler that I was ready to respect, if only I could have learned certain things about him.

The drawlers that I could readily despise were such as the greyhaired man that I heard one day drawling his opinion of an American film or play that he had seen recently. The man lived in one of the two roads that I named earlier and was wealthy as a result of events that had happened before his birth in places far from the two roads. The chief of these events were the man's greatgrandfather's having brewed and then peddled on the goldfields of Victoria in the 1860s an impressively named but probably ineffective patent medicine.

The American film or play that the drawler had seen was named *The Moon Is Blue*. I had learned previously from newspapers that some people in Melbourne had wanted *The Moon Is Blue* to be banned, as many films and plays and books were banned in Melbourne in the 1950s. The people had wanted it banned because it was said to contain jokes with double meanings.

The drawler had said to three other men, while the four were walking among the complex arrangement of vistas of green fairways that I would later see in my mind from 1961 onwards whenever I would read in one or another volume of *À la recherche du temps perdu* the name of one or another wood or park in Paris,

"I've never laughed so much in my whole life. It was absolutely the funniest show I've ever seen!"

On the afternoon nearly forty years ago when I heard the grey-haired drawler drawl those words, I readily despised him because I was disappointed to learn that a man who had inherited a fortune and who might have taken his pleasure from the ownership of a vast library or a stable of racehorses could boast of having sniggered at what my school-friends and I would have called dirty jokes.

Six or seven years later, when I read for the first time about Swann, the descendant of stockbrokers, and his passion for Odette de Crecy, I saw that the Swann in my mind had the grey hair and wore the plus-four trousers of the great-grandson of the brewer and peddler of patent medicines.

The Swann in my mind was not usually one of the *despised* drawlers. Sometimes at the Metropolitan Golf Club, but more often when I looked at the owners of racehorses in the mounting yard of one or another racecourse, I saw a sort of drawler that I admired. This drawler might have lived for some time during each year behind a walled garden in Melbourne, but at other times he lived surrounded by the land that had been since the years before the discovery of gold in Victoria the source of his family's wealth and standing—he lived on his sheep or cattle property.

In my seventh book of fiction, *O, Dem Golden Slippers*, which I expect to be published during 1993, I will explain something of what has happened in the mind of a person such as myself whenever he has happened to see in the mounting yard of a racecourse in any of the towns or cities of Victoria an owner of a racehorse who is also the owner of a sheep or cattle property far from that town or city. Here I have time only to explain first that for most of my life I have seen most of the sheep or cattle properties in my mind as lying in the district of Victoria in my mind that is sometimes called the Western Plains. When I look towards that district in my mind while I write these words, I look towards the north-west of my mind. However, when I used to stand on the Warrnambool racecourse during my summer holidays in the 1950s, which is to say, when I stood in those days at a point nearly three hundred kilometres south-west of where I sit at this moment, I still saw often in the north-west of my mind sheep or cattle properties far from where I stood, and doubly far from where I sit today writing these words.

Today, 26 July 1989, I looked at a map of the southern part of Africa. I wanted to verify that the districts where the chief character in my father's favourite book of fiction arrived with his flocks and herds at what might be called his sheep or cattle property would have been in fact north-west of the settled districts. After having looked at the map, I now believe that the owner of the flocks and herds was more likely to have travelled north-east. That being so, when my father said that the man in southern Africa had travelled north-west in order to discover the site of his sheep or cattle property, my father perhaps had in mind that the whole of Africa was north-west of the suburb of Oakleigh South, where my father and I lived at the time when he told me about his favourite book of fiction, so that anyone travelling in any direction in Africa was travelling towards a place north-west of my father and myself, and any character in a book of fiction who was described as having travelled in any direction in Africa would have seemed to my father to have travelled towards a place in the north-west of my father's mind. Or, my father, who was born and who lived for much of his life in the south-east of Australia, may have seen all desirable places in his mind as lying in the north-west of his mind.

Before I mentioned just now the map of the southern part of Africa, I was about to mention the second of two things connected with my seeing on racecourses the owners of distant sheep or cattle properties. I was about to mention the first of those owners that I can recall having seen. The owner and his horse and the trainer of his horse had come to the summer meeting at Warrnambool, in one of the early years of the 1950s, from the district around Apsley. At that time I had seen one photograph of the district around Apsley: a coloured photograph on the cover of the *Leader*, which was once the chief rival of the *Weekly Times* for the readership of persons in rural Victoria. The photograph showed grassy country-side with a few trees in the distance. Something in the colours of the photograph had caused me to remember it afterwards as having been taken during the late afternoon.

The only map that I owned in the 1950s was a road map of Victoria. When I looked at that map, I saw that Apsley was the furthest west of any town in the Western District of Victoria. Past Apsley was only a pale no-man's-land—the first few miles of South Australia—and then the end of the map.

The man from the district around Apsley stood out among the owners in the mounting yard. He wore a pale-grey suit and a pale-grey hat with green and blue feathers in the band. Under the rear brim of his hat, his silvery hair was bunched in a style very different from the cropped style of the men around him. As soon as I had seen the man from the district around Apsley, I had heard him in my mind speaking in a world-weary drawl but I was far from despising him.

I have always become alert whenever I have read in a book of fiction a reference to a character's country estates. The ownership of a country estate has always seemed to me to add a further layer to a person: to suggest, as it were, far-reaching vistas within the person. "You see me here, among these walls of pale stone topped by pink blossoms," I hear the person saying, "and you think of the places in my mind as being only the streets of this suburb—or this *faubourg*. You have not seen yet, at a further place in my mind, the leafy avenue leading to the circular driveway surrounding the vast lawn; the mansion whose upper windows overlook grassy countryside with a few trees in the distance, or a stream that is marked on certain mornings and evenings by strands of mist."

I read in *Swann's Way* during January 1961 that Swann was the owner of a park and a country house along one of the two ways where the narrator and his parents went walking on Sundays.

According to my memory, I learned at first that Swann's park was bounded on one side at least by a white fence behind which grew numerous lilacs of both the white-flowering and the mauve-flowering varieties. Before I had read about that park and those lilacs, I had seen Swann in my mind as the drawler in plus-four trousers that I described earlier. After I had read about the white fence and the white and lilac-coloured flowers, I saw in my mind a different Swann.

As anyone who has read my first book of fiction, *Tamarisk Row*, will know, the chief character of that book builds his first racecourse and first sees in his mind the district of Tamarisk Row while he kneels in the dirt under a lilac tree. As anyone will know who has read the piece "First Love" in my sixth book of fiction, *Velvet Waters*, the chief character of "First Love" decides, after many years of speculating about the matter, that his racing colours are lilac and brown. After I had first read about the park and the lilacs at Combray, I remembered having read earlier in *Swann's Way* that Swann was a good friend of the Prince of Wales and a member of the Jockey Club. After I had remembered this, I saw Swann in my mind as having the suit and the hat and the bunched silver hair beneath the brim of his hat of the man from Apsley, far to the north-west of Warrnambool. I decided that Swann's racing colours would have been a combination of white and lilac. In 1961 when I decided this, the only set of white and lilac colours that I had seen had been carried by a horse named Parentive, owned and trained by a Mr A. C. Gartner. I noticed today what I believe I had not previously noticed: although the one occasion when I saw the horse Parentive race was a Saturday at Caulfield Racecourse at some time during the late 1950s, Mr Gartner and his horse came from Hamilton, which, of course, is north-west from where I sit now and on the way to Apsley.

One detail of my image of Monsieur Swann, the owner of race-horses, changed a few months later. In July 1961, I became the owner of a small book illustrated with reproductions of some of the works of the French artist Raoul Dufy. After I had seen the

gentlemen in the mounting yards of the racecourses in those illustrations, I saw above the bunched silvery hair of Monsieur
Swann in my mind not a grey hat with blue and green feathers but
a black top hat.

I first read the first of the twelve volumes of the 1969 Chatto
and Windus edition of *À la recherche du temps perdu*, as I wrote
earlier, in the late summer and the autumn of 1973, when I was
thirty-four years of age. On a hot morning while I was still reading the first volume, I was lying with the book beside me on a patch
of grass in my backyard in a north-eastern suburb of Melbourne.
While my eyes were closed for a moment against the glare of the
sun, I heard the buzzing of a large fly in the grass near my ear.

Somewhere in *À la recherche du temps perdu*, I seem to remember, is a short passage about the buzzing of flies on warm mornings, but even if that passage is in the part of the text that I had
read in 1961, I did not recall my having previously read about the
buzzing of flies in Marcel Proust's texts when the large fly buzzed
in the grass near my ear in the late summer of 1973. What I recalled at that moment was one of those parcels of a few moments
of seemingly lost time that the narrator of *À la recherche du temps
perdu* warns us never deliberately to go in search of. The parcel
came to me, of course, not as a quantity of something called time,
whatever that may be, but as a knot of feelings and sensations that
I had long before experienced and had not since recalled.

The sensations that had been suddenly restored to me were
those that I had experienced as a boy of fifteen years walking alone
in the spacious garden of the house belonging to the widowed
mother of my father in the city of Warrnambool in the south-west
of Victoria on a Saturday morning of my summer holidays. The
feelings that had been suddenly restored to me were feelings of expectancy and joy. On the Saturday morning in January 1954, I had
heard the buzzing of a large fly while I had been looking at a bush
of tiger lilies in bloom.

As I write this on 28 July 1989, I notice for the first time that the
colour of the tiger lilies in my mind resembles the colour of the

cover of the biography of Marcel Proust by André Maurois that I quoted from in my fifth book of fiction, *Inland*. The passage that I quoted from in that book includes the phrase *invisible yet enduring lilacs*, and I have just now understood that that phrase ought to be the title of this piece of writing . . . *Invisible Yet Enduring Lilacs*.

My book *Inland* includes a passage about tiger lilies that I wrote while I saw in my mind the blooms on the bush of tiger lilies that I was looking at when I heard the large fly buzzing in January 1954.

I had felt expectancy and joy on the Saturday morning in January 1954 because I was going to go later on that day to the so-called summer meeting at Warrnambool racecourse. Although I was already in love with horse-racing, I was still a schoolboy and seldom had the money or the time for going to race meetings. On that Saturday morning, I had never previously been to a race meeting at Warrnambool. The buzzing of the fly was connected in my mind with the heat of the afternoon to come and with the dust and the dung in the saddling paddock. I had felt a particular expectancy and joy on that morning while I had pronounced to myself the name *tiger lily* and while I had stared at the colours of the blooms on the bush. The names of the racehorses of the Western District of Victoria and the racing colours of their owners were mostly unknown to me in 1954. On that Saturday morning, I was trying to see in my mind the colours, unfamiliar and striking, carried by some horse that had been brought to Warrnambool from a hundred miles away in the north-west, and I was trying to hear in my mind the name of that horse.

During the morning in the late summer of 1973 when I heard the buzzing of the large fly soon after I had begun to read the first of the twelve volumes of *À la recherche du temps perdu*, the feelings that came back to me from the Saturday morning nineteen years before only added to the feelings of expectancy and joy that I had already felt as I had prepared to read the twelve volumes. On that morning in my backyard in 1973, I had been aware for twelve years that one of the important place-names in À *la recherche du temps perdu* had the power to bring to my mind details of a place such as I had wanted to see in my mind during most of my life. That place was a country estate in my mind. The owner of the estate spent his mornings in his library, where the windows overlooked grassy countryside with a few trees in the distance, and his afternoons exercising his racehorses. Once each week, he travelled a hundred miles and more with one of his horses and with his distinctive silk racing colours south-east to a race meeting.

At some time during 1949, several years before I had attended any race-meeting or had heard the name of Marcel Proust, my father told me that he had carved his name at two places in the sandstone that underlies the district of Allansford where he was born and where his remains have lain buried since 1960. The first of the two places was a pinnacle of rock standing high out of the water in the bay known as Childers Cove. My father told me in 1949 that he had once swum through the fifty yards of turbulent water between the shore and Steeple Rock with a tomahawk tied to his body and had carved his name and the date on the side of Steeple Rock that faced the Southern Ocean. The second of the two places was the wall of a quarry on a hill overlooking the bays of the Southern Ocean known as Stanhopes' Bay, Sandy Bay, and Murnane's Bay, just south-east of Childers Cove.

During the first twenty-five years after my father had died, I thought about neither of the two places where he had once carved his name. Then, in 1985, twenty-five years after my father had died, and while I was writing a piece of fiction about a man who had read a story about a man who thought often about the bedrock far beneath his feet, an image of a stone quarry came into my mind and I wrote that the father of the narrator of the story had carved his name on the wall of a quarry, and I gave the title "Stone Quarry" to my piece of fiction, which until then had lacked a title.

At some time during the spring of 1985 and while I was still writing "Stone Quarry," I received through the post a page of the *Warrnambool Standard* illustrated by two reproductions of photographs. The first of the two photographs was of Childers Cove as it had appeared for as long as European persons had looked at it, with Steeple Rock standing out of the water fifty metres from shore and the Southern Ocean in the background. The second photograph showed Childers Cove as it has appeared since the day or the night in 1985 when waves of the Southern Ocean caused Steeple Rock to topple and the surfaces of sandstone where my father had carved his name to sink beneath the water.

In the autumn of 1989, while I was making notes for this piece of writing but before I had thought of mentioning my father in the writing, a man who was about to travel with a camera from Melbourne to the district of Allansford offered to bring back to me photographs of any places that I might wish to see in photographs.

I gave the man directions for finding the quarry on the hill overlooking the Southern Ocean and asked him to look on the walls of the quarry for the inscription that my father had told me forty years before that he had carved.

Two days ago, on 28 July 1989, while I was writing the earlier passage that has to do with the buzzing of a fly near a bush of tiger lilies at Warrnambool in 1954, I found among the mail that had just arrived at my house a coloured photograph of an area of sandstone in which four letters and four numerals are visible. The four numerals 1-9-2-1 allow me to believe that my father stood in front of the area of sandstone in the year 1921, when he was aged seventeen years and when Marcel Proust was aged fifty years, as I am today, and had one year of his life remaining. The four letters allow me to believe that my father in 1921 carved in the sandstone the first letter of the first of his given names followed by all the letters of his surname but that rainwater running down the wall of the quarry caused part of the sandstone to break off and to fall away at some time during the sixty-eight years between

1921 and 1989, leaving only the letter *R* for *Reginald* followed by the first three letters of my father's and my surname.

I have a number of photographs of myself standing in one or another garden and in front of one or another wall, but the earliest of these photographs shows me standing, in the year 1940, on a patch of grass in front of a wall of sandstone that is part of a house on its sunlit side. The wall that I mentioned earlier—the wall that appears as an image in my mind together with the image of a small boy and the image of a bed of tall flowers whenever I try to imagine myself first reading the first pages of *À la recherche du temps perdu*—is not the same wall that appears in bright sunlight in the photograph of myself in 1940. The wall in my mind is a wall of the same house that I stood beside on a day of sunshine in 1940, but the wall in my mind is a wall on the shaded side of the house. (I have already explained that the image of the boy in my mind is an image of a boy who was first photographed thirty years before the day of sunshine in 1940.)

The house with the walls of sandstone was built by my father's father less than one kilometre from where the Southern Ocean forms the bay known as Sandy Bay, which is next to the bays known as Murnane's Bay and Childers Cove on the south-west coast of Victoria. All the walls of the house were quarried from the place where the surname of the boy who appears in my mind as listening and staring whenever I remember myself first reading about Combray now appears as no more than the letters MUR . . . the root in the Latin language, the language of my father's religion, of the word for *wall*.

At the summer race meeting at Warrnambool racecourse in January 1960, which was the last summer meeting before the death of my father and the second-last summer meeting before my first reading the first part of *À la recherche du temps perdu*, I read in my racebook the name of a racehorse from far to the north-west of Warrnambool. The name was a place-name consisting of two words. The first of the two was a word that I had never previously read but a word that I supposed was from the French language.

The second word was the word *Bay*. The colours to be worn by the rider of the horse were brown and white stripes.

I found the name and the colours of the horse peculiarly attractive. During the afternoon, I looked forward to seeing the owner of the horse and his colours in the mounting yard. However, when the field was announced for the race in which the horse had been entered, I learned that the horse had been scratched.

During the twelve months following that race meeting, I often pronounced in my mind the name of the racehorse with the name ending in the word *Bay*. During the same time, I often saw in my mind the brown and white colours carried by the horse. During the same time also, I saw in my mind images of a sheep or cattle property in the far west of Victoria in my mind (that is, north-west of the south-west of Victoria in my mind) and of the owner of the property, who lived in a house with a vast library. However, none of the images of the sheep or cattle property or of the owner of the property or of his vast library has appeared in my mind since January 1961, when I read in *Swann's Way* the first of the two words of the horse's name.

In January 1961, I learned from the paperback volume with the title *Swann's Way* that the word that I had previously known only as part of the name of a racehorse that had been entered in a race at Warrnambool racecourse, as though its owner and its trainer were going to bring the horse out of the north-west in the same way that the horse had been brought in the dream that had mattered most to my father, was the name of one of the places that mattered most to the narrator of *Swann's Way* from among the places around Combray, where he spent his holidays in each year of his childhood.

After I had learned this, I saw in my mind whenever I said to myself the name of the horse that had not arrived at Warrnambool racecourse from the north-west, or whenever I saw in my mind a silk jacket with brown and white stripes, a stream flowing through grassy countryside with trees in the background. I saw the stream at one point flowing past a quiet reach that I called in my mind a bay.

A bay in a stream might have seemed a geographical absurdity, but I saw in my mind the calm water, the green rushes, the green grass in the fields behind the rushes. I saw in the green fields in my mind the white fence topped by the white and lilac flowers of the lilac bushes on the estate of the man with the bunched silvery hair who had named one of his racehorses after a geographical absurdity or a proper noun in the works of Marcel Proust. I saw, at the place named Apsley in my mind, far to the north-west of Warrnambool in my mind, enduring lilacs that had previously been invisible.

At some time during the seven years since I last read the whole of *À la recherche du temps perdu*, I looked into my *Times Atlas of the World* and learned that the racehorse whose name I had read in the racebook at Warrnambool twelve months before I first read *Swann's Way* had almost certainly not been named after any geographical feature in France or after any word in the works of Marcel Proust but had almost certainly been named after a bay on the south coast of Kangaroo Island, off the coast of South Australia.

Since my having learned that the horse that failed to arrive from the north-west at Warrnambool racecourse in the last summer of my father's life and the last summer before I first read the fiction of Marcel Proust was almost certainly named after a bay on Kangaroo Island, I have sometimes seen in my mind, soon after I have pronounced in my mind the name of the horse or soon after I have seen in my mind a silk jacket with brown and white stripes, waves of the Southern Ocean rolling from far away in the direction of South Africa, rolling past Kangaroo Island towards the south-west coast of Victoria, and breaking against the base of Steeple Rock in Childers Cove, near Murnane's Bay, and causing Steeple Rock at last to topple. I have sometimes seen in my mind, soon after Steeple Rock has toppled in my mind, a wall of a stone house and near the wall a small boy who will later, as a young man, choose for his colours lilac from the white and lilac colours of the Monsieur Swann in his mind and brown from the white and brown colours of the racehorse in his mind from far to the north-west of Warrnambool: the racehorse whose name he will read for the first time in a racebook in the last summer before he reads for the first time a book of fiction with the title *Swann's Way*. And I have sometimes seen in my mind, soon after I have seen in my mind the things just mentioned, one or another detail of a place in my mind where I see together things that I might have expected to lie forever far apart; where rows of lilacs appear on a sheep or cattle property; where my father, who had never heard the name *Marcel Proust*, is the narrator of an immense and intricately patterned work of fiction; where a racehorse has for its name the word *Bay* preceded by the word *Vivonne*.

As It Were a Letter

On the day before I began to write this piece of fiction, I received in the post two items from a man who was born when I was already eleven years of age. That man, whose name is not part of this piece of fiction, has the same urge that Vladimir Nabokov attributed to himself in the early pages of his book *Speak, Memory*: the urge to learn more and more about the years just before his conception and birth. The man often questions me about what I remember from the eleven years when I was alive and he was not. The man claims that what I tell him adds to the sum of what he knows about himself.

The first of the two items sent by the man was a clipping from a recent edition of a Melbourne newspaper that I do not read. The clipping consisted of a feature article and a reproduction of a photograph. The author of the feature article was, I supposed, a reader of the newspaper who had written the article and offered it for publication to make known the forthcoming celebration of the fiftieth anniversary of the founding, in the year when I became eleven years of age and the sender of the clipping was born, of a communal settlement in a remote district of south-eastern Victoria by a group of Catholic persons who wanted to live self-sufficiently and to bring up their children far from what they, the Catholic persons, considered a corrupt civilisation. The photograph reproduced as an illustration for the article showed about forty persons of all ages and both sexes. The persons seemed to be part of an audience in a hall and to be waiting eagerly to be addressed by someone who had inspired them in the past and was about to do so again.

The second of the two items sent by the man was a note from him to me. In the note, the man told me that he still recalled from time to time a certain few pages in an early book of fiction of mine. In those pages, the chief character of the fiction was reported as having visited, at some time in the early 1950s, a place called Mary's Mount in the Otway Ranges, in south-western Victoria. The place was a communal settlement founded by a group of Catholic persons, and the chief character found everything about the place inspiring. The man told me further that he had sometimes wondered whether or not this passage of fiction had been based on an actual experience of mine. Now, the man told me, he believed he had discovered the original, as he called it, of the place in the Otway Ranges of my fiction. He had been struck, wrote the man, by the similarity between the name of the place in my fiction and the name of the place in the feature article. He concluded, so the man wrote, that I had varied the name slightly and had moved the place, as he put it, to the opposite side of the state of Victoria.

Within an hour after I had read what the man had written, I had begun to make notes and to write the first draft of this piece of fiction. Then, although I understood that the man who had sent me the newspaper clipping might be only a minor character in this piece of fiction, I found myself making notes about him for including in the fiction.

Since the previous sentence is part of a piece of fiction, the reader will hardly need to be reminded that the man mentioned in that sentence and in earlier sentences is a character in a work of fiction and that the newspaper clipping and the note mentioned in some of those sentences are likewise items in a piece of fiction.

While I made the notes mentioned above, I first noted that the man is himself the author of published pieces of fiction. I noted this in order to remind myself of the only conversation that the man and I had had about the writing of fiction. During that conversation, the man and I had agreed that the chief benefit to be got from the writing of a piece of fiction was that the writer of the fiction discovered at least once during the writing of the fiction a connection between two or more images that had been for long in his mind but had never seemed in any way connected.

I noted further, in my notes for my piece of fiction, that the man in question had at one time begun but had soon afterwards given up a course for the degree of Bachelor of Laws in a university and had often afterwards made remarks that caused me to suppose he held in contempt the persons who are sometimes called collectively the legal profession.

I noted further in the notes that later became part of this piece of fiction that the man who is now a character in this piece of fiction had become, when he was a young man, the owner of a guitar and that he had played his guitar often since then. The man owned many books of music for the guitar and many books about famous players of the guitar and many recordings of guitar music. The man had sometimes played his guitar in my hearing, although I had told him politely when I had first seen his guitar that I consider myself a musical person but that I have never been inspired by any sound of strings being plucked or otherwise handled.

I noted further in my notes that the man had at one time taken a course of lessons in the Spanish language and had told me at the time that he found the sound of the language inspiring. When I was making that note, I recalled for the first time in many years that I had spent more than a few hours at the age of eleven in looking through a newspaper printed in the Spanish language.

Towards the end of my notes, I noted that I had sometimes

admired the subject of the notes as a result of my suspecting that he had been connected sexually with many more women than I had been, even though I had been alive for eleven more years than he had been.

I noted finally in my notes that the man had been for many years the owner of forty-five hectares of virgin bushland in the Otway Ranges and that he had sometimes told me that if only he could have found what he called the right sort of woman, he would have built on his bushland property a simple but comfortable house and would have moved there with the woman and afterwards lived what he called his ideal life.

I did not note as part of my final note, but I note here that I have never visited the Otway Ranges or wanted to visit them. I once wrote a passage of fiction the setting of which was a place in the Otway Ranges, but I have written many pieces of fiction the settings of which are places where I have never been.

After I had finished the notes mentioned above, I looked into the illustration of the persons who seemed to be waiting in a hall for the person who inspired them from time to time. I was looking for what I looked for whenever I looked into one or another photograph or reproduction of a photograph of persons who had been alive during the first twenty-five years of my own life and who might have lived during those twenty-five years in places such that I might have met up with one or another of the persons while I was living at one or another of the twenty-five and more addresses that I lived at during those twenty-five years and before I decided to live for the remainder of my life at the one address. I was looking for the face of a female person who might have met up with me, or might merely have come to my notice, and whose words or deeds, or whose face observed merely from a distance, might have inspired me to become one of the many persons I might have become and to live for the remainder of my life in one of the many places where I might have lived.

In the illustration that I looked at, the female faces seemed to be those of married women or very young children. (I took no interest in the faces of the two nuns in the front row.) I supposed that the early settlers at the settlement had been families with small children. And then I read the text of the feature article beside the illustration. I found the text sentimental and dishonest, but in order to explain this finding of mine I would have to report certain facts that are not part of this piece of fiction.

After I had done all the things so far reported I made notes for, and later wrote, the following pages, which themselves make up a complete piece of fiction within the whole of this piece of fiction.

I was eleven years of age when I first heard of the settlement that I shall call hereafter Outlands. The settlement was in neither the south-east nor the south-west of Victoria but in the far north-east of the state, and it had already been established for several years before I first heard of it.

When I first heard of Outlands, one month short of fifty years ago, I was already living at a place that had been until recently a sort of settlement founded and managed by a small group of Catholic laypersons who were, in their own way, inspired. This place, which I shall call hereafter the Farm, was in a northern suburb of Melbourne. From the front gate of the Farm I could see, only a short walking distance away, a tram terminus; and yet the suburbs of Melbourne reached in those days so little distance from the city that I could look out from the rear gate of the Farm across a paddock where a few dairy cows had been kept until recently. On either side of this gate were sheds where tools and cattle feed had been stored, and one shed that had been the dairy. Between the sheds and the house was a neglected orchard overgrown with long grass. Where the orchard adjoined the kitchen garden of the house was a small bluestone building that had been the chapel.

I was living at the Farm as a poor relation of the family whose home it then was. That family consisted of an elderly husband and wife, their only son, who was a widower in early middle age, and his only son, who was five years younger than myself. My own family—my parents and my sister—were scattered among relatives and friends because we had no house of our own. A few months before, my parents had had to sell the house they partly owned in a suburb not far from the Farm. They had needed the money to settle my father's debts. He had incurred these debts as a part-time trainer of racehorses and as a punter. When my parents had put up the house for sale, they had believed they could move after the sale to a partly built house in an outer south-eastern suburb. Not all of my father's racing friends were luckless gamblers. One friend was what was called in those days a speculative builder. He was going to let my family live in one of his partly built houses while my father tried to arrange a loan from a building society. But something had delayed this plan, and we found ourselves for the time being homeless. My mother and my sister went to stay with one of my mother's sisters. My father boarded with friends of his. I went to the Farm.

I remember no feelings of misery or even discontent. The Farm was a haven of order and neatness after the latest of the many crises that my father's gambling had caused. I was especially pleased not to have to attend school. I was tired of going to one after another school and being always someone newly arrived or soon to leave while everyone else seemed settled. I arrived at the Farm in the first week of November, and it was decided that I could do without school for the last months of the year. In the main room at the Farm was a tall cupboard full of books. I promised my father when he left me at the Farm that I would read every day, even though he seemed too concerned about his own problems to care how I might spend my time.

I was a relation of the people at the Farm because the widower's dead wife had been one of my father's sisters. I shall call the widower hereafter Nunkie. The name suits my memory of him as being always cheerful and helpful towards his nephew, myself. Nunkie might have been a scholar on the staff of a university if he had been born in a later decade, but he had been obliged during the Great Depression to train as a primary teacher for the Education Department of Victoria. He had met his future wife when he was teaching at the small school near the farm where my father and his sisters grew up. The school had a residence beside it for a married teacher, but Nunkie lived in the residence with his parents. Nunkie's parents had come with their son to the far southwest of Victoria for the time being because the father could no longer get work as a musician in picture theatres after the silent films had been replaced by talkies, and because he had been a reckless gambler on racehorses for as long as he had lived in Melbourne. I shall call this man hereafter the Reformed Gambler, because his years away from Melbourne had apparently reformed him. I never saw him looking at a form guide or listening to a race broadcast while I was at the Farm, and every Saturday he went off to umpire one or another local cricket match.

Nunkie and his mother always seemed united against the Reformed Gambler. The son and the mother mostly ignored him, or, if he tried to break into one of their many long discussions, put him off with short answers.

Every evening the people at the Farm, together with their many visitors, recited the rosary and a portion of the divine office for the day. The Reformed Gambler was obliged to take part in these prayers, although I could see that they bored him. He was a gentle, likeable man whose religious observance consisted of Sunday mass and an occasional confession and communion. One evening, after twenty or thirty minutes of prayer during which the word *Israel* had occurred a number of times (*Remember, O Israel . . . I have judged thee, O Israel . . .* and the like), the Reformed Gambler looked in the direction of his wife and son and asked innocently who was this Israel, anyway: this chap who was always turning up in our prayers.

Much of what I know about the family at the Farm I learned at one or another later time from my father. According to him, the father at the Farm was the salt of the earth, the mother looked down her nose at the world, and the son meant well but had been turned by his mother into an old woman himself. On the evening when the Reformed Gambler had asked who Israel was, I actually saw his wife look down her nose. There is no better form of words to suggest the pose that she struck. Her son, Nunkie, tried to relieve the tension by saying, not directly to his father but into the air, that Israel was not a man but a people, and not even a people but a symbolic people . . .

The Reformed Gambler has no further part in this piece of fiction, but I would like to report here that he lived a long life and that he spent much of his time in later life far from his wife and son and in the company of congenial relatives of his.

The person who looked down her nose sometimes I shall call hereafter the Holy Foundress. I call her this not only because she had founded the Farm, but because I believe she would have been, in many an earlier period of history, the foundress of a religious order dedicated to one or another special task within the Church; would have written without help from any adviser the compendious Rule and Constitution of the Order; would have travelled to Rome under trying conditions; would have gained at last official approval for her new order; and would have died long afterwards in what was called in earlier times the odour of sanctity.

My father had warned me before he left me there that I must not ask questions about what he called past goings-on at the Farm. I asked no questions, but I saw much evidence that the Farm had been, until recently, a small farm with a few dairy cows. I guessed that the cows had been milked and other farming tasks performed by the five or six male persons who had slept in the wing of the house which was obviously a later addition and which Nunkie sometimes called absently the boys' wing. I guessed that the boys, whoever they had been, had attended daily mass every morning in the bluestone chapel that was always locked whenever I tried the door but which Nunkie unlocked for me one afternoon, after I had questioned him about the chapel yet again, so that I was able to look at the empty seats and the bare altar and the cupboard where the priest's vestments had been stored and at the windows of orange-gold frosted glass that made a mystery of each view of trees or sky outside the place.

At the age of eleven, I never doubted that I would live for the rest of my life as a faithful Catholic, but I found it tedious to sit each Sunday in a parish church crowded with parents and their squirming clusters of children; to hear the priest preaching that the parish school needed money for an extra classroom; to read in the Catholic newspaper that the archbishop had made a speech attacking communist-controlled unions after he had blessed and opened a new church school building in a faraway outer suburb where the streets were dust in summer and mud in winter. From here and there in my reading, I had put together a collection of expressions that inspired in me what I supposed were pious feelings: *private oratory*; *private chaplain*; *gothic chasuble*; *jewelled chalice*; *secluded monastery*; *strict observance*. I seem to have been dreaming of a private place where I could enjoy my religion with a few like-minded persons. At the centre of the place was, of course, the oratory or chapel, but I was also concerned that the place should be surrounded by an appropriate landscape.

After I had been at the Farm for a few days, I heard for the first time about Outlands. The day was a Sunday, and a visitor from Outlands had arrived for the midday meal. The visitor was a young man perhaps not yet thirty years of age. He was pale and rather plump, and I was surprised when I learned that he came from a settlement of farmers but very interested when I saw that the newspaper he carried with his luggage was in a foreign language. Before I could learn much about the man or about Outlands, my father arrived to take me for a walk and to tell me news of our family.

While I walked with my father, I tried to learn what he might have known already about the Farm and about Outlands. My father would tell me only that Nunkie and his parents had been very kind to take me in but that I must not let them turn me into a religious maniac. My father, who could well be called for the purposes of this piece of fiction the Unreformed Gambler, was a Catholic in the same way that the Reformed Gambler was a Catholic. My father went to mass every Sunday and to confession and communion once each month and seemed to suspect the motives of any Catholic who did any more than this.

While we walked on the Sunday, my father told me that he knew about Outlands only that it was doomed to fail, just as the Farm had failed. Such places always failed, my father said, because their founders were too fond of giving orders and not prepared to listen to advice. He then told me that the Farm had been intended by its founder, the person called in this fiction the Holy Foundress, to be a place where a few men who had recently completed long terms of imprisonment could live and work and pray while they prepared themselves to find homes and jobs in the world at large. The Farm, my father reminded me, was only a few tram stops away from the large prison where he himself had been a warder when I was born and where he had learned, as all the other warders, his mates, had learned, that almost every person who had been imprisoned for a long term was by nature the sort of person who would be later imprisoned again.

My father had ceased to be a prison warder in one of the first years after I was born, but he had remained friends with many warders. He told me on our Sunday walk, in the streets of the suburb where the Farm was at the end of the tramline that passed the front gate of the large prison, that all the warders who had heard of the founding of the Farm had predicted that the Farm would fail and that the warders' predictions had been fulfilled. The Farm had failed, my father said, because most of the men who had gone from the prison to the Farm had not been reformed but had gone on planning—and even committing—further crimes while they lived at the Farm.

My father told me the story of the Farm with seeming relish, but I tried while he talked to compose in my mind arguments in defence of the Farm. I had lived at the Farm for only a few days, but each morning I had gone with Nunkie and his son, my cousin, and the Holy Foundress to early mass in the semi-public chapel of a nearby convent; each evening I had prayed with the others at dusk in the room where the big bookcase stood; each day I had walked between the fruit trees for ten minutes, imitating the even paces of one or another priest I had once seen walking on the paths around his presbytery while he read the divine office for that day. Perhaps I was discovering the power of ordered behaviour, of ritual. Perhaps I was merely devising for myself one more of the imagined worlds I had devised throughout my childhood. Although I was hardly fond of the Holy Foundress, I admired her for having tried to set up what I thought of as a world of her own, a world apart from or concealed within the drab world that most people inhabited, a small farm almost surrounded by suburbs.

My own imagined worlds before then had been located each on an island of the same shape as Tasmania, which was the only suitable island I knew of. The people of those worlds had been devoted to cricket or to Australian Football or to horse-racing. I had drawn elaborate maps showing where the sportsgrounds or racecourses were situated. I filled pages with coloured illustrations of the football jumpers of the many teams or of the coloured caps of the cricket teams or of the racing silks of the racing stables. I had spent so much time in preparing these preliminary details for each of my imagined worlds that I had seldom got as far as to work out results of imagined football or cricket matches or of imagined horse-races.

I had destroyed or lost all the pages showing the details mentioned above, but sometimes during the year before I arrived at the Farm I had felt a peculiar longing and had wanted my adult life to be so uneventful and my future home to be so quiet and so seldom visited that I could spend most of my life recording the details of an imaginary world a hundred times more complicated than any I had so far imagined.

The people at the Farm seemed not to read newspapers, although I feel sure today that Nunkie and the Reformed Gambler must have looked through the results and reports of cricket matches during the summer. Perhaps they kept the newspaper out of sight of the children, or cut out the sporting pages and burned the rest. When I asked Nunkie, on my first day at the Farm, where the newspaper was, he told me that the people of the Farm were not especially curious about events in the secular world. Nunkie's expression, "the secular world," gave me even then, on my first day, the pleasant sensation that I was inside a world inside what others considered to be the only world.

After Nunkie had answered my request for a newspaper, he had taken me to the bookshelves in the main room at the Farm. He told me I was welcome to read any book from what he called the library, provided that I first sought his approval of my chosen book. I saw names of authors such as Charles Dickens and William Thackeray on some of the nearest books, and I asked Nunkie whether the library contained any modern books. He pointed to a shelf containing many of the works of G. K. Chesterton and Hilaire Belloc.

On the day after Nunkie had shown me the library, I looked more closely at the books. When he arrived home that afternoon from the state school where he taught, I asked him whether I could read a book from an upper shelf: a book the spine of which I had looked at often during that day. The title of the book was *Fifty-two Meditations for the Liturgical Year*.

As soon as I had seen the title mentioned above, I had done, probably for the first time, two things that I have done many times since then: I first imagined the contents of a book of which the title was the only detail known to me; and I then derived from my imagining much more than I later derived from my looking into the text of the book.

I have to remind the reader that this piece of fiction is set in the year 1950. In that year, and for many years afterwards, the word *meditation* denoted only a little of what it has since come to denote. In the year in which I wanted to read the book mentioned above, there were no doubt a few scholars or eccentrics in the city of Melbourne who knew something about meditation as it was practised in so-called eastern religions, but neither Nunkie nor I knew of the existence of those scholars or eccentrics. The only sort of meditation that he or I was aware of was an exercise such as Ignatius Loyola, founder of the Society of Jesus, had devised: an attempt by the person meditating to bring to mind as clearly as possible one or another of the events reported in one or another of the four Gospels and then to ponder on the behaviour and the words of Jesus of Nazareth as reported in connection with that event and then to feel certain feelings as a result of the pondering and finally to make certain resolutions for the future as a result of the feelings.

Thirteen years after I had asked to be allowed to read the book mentioned above, I was anxious to have as my girlfriend a certain young woman who worked in a certain second-hand bookshop in the central business district of Melbourne. While I was thus anxious, I used to visit the bookshop every Saturday morning and to spend an hour and more looking around the shelves before buying one or another book and then trying to begin with the young woman while she sold me the book such a conversation as would persuade her that I was a young man who dressed and behaved unexceptionally but who saw inwardly private sights the descriptions of which would become in the near future the texts of one after another of the works of fiction that would make him famous. Whether or not I can claim that the young woman became my girlfriend, I can state that she and I went out together, as the saying used to go, for a few weeks during which time she sometimes described to me what she had seen inwardly as a result of her having read one or another book while I described often to her what I foresaw as the contents of one after another of the works of fiction of mine that would later be published, one of which works, so I promised the young woman, would include a character inspired by her. At the end of the few weeks mentioned in the previous sentence, the young woman went to live in another city, and she and I have never met up with one another or written to one another since then. However, I have learned from newspapers that the young woman later became a famous author, although not an author of fiction. The young woman later became a much more famous author than I became, and during the year before I began to write this piece of fiction, her autobiography was published. I have been told by a person who has read the autobiography that no passage in it refers to myself. Even so, the publication of the autobiography of the famous woman who had once been the young woman in the second-hand bookshop reminded me that I had still not kept the above-mentioned promise that I made. I am able to introduce the young woman into this paragraph, and so to keep my promise to her, for the reason that one of the books that I bought in the shop where she worked was a copy of the same book that I had wanted Nunkie's permission to read, as was reported above. I had bought the book, and had given the young woman in the shop to understand that I would look into the book, because she was still a faithful Catholic and I wanted her to suppose that I had not lost all interest in religion and even that she might win me back to a certain degree of belief in the Catholic faith if she became my girlfriend. The paragraph that ends with this sentence is, of course, part of a work of fiction.

After I had asked Nunkie whether I might read the book mentioned earlier, he had smiled and had told me that meditations were not for boys. He had then reminded me that it was time for our daily cricket match. This was played every evening between Nunkie and his son on the one side and the Reformed Gambler and myself on the other. We bowled underarm with a tennis ball on a paved area near the former dairy, and we observed complicated local rules as to how many runs were scored if the ball was hit into this or that area of the long grass in the orchard.

Even though I knew nothing about non-Christian sorts of meditation, I had already, at the age of eleven, heard or read enough about certain great saints of the Church to know that those persons saw more in their minds while they prayed or meditated than mere illustrations of the gospel story. I had heard or read that certain great saints had sometimes gone into trances or been transported. No priest or religious brother or nun had ever, in my experience, suggested that his or her congregation or pupils should do more while praying than talk to one or another of the Persons of the Holy Trinity or the Blessed Virgin Mary, or one or another of the saints. I sensed as a child that my priests and teachers were uncomfortable when questioned about anything to do with visions or with unusual religious experiences. Those same priests and teachers were never reluctant to talk about hell or purgatory and the punishments meted out to the residents of those places, but they were reluctant to speculate about the joys of heaven. A child who asked for details about the celebrated happiness of the residents of heaven might well be told that the souls in heaven were content forever to contemplate the Beatific Vision. This was the term used by theologians, so I learned as a child, for the sight that one saw when one saw Almighty God.

For all that I was most curious to know what the souls in heaven enjoyed and what the great saints sometimes saw while they prayed or meditated, I was in no way curious to see God Himself. I write this in all seriousness. I had never wanted to meet God or to have with Him any more dealings than were absolutely necessary. I believed in Him; I was pleased to belong to the organisation that I believed to be His One, True Church; but I had no wish to meet Him and to have to make conversation with Him. I was much more interested in the place where God lived than in the Deity Himself.

For most of my childhood, I could only dare to hope that I might one day see the landscapes of heaven. I was rather more confident that I would one day glimpse some of those landscapes while I prayed with intensity or while I meditated. And, of course, I was able to imagine beforehand something of what I hoped to glimpse in the future. The landscapes of heaven were lit by a light that emanated from God Himself. Near its source, this divine light was of an almost unbearable fierceness, but in the distant zones of heaven where I was most at home, it shone serenely, although by no means unwaveringly, so that the sky above the landscapes seemed sometimes like a sky at early morning in summer in the world where these details were being imagined, and sometimes like a sky at mid-afternoon in late autumn in that same world. The details of the landscapes themselves were by no means elaborate. I was content to compose my heavenly vistas by extending further and further into the background the simple green hills, some of them with a few stylised, tufted trees on top, that I had enjoyed staring at in pictures in the earliest of my picture books; by having a pale-blue stream wind between some of the hills; by situating on this or that hillside a farmhouse or a few cattle or horses, and behind just one of the furthest hills the church steeple or the clock tower of a peaceful village.

The person who imagined the landscapes described above could hardly have been satisfied to contemplate mere details designed for infants, nor was he. My looking at the landscapes of the outer zones of heaven was always accompanied by the reassuring knowledge that heaven extended endlessly. My looking over a vista of green hills was only an introduction to the place that contained all places, even all unimaginable places. Soon, the simple green countryside would give way to unknown landscapes. And even more encouraging than the knowledge just described was a certain feeling that I often felt during my surveys of the little I had so far imagined.

The feeling mentioned above was a feeling of being accompanied by and watched over by not so much a person as a presence. This presence was unquestionably a female presence. Sometimes I imagined that the presence and I were no more than children who had agreed to be girlfriend and boyfriend. Sometimes I imagined, though I was still a child myself, that the presence and I were adults and were wife and husband. Sometimes I imagined the face of the presence, sometimes even the clothes that the presence wore or the few words that the presence spoke to me. Mostly, I was content to feel the presence of the presence: to feel as though she and I were sharers in a pact or understanding that bound us together intimately but could not have been expressed in words. Although I would never during my childhood have asked such a question of myself, it occurs to me now to ask of the fictional child who is the chief character of this part of this piece of fiction the question

what seemed to him the most desirable of the likely pleasures that
he might enjoy in his imagined heaven. It is, of course, easy to ask
a question of a fictional character but unheard of to receive an
answer from such a character. Even so, I believe I should report
here my belief that if the chief character mentioned above could
be imagined as being able to answer the question mentioned
above, then he could be imagined as answering that he most de-
sired to discover, in a remote district of the landscapes mentioned
previously, a place in which he and the presence that accompanied him always could settle.

If this piece of fiction were a more conventional narrative, the
reader might be told at this point that the parenthetical passage
that began in the fifteenth paragraph before this paragraph has
now come to an end and that I, the narrator, am about to continue
narrating the events of the Sunday when the chief character of
this piece of fiction was walking with his father after having seen
an hour beforehand at the Farm a pale and plumpish young man
who was the first of the settlers at Outlands that the chief character had seen. Instead, the reader is hereby assured that nothing
of significance took place during the rest of the Sunday just
mentioned, and the same reader is further assured that the next
paragraph and many subsequent paragraphs will contain not a
narrative of certain events but a summary of the significance of
those events and of much more.

I asked few questions about the settlement of Outlands while
I was at the Farm, but I listened whenever a resident of the Farm
or a visitor from Outlands said anything about the settlement in
the far north-east of the state. Even years later, I was still able to
learn details from one or another of my father's relatives.

The writer of the feature article mentioned much earlier seemed
to have believed that the settlement in south-eastern Victoria
was the oldest or even the only such settlement of its kind. That
settlement was founded in the year when I was staying at the
Farm, by which time Outlands had been in existence for at least
one year. I have heard of another such settlement that was founded

in the late 1940s. These settlements were hardly rivals, but I suspect that the settlers in the south-east, many of whose faces I had seen images of in the illustration mentioned earlier, might have been called mostly working-class persons, whereas the Outlanders might have been called mostly middle-class persons. I suspect further that the Outlanders would have wanted to be called a group of Catholic intellectuals. My father called them long-hairs, in accordance with his belief that men who had been to university wore their hair longer than did other men, had less common sense, and were less able with their hands.

On the day after I had first met an Outlander and had learned something about the settlement of Outlands, I walked far out into the long grass between the neglected fruit trees at the Farm and founded a settlement of my own. I thought of my settlement as having the same name as the settlement that had inspired me, but for the sake of convenience I shall call my own settlement hereafter Grasslands.

The founder of the settlement of Grasslands had never met any other child or adult who was less skilled than he was at representing things by drawing or painting or modelling. Other children had often laughed, and even teachers had smiled, at the distorted pictures and lumpish objects that the future founder of Grasslands had produced in art and craft classes. The same children and teachers praised the essays and stories that the future founder wrote in English composition classes. On the day when he prepared to found his settlement, the founder might have been expected to call on his skills as a writer and so to write a detailed description of the settlement and the settlers. But the founder knew he had much more to fear if his writing were discovered by one of the adults at the Farm than if one of those adults stumbled on his model in the grass. The founder knew that his writing would report what the settlers saw inwardly as they lived their lives at the settlement and so, by implication, what he, the writer, had seen inwardly while he wrote.

And so the settlement of Grasslands was founded not as the subject of a piece of writing but as a model or toy. And because the founder was so little skilled with his hands, he was unable to make from the excellent clay of the northern suburbs of Melbourne any sort of building other than a rough cube or trapezoid that later cracked apart in the sun. The animals in the paddocks at the settlement were pebbles. The settlers themselves were forked twigs found among the branches of the orchard trees.

I never learned how many persons had settled at Outlands. While I stayed at the Farm I saw two young men and three young women who might have been newly recruited to Outlands or, perhaps, returning briefly to Melbourne to settle some private business or who might even have been on their way back to the secular world after having decided to leave Outlands. The young men seemed thoughtful; the young women seemed more ready to smile or joke, but I noted that they were all what my father called plain Janes. All of these young persons were unattached. I never heard of any married couples at Outlands, although I cannot believe couples would have been prevented from joining the settlement.

I never met any of the leading settlers from Outlands. There seemed to have been two men prominent in the founding of the settlement: one a medical practitioner and the other a barrister and solicitor. Of these two, the legal man was much more often talked about at the Farm, and always with reverence. His surname ended with the fifteenth letter of the English alphabet. So, too, did the surname of the Reformed Gambler. (And, so too, of course, did Nunkie's surname.) I understood that the Reformed Gambler had come to Australia from Italy as a young man. I concluded from all this—wrongly, as I shall explain later—that the surname of the admired legal man was an Italian surname.

The founder of Grasslands would have said at the time that he had founded his settlement as a place where he and his like-minded followers could live prayerful lives far from the dangers of the modern world. Or, he might have said that Grasslands was intended as a place from which heaven would be more readily visible.

If the founder of Grasslands had been asked at the time what were the chief dangers of the modern world, he would have described in detail two images that were often in his mind. The first image was of a map he had seen a year or so previously in a Melbourne newspaper as an illustration to a feature article about the damage that would be caused if an Unfriendly Power were to drop an atomic bomb on the central business district of Melbourne. Certain black and white markings in the diagram made it clear that all persons and buildings in the city and the nearest suburbs would be turned to ash or rubble. Certain other markings made it clear that most persons in the outer suburbs and the nearer country districts would later die or suffer serious illness. And other markings again made it clear that even persons in country districts rather distant from Melbourne might become ill or die if the wind happened to blow in their direction. Only the persons in remote country districts would be safe.

The second of the two images mentioned above was an image that often occurred in the mind of the founder of Grasslands although it was not a copy of any image he had seen in the place he called the real world. This image was of one or another suburb of Melbourne on a dark evening. At the centre of the dark suburb was a row of bright lights from the shop windows and illuminated signs of the main shopping street of the suburb. Among the brightest of these lights were those of the one or more picture theatres in the main street. Details of the image became magnified so that the viewer of the image saw first the brightly lit picture theatre with a crowd milling in the foyer before the beginning of one or another film and next the posters on the wall of the foyer advertising the film about to be shown and after that the woman who was the female star of the film and finally the neckline of the low-cut dress worn by that woman. This image was sometimes able to be multiplied many times in the mind of the viewer, who would then see images of darkened suburb after darkened suburb and in those suburbs picture theatre after picture theatre with poster after poster of woman after woman with dress after dress resting low down on breasts after breasts.

If the founder of Grasslands had been asked at the time why he had founded his settlement, and if he had been able to describe in detail to his questioner the images mentioned above, he would have assumed that the questioner would not need to question him further and would understand that he, the founder of Grasslands, wanted to live in a place where he need no longer fear the bombs of an Unfriendly Power and need no longer try to imagine the details concealed by low-cut necklines of dresses of female film stars.

One of the young men who called at the Farm from Outlands wore a beard. Until I met him, I had never seen a beard on any but an aged man. I watched the bearded man while he worked with rolled-up sleeves to load some timber from a disused Farm building onto a truck that was going to Outlands. The bearded man joked and said such things as gave me to understand that he read often from the New Testament and the Fathers of the Church and Saint Thomas Aquinas. I thought of the bearded man as resembling a man from medieval times, and I supposed Outlands more resembled medieval Europe than modern Australia.

The newspaper carried by the pale and plumpish young man mentioned much earlier in this piece of fiction was in the Spanish language. Even before I stayed at the Farm, I had come to understand that Spain was the most admirable of all European countries, even though it was the most reviled by the secular press. It was the most admirable, so one of my father's sisters had once told me, because it was the only country in Europe where Communism had been fought to a standstill, and it was the most reviled because many journalists secretly sympathised with Communism.

Many years after both Outlands and Grasslands had ceased to exist, I read a statement by a man who had been a commentator on current affairs in various Catholic newspapers and on a Catholic radio program from the 1930s to the 1950s. The man had stated that he had taken many unpopular positions during his career as a commentator and had received many angry letters as a result but that the most numerous and the angriest letters by far had been those that reached him after he had written and had broadcast his opinion that the government of General Franco better suited the interests of Spain than any government that might have been installed if the Civil War had ended differently.

The founder of Grasslands knew nothing of the causes or results of the Spanish Civil War, but he sensed that in this connection, as in so many others, the sort of Catholic who wore a beard and chose to live on a remote settlement possessed an inner, private knowledge of moral issues which was almost the opposite of what passed for knowledge with other persons. The founder hung about the pale and plumpish young man while he read parts of his newspaper. He, the founder, asked to have the dialogue in the Felix the Cat cartoon translated for him and laughed at the humour of it and learned from it the only five Spanish words he was ever to learn. The same founder was not at all troubled when the same pale and plumpish young man returned to the Farm two weeks later for another short visit and took out the same edition of the same newspaper (the founder identified it from the Felix cartoon) and began to read parts of it.

When the liturgical season of Advent was about to begin in the world where the settlement of Grasslands appeared as a few rows of cracked mud blocks and its settlers as a dozen and more forked twigs, the uncle of the founder of Grasslands, in whose eyes the settlement was a thriving village whose residents sometimes angered their neighbours by speaking the Spanish language instead of the English, took his nephew and the nephew's cousin into the garden of the Farm in order to choose leaves for the weaving of an Advent wreath, which was a custom, so the uncle said, that European Catholics had kept up since the Middle Ages and earlier. They chose fig leaves for the wreath, wove the wreath, and hung it in the main room of the Farm. For a few days, the wreath looked well: a mass of green leaves hanging like a halo above the dining table. On each of those days, the residents of the Farm had gathered at evening and had prayed beneath the wreath and had sung an Advent hymn, some of the words of which can be found in a book of fiction that I wrote nearly twenty years ago.

Ten minutes ago, I took down from the bookshelves in this room a copy of the book of fiction mentioned in the previous sentence. I had not looked into that book for several years, although I see in my mind every day one or another of the images that caused me to begin to write the book, the title of which is *Inland*. I learned from my looking into the book *Inland* just now that the narrator of the book did not report that a certain wreath of fig leaves mentioned in the book had become brown and withered soon after the wreath had been hung in the living room of a certain house. I learned also just now that the narrator of *Inland*, which is a book of fiction in the same way that this piece is a piece of fiction, had reported in the book that a certain utopian settlement founded by certain characters in the fiction was situated between two rivers the names of which are identical to the names of two rivers on the maps of Victoria in the collection of maps in this room.

The wreath of fig leaves that is part of this piece of fiction became brown and withered after a few days. Afterwards, the leaves seemed so brittle whenever I looked up at them that I was often afraid some of them might crumble and fall as a result of the vibrations from our hymn singing of an evening. I was afraid that this would oblige Nunkie to have to explain to his son and to me that European people were able to make Advent wreaths that stayed green for much longer than ours had stayed, which was something that I might have found hard to believe, although I would never have said so.

All the settlers at Grasslands were unmarried. The founder of the settlement might have been only dimly aware of the power of sexual attraction between men and women, but he himself had for some years past felt a strong attraction towards one or another female person, which attraction he thought of as a falling in love, even though the female person was sometimes of a different age than his. Accordingly, the founder had designed the settlement so that females and males lived at opposite ends of the place, with the chapel, the library, and all the farm buildings between. They mostly worked at separate tasks, but they met for meals and for prayers of the divine office, which they recited during their several visits to the chapel each day. This chapel was so arranged that the males and females faced each other, with each sex occupying a set of stalls to the side of the building. Males and females were permitted to look freely at each other. The founder expected that many a male would feel attracted to one or another female, but he supposed that such a male would be affected as he, the founder, would have been affected in such circumstances: the male would be continually inspired by the image in his mind of the face of the female as she appeared in the chapel or in the dining room; he would work more strenuously in the paddocks in order to impress her; he would study harder in the library so that he could discuss theology and philosophy with her. In the fullness of time, every male settler would be continually aware of the face and person of a young woman who was sometimes visible on the opposite side of the chapel or the dining room and was at other times an inspiring image in his mind.

One of the explanations that I heard long afterwards for the failure of the settlement of Outlands was that the bishop of the diocese where the settlement was situated would never allow any of his priests to be stationed as chaplain in a place where the presence together of unmarried males and females might have given rise to scandal among non-Catholic neighbours. The Outlanders had tried by every possible means, so I was told long afterwards, to obtain a chaplain. They had drawn up an eloquent petition at one time, and a number of them had travelled by horse and cart— their only available transport—from Outlands to the palace of the bishop, which palace was in a suburb of the city that was named Bassett in my first published work of fiction. The Outlanders had travelled for two weeks and had arrived tired and dishevelled at the bishop's palace, but he had rejected their petition.

This piece of fiction is as it were a letter to a man who was mentioned earlier in the fiction. As soon as I have finished the final draft of this fiction, I will send a copy to the man just mentioned. I mentioned this now rather than at the end of the fiction so as not to lessen whatever effect the last pages might have or to suggest that the whole piece is anything but a piece of fiction. While I was writing the previous paragraph, I intended to put marks beside that paragraph in the copy that I sent to the man mentioned above so that the man would not fail to note that a party of dishevelled Outlanders must have passed close by the house where he lived in the first year of his life. I understand now, however, that my having written the previous sentence relieves me of the need to put any marks in the margin of this text.

No one at the Farm knew about the settlement of Grasslands. I was not anxious to keep the place secret, but I was mostly clearing the forest and building the buildings and keeping the twig-persons active during the daytime, while Nunkie and my cousin were away. Sometimes one of the young men or women from Outlands would be sitting with a book on the veranda or strolling up and down beside the house—praying, perhaps, or even meditating—and would ask me later what I had been doing out in the long grass. I would tell the questioner a half-truth: that I had a toy farm in the grass.

Grasslands had been already well established when a certain young woman arrived for the first time at the Farm. I shall call the certain young woman hereafter the Pretty-faced Woman. Perhaps I might not consider her so pretty if I saw her likeness today, but in the last month of 1950 she was the prettiest young woman I had seen. She was on her way to or from Outlands, busy on some secular or spiritual errand that I could never hope to know about. She bustled through the quiet rooms at the Farm, talking softly and earnestly to Nunkie or the Holy Foundress. Her noticeable breasts swung often behind her blouse. Her dark blue eyes and dark brown hair went strangely together. I stared often at the pale freckles above the high neckline of her dress.

The Pretty-faced Woman was different from the other young women from Outlands not only because she was pretty and they were plain but because she seemed more curious about me. She asked me who I was, how I was connected with the persons at the Farm, where my home was, why I was living away from my family. She asked these things as though she was truly interested.

On the day after the Pretty-faced Woman had arrived at the Farm, I looked through the branches of the fruit trees at the Farm in search of a twig to represent a new settler at Grasslands. The females at Grasslands were by no means all plain Janes; some of their faces had already begun to inspire some of the male settlers. But I had taken no special care in choosing any of the twigs that represented the females. Now, I found a twig with a certain shapeliness and symmetry and with a certain smoothness when the bark had been peeled away from the paler wood beneath. I placed this twig among the other representations of female settlers and looked forward to a series of events that would soon take place at Grasslands, the first of which events would be a long exchange of looks between the twig that represented myself and the twig that represented the new arrival when the settlers were next gathered in the chapel.

I did the things mentioned above on the morning of the day mentioned above. After lunch on that day, I was only just settling myself on my knees beside the settlement of Grasslands when I heard someone walking up behind me through the long grass.

I was a child, but I did not lack guile. I went on staring ahead. I pretended not to have heard her footsteps behind me. I sat back on my thighs and stared ahead of me as though I was contemplating fold after fold of an endless landscape. She remained for a short while a female presence just out of sight behind me, and then she stepped forward and asked me what I would have expected any visitor to the Farm to ask about my dirt clearings, my lumps of cracked mud, and my forked twigs standing crookedly here and there.

I told her as much of the truth as she needed to be told: that I had founded a settlement in a remote place; that I had been inspired by the example of Outlands, even though I had only heard a little about it . . .

She reached down and drew her fingers through my hair and

then told me she hoped to welcome me one day to Outlands, which was still hardly bigger than my own settlement in the grass but which would grow and thrive. And then she went back to the house.

After she had gone, I began to modify somewhat my original ground plan for Grasslands. Somewhere at the edge of the settlement there would have to be space for a house, and perhaps a small garden, for the first two of the settlers who were a married couple. Later, other such houses would be needed for other couples and their children. But these plans of mine were never carried out. On the next day, my father arrived without notice at the Farm. The electricity had been switched on in the partly built house on the far side of Melbourne where my parents and my sister and I were going to live happily together during the foreseeable future. (In fact, we lived there for four years, until my father, who had become for several years a reformed gambler, became again a gambler and had to sell the house in order to pay his latest debts.)

I suppose the last traces of Grasslands would have melted away several years after I had left the Farm. And yet, the settlement of Outlands did not outlast Grasslands by many years. At some time in the 1960s, I heard that the settlement no longer existed, although several of the married couples who had been among the last settlers still remained on the site. They had bought a share each of the land and had survived as farmers.

At some time in the early 1970s, after I had been married for several years and was the father of two children, I decided I had better make my Last Will and Testament with the help of a legal practitioner. While I was looking into the telephone directory at the pages where legal practitioners advertise their services, I saw a very rare surname that I had only once previously come across. I understood from what I saw that the bearer of the surname was the principal of a firm of legal practitioners in an inner eastern suburb of Melbourne, where the value of the most modest house was three times the value of my own house. After I had looked at the initial of the first given name of the principal just mentioned, I became convinced that the man I had heard of twenty and more years before as one of the founders of Outlands was now a prosperous legal practitioner in one of the best suburbs of Melbourne, so to speak.

Only a year or so after the events reported in the previous paragraph, I heard of the death of Nunkie. I had seen him only occasionally during the years since I lived briefly at the Farm, but I took steps to attend his funeral service.

I sat near the rear of Nunkie's parish church and saw hardly anything of the chief mourners until they came down the aisle with the coffin. Among the leading mourners was a man of middle age whose appearance could only be called commanding. He was very tall, strongly built, and olive-skinned. He had a mane of silvery hair and a nose like an eagle's bill. He looked continually about him, nodding to this person and that. He did not nod at me, but I was sure he took note of me. And while his black eyes measured me, I was aware of what a weak, ineffectual person I have always been and of how much I have needed to be guided and inspired.

At the side of the commanding man was a woman with a pretty face. She was perhaps ten years younger than the man and was herself approaching middle age, but I could readily recall how she had looked twenty and more years before. She kept her eyes down as she passed.

Behind the couple mentioned above were four young persons who were obviously their children. I estimated from the seeming age of the oldest that the parents had been married in the very early 1950s.

In one of the last years of the twentieth century, I pressed by mistake a certain button in the radio of my motor car and heard, instead of the music that I usually hear from that radio, the voices of persons taking part in what was probably called by its makers a radio documentary. I was about to correct the mistake mentioned above when I understood that the actors taking part in the program were reading the words previously spoken or written by several persons who had been among the settlers at Outlands almost fifty years before. After I had understood this, I steered into a side street and stopped my motor car and listened until the program about Outlands had come to an end. (The program was one of a short series. The following week I listened for an hour to a similar program about the place mentioned in the second paragraph of this piece of fiction.)

I learned less than I had expected to learn, except for what will be reported in the last paragraph of this piece of fiction. The details of the daily lives of the Outlanders seemed to have been hardly different from what I had imagined while I lived at the Farm. Even when the actors spoke the words of the early settlers (who would have been aged seventy and more when they were interviewed) explaining why they had left the secular world for a communal settlement, I was not surprised. The Outlanders too had felt that the world was becoming more sinful and that the cities of the world were in danger of being bombed flat. I was beginning to be disappointed while I listened. But then a number of younger female voices began to report the recollections of the earliest female settlers at Outlands while they asked themselves what had finally persuaded them to leave the world and to join the settlement in the mountains. The reports were at first rather predictable. But then a name was mentioned: the name of a man. The surname had a musical sound and ended in the fifteenth letter of the English alphabet. The reports from the young female settlers became more specific, more in agreement, more heartfelt. I shall end this piece of fiction with a paragraph reporting my own summary of what I understood the female actors to be reporting from the females who claimed still to remember their feelings of nearly fifty years before.

He was the sort of person who would be called today charismatic, truly charismatic. He had graduated in law but had declined to practise. He was a cultured European in the dull Australia of the 1940s and 1950s. He had a Spanish father, and he spoke Spanish beautifully. We had never heard such a musical language. And he played the guitar. He would sing Spanish folk songs for hours while he played the guitar. He was inspiring.

The Boy's Name Was David

The man's name was whatever it was. He was more than sixty years of age and he spent much of his time alone. He was never idle, but he was no longer in paid employment, and on the most recent census form he had described himself as a retired person.

He had never thought of himself as having any profession or following any career. From about his twentieth to about his sixtieth year he had written some poetry and much prose fiction, and some of the fiction had been afterwards published. During those same years, he had earned a living by several means. In his forty-first year, he had found a position as a part-time tutor in fiction writing in an insignificant so-called college of advanced education in an inner suburb of Melbourne. His first students were all adults, some older than himself. So far as he could tell, they were not impressed by his credentials or his teaching methods, and he responded by being wary with them and giving away little of himself.

He had been given to understand that he was only a stopgap;

that he would keep his tutor's position only until the college was able to appoint permanently as a lecturer one or another writer of note: someone whose reputation would lend prestige to the writing course. In the event he, whatever his name was, stayed on for sixteen years. By then, the place where he was employed had become a university and most of his students were not long out of school. How these things came about is no part of this piece of fiction.

This piece of fiction begins a few years after its chief character had ceased to be a teacher of fiction writing, and at a time when he sometimes lived through several days without remembering that he had formerly been such a teacher.

The man of this fiction had no interest in mathematics, but throughout his life he had loved arithmetic. He was fond of calculating such numbers as the approximate total of the breaths that he had drawn since the moment of his birth or of the bottles of beer that he had drunk since the well-remembered day when he had drunk the first of them. He had once arrived at a close estimate of the total length of time during which he had experienced the extremes of sexual pleasure. He daydreamed of quantifying things that had never before been measured. Whenever he was in a railway carriage or a theatre, he wished he could have been free to discover which person from among those present had the keenest sense of smell; which one had been most often frightened of another person; which one had the strongest belief in an afterlife . . .

Most of the man's arithmetical enterprises resulted in estimates only, but in some matters he was able to arrive at exact totals, for he was a diligent keeper of records. Calendars, bank statements, receipts, and such things he stored in his filing cabinets at the end of every year. And in keeping with his love of recording and measuring, he kept precise and detailed accounts of his work as a teacher of fiction writing.

He was obliged to keep certain records, of course, so that he could award grades to his students at the end of each semester, but he went far beyond this. Not only for his own satisfaction, but also to avoid disputes with students over their grades, he devised and perfected during his first years as a teacher what he supposed must have been a unique means of arriving at a mark (on a scale from 1 to 100) for each piece of fiction that he assessed. His method was to record in the margins of every page of every piece of fiction every instance of his having had to pause in his reading. Whenever he was stopped by a spelling mistake or a fault of grammar; whenever he was confused by a badly shaped sentence; whenever he lost the thread of the narrative; whenever he became bored by what he was reading; at every such time, he put in the margin what he called a negative mark and, if time allowed, he wrote a note to explain why he had stopped and had made the mark. At the foot of each page he put a running tally of the number of lines of fiction that he had so far read and of the number of negative marks that he had made in the margin. At the foot of the last page he set out in full his calculation of the percentage of the fiction that had been free of fault. This percentage figure became the numerical mark for the piece of fiction.

Of course, it was not only faults in the fiction that might have caused him to stop reading. He paused often from sheer enjoyment of a shapely sentence or from admiration of a thoughtful passage or from a wish to postpone the pleasure of reading further into a passage that promised much. Whenever he paused for reasons such as these he wrote a warm message to the author of the piece, but his method of assessment would have become too complicated even for him if he had tried somehow to have the outstanding passages cancel out some of the negative marks.

He was always ready and waiting to defend his method of assessment if some querulous student had challenged him over it but no student ever did so, although not a few disputed his comments on particular passages that he had assessed as faulty. For year after year, he went on assigning to hundreds of pieces of fiction percentage marks that claimed to rank the pieces precisely.

He was not required to keep any details of his assessment after he had sent the final results for all students to the administrative officers of the place where he worked. But being the person he was, he could never think of throwing away even a single page that recorded some of the workings of his mind. At the end of each year, he put into one of his filing cabinets the folders of ruled pages on which were recorded, among other details, the title of every piece of fiction submitted to him during the year, the number of words in each piece, and the percentage mark that he had allotted to the piece. The total of the pieces of fiction was never less than two hundred and fifty, and the total words in all the pieces was never less than half a million. Before he put his records away he would turn the pages, letting his eyes take in the columns of figures showing the percentage mark for piece after piece of fiction.

As a boy, he had kept pages filled with batting and bowling averages for cricketers; he had pasted into scrapbooks pictures showing the finishing order of field after field of horses in famous races. Always during these months-long tasks, his hope had been that some surprising discovery would be his final reward; that the first columns of figures might prove to have been misleading, or that the horse that seemed likely to be beaten in a close finish had won after all. Fifty years afterwards, he was much more adept at devising games to satisfy his lifelong love of protracted contests and delayed but decisive results. He would have taken care throughout the year not to compare any of the several hundred marks that he had awarded. He knew, of course, which were the dozen or so most memorable pieces that he had read, but he had been at pains never to think of one as better than another. Now, at the end of the year, and six weeks and more after the last student had been seen on campus, he placed a crisp sheet of white paper over each page of his folder of results while he looked at the page. The paper was so placed that he saw only the first of the two numerals of the percentage mark for each piece of fiction. When he looked down any page, he knew only which pieces of fiction had earned ninety percent or more but not which piece had earned the highest mark.

Of the half-formed images that came into the man's mind while he scanned the titles of the pieces of fiction with ninety or more marks apiece, he was taken most by a glimpse of the highest-scoring pieces of fiction as the leading horses in an impossible race. On some vast prairie or pampa, hundreds of horses were approaching a crowded grandstand and a winning post. He was fond of dwelling on this image, with its promise of something about to be decided after having been for long in doubt.

There was more to the exercise described just above than the comparatively simple experience of awaiting the outcome of a decisive event; more even than the more subtle pleasure of admiring the strong claims of each contender and marvelling or regretting that even such claims might be surpassed by the even stronger claims of another and yet another contender. There was also the question—simple for him to pose to himself but perplexing, if not impossible, to answer—what exactly was he thinking of whenever he claimed to remember each of these pieces of fiction? He saw on the page of his folder of pages a title, and sometimes he saw beyond this no more than an image that the title had given rise to. (He had always encouraged his students to choose as the title for a story a word or words connected with a central image or a recurring theme in the fiction. He discouraged them from choosing abstract nouns or phrases that related only in a general way to the fiction. Among the titles of the leading pieces, therefore, he was much more likely to see such as "Killing Ants," "A Long Line of Trees," or "Six Blind Mice" than "The Request," "Secrets," or "The Tourist.") Sometimes, other images would appear in his mind following on from the image connected with the title. Sometimes the succession of images was long enough for him to be able to say that he recalled the plot of the piece of fiction or the story. Sometimes he saw, in what he thought of as the background of his mind, an image of the author of the piece of fiction while one or another of the previously mentioned images remained in the foreground. Sometimes, whether or not he had seen in his mind any of the previously mentioned sorts of images, he saw an image of the classroom where he and a group of students had read the piece of fiction and had afterwards discussed it on one or another morning or afternoon of the past year. At such times, he sometimes heard in his mind particular comments from one or another reader or even the distinctive hush that always settled over a class soon after they had begun to read a piece of fiction that was far beyond the ordinary.

The sort of image that hardly ever occurred in his mind while he read the title of a piece of fiction was the very image that he most wanted to occur. This was the image in his mind of parts of the actual text of the fiction: of a sentence or a phrase, or even of disjointed words.

As a teacher, he had been fanatical in urging his students to think of their fiction, of all fiction, as consisting of sentences. A sentence was, of course, a number of words or even a number of phrases or clauses, but he preached to his students that the sentence was the unit that yielded the most amount of meaning in proportion to its extent. If a student in class claimed to admire a piece of fiction or even a short passage of fiction, he would ask that student to find the sentence that most caused the admiration to arise. Anyone claiming to be puzzled or annoyed by a passage of fiction was urged by him to find the sentence that had first brought on the puzzlement or the annoyance. Much of his own commentary during classes consisted of his pointing out sentences that he admired or sentences that he found faulty. At least once each year, he told each class an anecdote that he had remembered from a memoir of James Joyce. Someone had praised to Joyce a recent novel. Joyce had asked why the novel was so impressive. The answer came back that the style was splendid, the subject powerful . . . Joyce would not listen to such talk. If a book of prose fiction was impressive, the actual prose should have impressed itself on the reader's mind so that he could afterwards quote sentence after sentence.

The teacher who set such store by sentences, whenever he visualised as the last fifty metres of a mighty horse-race his looking for the piece of fiction that had most impressed him, regretted that he *heard* so little in his mind. If the images mentioned in a recent paragraph were few enough, the memories of sentences or phrases were fewer by far. He would have rejoiced if he could have witnessed a contest of sentences alone: if he could have repeated aloud to himself even a short sentence from each of the leading pieces of fiction so as to have had in his mind as the race came to an end only such visual images as arose from the remembered sentences. But he seldom recalled a sentence. The blurred and overlapping visual images took over his mind.

During the first few years after the man, whatever his name was, had ceased to be a teacher of fiction writing, he remembered some of the images mentioned in the previous few paragraphs of this piece of fiction: the images that had arisen in his mind whenever he had watched the details of an impossible horse-race in his mind. In later years, the man found himself remembering many fewer images than he might have expected to remember. In one of those years, the man began to understand that his failing more and more to remember details connected with more than three thousand pieces of fiction might itself be imagined as the finish of a horse-race.

The race just mentioned would be the last of all such races to be decided in the mind of the man, whatever his name was. The finish of the race would be very different from the finishes of the races that had been run in his mind at the end of most of his sixteen years as a teacher of fiction writing. In those earlier races, a closely bunched field had approached the winning post with first one and then another likely winner appearing. The last part of this last race would more resemble the last part of a long-distance steeplechase, when all but two or three entrants had dropped far behind. The entrants in the race would be every one of the more than three thousand pieces of fiction that the man had read and assessed while he was a teacher of fiction writing. No, the entrants would be every *detail* that the man might conceivably have remembered in connection with any of the more than three thousand pieces of fiction that he had read during sixteen years of his life. And the finish of this last race might itself last for a year at least, which would be in keeping with the duration of the whole race, which had already been in progress for more than five years before it came to the attention of the man in whose mind it was being run.

The man could take his time over this race; could even forget about the existence of the race for days or weeks on end. The less he thought about the race, the fewer contestants might appear in his mind when he next looked out for them.

At the fictional time when this piece of fiction began, the man, whoever he was, had been aware for more than two years that this last race, this race of races, was being decided in his mind. He was especially careful not to interfere with the fair running of the race. He wanted to give no help to any of the entrants, of which a dozen or more were in his view when he first became aware that they were, in fact, entrants in the most decisive of races. Whenever he looked at the progress of the race, which was only once in every few weeks, perhaps, he merely took note of which entrants were at the front of the field and then turned his attention to other matters, which is to say that every few weeks he asked himself what details he could still call to mind from all the pieces of fiction that he had read during his sixteen years as a teacher. Having asked this question of himself, he waited during an interval of a minute or two and observed the while what occurred in his mind.

The man thought it would have been unfair of him to give any encouragement to any of the struggling leaders in the race. And so he took care to do nothing that might help to fix in his mind one or another image arising from one or another piece of fiction and might therefore help to unfix one or another image arising from some other piece of fiction. But even though he tried to do no more than observe, his many years as an observer of actual horse-races made it impossible for him not to try to predict the actual winner. He had sat in so many grandstands at so many race-courses and had foreseen the eventual winner in each of so many closely contested races that he could not keep himself from trying to predict the winner of the race in his mind.

At the time when this piece of fiction began, no more than half a dozen contenders were in sight, and several of these were drop-ping back. The man who observed from time to time the progress of these stayers towards the finish line was surprised whenever he asked himself why these few and not some of countless other im-ages were still in his view. The man could not remember the expe-rience of reading for the first time any of the words and sentences that had first caused any of these images to arise in his mind. This failure to remember suggested to the man that he had never ex-pected any of the images to remain in his mind long after count-less other images no longer appeared in his mind.

A young Australian man is drinking in a bar in East Africa. He finds himself staring more and more often at two young women of striking appearance, even while his African drinking mate warns him to take no notice of the Somali prostitutes.

A young woman sits in a small boat in the shallows of a lake on a summer morning. The rest of her group are on a sandbar nearby. Among the group are a man who loves the woman and a man she hates. The two men are friends. The young woman is ill from the beer that she drank on the previous night in the company of the two men. At a certain moment while she tries to recall the details of the previous night, the young woman leans over the side of the boat and vomits into the lake.

A young girl comes home from school and finds, as on most other afternoons, that her mother has spent the day in her room smoking, drinking coffee, and entertaining delusions.

Late on a summer evening in the 1940s, a girl of twelve or thir-teen years tries to explain herself to her mother. A few minutes before, the girl had been playing cricket in the backyard with some boys from the neighbourhood. The girl had often played cricket with the boys. She was known as a tomboy and was innocent of sexual knowledge. During the latest game, she had chased the ball into a shed. The eldest boy had followed her. He had taken out his erect penis and had tried to undo her clothes. The girl's mother, who might well have been spying on the cricketers for some time previously, had come into the shed. Later, when the girl tried to explain herself, she had seen that her mother thought her partly to blame, even complicit.

Each of the four previous paragraphs reports details of a central image surrounded by a cluster of lesser images that had arisen from several sentences of one or another piece of fiction. In none of those paragraphs are words quoted from any piece of fiction. For as long as the man who was aware of those images was aware of them, he was unable to quote in his mind from any of the sentences that had caused those images to arise.

This continued to be a disappointment to the man, whatever his name was. In gloomy moments, he was ready to suppose that he had argued as a teacher of fiction to no purpose when he had argued that fiction was made up of sentences and sentences alone. In those gloomy moments, he was ready to suppose that he had got from the several thousand pieces of fiction he had taught his students to write only a cluster of images such as he might have got if his hundreds of students, instead of writing fiction, had met for a few weeks in his presence and had talked about their memories and imaginings.

But the man could always put an end to his gloom by looking along the far-reaching home-straight of the vast racecourse in his mind and observing a fifth contender for the Gold Cup of Remembered Fiction. As a racing commentator might have said, this contender was going strongly—as strongly as anything else in the field. The man in whose mind this fifth contender had arisen and who could not keep himself from trying to foresee the outcome of any race-in-progress, this man foresaw that the finish might be, in the language of racing commentators, desperately close, but he foresaw that the fifth contender would be the winner at last.

The fifth contender was a sentence: the opening sentence of a piece of fiction. A few vague images hung about the man's mind whenever he heard the sentence in his mind, but they meant little to him. The man was not even sure whether the images had arisen when he had first read the fiction that followed on from the opening sentence or whether he had imagined them, so to speak, at a much later date. The man seemed to have forgotten almost all of the fiction except for the opening sentence: *The boy's name was David.*

Whatever else the man might have forgotten from his experience of reading the fiction that followed on from the sentence just above, he had not forgotten the exhilaration that he had felt as he read the sentence for the first time; and he recalled the substance of the long message that he had written to the author of the fiction as part of his, the teacher's, assessment of the piece; and he recalled the substance of the comments that he had later made to the class where the fiction was read and discussed.

The boy's name was David. The man, whatever his name was, had known, as soon as he had read that sentence, that the boy's name had not been David. At the same time, the man had not been fool enough to suppose that the name of the boy had been the same as the name of the author of the fiction, whatever his name had been. The man had understood that the man who had written the sentence understood that to write such a sentence was to lay claim to a level of truth that no historian and no biographer could ever lay claim to. There was never a boy named David, the writer of the fiction might as well have written, but if you, the Reader, and I, the Writer, can agree that there might have been such a boy so named, then I undertake to tell you what you could never otherwise have learned about any boy of any name.

This and much more the man, whatever his name was, had understood from his first reading of the first sentence of the piece of fiction by a man whose name he soon afterwards forgot. And in his comments on that sentence the man, so he had thought at the time and for long afterwards, had come as close as he would ever come to explaining the peculiar value of fiction and why persons such as himself devoted much of their lives to the writing and the reading of fiction.

During a lifetime of watching horse-races or televised images of horse-races and of listening to radio broadcasts of horse-races, the man mentioned often in this fiction but never named had seen a comparatively small number of a sort of finish in which the eventual winner had not been considered even a likely placegetter a short distance from the winning post. Racing commentators described such a winner as having come from nowhere or from the clouds or from out of the blue. The man liked this sort of finish above all other sorts. Even if he had lost money on one of the beaten horses in such a finish, he could later appreciate the complex interplay of feelings that the last part of the race and, at the very last, the finish of the race had caused to occur in the minds of the persons interested in the race.

Finishes such as those described just above were rare enough in races over shorter distances and almost unheard of in long-distance races. In those races, the leading few usually remained in the lead during the last phase of the race, the rest having tired and fallen far behind. But the man of this fiction had seen occasionally a group of leaders unexpectedly tire and falter near the end, and an unthought-of horse arrive ahead of them. And towards the end of the race mentioned most often in this piece of fiction, the man became aware of the arrival on the scene, as a racing commentator might have said, of a previously unthought-of contender.

Perhaps ten years before the fictional time when this piece of fiction began, the man most often mentioned in this piece had been in his office on a cold, cloudy afternoon during the mid-year break between the first and second semester. Few students were on the campus. This was one of the few periods of the year when the man could sometimes read or write fiction for several hours without interruption. Then, while he was reading or writing, the man was visited, as he was liable to be visited at any time during the year, by a person who had heard about his course and wanted to learn more about it before applying to enrol.

The person visiting was a young woman. Something about her made him feel warmly towards her at once, and what she told him made him feel even more so, but he tried to deal with her in the same calm and courteous way in which he tried to deal with all his students. He and the young woman talked for perhaps twenty minutes, after which time they farewelled each other and the young woman went away. At the time when the man supposed that an important race in his mind was approaching its end, he had never seen the young woman or had any communication with her since the cold and cloudy afternoon when she had visited him in his office, perhaps fifteen years before.

Most of what the young woman had told the man is no part of this piece of fiction. The reader needs to know only that the young woman had not long before been disowned, as she expressed it, by her parents because she would not follow some or another career or profession. She had then left her parents' house in a northern state of Australia and had moved to Tasmania and had found employment as an assistant to the chef in a fashionable restaurant. Only recently, so she explained to the man in his office, the chef in the fashionable restaurant, together with his wife, had invited her to join them in establishing a restaurant of their own with all three of them as partners. The young woman had been flattered by this offer, so she told the man in his office, but she had not yet accepted it. She was unable to think of herself as having any career or profession. For some years past, she had wanted to devote herself to writing fiction. She had heard of the fiction-writing course conducted by the man, and she had travelled from Tasmania on that cold and cloudy afternoon to learn more about the course and to help her chances of gaining entry to the course.

The man, whatever his name was, remembered perhaps fifteen years afterwards only a summary of the advice that he had given to the young woman, whatever her name was, after she had reported to him what was summarised in the previous paragraph. The man remembered that he had told the young woman that he would never advise any person to give up the opportunity to follow some or another career or profession so that the person might write fiction; that she ought to go back to Tasmania and to become a partner in the establishing of the new restaurant; but that she ought to write during the next few months a piece of fiction. If she wrote such a piece of fiction, so the man told the young woman, and if she sent the fiction to him during the next few months, he would read it at once and would tell her soon afterwards in writing whether or not he had been impressed by the fiction. If it happened that he had been deeply impressed, so the man said, then she might with good reason apply to enrol in his writing course.

During the months following the cold and cloudy afternoon mentioned above, the man would sometimes note, while he was opening his mail in his office of a morning, that none of the envelopes seemed likely to have been sent from Tasmania and to contain the typescript of a piece of fiction. During the years following the afternoon mentioned, the man would sometimes recall one or another moment from the afternoon.

The man had never been able to recall clearly the appearance of any person. What he recalled were what he called details connected with the presence of the person. What he recalled in connection with the young woman who had visited him from Tasmania was the earnest tone of her voice and the paleness of her complexion and a wound on her wrist that he had found himself often staring at during their interview. Down the side of her pale left wrist was a long mark made, he supposed, by a knife that had slipped while she worked as a chef. A scab had formed over the wound, but a narrow zone of red remained around the scab.

During the years when he was a teacher of fiction writing, the man of this fiction had read aloud to his students and had urged them to consider many hundreds of statements by writers of fiction or anecdotes about those writers. In the years after he had ceased to be a teacher of fiction writing the man had forgotten most of those statements and anecdotes, but he sometimes remembered having told one or another class that the writer Flaubert had claimed, or was reported as having claimed, that he could hear the rhythms of his still-unwritten sentences for pages ahead. Whenever the man had told this to a class, he had hoped to cause his students to reflect on the power of the sentence over the mind of a certain sort of writer; but he, the man, had often supposed that the claim, or the reported claim, by Flaubert was much exaggerated. Then, about five years after he had ceased to be a teacher of fiction writing, and while he was watching in his mind the last part of what he sometimes called the Gold Cup of Remembered Fiction, he recognised that a previously unthought-of contender in that race was a sentence as yet unwritten.

If the man had had an ear for sentences as acute as Flaubert had had, or was supposed to have had, he, the man, might have heard in his mind the rhythm of the sentence mentioned above long before it had joined in with the other contenders in the race in his mind. But the man could hardly claim that he heard the rhythm of the unwritten sentence in his mind even while he was aware of the sentence as a late contender in the race. What the man might have claimed instead was that he was aware of what he might have called details connected with the meaning of the sentence. While the still unwritten sentence seemed about to claim the leaders, as a racing commentator might have said, the man in whose mind the race was being run was still unaware of the meaning of the unwritten sentence. But the man was aware that the meaning would be connected with the greenness of the island of Tasmania in his mind, with the white and the red of skin marked by a knife in his mind, and with a person in his mind who had not written any fiction or who had begun long ago to write a piece of fiction but had since left off writing.

Last Letter to a Niece

My Dearest Niece,

With this letter, our long-standing correspondence comes to an end. The reasons for this will become clear while you read the following pages. Yes, this letter must be my last, and yet I begin it with the same message that I sent in all my earlier letters. I remind you yet again, dear niece, that you are not obliged to reply to me; and I add yet again that I almost prefer not to hear from you, since this allows me to imagine many possible replies.

This letter has been the hardest to compose. In all my earlier letters I wrote the truth, but in these pages I have to write what might be called a higher truth. First, however, I must set the scene for you, as usual.

The time is evening, and the sky is almost dark. The day was fine and calm, and the stars will all be visible shortly, but the ocean is strangely loud. The weather must be bad far away in the west, because a heavy swell is running and I can hear, every half-minute, the loud crack as some huge wave breaks against the cliffs. After each crack, I imagine I feel under my feet the same tremor that I would feel if I were standing on one of the cliffs; but of course the cliffs are nearly a kilometre away, and the old farmhouse stands rock-solid as always.

As a child and a young man, I was known as the reader of the family. While my brothers and sisters were playing cards or listening to the gramophone, I would be sitting in a corner with a book open in front of me. I was always lost in a book, so my mother used to say. She, the wife of a dairy farmer and the mother of seven children, had little opportunity to read, but that simple remark of hers stays in my thoughts as I write this last letter. What did my mother understand of body, mind, soul, that caused her to report of her eldest son, while his body and face and eyes were clearly in her sight, that he was somehow within the confines of the smallish object held in his hands and, moreover, unsure of his whereabouts?

Something else my mother said of me: I was a bookish person. After you have read this letter, niece, you may choose to understand my mother's remark in other than its obvious sense. My mother would have meant that I read a great many books, but she was, in fact, wrong. If my hard-worked mother had cared to look closely, she might sometimes have seen that the book I held up to the kerosene lamp at the kitchen table on some evening in winter was the same that I had shielded with my hand from the sunlight on the back veranda on some Sunday morning of the previous summer.

When I write "book," I mean, as you surely know, the sort of book that has characters, a setting, and a story. I have seldom troubled myself over any other sort of book.

In many a letter during past years, I named for you one or another book that had affected me. As well, I mentioned certain passages in each book and told you that I often took pains to recall my first reading of each passage. I wonder how much you divined of what I am now about to tell you in full. The truth is, dear niece, that I have been, from an early age, powerfully drawn towards certain female characters in books. I am almost reluctant, even in such a letter as this, to write in everyday language about my feelings towards these personages, but you might begin to understand my situation if you think of me as having fallen, and ever since remained, in love with the personages.

Picture me on the day when I first learned what it was that would inspire and sustain me from then onwards. I am hardly more than a child. I am sitting on the lowest of the tier of sandstone blocks that support the rainwater tank on the shady, southern side of the house. This is my favourite place for reading by day in mild weather. The bulk of the tank-stand protects me from the sea wind, and if I lean sideways I sometimes feel against my face a trailing leaf or petal from the nasturtiums that grow out of the cracks between the topmost stones and down over the cream-coloured surface behind me. I am reading a book by an Englishman who died nearly fifty years before my birth. The book was presented to me as suitable for older children, but I was to learn much later that the author intended the book for adults. The action of the book was purported to have taken place nearly a thousand years before the author's birth. Among the major characters of the book was a young woman who later became the wife of the chief character and, later again, was rejected by him. At one or another moment while I was reading from the later pages of the book a report of the circumstances of this female character, I had to stop reading. Rather than cause embarrassment to either of us, I will describe my situation at that moment by calling on one of those stock expressions that can yield surprising meaning if one ponders them word by word. I tell you, dear niece, that my feelings got the better of me for a few moments.

Do not suppose that a few moments of intense feeling of themselves revealed much to me. But after I had reflected for long on the events just described, I began to foresee the peculiar course that my life would take in the future: I would seek in books what most others sought among living persons.

I reflected as follows. My reading about the personage in the book had caused me to feel more intensely than I had previously felt for any living person . . . At this point, dear niece, you may be preparing to revise your previous good opinion of me. Please, at least, read on . . . If I had been utterly candid with you from the beginning of our correspondence, you might have broken with me long ago. To whom, then, could I have written my many hundreds of pages? To whom could I have addressed this most decisive of letters? My being able to write even these few pages today is justification a hundredfold for whatever reticence and evasion I may have practised before now.

You read and interpreted rightly just now. I declare to you freely that I felt as a child and have felt ever since more concern for certain characters in books than for my own sisters and brothers, more than for my own mother and father even, and certainly more than for any of the few friends I have had. And in answer to your urgent question: you, dear niece, stand somewhat apart from the persons just mentioned. You are, it is true, a blood relation, but our having never met and our agreement that we should never meet allows me often to suppose that we are connected through literature only and not through your father's being my younger brother. Then again, that you are a blood relation of mine should lessen the strangeness of my revelations. You must have been from an early age not unfamiliar with aloofness and solitariness among the branches of our family. I am by no means your only unmarried uncle or aunt.

If you are still inclined to judge me harshly, dear niece, remember that I have done little harm to any living person during my bachelor's life. I was never a brute or unfaithful to any wife; I was never a tyrant to any child. Above all, consider my claim that I never chose to live as I have lived. My own conscience has reassured me often that I have dreamed and read only in an effort to draw nearer to the people who are my true kindred; the place that is my true home. My acts and omissions have had their origins in my nature and not in my will.

And now you wonder about my religious faith. I was not deceiving you whenever I mentioned in earlier letters my weekly churchgoing, but I have to confess to you that I long ago ceased to believe in the doctrines of our religion. I have read as much as I could bring myself to read of the book from which our religion has been derived. I was able to feel for no character in that book the half of what I have felt for many a character in books scarcely mentioning God.

Do not be dismayed, niece. I have sat in church every Sunday while our correspondence has gone forward, although stolidly rather than devoutly, and more as some English labourer of the previous century sat in his village church in one or another of my most admired books. I use my time in church for my own purposes but I cause no scandal. From under my eyebrows, I look at certain young women. My only purpose is to take home to my stone farmhouse and my bleak paddocks a small store of remembered sights.

You must remind yourself, niece, that I see very few young women. I spend a few hours each week in the town of Y—, where numerous young women are to be seen in shops and offices and on the footpaths. But I have observed during my lifetime a great change in the demeanour of young women. The weatherboard church in this isolated district is perhaps the last place where I could hope to see young women dressed modestly and with eyes downcast.

But I have not explained myself. I am interested in the appearance and deportment of young women in this, the everyday visible world, for the good reason that the female personages in books, like all other such personages together with the places they inhabit, are quite invisible.

You can hardly believe me. In your mind at this very moment are characters, costumes, interiors of houses, landscapes and skies, all of them faithful images of their counterparts in descriptive passages in books you have read and remembered. Allow me to set you right, dear niece, and to make a true reader of you.

I have had no education to speak of, but a man may learn surprising things if he spends all his life in the same house and most of that life alone. With no chatter or argument in his ears, he will hear the persuasive rhythms of sentences from the books that he keeps beside his bed. With his eyes undistracted by novelty, he will see what those sentences truly denote. For long after I had first fallen in love as a result of my reading, I still supposed that the objects of my love were visible to me. Did I not see in my mind, while I read, image after image? Could I not call to mind, long after I had closed this or that book, the face, the clothing, the gestures of the personage I loved—and of others also? Whenever I think of how readily I deceived myself in this simplest of matters, I wonder in how many other matters no less simple are persons deceived who will not inspect the contents of their own minds nor look for the source of what appears there. And I beg you, dear niece, not to be prevented by the welter of sights and sounds in the great city where you live; not to be deceived by the glibness of the educated; but to accept as truths only the findings of your own introspection.

But I am preaching at you, when my own example should serve. You will believe me, niece, when I tell you that I learned, in time, that all the contents of all the books that I had read or would read were invisible. Whatever personages I had loved, or would love in the future, were forever hidden from me. Certainly, I saw as I read. But what I saw came only from my poor stock of remembered sights. And what I saw was only a scrap of what I believed I saw. An example will serve.

Last night, I was reading yet again from a book the author of which was born before the midpoint of the previous century but lived until the year before my own birth. I had read only a few words referring to the chief female personage of the book before the appearance in my mind of the first of the images that another sort of reader would have supposed to have originated by some means in the text of the book. Being by now well skilled in such tasks, I needed only a moment of mental exertion before I recognised the source of the image just mentioned. Note first that the image was of a detail only. The text referred to a young woman.

Would you not expect that any image then arising in my mind would be an image of a young woman? But I assure you that I saw only an image of a corner of a somewhat pale forehead with a strand of dark hair trailing across it. And I assure you further that this detail had its source not in any sentence of the text but in the memory of the reader of the text, myself. Some weeks before, while I sat in my usual seat in a rear corner of the church, I observed from under my eyebrows a certain young woman as she returned to her seat from the communion rail. I observed many details of her appearance, and all were of equal interest to me. Neither in the church nor at any time afterwards did I think of any of those details as being connected with any personage in any book that I had read. And yet, dear niece, the image of a strand of dark hair and a corner of a forehead are all that I can see, for the time being, of a personage who has been dear to me for longer than I have been writing my letters to you.

Much might be learned from all this, dear niece. I myself have certainly learned much from many similar discoveries. Item: if, for the sake of convenience, we call the subject matter of books a world, then that world is wholly invisible to the residents of the world where I write these words and where you read them. For I have studied the images not only of personages but of those details we suppose to be the settings of books and suppose further to have arisen from words in the text. The same book whose chief female character is visible to me presently as only a strand of hair trailing across a forehead, that same book contains hundreds of sentences describing a variety of landscapes in the south of England. I have observed myself to read all of those so-called descriptive sentences while seeing in my mind only one or another of precisely four details from the scattered coloured illustrations in a magazine that had belonged to my dead sister and still lay about this house. All of the illustrations were of landscapes in the midlands of England.

But you have read enough of arguments and demonstrations, and I have almost lost my thread. Trust me to know that the personages I have been devoted to since boyhood have been invisible to me, as have their homes, their native districts, and even the skies above those districts. At once, several questions occur to you. You assume, correctly, that I have never felt drawn towards any young woman in this, the visible world, and you want me to explain this seeming failure in me.

I have often myself considered this question, niece, and I have come to understand that I might have brought myself to approach one or another young woman from this district, or even from the town of Y— if even one of the following two conditions could have been fulfilled: before I had first seen the young woman, I would have had to read about her, if not in a book then in passages of the sort of writing such as appears in the sort of books that I read; alternatively, before I had first seen the young woman I would have had to know that the young woman had read about me as described earlier in this sentence.

You may consider these conditions overly stringent, niece, and the chance of their being fulfilled absurdly remote. Do not suspect for a moment that I devised these conditions from a wish to remain solitary. Think of me, rather, as a man who can love only the subjects of sentences in texts purporting to be other than factual.

There has been only one occasion when I felt myself drawn to treat with a young woman of this, the visible world without any bookish preliminaries. When I was still quite young, and still not reconciled altogether to my fate, I thought I might strengthen my resolve by learning about other solitaries: monkish eremites, exiles, dwellers in remote places. I happened to find in a pile of old magazines that someone had lent to one of my sisters an illustrated article about the island of Tristan da Cunha in the South Atlantic. I learned from the article that the island is the loneliest inhabited place on earth, lying far from shipping routes. The cliffs around the island allow no ship to berth. Any visiting ship must anchor at sea while the men of Tristan row out to her. These things alone were enough to excite my interest. You know the situation of this farm: a strip of land at the very southern edge of the continent, with its boundary on one side the high cliffs where I often walk alone. You should know also that the nearest bay to this farm is named after a ship that was wrecked there during the previous century. But my interest in the lonely island increased after I had learned from the magazine article about a disaster that had happened some forty years before my birth. A boat carrying all the able-bodied men of the island was lost at sea, and Tristan became a settlement of mostly women and children. For many years afterwards, so I read, the young women prayed every night for a shipwreck to bring marriageable men.

There came into my mind an image of a certain young woman of Tristan da Cunha, and whenever I looked up from my paddocks to the cliffs I thought of her as standing on the highest cliff of her island and staring out to sea. I was impelled to visit the library in the town of Y— and to consult a detailed atlas. I learned, with much excitement, that the island of Tristan da Cunha and the district where this farm is situated lie almost on the same latitude. I learned further that no land—not even the speck of an island— lies between Tristan and this coast. Now, dear niece, you must know as I know that the prevailing winds and currents in this hemisphere are from west to east, and so you can anticipate the conjectures that I made after I had studied the atlas. If the young woman on the cliff tops of the island of Tristan had written a message and had enclosed the message in a bottle and had thrown the bottle into the Atlantic Ocean from a cliff on the western side of her island, then her message might well have been carried at last to the coast of this district.

You may be inclined to smile as you read this, niece, but after I had first conjectured thus, I began the habit of walking once each week along the few beaches near this farm. While I walked, I composed in my mind various versions of the message from the young woman of Tristan. I found no bottle, which should hardly surprise you, but I was often consoled to think that a message such as I had imagined might lie during all my lifetime in some pool or crevice beneath the cliffs of my native district.

You have another matter to raise. You want to argue that each of the personages I have devoted myself to had her origins somewhere in the mind of the author of the writing that first brought her to my notice. You suggest that I might have studied the life and the pronouncements of the author in order to discover the reality, as you might call it, beneath my illusions, as you might call them. Better still, I might read a suitable work by a living author and then submit to him or her a list of questions to be answered in writing and at length.

In fact, dear niece, I tried long ago but soon abandoned the line of investigation noted above. Most of the authors concerned wrote their books during the previous century and died before my birth. (You must have observed that I learned my own style of writing from those worthies.) I read just enough about the lives of the authors of my admired books to learn that they were vain and arrogant persons and much given to pettiness. But what of the present century? A great change has occurred in books during this century. The writers of those books have tried to describe what they had better have left unreported. The writers of the present century have lost respect for the invisible. I have never troubled myself to learn about the writers themselves. (I exclude from these remarks a certain writer from a small island-republic in the North Atlantic. I learned of the existence of his books by a remarkable chance and read several in translation, but I could not bring myself afterwards to compose any message for him in his cliff-bound homeland.)

I have come to hope, dear niece, that the act of writing may be a sort of miracle as a result of which invisible entities are made aware of each other through the medium of the visible. But how can I believe that the awareness is mutual? Although I have sometimes felt one or another of my beloved personages as a presence nearby, I have had no grounds for supposing that she might even have imagined my possible existence.

On a day long ago, when I was somewhat cast down from thinking of these matters, I wrote my first letter to you, dear niece.

I sought a way out of my isolation by means of the following, admittedly simplistic, proposition: if the act of writing can bring into being personages previously unimagined by either writer or reader, then I might dare to hope for some wholly unexpected outcome from my own writing, although it could never be part of any book.

How many years have passed since then you and I alone know, and this, as I have told you, is my last letter. However little I may know of it, I remain hopeful that something will come of this writing.

Something will come of this writing. I was born in Transylvania in the seventeenth century of the modern era. I became in my youth a follower of Prince Ferenc Rákóczi. When the Prince went into exile after the War of Independence, I was one of the band of followers who went with him. In the second decade of the eighteenth century, we arrived at the port of Gallipoli as invited guests of the Sultan of Turkey. Shortly afterwards, I wrote the first of my letters to my aunt, the Countess P—, in Constantinople. We followers of Prince Rákóczi had hoped that our exile might not be for long, but almost all of us remained for the rest of our lives in Turkey, and even those few who left Turkey were never allowed to return to their native land, my native land. For forty-one years, until almost the last year of my life, I wrote regularly to my aunt. I wrote to her almost a full account of my life. One of the few matters that I chose not to write openly about was my solitary state. Only a few of the exiles were women, and all of these were married. Most of us men remained solitary throughout our lives.

Dear Reader

The following is adapted from one of the seven pages about the life and the writing of Kelemen Mikes in the *Oxford History of Hungarian Literature*, 1984.

The *Letters from Turkey* were regarded by critics for a long time only as a source for the history of the exiles. Much futile re-search was done in an attempt to find traces of the mysterious Countess P— who proved never to have existed. Mikes never sent his letters to any 'aunt' but copied them into a letter-book, which was found after his death.

Acknowledgments

Certain texts in this volume originally appeared in the following books and periodicals: "When the Mice Failed to Arrive," *Sport*, Autumn 1989 (Victoria University, NZ); "Stream System," *Age Monthly Review* 8, no. 9 (December 1988–January 1989); "Land Deal," *Educational Magazine*, no. 3 (1980); "The Only Adam," *Scripsi* 3, nos. 2–3 (1985); "Stone Quarry," *Meanjin*, no. 4 (1986); "Precious Bane," *Strange Attractors*, ed. Damien Broderick (Hale and Iremonger, 1985); "Cotters Come No More," *Footprint New Writers* 2 (1987); "There Were Some Countries," *Tabloid Story*, in the *Valley Voice* 28 (March 1979); "Finger Web," *Expressway*, ed. Helen Daniel (Penguin, 1988); "First Love," *Scripsi* 5, no. 4 (1988); "The White Cattle of Uppington," *Southerly* 55, no. 3 (1995); "Pink Lining," *Scripsi* 8, no. 2 (1992); "Boy Blue," *World Literature Today* 67, no. 3 (1993); "As It Were a Letter," *Southerly* 61, no. 1 (2001); "The Boy's Name Was David," *The Best Australian Short Stories 2002*, ed. Peter Craven (Black Inc., 2002); "Last Letter to a Niece," *The Best Australian Short Stories 2001*, ed. Peter Craven (Black Inc., 2001).

All but "The White Cattle of Uppington" appeared in the following collections: *Velvet Waters* (McPhee Gribble, 1990); *Emerald Blue* (McPhee

Acknowledgments

Gribble, 1995); *Invisible Yet Enduring Lilacs* (Giramondo, 2005); and *A History of Books* (Giramondo, 2012). The extract quoted on pages 324–25 is from *Woodbrook*, by David Thomson, published in 1991 by Vintage, London.

A Note About the Author

Gerald Murnane was born in Melbourne in 1939. One of Australia's most highly regarded authors, he has published eleven volumes of fiction to date, including *The Plains*, *Inland*, *Barley Patch*, and *Border Districts*, as well as a collection of essays, *Invisible Yet Enduring Lilacs*, and a memoir, *Something for the Pain*. He is a recipient of the Patrick White Literary Award, the Melbourne Prize for Literature, and an Emeritus Fellowship from the Literature Board of the Australia Council. He lives in a small town in Western Victoria, near the border with South Australia.